J.D. Crist

Chains of the Union

Dedication

To everyone who hid their strength and fire to be what was expected of them. Remember, they try to control you because they are afraid you will realize you are better than they could ever dream of being.

<u>Trigger Warnings</u>

This story contains some themes and scenes that some readers may find uncomfortable or triggering. Your mental health is most important. Please ensure that you are comfortable with the list below before continuing.

- Thoughts/Mentions of Suicide
-
- Arranged Marriage
-

Grooming of Women (Adult, not children)

Strong Language

Use of Restraints During Sex

I figure there are 2 reasons people read this page. Either they are making sure the content will not affect their mental health, or they are reading it like a menu. Either way, once you turn this page, you will be thrust into the world of The United Union. I hope you enjoy it as much as I did creating it.

THE UNION

The Capital
Ring 1
Ring 2
Ring 3
Ring 4
Ring 5
Ring 6
The Edge
Twain

Prologue

"*C*al, I swear to whatever god still exists if you don't open this fucking door, I will break it down and kick you in the balls!"

Maddie's threat cut through the silence of my office. She had been banging on the door for the past ten minutes. I knew what she wanted to talk about. Everyone had been asking me if I was alright all week, and I was tired of it. I was tired of the pity in their eyes and the vice it put in my chest. Sighing, I stood up from the small couch and looked around at the destruction in my office. Books and papers lay scattered across the floor, and shattered glass was sprinkled throughout. I twisted the lock on the door and stepped back, hearing the crunch of something under my foot.

Maddie burst through the door, her fiery red hair flying behind her. "I was beginning to think you died in here." She looked around my disheveled office as she spoke. My office was normally tidy and meticulously organized, but today, I needed destruction, or I feared what I wanted to do. I had locked myself in here for just that. To destroy and release my frustration and anger. No one was supposed to see, but she had insisted. The look on her face was pity, and I felt the anger I thought I had dispersed returning.

"What do you want?" I asked in a low tone. Maddie didn't deserve my anger. She and I had been friends since we were children. She knew the source of my pain and would have done anything to help me stop it. I just needed her to speak her peace and leave. There were still some things that I could break in here and not feel regret.

"We have a request for extraction tonight," she said as she turned to me. She was trying to look serious, but the look in her eyes gave her away - hope, something that she dared not speak, and I was in no mood to entertain.

"It will have to wait until tomorrow." Maddie knew the rules. Security was too tight the night of the bride auction. It put too much at risk. Whoever wanted out would have to wait one more day.

Maddie eyed me up and down before holding out an envelope. "Even for her?" The neat script on the plain envelope told me who it was from. It had been two years since I last spoke with her. She had seen to it that my suffering would continue, that this night would happen. My hands shook with anger as I ripped the letter out of Maddie's hands. I read the words slowly, each seeming to cut into my heart like a knife.

My body slumped into the couch as soon as I finished, the letter still clutched in my hand. This couldn't be real. It had to be a trap. Had she known all along that it would come down to this? Why hadn't she told me years ago? Instead, she had left me to suffer and now asked me to do the impossible. But that's what I did - the impossible. For her, I would do whatever it took.

"Well," Maddie asked, drawing my attention back to her. I crumpled the paper in my hand before dropping it to the ground. Maddie knew what I would do. She just needed me to give the word so she could put things in motion.

"Looks like we're crashing the ball," I replied as I stood.

"We leave in an hour."

Maddie left the room without hesitation, barely containing her excitement. The others wouldn't hesitate either. They had all wanted to get her out years ago. They all loved her just as much as I did, just in a different way. I picked up a framed picture on my desk. It was a little blurry, but I could still see her face. Her dirty blond hair was blown around her face by the wind. The way she smiled, hiding something she was planning to do behind that pretty face. Her dark brown eyes seemed to be looking into my soul. I brushed my thumb over her face, wishing to feel her soft skin once again.

"I'm coming for you," I said softly. "I may not be able to have you, but I will set you free."

Chapter 1

A cool breeze flowed through the open window of our small one-room shack. Summer was in full swing, and these moments were becoming fewer every day. For most people, summer signaled a chance, a chance at life. The warm weather provided more work and an opportunity to grow crops in the poor soil. Though crops were rare, the extra work did provide the money needed to keep a family from starving. For me, summer signaled a heat that would feel like my skin was burning and an anxiety I wouldn't be able to shake until fall arrived and the cool air returned.

Compared to most who lived on The Edge, my struggles were minor. We were still poor, but we always had enough to ensure that we were able to eat. Nothing fancy, most of the time it was a simple soup that consisted mostly of water and herbs. Life on The Edge wasn't easy for anyone who called it home, but we all tried to make it as pleasant as possible. As part of the United Republic, we were looked down on by those in the inner rings and the capital. Everyone this far out had mutations, some more ghastly than others, and fought to survive. But we accepted each other without prejudice, content to leave the petty fights and drama to those who could afford to waste their time on such things.

I looked over at Grams, who sat in a wooden chair beside me, sewing a hem on a dress that no one who lived here could afford. I had been trying since I was a child to figure out what her mutation was. Looking at her, she looked to be a normal but the fact that she lived here told that she wasn't. She had explained to me years ago that not all mutations were physical. That some mutations lived in the blood, like hers. I had never met anyone like her, but had no reason to doubt her explanation.

It also explained about myself when I was younger. I showed no physical mutation and always assumed that mine must be one of the blood as well. The required genetic test on my sixteenth birthday had proven that to be wrong. I was a normal. Everyone I knew had celebrated when I got my results. It meant that I would marry into one of the inner rings and live a life away from the struggles and poverty I had known my whole life. To me, it felt like a death sentence.

I was required by law to marry someone who was also mutation-free and produce at least one child. The requirement was to ensure that those without mutations thrived. After all, mutants were not allowed to lead or have any say in how the city was run. The explanation was that those with mutations were also affected in the mind. They couldn't make the rational decisions that were needed to ensure the Union thrived.

Marrying into the inner rings did come with comforts, but also restrictions. Once I was married, I would not be allowed to return to The Edge, and Grams was not allowed to come with me. I was being forced to leave the only family I had and the only person who loved me. I watched her as her fingers shook while she continued to sew. She had done what most people wouldn't when my parents died. Life on The Edge was hard enough for most folk without taking in orphans to feed. Most were placed in the orphan camp where they worked for scraps, and few survived to adulthood.

Grams hadn't hesitated to take me in. She took on extra work to ensure I never went hungry and even managed to afford for me to get a basic education. After everything she did, I wanted to ensure that she lived a comfortable life. I had been given until my twenty-first birthday to find a husband - a deadline that had already passed. I had chosen instead to be auctioned off at the Union Ball. There, men would bid on me, and I would be given to the highest bidder. However, most of the money would be given to my guardian for raising me, for their sacrifice and dedication. I may not be able to stay with Grams and take care of her, but I could ensure that she would live out the rest of her days comfortably. She deserved it after all the sacrifices she made for me.

A gentle chime sounded from the silver bracelet around Gram's wrist just as she finished the dress. She looked down at the small screen, wiping a strand of her silver hair out of her face. "They want these things early," she said with a sigh. "Are you about finished?"

I quickly moved the needle through the last few stitches and added it to the box of other garments we had completed. This was the last time Grams would have to do this work. Tomorrow was the ball, and she would be set for the rest of her life.

"Take these to the depot," Grams continued. "And then come straight home. I want to spend tonight together and have planned a special supper."

I nodded, afraid to speak as I picked up the box and walked towards the door. I didn't want Grams to know how much I hated having to leave her, and I knew my shaky voice would betray me. The wooden door creaked on its hinges as I opened it and stepped out into the sun. Glancing back at Grams, I could see that she was already setting to work in our makeshift kitchen, lighting a fire to cook whatever she had planned. I prayed that the heat would die down when I returned, as I closed the door. I didn't want my nerves to be any more on edge on our final night together.

As I walked the road, my steps kicked up small puffs of dust. The Edge reminded me of an old wild west town that I had read about in school. All of the buildings were put together from scrap wood, most threatening to fall at any moment. People wore plain clothes, most without shoes, as they worked. The only building that showed how things were different for those with wealth and power was the medical facility. Its shiny, smooth walls stood out and looked out of place near the gate. I, like most people, had only been inside once, and that was for my genetic test. That day was such a blur that I couldn't remember any of the details of the inside. The only evidence that I had been there was the silver bracelet on my wrist.

It seemed such a waste to have the facility here at all. It mocked us all with its grandeur and denied us the one thing it should have offered - medical treatment. We were only allowed to enter for genetic testing. No injury or illness would be treated there, not for us. Instead, we relied on our basic knowledge and resources to treat our ailments. When it was something minor, it seemed fine. But when something major happened and we were forced to watch another die, knowing that they could be saved by those in the facility, it caused people to become dangerous. There had been several attempts to raid the facility over the years. All it gained was more deaths and increased soldiers to guard it. Further proving that the Union saw us as nothing more than servants, easily expendable and only needed for what we could provide.

I made my way through the familiar streets and reached the depot just before the sun began to set. The door stood propped open, and I could see Joe standing behind the counter inside. Even from a distance, I could see the frustration on his face as he talked to a man in a tailored suit. Joe was a kind man, always there for me and Grams when we needed help. I hated to see someone think they were superior to him. He never let his deformity hold him back. He volunteered for his position at the depot. Most people refused because they didn't want to deal with the constant judgment and ridicule that came when working with people from the inner rings.

Joe accepted the challenge, unfazed by those who looked down on him for his deformity. Most people found ways to try and hide theirs - a long sleeved shirt to hide their arms or growing out their hair to hide their deformed skull. Joe's, however, was impossible to hide. He was unfortunate enough to have a facial deformity. The left side of his face sagged down, looking almost as if it had begun to melt. His eyes were sharp, though, and he stared at the man with shame.

"Pick up was set for first thing in the morning," Joe said firmly. "They are doing you a favor by agreeing to bring it tonight."

"Favor?!" the man snarled. "The favor is allowing scum like them to have any work   at all!"

"I'd watch your tone if I were you," I said as I walked up to the counter and dropped the box. "Joe here may have trouble finding you a new seamstress to fix your wife's pretty clothes."

The man's face turned red as he looked at me with a stony expression. I knew his type, thinking he was better because he lived in the inner rings. A pain in my head threatened a new migraine, but I ignored it and stared back at him. I knew better than to talk back or do anything other than what was expected of me. It always led to a headache, but I couldn't just let this man talk to Joe like he was trash. I didn't have to know this man to know that Joe was better than him in every way that mattered.

"You little bitch!" the man snarled as he raised his hand. It was a typical power move for someone like him. He couldn't form an intelligent argument, so he planned to slap me into line.

"I would think twice about that," I warned, doing my best to look bored.

"And why's that?" The man's face still showed his anger, but his hand hung still in the air, ready to slap me.

"Joe, isn't it true that the governors take it seriously if someone diminishes the value of a bride, especially the night before the ball?"

Confusion washed over the man, but he remained firm in his position.

12

"It is," Joe nodded. "I expect it would be worse if someone diminished the value of the first bride from The Edge."

The man's face went white as he looked at me. "Ms. Elizabeth Allard," he asked in a shaky voice as he lowered his hand. It was sad how just a few well-placed words could cause a man like him to tremble.

"The one and only," I smiled at him as I winked. I heard Joe let out a low chuckle, enjoying watching the man try to save face.

His gaze moved to the box I dropped on the counter, realization washing over his face. "I do apologize," he began. "Thank you for agreeing to deliver the goods early." I watched as he put a large bag of silver on the counter. "I believe double payment is needed for the inconvenience I caused you."

"Much appreciated," I smiled back. "My grandmother will be thrilled. However, as I'm sure you've been informed, she is retiring after today. I'm not sure your poor manners today have given Joe much of an incentive to find you a new seamstress with half her skill."

The pain in my head grew stronger, but I managed to keep my face neutral. The man nodded and slid a smaller bag of silver to Joe, who took it with a nod. Desperate to get out of the depot, the man quickly grabbed the box and left. Joe and I both burst out into laughter as soon as he was gone. The man had acted like his life depended on not insulting me. I was good at carrying myself like I mattered, but the truth was I didn't. I would be married off tomorrow, forced to have children, and no one would remember me when I was dead and gone. I was okay with it, as long as I used what little influence, I had to help people like Joe.

"I'm not sure you made a friend in that one," Joe said once we calmed down.

"Wasn't looking to," I replied. "No matter who I marry, I won't forget where I come from."

"Of that I have no doubt," Joe said as he put the bag of silver into his pocket. "Are you excited about tomorrow?"

"I'm ready to do my civil duty," I said with a half-hearted grin. I had already caused myself enough pain; no need to tell the truth. I would rather run off into the Deadlands than marry whatever pompous jerk was so desperate for a wife that he had to buy one. But Grams needed the money, and I would do what I must to ensure she was provided for. Telling the truth would only lead to the dull ache in my skull turning into a serious pain that felt like someone was trying to tear it open.

Joe raised an eyebrow at me, as if he knew there was more I wanted to say. "Will you do me a favor and watch out for Grams when I'm gone?" I was desperate to change the subject. Joe looked at me knowingly but didn't push. "Of course," he smiled with a nod.

I nodded back and turned to head outside. There was no need for a tearful goodbye. I would never forget Joe or the others I cared about here.

Staying to cry and hug it out wouldn't change anything. Tomorrow, I would be dressed up and trotted out for men to drool over and bid on. It was easier just to leave things as they were, cleaner in fact.

The sun had begun to set, and I would need to hurry if I was going to make it home before dark. Workers were still busy setting up supplies in the gathering area in front of the depot. For the first time, the Union Ball was being held in The Edge. A celebration of the first normal to come out of the forgotten ring of the Union. Based on the number of crates that were scattered about, they would be working through the night and right up until the ball started. Pride showed on the faces of those who were working - prideful ignorance. They were all working hard, proud to be hosting a ball that none of them would be deemed worthy to attend. People on The Edge were so desperate to be accepted and seen, they ignored the fact that they were being used.

I rushed through the workers, making my way down the makeshift streets. I smiled at those who looked at me as I ran. No need to take away the small amount of happiness they had found. It wasn't my place to tell them that it was wrong or how much of a fool they were. It didn't matter how hard they worked or how loyal they were; The Union would never accept them.

I managed to reach home just as the last of the sun's light disappeared. I stood outside and looked at the small shack that was the only home I could remember having. The windows were just holes in the wood, covered by a curtain that blew in the breeze. During the winter, Grams and I would board up the holes and nail the curtain down to help keep the cold out. I walked towards the crooked wooden door and gently pushed it open.

Inside, Grams had doused the fire, and the breeze had taken away most of the heat. I watched her as she ladled something into two bowls. As she turned, she spotted me standing in the doorway. She nodded her head, signaling for me to come in. I closed the door and walked over to where she waited. Once I was seated at the table, she set one of the steaming bowls down in front of me before sitting down with her own.

She had promised a special meal, but soup was something we had most nights. Water was the only abundant resource we had that didn't cost an exorbitant amount. I would often search around The Edge, looking for odd plants that dared to grow in the harsh soil. Grams would always praise what little I found and add them to the boiling water as if it was precious herbs.

I smiled at her as I picked up my spoon and began to stir the contents of my bowl. I knew what she had made had been the best she could, and that was enough to make it special. As I stirred through, I realized that this was not our normal soup. I lifted my spoon, surprised at the sight that greeted me.

"Are these vegetables?" Grams smiled and lifted a spoonful to her mouth and softly blew on it. "It's tradition," she smiled. "Every woman in our family has had this meal on the night before they took their place in this world."

I felt tears sting at my eyes, but quickly blinked them away. This soup must have cost her a fortune. Part of me wanted to scold her for spending the money, but I couldn't bring myself to do it. Besides, I had the extra silver from that asshole at the depot; there was no need to ruin this moment.

I took a bite of the hot soup, allowing the flavors to explode across my tongue. No matter how good the food would be after tomorrow, nothing would compare to this. This would be the meal I compared all other meals to, and nothing would ever be able to best it.

The next morning came too soon. Sunlight was barely peeking through the window when Grams woke me. "We have a lot to do before your evaluation," she said in a hurried voice, "And you can't be late." I stretched, trying to shake the sleep from my body in the small bed. The straw that made up the mattress was poking into my skin. This would be the last time its gentle jabs poked me awake.

Chapter 2

As I sat up, I noticed that Grams had already been busy. My attention was drawn to her bed, just a few feet away from my own. It was impeccably made, as always, but a silky white dress lay on it. I stood, my feet used to the feel of the rough floor, and walked closer. My hands brushed the material as Grams appeared behind me. "It was your mother's," she said softly.

A lot of people would have cried at the sentiment the dress represented, but not me. I hadn't cried since my parents were killed by raiders when I was seven. After that, nothing seemed deserving of my sorrow. I probably wouldn't cry again until news reached me when Grams passed, but at the sight of my mother's dress, I was tempted to make an exception. The design was simple but elegant, with a low-cut bust that was form-fitting and a flowy bottom that would stretch down to the floor. Even with all the fine clothes I had helped tailor over the years, it was the most beautiful thing I had ever seen.

"Let's get you cleaned up and your hair done," Grams said as she turned me away from the dress. "Then we can see how it looks on you."

I turned away and allowed Grams to get to work. The next few hours were a mixture of scrubbing and brushing knots from my dirty blonde hair. I didn't complain as Grams worked despite the pain in my scalp from her tugging on my hair and the raw redness of skin from her scrubbing away that lay on her bed. While it was beautiful, I couldn't understand how my mother afforded it. No one in The Edge had that kind of money, especially for something like a wedding dress. Most said their vows in private. The odd ones who wanted it make it feel extra special would go to the abandoned cathedral.

I'm sure unions were more glamorous in the capital. If the ball for the bride action was any indication, they sealed things with contracts and grand celebrations. I had learned in my studies that while unions were made on The Edge out of love, the Capital saw them as being more practical. Feelings rarely came into play. People were matched based on social standing and for strategic moves. That is the life my future children would be brought into. I would try my best to teach them love and respect, but in the end, they would just be pawns that were used to further the Capital's agenda.

"Perfect," Grams smiled as she took a step back. I smiled at her as I was pulled out of my thoughts and back to the moment. "Time for the finishing touches."

I watched as she walked over to the bed and carefully picked up the dress. I slid off my nightgown and stepped into the smooth fabric. The fit was perfect, and I felt sure that Grams had made some alterations. There was no way that my figure could be exactly as my mother's had been. As I ran my hand over the smooth fabric, thoughts of my mother raced through my mind.

"How?" I finally spoke. Grams raised an eyebrow at me in confusion. "How did my mother afford something like this?"

Gram's face softened as she sat down in one of our wooden chairs. "Your mother wasn't from The Edge," she began. "She was born and raised in the Capital." I felt myself sink into the other chair as all the air rushed out of my lungs. I had never met anyone from my mother's family, but I assumed that it was because they had died. Death was common on The Edge, especially during lean years. It never occurred to me that she might not have been from here.

"Your grandparents are very influential in the Capital," Grams continued. "Your mother's life was planned out from the moment she was born. On her sixteenth birthday, they gave her that dress and took her for her testing. When it was over, she was going straight to a marriage ceremony with a man they had chosen."

"What happened?" I asked so softly that I wasn't sure if Grams heard me. It was hard to imagine my mother being so complacent with that sort of arrangement. The few memories I had of her, she was strong, stubborn, and resourceful. I could still remember my father telling me he would rather fight the entire Union army alone than go toe to toe with my mother. Things hadn't gone according to her parents' plan. Had she found a way to escape and run away to The Edge?

"Her test results were not as expected," Grams sighed. "It turned out that she had a mutation. This nullified the marriage they had arranged and brought shame to their family name. They disowned her on the spot and sent her to The Edge with nothing but this dress."

I looked down at the dress, feeling a hint of disgust at what it represented. "They disowned her for something she had no control over?"

Grams nodded. "Their pride meant more to them than she ever did. They were already disappointed that they had a daughter instead of a son. Their only hope of keeping their high standing was a prestigious marriage. When that fell through, they had no use for her."

I sat, letting the anger well up inside me. Her parents had dismissed her like she was nothing. My mother was a wonderful woman, and everyone who knew her always reminded me of that. The thought of even being related to such people made my stomach churn.

"She brought it to me, hoping I had a client who would want to buy it." A smile spread across Gram's face as she thought of the memory. "But she met your father, and they took their vows a few months later. I still remember her wearing that dress as if it symbolized she had made it without them."

"She was strong," I said as I took Gram's hand.

"As are you," she smiled back. "One last thing, and we'll be ready to go."

Grams pulled a folded piece of cloth from her pocket and placed it on the table. I watched as she unfolded it, expecting maybe a piece of jewelry or some sort of family heirloom. I did not expect to see the small blade tucked into a leather holder with two straps attached to it.

"What's this?" I asked, touching my fingers against the metal handle.

"A gift," Grams said as she picked up the knife and put it in my hand. "Secure the straps around your upper thigh."

"A gift," I asked, looking at the small knife that felt oddly familiar. It couldn't have been, though. Grams hadn't allowed me to take part in combat training, and I had never held a weapon in my life. Even now, it felt like I was breaking some kind of rule by even holding it. Why would Grams want me to have this on my wedding day? Surely it was not another tradition. I had never heard of a bride being armed before taking her vows.

"From an old family friend," she nodded, motioning for me to attach the blade.

My hands were surprisingly steady as I lifted the dress and secured the knife as she watched. While I didn't understand, I decided it was best to humor her. If she wanted me to have the knife, I would take it. If my future husband asked, I could just tell him that it is an old Edge tradition and dismiss it. After tonight, I will keep it in a drawer as a keepsake of Grams.

"I don't see myself needing to defend myself," I teased as I secured the straps, ensuring they wouldn't slip when I walked.

"You never know," Grams said in a sterner tone. Her face was suddenly more serious as she watched me finish. "If the groom tries to hurt you after the ceremony, you remove the one thing every man cares about." She raised an eyebrow at me, and I nodded that I understood. I couldn't hide the shock her words had on me. "There's also a chance that your mother's parents will learn who you are and seek you out. They will want to use you to regain some of the glamour they lost because of your mother."

I let the dress fall to the ground, touching where the knife was hidden. I could never avenge my parents' deaths. No one knew who killed them exactly, just raiders that could have starved in the Deadlands years ago. But my grandparents were here. If they did seek me out, I would show that I was my mother's daughter. I didn't care if the migraine from it killed me; it would be worth it. Perhaps I would have a use for this blade after all.

"Enough of that," Grams said with a forced smile. "Now, gather up that skirt so it doesn't get filthy. We don't want to be late."

Carefully, I gathered up the dress so the fabric didn't go any lower than my knees. It was just high enough to keep it from getting dirty, but also hide the knife I now had strapped to my thigh. Not a proper look for a lady, but I didn't care. The people of this ring had seen me running around in non-ladylike form since I was a child. Dresses and frilly things just slowed you down when you were running or trying to jump over things.

I followed Grams outside, stealing one last glance back at the shack that was my home. These worn walls and simple pieces of furniture held memories that no one else would see. I couldn't remember the house I had lived in with my parents. Grams explained that it had burned down after they were killed. I thought it took everything of theirs with them, but it hadn't. Grams had managed to save the dress for me. I wouldn't have blamed her for selling it and using the money to keep us going. But she didn't; she kept it and saved it for me all these years.

Grams raised me with nothing but her sacrifice and determination. This small shack may be nothing to some people, but to me, it was and always would be home. All of my memories of home were here. As I shut the door, I felt a feeling wash over me that I did not expect. Where there should have been sorrow or grief, I felt determination and freedom. Guilt immediately took over. How could I feel such things when I was leaving everything behind? When I was leaving Grams behind? I placed my hand on the old door and closed my eyes. I had to let it go, no matter how much it hurt.

As I turned, I could see that she had already made it a distance up the dirt road. I turned and ran to catch up with her. She moved surprisingly fast for her age. She was probably where I learned that sentiment in times like these was pointless. It didn't change what needed to be done, just dragged it out and made it hurt more.

The streets of The Edge were busy with people setting up for the ball. All of them were working so hard for an event that they wouldn't be allowed to attend. Even Grams was not able to go with me. After she delivered me for inspection, I would not see her again until the

ceremony, once I was purchased. The thought of
it twisted my stomach, but I kept moving. After
the ceremony, I would move to the ring where
my new husband lived, never to return to The
Edge or Gram's again.

Our normal path to the depot was blocked
by a giant tent. Grams looked back and forth,
deciding the best way around. I stood behind her,
watching as people carried in tables and
decorations like nothing I had ever seen. As if the
tent itself didn't look out of place enough with its
deep red color, the decor being carried in
belonged here even less. Fancy-looking wooden
tables with a shine that reflected the sunlight and
flowers so bright and colorful, I would have
thought they were fake if not for their strong
floral scent that filled the air.

"This way," Grams said as she took off to
the right. We wove our way around workers and
crates until we finally reached the depot. When
we arrived, the door that was normally propped
open was closed with two soldiers standing
outside. I knew that when I went in, Joe wouldn't
be there to greet me like he had been the day
before. Instead, I would be put through exams
and tests to determine what the starting bid
would be. I turned to Grams, expecting to see
sorrow on her face, but she remained calm and

steady. I felt my resistance bolstered because of it. If Grams could be strong, so could I.

"Everything will be fine," Grams assured me as she glanced at the building. "Just go in there and be honest. I will see you at the ceremony."

I wrapped one arm around her in a hug while the other held up my dress. Grams hugged me back tightly with both arms, and I didn't want to let go. "Don't lose the blade," she whispered in my ear.

I pulled back and looked at her, confused. I understood her desire for me to be able to defend myself, but there seemed to be more behind her words. It was as if this weapon were significant in some way that I was unaware of. I opened my mouth to speak, but Grams held up a hand to hush me as footsteps sounded behind me.

"Ms. Allard," a deep voice that sent a shiver down my spine asked. I turned to see one of the soldiers who had been guarding the door standing directly behind me. He was at least a foot taller with dark eyes that were void of emotion. I guess that's how they are trained. Emotions and the like were dangerous for soldiers. Even still, it wouldn't have killed to show some compassion as

I had arrived to be sold off in the name of the Capital.

"Yes," I replied, ashamed of how meek my voice sounded. It wasn't he that frightened me, because not much did. But the thought of the ball suddenly terrified me down to my bones. I had chosen to be married off this way. Many men had approached me over the years, attempting to court me and making offers of marriage. I turned them all down. I decided that just because I couldn't marry for love didn't mean I couldn't make sure my marriage benefited someone I loved. Even still, standing here now, terror shook me even though my hands remained steady.

"They are ready for you." The soldier turned and motioned towards the door. I looked back at Grams, searching her face for anything that would answer my questions. Part of me hoped she would grab my hand and tell me to run. Instead, she gave me a small smile and stepped back, leaving me alone with my questions and fears. Clutching my dress, I turned and walked towards the open door. Each step seeming more heavy than the last. I kept my head high and walked with as much confidence as I could muster. All of the sounds and people around me faded into the distance the closer I got to the door. Once inside, my fate was sealed. I would be poked, prodded, and tested to ensure that my starting bid was set at a fair amount. They would see me as nothing more than a prized heifer.

Stepping inside the door, I stole one last glance back at Grams. My heartbeat was pounding in my ears as I looked at her. She raised her hand and blew me a kiss. I quickly returned the gesture just before the door slammed shut, sealing me inside. My hand fell back to my side as my heart continued to pound in my chest. I was trapped, and instantly my anxiety grew. I had heard of people being claustrophobic, but I had never known before that moment that I was. Closing my eyes, I forced myself to take several deep breaths. I wasn't claustrophobic; it was just the crushing feeling of being trapped that was swallowing me whole. I forced myself to take several deep breaths in an attempt to calm my nerves. I may be trapped, but I wouldn't let them break me. No, I was stronger than that. I felt my muscles begin to relax as I took several more deep breaths.

"Just get through this," I whispered to myself. "After this, things will get easier."

My stomach knotted as if to call me out on my lie. This was the easy part. All I had to do was smile and go through some exams. It was afterwards that things would get hard. My husband would expect to have an obedient wife. He would be paying for one after all. I would be forced to play my role and do my duty or face not only his wrath, but the pain of the migraine I would get from being defiant. I was alone and trapped now, and that's what I would be for the rest of my life.

Chapter 3

The depot was dark; all of the windows were shut and blocking out the sun. The only light came from the old bulbs that hung on the ceiling. If they were trying to set the mood to show my impending doom, they succeeded. It was hard to believe that just the day before, I had stood in here laughing with Joe.

"Ms. Elizabeth Allard," a confident male voice spoke, startling me. I turned to see a man in a fine suit, one that I thought we may have tailored, standing there with a sickening white smile. His smooth hands were holding a clipboard as he stepped towards me. "I had to be the first to meet you. Someone of your genetic makeup coming from Ring Five, you truly are going to be the crowning jewel of my first auction."

I let go of my skirt, allowing it to fall to the ground. For some reason, his complimenting my beauty made my stomach churn. I forced a smile on my face as I turned to fully face him. "I didn't think we were to see the grooms until the ball," I asked.

"Forgive me," the man laughed. "I am not a groom. I am Alexander Pyne, coordinator of this year's Union Ball."

I nodded, hiding my embarrassment at not knowing who he was. He was the man who would set my starting bid and handle all the grooms throughout the night. In short, this man held my fate in his hands. Despite how much his wandering eyes made me sick, I had to be polite and make myself seem like a lady. I felt like a fool as I stood there with my smile, letting him look me up and down.

"You are a beauty," he said after a few moments. I felt a shiver run up my spine as he licked his lip and nodded with approval. "That will drive your price up." I stood still as he looked over the clipboard. "Also educated and ... unspoiled?" He looked at me with a raised eyebrow in disbelief.

"That's correct. Life on The Edge is full of hard work and late nights. It left little time for sexual activities. I have spent every day since I was sixteen working to ensure my grandmother would be taken care of financially. When I learned that saving myself would help ensure a higher price, I did just that."

He nodded as he made some quick notes on the paper. I could tell by his dismissal that he didn't believe me. "Well, as much as we would like to take your word, we have to be positive. We will start with the physical examination that will check both that and other health issues."

Without looking at me again, he turned and walked down the hallway. I followed him, resisting the urge to slap him on the back of the head for what he said and how he treated me. Why was it so hard to believe that I was a virgin? Did girls in the Capital just spread their legs for anyone who asked?

He stopped at a door that normally would have contained grain. I had helped Joe a few times when his workload was heavy. I knew this building inside and out. He opened the door, revealing that the grain room had been transformed into a makeshift exam room. A metal table sat in the center with a tray of tools next to it. I couldn't help but smile as I noticed small pieces of grain in the corners of the room. They had tried to erase what this place was, but couldn't. The Edge was here, whether they liked it or not.

"This is Dr. Griffith," Mr. Pyne said, motioning to a man about the same age as my grandmother. "I will be right outside when you are finished."

I stepped into the room as Mr. Pyne closed the door behind me. The click of the door closing sent another sense of dread through me. I held my head high as Dr. Griffith stood from his chair with a sigh, adjusting his glasses. He looked just as happy about being here as I felt.

"I'm sorry you have to do this," he said in a kind voice. "I promise to be as gentle and quick as I can. If you could just step behind the curtain and remove your dress. There is a blanket back there for you to cover yourself with when you are done." I looked at the curtain and walked behind it slowly. Carefully, I slipped off my mother's dress and hung it on a hook that I knew sacks usually hung on. I glanced around, making sure the doctor couldn't see me as I untied the blade and tucked it inside my worn white shoes. The shoes were something that Grams and I had agreed not to trouble ourselves over. They were comfortable, and no one could see them under my dress. The blanket did little to help me feel less exposed. I clung to its itchy fabric as I walked back out to where Dr. Griffith waited. When he saw me, he gave me a sympathetic smile and motioned towards the table.

I climbed on top, the cool metal against my bare skin bringing me comfort, probably the only comfort I would find today. The depot was uncomfortably hot with all the doors and windows shut. I felt my muscles relax as the cool feeling spread through them. It was weird how heat triggered panic in me, but cold brought a sense of comfort.

Dr. Griffith slowly examined my body, marking every scar he found on paper. I lay staring at the ceiling, trying to ignore what was happening. I had never let a man see me like this. Despite it being a medical exam, it still felt invasive, and I wanted it over with as quickly as possible. I breathed a sigh of relief as he covered me with the blanket and took a step back.

"Just one last thing," Dr. Griffith said with hesitation in his voice. "I have to ensure that you are intact."

Of course, it wasn't over. He had seen every inch of my flesh, but now he needed to see more. I nodded as I moved my feet into the stirrups he pulled up. He positioned himself at the edge of the table and grabbed a metal instrument from a table that I had never seen before. He gave me an apologetic look as he moved between my legs and set to work on his final exam. Who would have thought the first time I let someone near my lady parts, it would be an over-the-hill doctor? I winced as he placed something inside me, and an uncomfortable pressure spread. I gripped the edge of the table, begging for this humiliation to be over.

"Done," he said as he removed the device and set it on the table. "I must say, you are the first bride in all my years of doing this who was telling the truth, though I'm not surprised. I'm sure being out here, working to survive, you have some self-respect, unlike my usual brides."

"Can I get dressed now?" I asked, ready to end this humiliation. He nodded and motioned towards the curtain. I held the blanket against me, as if he hadn't just seen every inch of me, and walked behind it. Heat spread through my face at the embarrassment of everything that had just happened. I took a few breaths before placing the blanket on the chair and pulling my dress off the hook. It felt like I was slipping into armor as I slid the dress back on. Once the knife was secured to my thigh again, I stepped into my shoes and back out into the makeshift office. Mr. Pyne was back in the room, speaking in a hushed voice with the doctor. Somehow, his being here while I was getting dressed only made me feel more violated.

"Truly a miraculous creature," he grinned at me as he took the doctor's report and added it to his clipboard. I resisted the urge to slap him that suddenly surged throughout me. At least the doctor had tried to let me keep some of my dignity and pride. Mr. Pyne saw me as nothing but a prized hog to help him secure his reputation. My face turned hard as I glared at his too-perfect smile. I wasn't just some piece of meat for him to earn his reputation on. Any hope I had of him showing compassion and choosing my husband based on anything but silver was gone.

Mr. Pyne seemed unfazed and motioned for me to follow him as he walked out of the room. I walked out, nodding at the doctor as he gave me a kind, knowing smile. In the hall, an older woman waited, eyeing me with disgust as soon as she saw me. Her hair was pulled back in a bun that was too tight. I could see where the hair was pulling against her skin and changing the contours of her face. It made her look like a cloth stretched too tight over a frame. She looked at me over her wire-rimmed glasses, looking like she smelled something sour.

"This is Ms. Rynal. She will be taking you through the rest of your exam."

With that, he handed her his clipboard and left. The silence was crushing as Ms. Rynal looked over the clipboard, making a few sighs as she read. I resisted the urge to ask her what her problem was. This woman would play a role in determining my starting bid. For Gram's sake, I needed to keep my mouth shut.

"Educated," she finally spoke. "A rat from Ring Five claims to be educated. We will see about that."

My anger threatened to burst out of me, and my fists clenched at my sides. I could tolerate a lot, but her insults questioned not only my integrity but my grandmother's. Instantly, a familiar pain began in my head. I couldn't afford a migraine today of all days. I forced myself to take a deep, shaky breath and relax. It was just words. She could spit out all the vile things she liked. Soon enough, I would prove her wrong. That revenge would be so much sweeter than the one I would get from slamming her face into the wall.

I followed Ms. Rynal to a room with a small desk and a couple of chairs. This is where Joe used to keep outgoing deliveries. Again, all evidence of its true purpose had been removed, and it had been set up for the Union's needs.

I took a seat on one side of the table and waited as Ms. Rynal set up a stack of papers. For the next two hours, I sat as she quizzed my knowledge and skills. I answered each question, making sure to give detailed explanations for each of my answers. Every time I proved to her that I wasn't lying about my education, I took satisfaction in watching her face twist in disgust.

Most of her history questions were to ensure that I understood how the United Union was founded and run. It wasn't that hard to understand. Over a hundred years ago, mankind went to war and nearly caused the human race to go extinct. No written record tells why the war started, and there are none alive who remember. What was left of the world was mostly a wasteland. The lands were unable to be worked as it was killed by the radiation. The animals and the humans that remained were also changed. Three men, the original governors, discovered a section of land that had managed to survive. They founded the United Union. Over the years, the Union expanded five rings. Ring Five, or The Edge, was said to be a regret as the soil was too poor to produce anything of value.

To ensure that people thrived, those with the best genetic makeup were given lives in the best part of the Union, while those with mutations were banished to the outer rings - only allowed to remain because they provided the manual labor that the normals were too good to perform. In truth, the whole system seemed broken to me, but no one cared what I thought. I just repeated everything as I was supposed to, playing the part of a perfect citizen. Ms. Rynal listened to my answers before writing something down on the papers in front of her. I watched with satisfaction as she finished writing on the final paper and added it to a stack with the others.

"You did well enough," Ms. Rynal said as she set down her clipboard. "I assume by your attire that you are wishing for the Union to provide you with a dress?"

My mother's dress was more elegant than anything they could have offered. How dare she look down at it with disgust and assume it was trash? I clenched my teeth together, trying to contain my anger.

"No, thank you," I growled. "I am ready."

Ms. Rynal eyed me with skepticism but didn't argue. She stood and opened the door to her makeshift office. I followed her back to the entryway of the depot, where Mr. Pyne waited with an eager smile. She motioned for me to sit in a chair while she walked towards him. I watched, twisting my fingers in the fabric of my dress as I waited. I knew the minimum amount I needed to be valued at for Grams to have all the money she needed. If I could get close to that as a starting bid, this would be all worth it.

The decision between them seemed to become heated. Yet, they kept their tones low enough that I couldn't make out what they were saying. In the end, Ms. Rynal threw up her hands and walked away in frustration. Mr. Pyne seemed unfazed as he made a note and turned to look at me. I felt myself go stiff in their chair. This was it, the moment I would know if everything I was doing would be enough.

"You are truly a gem," Mr. Pyne smiled as he walked towards me. "We have agreed that your starting bid will be set at two hundred thousand silver, but I expect you will go for at least double that."

I forgot how to breathe as I stared at him in disbelief. That was more than double the minimum amount I needed. Based on his demeanor, I could tell that Ms. Rynal had not agreed with his high value of my worth. Not surprisingly, I had passed all of her tests, but she still saw me as nothing more than a rat from The Edge. I felt a surge of pride go through me at knowing she was upset. She thought she was better than me, but I had proven my worth.

43

"Is everything alright with Ms. Rynal?" I asked with fake concern. "She seemed upset before she left."

"Perfectly fine," Mr. Pyne assured me. "She just has trouble seeing the bigger picture sometimes."

I nodded, trying to contain the smile on my face. For a moment, the terror of what was to come next was banished by the glee I felt in making the old bat so upset. I could practically see her still in a huff as she told everyone that my starting bid was a mistake. Let her wallow in her despair.

"The ball will be starting in a few minutes," Mr. Pyne said as he tucked his clipboard under his arm. "You will be introduced last as the crown jewel of the event."

I looked around the empty depot, confused. "What about the other brides?" I asked.

"They were examined in the Capital and then transported here," Mr. Pyne explained. "We only did your examination here because your communicator will not grant you access to the inner rings until after you are purchased."

The glee I had felt from Ms. Rynal's obvious resentment towards me vanished, and the dread returned. This was it, the final moments before I became some rich man's wife and gave up everything I had ever known.

"It will be at least an hour before we are ready for you," Mr. Pyne continued. "You will remain here until it is time. Ms. Rynal will come to get you and deliver you to the tent."

With that, he turned and walked out of the depot. I felt like a block was sitting on my chest, slowly crushing the air out of my lungs as I stared at the door. Other brides were being introduced, walking into the glitz and glamour of an event that they had prepared their entire lives for. All were seeking the perfect match that would earn them the position and respect that their families desired. They all probably knew each other, in one way or another. I would be walking into the lion's den alone, without a friendly face in sight. They would all surely hate me. I was the reason they were forced to come to The Edge for the ball. Not only that, but I was also being billed as the most valuable and desired. My introduction to high society was going to be a party full of women who hated me and men who hoped they could afford enough to get into my pants.

My eyes remained fixed on the door as my heartbeat thudded in my ears. Each beat marked another second closer to my fate. They may hate me, and I could live with that, but I wouldn't let them change me. I was Elizabeth Allard, and I would not cower before them. I wasn't doing this for social standing or personal benefit. I was doing this for Grams. I could hold my head high knowing that none of them were above me tonight.

Chapter 4

$\mathscr{T}$he sounds of the ball drifted in as the door opened. The sound of string instruments playing a tune I was unfamiliar with could be heard over the murmur of voices. I looked up to see Ms. Rynal appear in the doorway. The look of disgust seemed to be permanently glued to her face, but it brought me no joy in knowing that I was the reason for it.

She motioned for me to follow as she turned and walked away. I gathered my dress and hurried to follow her. Despite her obligation to take me, she showed no signs of waiting for me if I fell behind. Outside, a gentle breeze brushed against my skin as I hurried to catch up with Ms. Rynal. I followed her to a giant tent that had been set up in front of the depot, and the sounds of the ball were flowing out. I walked through the light of the setting sun behind her, my nerves threatening to take over at any moment. We walked through a flap into a small area just large enough for us to stand in. The light was dim, adding to the dread that was growing inside me.

"Wait here," Ms. Rynal said with no emotion. "You will be announced in a few moments. When you hear your name, walk through that curtain and go straight to Mr. Pyne."

I looked at the red curtain that separated me from the ball. When I looked back, Ms. Rynal was gone. She hadn't provided me with any real comfort, but her presence was still better than being alone. Smoothing my dress to try to get rid of the wrinkles from earlier, I waited. Standing alone in the small, dim space was unsettling. I had to resist the temptation to pull back the curtain and peek inside. I didn't like not knowing what I was walking into, and right now, I had no clue.

Thankfully, I didn't have to wait long, as with each passing moment, the temptation and fear only grew. I held my breath as the sounds of the music and chatter died down. The silence on the other side of the curtain was unnerving. I took a deep breath, preparing myself for what was about to happen.

"Finally!" Mr. Pynes' voice rang out. "The moment you've all been waiting for. The belle of the ball. Certified pure and not too bad on the eyes if I say so myself. Ms. Elizabeth Allard!"

My breath caught in my chest as I stepped through the curtain. The lighting on the other side was glaringly bright. I resisted the urge to hold up my hand to shield my eyes. Instead, I forced myself to stand tall as I glided in. Immediately, all eyes fell on me. The men looked primal, as if I were a lamb they all wanted to devour. The women were different. Still primal in a way, but they looked as if I were someone intruding on their territory that they needed to destroy. So far, it was exactly as I expected.

I ignored them all as I focused and found Mr. Pyne. I forced myself to keep my eyes locked on him and walk towards him with more confidence than I felt. Taking his outstretched hand in mine, it felt like I was holding hands with the devil. Mr. Pyne turned me in slow circles, showing off the prize of the ball to everyone. Strange men, ranging from teenagers to grandfathers, ogled me without shame. The other women, all brides, glared daggers at me.

Ignoring their gazes, I took in my surroundings. For being a place to auction women, it was quite beautiful. Dark wooden tables with gloss lined the outer perimeter, with large centerpieces of flowers I had never seen before. Each centerpiece probably cost more than Grams made in a year, but at the end of the ball would be discarded like they had no value. The dirt ground had been covered with a smooth wooden floor, the center of which was clear for dancing. Overhead, chandeliers hung from iron beams, their light almost magical as it danced around the enormous tent. If it wasn't for the fact that I was being actioned off, I would have found it breathtaking. Instead, each beautiful piece seemed to mock and judge me as if it knew I didn't belong.

Mr. Pyne led me to the center of the dance area and motioned to the band, who started playing. I resisted the urge to pull away as he pulled me closer and began to dance. He moved gently and slowly, making sure that everyone got a good view of me as we went. I kept my touch on him light, though I would have preferred not to be touching him at all. I would need to get used to this discomfort. It was a necessary part of the evening. I would dance with all those who requested, answering their questions and trying to sell myself.

"Every man here has requested an audience with you tonight," he said in a hushed tone. "Bids will start as soon as our dance ends."

I nodded as he continued to slowly move us across the empty dance floor. I knew what my part was in all this. I was here, dressed to impress, and now I would have to suffer through my dance card. Each man on it was granted ten minutes of my time. I would dance or talk, whichever they preferred, and try to sell myself to each one of them. I was already ready for this to be over. Why did I have to go through this show? I didn't understand. None of them cared what I had to say, not really. They would bid based on my looks and their perceived value of me. Putting me through this just seemed like an unnecessary practice in torture.

Suddenly, I no longer wanted the dance with Mr. Pyne to end. At least with him, there was no chance of him trying to grope me or imagining what I looked like out of my dress. Well, maybe he still imagined, but there was no danger in him trying to act on his fantasies. The music came to an end, and the crowd clapped politely around us. I stood with Mr. Pyne as the other brides walked onto the dance floor, forming neat lines. Once they were in place, a man walked in front of each of them.

Mr. Pyne led me to the only man who stood alone. The man looked old enough to be my grandfather. Yet, his eyes traveled over my body in a way that made my skin crawl. When we

<u>51</u>

reached him, he seductively licked his lips, forcing me to choke back a gag. Bile burned at the back of my throat, and I could only hope my smile hid how disgusted I was.

"This is Mr. Theadore Retman." I did my best attempt at a curtsy before taking the man's hand. The man grabbed it readily and placed a wet kiss on the back. I fought hard to resist the urge to recoil and pull my hand away. Mr. Pyne smiled at me before walking away and disappearing behind a curtain. Before I realized what was happening, the music had started, and Mr. Retman had pulled me too close as he clumsily led me around the dance floor.

The next ten minutes were humiliating. Mr. Retman was a widower with six children, four of them grown and married. However, he wished for a young bride who could help bring his total to an even dozen. He asked nothing about me but explained what my duties and expectations would be as if I were already his. His breath smelled of stale whisky and rot. I could only assume that the rot was due to his teeth, which appeared to be disintegrating in his mouth.

I sighed a breath of relief as the chime signaling ten minutes up sounded. I bid goodbye to Mr. Retman, hoping that I would never have to see him again. I joined the other brides on the dance floor as we waited for our next partners. As soon as everyone was paired up, a chime sounded once more, signaling the start of our time.

This time, my partner was no more than seventeen. He explained that he was only here because his father required it. He had no say in the bidding whatsoever. I felt sorry for him as it was obvious that he wanted to be here less than I did. At least he chose for us to sit at a table, giving me a break from the dance floor. Silence filled the air between us, but I did not mind, and he didn't seem to either. There was something comfortable about it. In truth, it wasn't for his age, I wouldn't have minded being sold to him. He seemed gentle and respectful, something I was feeling sure was rare among the men in attendance.

"Ms. Elizabeth," a woman's voice spoke beside me. I looked at the woman, dressed in a plain black dress with hair pulled up in a tight bun. She looked as if she had taken fashion advice from Ms. Rynal, the poor girl. "Mr. Pyne requires your presence."

My heart began to pound in my chest as I said goodbye to the boy and followed the woman. The music stopped, and everyone was watching me as I walked across the tent and through a dark curtain. The men looked at me as if they were

53

being robbed of something, and the women smiled.

All of them were grateful to see me go, as it increased their chances. With the attention no longer on me, they would have a better chance at finding a desirable husband. Being pulled out could only mean one thing: my deal was done. My groom had finalized the deal, and my torture at the ball was over. Mr. Pynes' excitement when he saw me confirmed my suspicions.

"You, my dear, have made sure that my name will never be forgotten," he celebrated. "Your deal is done, and your groom is waiting with both your families and a governor to finalize the contract."

I forced myself to smile and try to appear grateful. His excitement about me cementing his legacy was ridiculous. As if I were doing any of this for him. Still, I needed to play my part. The contract wasn't signed yet, and Grams was counting on me.

"I thought it would take longer," I said honestly as he took a sip from a champagne glass.

"Normally it would have," he beamed. "I expected a regular bidding war, but when he offered one million silver..." Mr. Pyne clapped excitedly, unable to finish his sentence. "That is more than any other coordinator has made for an entire ball!"

"And who is my new husband?" I asked, a sinking feeling in the pit of my stomach. I had only met two grooms so far, and I felt the familiar burn of bile at the back of my throat. If I now belonged to Mr. Retman, I had a feeling I would need the knife Grams had given me. The weight of it around my thigh brought me strange comfort.

"I don't want to ruin the surprise," Mr. Pyne said with a wink as he continued to smile, his excitement showing that he had no idea about the turmoil I was feeling. "But you are a very lucky woman, my dear, very lucky."

I felt anything but lucky as I was ushered out of the tent and over to a small one set up a few yards away. There were rows of them set up. Almost as if there was a tent for each bride in attendance tonight. I felt like I was walking to the gallows with each step, my eyes darting around for a way to escape. While I knew I couldn't run, it helped my nerves to imagine doing just that.

When Mr. Pyne reached the tent meant for me, and gave me another big grin before pulling back the flap. My eyes immediately fell on Grams, and all thoughts of running disappeared. She had sacrificed so much for me after my parents died. It was a debt that I could never fully repay. But if marrying meant I could make sure she lived out the rest of her days in comfort, then that's what I would do. Her face was tight, and she looked uncomfortable. I couldn't blame her. I had been uncomfortable since I arrived at the depot that morning.

Besides, Grams were two people I didn't recognize, probably the groom's parents. Their faces were cold, and their eyes did not meet mine. A sign to me that they viewed this ceremony as nothing but a transaction. I hadn't expected more, but some small part of me had hoped for it.

I glanced around the tent, desperate to stall off looking at the groom as long as possible. The outer edge was filled with large, fancy pillows, some covered in expensive-looking blankets. Towards the back, I noticed an elaborate bed.

Realization struck me, and my gaze flicked back to Grams. The shame in her eyes confirmed my suspicions. I was right about there being enough tents for each bride. The contract was not enough to finalize the deal. My new husband would then claim his bride right here, with witnesses. I knew

I would have to give my body to him, but I didn't think it would be in front of an audience.

Slowly, I turned my attention to where a man stood with his back turned to me. He was in a fine suit with his dark hair slicked back, which reached his neck. I felt a small amount of relief that it wasn't Mr. Retman. I swallowed my nerves as I walked up to join him. In front of him was a small podium set up with a marriage contract laid out. A man in black robes, one of the governors, though I did not know which one, stood on the other side to officiate. The governor began to speak, stating all the terms of the marriage, including the sale price and expectations of each of us. I slowly tried to sneak a glance at my groom, but my attention was called back before I even got a peek.

"Ms. Elizabeth Allard, do you agree to the terms stated for your marriage to Mr. Ryan Pertug?"

My hands began to shake as I turned and looked at the man beside me. I may not have known who the governors were on sight, but I knew their names. Ryan Pertug was the eldest son of Governor Pertug. Most women would have said that he was a dream match. Wealthy, handsome, and influential. However, I had heard the truth about the type of man he was. His cruelty, especially towards women, had many saying that he was born without a soul. Women who gave him what he wanted were blessed with only receiving cuts and bruises or maybe a few broken bones, as a thank you. Those that didn't seemed to always turn up dead. Of course, he was never charged with any crimes. His father always made sure that his precious son's innocence was well known.

I wasn't one to believe in rumors. But when my friend Charlette was sent back to The Edge after taking a job as a maid at the Pertug estate, I saw his wickedness for myself. Charlette was able to hide her mutation well under her clothing. Her pretty face and slim figure made her attractive to most men who laid eyes on her. She had only been gone for a month when I heard that she was back. I had been eager to see her, but when I arrived at her mother's shack, the reality of her situation could not be ignored. Deep gashes covered her face, and her left leg was bent at an unnatural angle. When I asked her what happened, she broke down in tears. I held her while she cried and told me that Ryan had forced himself on her. When she tried to push him off, he attacked. He took her innocence and then ordered her to be returned to The Edge, bragging to the guards that no one else would want her now that he had ruined her.

She remained held up in her mother's shack for months, refusing to come outside even after her leg and cuts were healed. I could still remember the day in great detail when I went to check on her, and I learned that she had killed herself. Her mother was a wreck, telling me that Charlette had learned she was pregnant with Ryan's baby. The shame of what he had done to her and being forced to have his child was too much. Charlette had slit her wrists during the night, bringing an end to her suffering.

My hands shook with a mixture of rage and fear as I looked at him. His cold eyes were locked on mine as a slight smile played on his lips. He had no way of knowing that I knew Charlette, what he had done to her, not that he would have cared. He knew I had no choice tonight. The question was just a formality, and my signature nothing more than a symbol. Ryan had just used his father's money to purchase a woman that he could use for his sick delights for the foreseeable future.

My hand traveled to where the knife lay just under my dress. I stopped myself and forced my instincts to calm down. Killing him wasn't an option tonight. Grams would lose the money and probably be killed. But once the contract was signed, my life would be simple enough. I thought of and realized what needed to be done.

59

Once the contract was signed, two quick cuts on the arms would be all it took. Grams would have the money, and I would be free of whatever sick fantasies Ryan had planned.

Chapter 5

$\mathcal{N}$ight was settling in, and everyone was in position. Sneaking in had been easier than I thought. All of the soldiers' attention was focused on the auction tent. The guards stood lazily around the perimeter, enjoying what they thought was an easy assignment. The fools never expected someone to sneak in from the Deadlands and crash their precious ball. In truth, they were right. If it wasn't for her, I would have never dared to try to enter the city tonight.

The sound of the music and voices inside had only stopped as each knew bride was introduced. My heart stopped in my chest, knowing that at any moment I would hear her name. As time passed, I grew more and more anxious. The sooner she was announced, the sooner she would be purchased, and then we could get her out. It was too risky to try to take her at the ball. We had to wait until she was taken to the ceremony. There would be less security, and we could use the ball as a distraction. The majority of my fighters would converge on their party. Their orders were to avoid killing if possible. I needed them to cause chaos, not shed blood. Besides, the blood of a bunch of young, rich bitches wouldn't do anything to help our cause.

The pompous ass in charge of this year's action rung out once more as he described the newest bride. His voice dripped with a condescension that made my skin crawl. He spoke of each woman like they were nothing. That's probably how he viewed them. To him, they were nothing more than a payday. He would receive a percentage of each bride's purchase. I was only half-listening when I heard her name.

"Ms. Elizabeth Alard!"

Her name echoed in my mind as I stared at the tent. I couldn't help myself as I lifted the flap and ducked inside the tent. The coordinator's area was separated from the main ballroom, set up for him to start negotiating and accepting the price of each bride. The area was filled with plush chairs, filled champagne flutes, and smugness in the air that was nearly suffocating. I ignored it all as I snuck over to the curtain and pulled it back just far enough to see. Even amongst the sea of people, my eyes locked on her instantly. Her flowing white dress and confidence demanded the attention of everyone there. It had been three years since I last saw her, and I couldn't look away.

Something twisted inside me as I watched her take the coordinator's hand and begin to dance. The way he touched her may have looked innocent, but I still wanted to remove his hands and leave bloody nubs. She seemed to detest his touch on her as much as I did. Her hands barely made contact as he moved her around the dance floor. I watched with my fists clenched at my side.

The music stopped, and the brides all scurried onto the dance floor like puppies eager to prove their worth to their master. I watched as Elizabeth was led over to a man easily three times her age. The way he looked at her showed his intentions. She was nothing but a body for him to use in any way he saw fit. I could practically feel the blood on my hands as I imagined ripping out his throat for even daring to have those types of thoughts about her.

"Cal?"

Malic's whispering voice carried a sense of both urgency and worry. I was out of position, dangerous for a plan that depended so much on everyone meeting their marks. I looked at Elizabeth one final time before dropping the curtain and rushing back outside.

"Everyone ready?" I asked, causing Malic to jump. He looked at the tent and then back at me. Of course, he knew I was inside. Malic had been one of my best friends since before I could walk. He was the logical one between us, always trying to talk me out of bad ideas and helping me when I went through with them anyway. He had given me an earful when we were planning tonight. Reminding me that I had to stay objective and focused on the task. I had promised to do that, and he had caught me slipping already.

"They are," he said, nodding his head. "There are whispers that she won't be on the floor long. It looks like someone is offering more than any man here can match."

Of course, someone was. She was worth more than whatever amount they were offering. Little did they know that they were purchasing a bride whom they couldn't have.

"Then we won't have to wait long," I
sighed. "Remember, no one moves until she is in
the ceremony tent."

Malic nodded, not pointing out how many
times I had gone over the plan with all of them
on the way here or that I had already left my
mark. I looked back at the tent as Malic
disappeared into the night. I had waited five years
for this chance to save her. Now, in just a few
minutes, I would be able to do just that. It didn't
matter if she didn't remember me; if I could never
have her. I would protect her and make those
who hurt her kneel as they begged for mercy.
They wouldn't find it, but I would find peace in
their screams as they died for what they did to
her.

Chapter 6

" *M* s. Elizabeth?"

The officiating governor's voice pulled my attention back to the contract.

"Do you understand the terms of this marriage?"

I nodded, my hands balling up into fists at my side. Of course, I understood. I was being purchased by a man who caused my friend to kill herself and viewed women as nothing more than objects for sick pleasure. The governor seemed to accept my response as he turned to Ryan.

"Do you understand the terms of the marriage?"

"I do." The smile that Ryan gave me as the words oozed out of his mouth made me sick. Ryan turned to who I assumed was his father and took a large black case. He handed it over to the officiating governor, who accepted it with a nod before handing off to someone I hadn't noticed standing behind him. The man who took the case looked out of place. Everyone was dressed in their finest clothes and was well-groomed. He looked like he was trying to fit in, but I could see the ways he didn't.

His clothes were nearly threadbare, with rips in places that were sloppily stitched. His pants looked to be too big around his small frame. As he reached for the case, my suspicions were confirmed by a bit of rope that he seemed to be using as a belt. As he took the case, I could see a layer of dirt on the tips of his fingers and under his nails.

I looked at him with surprise and was met with a smile. Not the polite smile I expected, but one that said mischief was the reason he was here. No one else seemed to notice. I don't think any of them looked at him. But for a representative of the Capital, he did not look the part. I glanced around at Grams, who suddenly shook her head at me. Something was wrong, I could feel it.

"Once the contract is signed, Ms. Gertrude Allard will receive seventy percent of the price, fifteen percent will be given to Mr. Pyne for his services, and the remaining fifteen percent will be deposited into the United Union."

Everyone else was still focused on the ceremony, while my attention was drawn to the stranger who now held the silver I sold myself for. I couldn't help but fear that he would attempt to run off with the case at any moment. My gaze didn't seem to bother him as he stood and watched the ceremony continue. I didn't look away until he met my eyes and nodded towards Ryan. There were soldiers everywhere. If he tried to run, he wouldn't make it far.

I turned my attention back to the ceremony. I watched as Ryan picked up the pen and signed the contract. He didn't seem to have a care or concern about what we were doing or the stranger who was holding the silver. He just gained a toy that could never say no or run away. He was probably too busy thinking of all the ways he would make my life a living nightmare. Little did he know that once Grams had her silver, he would never get to lay a hand on me.

I watched as he signed his name with a big, flamboyant script. Of course, he had to make a big show of everything. When he finished, he held the pen out to me with an evil grin. With a shaky hand, I slowly reached out and took it. The urge to bury it in his neck was strong, and I struggled to keep my composure. I probably looked nervous to everyone else, but it was a mixture of anger and fear that caused my hand to be unsteady. I turned to the contract and looked down at the line that awaited my signature.

Everyone was watching me as I stared at the paper. My heart was hammering wildly. Knowing what would happen once I signed it did not make what I had to do any easier. Beside me, Ryan let out a frustrated huff. I knew I couldn't stall off what had to be done any longer. Cautiously, I put the tip of the pen to the paper and closed my eyes.

I thought of Grams, all the late nights she worked by candlelight to do extra jobs to pay for my schooling. All the times she went hungry because she couldn't afford enough food for both of us. When I opened them, my head felt clearer about what I had to do. My hand steadied as I tightened my grip on the pen. I could do this for her. I could give her the life she deserved and then free myself. My hand went steady as I opened my eyes. I began to move the pen to sign my death warrant.

BOOM!!

An explosion outside shook the tent, knocking the pedestal with the contract to the ground. I held the pen, still poised to sign as chaos erupted around us. The sounds of fighting and screams filled the night air, where music and voices had just been earlier. I stood in shock as everyone in the tent began yelling in panic.

"Let's go!" Ryan growled as he gripped my arm, causing me to wince. The pain brought me back to the reality of what was going on.

"She hasn't signed!" Grams interjected. "She cannot leave The Edge until the contract is finalized."

The sounds of the battle outside drew closer as Ryan tightened his possessive grip on my arm. Grams was stalling, but I didn't know why. The contract didn't mean anything. Ryan could force me to sign one once we returned to the Capital. I watched as the officiating governor picked up the pedestal and placed the contract back on it.

"Sign!" Ryan demanded as he shoved me closer. The panic swirling around us seemed to have made everyone forget that it wasn't needed. My eyes flicked to where the stranger with the case still stood. He seemed unfazed by everything that was happening. Grams' plan was working, and I had no idea what to do. I gripped the pen in my hand so tightly that it began to dig into my skin. Grams began shaking her head, her eyes pleading with me not to sign. Ryan's grip tightened as his patience ran out.

"Sign," he snarled. "Or I will slit the old woman's throat right here."

He knew exactly where to strike. I looked at Grams, still silently pleading with me not to. I whispered an apology to her as I turned and placed the pen on the contract once more. All I had managed before the chaos was to sign my first initial. I moved the pen to finish where I had left off.

"I wouldn't do that, dear."

Something about the stage man's voice caused my heart to flutter in my chest. I suddenly felt safe despite Ryan's burning grasp on my arm. The man with the case smiled as he dropped the case to the ground and took a few steps forward. I watched as he rushed up behind the officiating governor and placed a knife to his throat. As horrible as it was, I knew that he hadn't been the one to speak. The strange voice had come from behind me. I tried to turn and see who he was, but Ryan held me firmly in place.

"This is no business of yours, rogue!" Ryan shot back. "She put herself up for auction, and I purchased her. If you want her, I will loan her out for a price once I've taken what I paid for."

I was beginning to lose feeling in my arm and tried to pull away. As if the knowledge that he would touch me wasn't enough, hearing him talk about loaning me out was more than I could take. I could see the case of silver on the floor in front of me. If I could get free, I could grab it and run with Grams.

Ryan's grasp only grew tighter as he pulled me back. As he pulled me close to him, I could turn just enough to see the man. The confidence around him was breathtaking. Despite Ryan's threats and possessiveness, he seemed unbothered as he took a few steps closer.

"Let her go." The rogue's voice dripped with hate, and I could hear the warning in it. Ryan seemed unfazed as he continued to hold me close to him. I felt like a chew toy being fought over by two selfish dogs. I didn't belong to either of them, not really. Yet, they were both acting like they had some sort of claim over me.

I stared at the rogue, trying to muster the hate and anger I should feel about what his kind did to my parents. Instead, his ice blue eyes stirred something inside me. I looked closer, feeling as if he were familiar to me in some way. His disheveled, black hair and tall, muscular build made him someone who was not easily forgotten. But it was his eyes that held my attention. I couldn't know him; those eyes were something I wouldn't forget.

"And if I don't?" Ryan boomed beside me. His confidence in being untouchable was nauseating. I tried to pull away, positive that my arm would have a deep bruise where he held it. Ryan's grip was too strong, and he held me firmly in place. I let out a whimper as the pain in my arm intensified. I feared that if he squeezed any tighter, my bone would snap under his grip.

The rogue's face changed to one of pure rage at the sound of my pain. He moved swiftly as he charged at Ryan. Ryan's hold on me disappeared as he shoved me violently to the ground. I let out a puff of air as I hit, the pain still stinging in my arm. I pushed myself back up, gasping for air, in time to see them both crash to the ground, a flurry of blows and swear words. I remained frozen as they fought through the tent, neither willing to give up an inch for the other. The other man still stood with a knife to the officiating governor's throat, seeming to enjoy the fight that was unfolding before him.

The knife against my thigh suddenly felt like it was burning into my skin. I lifted my dress and pulled the blade out. I tightened my grip on the handle as I pushed myself up to my feet. I watched as the rogue pinned Ryan to the ground and began to hit him relentlessly. Blood splatter sprayed with each blow the rogue landed on Ryan's face. With as much damage as the rogue was doing, Ryan would be dead in a matter of moments. Ryan may have been one of the worst people in the Union, but he was still better than a rogue.

I felt the familiar tug at the back of my head. It felt like a small voice trying to speak to me. I understood what it was saying; the rogue needed to die. I strode with confidence towards the fight, my blade raised and ready to sink into the rogue's back. My hand began to shake once more, but I fought myself to steady. The rogue had to die, that was certain. My hand continued to shake as I began to bring the blade down.

"Stop!"

Grams' commanding voice broke through the sounds of the fight, causing both me and the rogue to go still. My gaze snapped to where she stood. I was surprised to see Ryan's parents on their knees, Grams holding a gun on both of them. She wasn't caught up in the chaos like the rest of us. She was part of it.

"Elizabeth," Grams breathed as she cautiously took steps toward me. "You will regret this for the rest of your life."

Confusion washed over me as I looked down at the rogue who was now staring up at me with a look of worry and hurt. I looked back at Grams, who was now only a few steps away. I felt like a small child again with the way she yelled my name and looked at me. It was as if I had done something wrong and she was preparing to scold me. I stared at her, confused, and watched as her face softened.

I stared at her as she lowered the gun and tucked it into the folds of her dress. Ryan's parents remained kneeling behind her, frozen in terror by the looks of it.

"Put down the knife, child," she said softly. "There is so much you don't know. Trust me when I say that killing him will bring you nothing but pain and regret."

The shake in my hand intensified. It grew worse until the tremble shook the knife out of my hand, and it clattered on the floor. The rogue instantly moved to pick it up, tucking it into his pocket as he stood. The familiar pain in my head appeared, obviously signaling that I had done something that was against the Union. I rubbed my temples as I took a step back. I should have killed him, both the rogue and Ryan. Saved myself this pain and future pain in one swoop.

An unfamiliar set of hands grabbed my arms firmly, but not enough to cause me pain. Still, I struggled against the grasp. I had been manhandled enough for a lifetime. The last thing I wanted was another set of hands on me.

"Let me go!" I demanded as I tried to fight my way free. Whoever was holding me was trying their best not to hurt me. But the splitting pain in my head was draining my strength quickly.

I looked down at the hands and realized that it was the stranger who had held the case. As I fought against his grasp, I saw that the officiating governor was kneeling with Ryan's parents. More people had appeared, each with a weapon trained on them. The pain in my skull was more than I could bear. I didn't know what else it wanted from me. I was trying to fight back, to escape, but it wasn't enough to stop the attack in my mind.

"We're going to make it so this doesn't hurt you," the rogue said in a deep voice as he stood in front of me. "That no one ever hurts you again."

His voice was gentle, like someone trying to calm a spooked animal. I would have found it comforting if it weren't for the immense pain I was in. I wanted it to end. I needed it to end.

"It already does," I cried through clenched teeth as the pain in my head intensified. "Everything will be fine," the stranger behind me whispered. "You are going to fall asleep. You will not wake until the king tells you."

I felt a slight tingling where his hands gripped my arms, and then every muscle in my body relaxed. The migraine that was tearing through my mind disappeared, and my eyelids became heavy. I searched around until I found Grams. She was standing beside a woman with red hair, another rogue. Her eyes looked tired as she gave me a weak smile. Had she been part of this? How else could they have known about the migraine that was ripping me apart? Why would she help the rogues when she knew they killed my parents?

"Grams?" I said softly as the stranger held me, and I slid to the ground. "Why? Why are you..." My words trailed off as my eyes grew heavier. I wasn't tired before, but something about what the stranger had said was causing me to barely stay awake.

"I'm sorry," Grams whispered as she knelt and brushed her hand over my hair. "This is the only way to save you."

"Save me?" The light from the tent began to dim as my eyes closed. "Save me from what?"

Tears glistened in Gram's eyes as she gently stroked my hair. She was trying to comfort me just like she did when I was a child. But this nightmare was real, and going to sleep was the last thing I needed to do. "There will be time for that later," she assured me. "For now, don't fight it. Rest, my child. You will need it for what's to come."

"What's coming?" I breathed out as my eyes closed. Her words didn't make any sense. We had talked about everything. If there was some type of danger, why hadn't she told me before? Darkness began to invade my mind, but I could still hear the whisper of voices around me. They thought I was asleep. I continued to fight against whatever had been done to me. I wasn't able to open my eyes or speak, but my mind was still listening.

"Get her out," Grams said firmly. "I will stay to protect as many as I can. He won't let her go easily."

"She won't understand," I heard the rogue growl. "You are all she knows!"

I felt Gram's hand brush my hair once again. I wanted to find comfort in her touch, but I suddenly felt like she was a stranger. The way she spoke to these invaders, the way she worked with them. This wasn't the grandmother I knew. How could I not have seen that she was hiding something this big? The woman who held me when I cried for days after my parents died. The woman who promised me that one day those who killed them would get what they deserved. She was working with the murderers and their people the entire time.

"She will remember," she said confidently. "Just give her time and don't push. And when she does, watch her. The realization of what she's been through may be more than she can handle."

I didn't want to hear anymore. The more I listened, the less I understood. I stopped fighting against the darkness and allowed it to swallow me whole. Perhaps when I woke, I would learn that this was all just a terrible nightmare. It would be the morning of the ball, and this all was nothing more than my mind playing out my worst fears.

Chapter 7

"*Time* to wake up."

My eyes flew open at the sound of the voice. A field of stars was above me as my eyes fluttered open. I could hear the crackle of fire close by and knew immediately that what had happened was not just a nightmare. I pushed myself and looked around in a panic. Gone were the tents and comforts of the ball. Gone was Ryan and the marriage contract. I had been taken. I looked around at the wasteland, the few dead trees that stuck up out of the dead soil, trying to grow where life was snuffed out before it began. My eyes eventually locked with his - the rogue.

He sat by the fire, watching me from a distance like a vulture. I grabbed at the dirt, trying to find something to defend myself with. My hands found nothing but useless soil, not a rock to be found. He had taken my knife, and Grams had let him take me. Now, I was out in the middle of nowhere with no way to defend myself.

The rogue remained still as he watched me search the area around me. He probably expected me to be scared. Well, I wouldn't give him the satisfaction. I steadied my breathing and kept my face stern as I met his gaze.

"You need to drink," the man said firmly as he tossed a water bottle to me.

I stared down at the bottle for a moment before kicking it back to him. He laughed lightly as he picked it up. I watched as he opened the lid and took a slow drink. After he swallowed several times, he put the lid back and tossed it back to me. I caught it and looked at him, confused. He thought I was refusing it because it may have been poisoned. How could he not see that I was refusing it because he had kidnapped me? I wanted nothing from him. I wanted to go home.

I felt myself relaxing and looked down at the bottle. Somehow, despite the heat around us, it was cold. I glanced back up at him to see him watching me intently. Slowly, I took off the lid and lifted the bottle to my lips. I needed to get home, back to Grams. She would be able to explain everything. I had to have misunderstood what happened in the ceremony tent. But my only way home was this rogue. As much as I despised him, I needed him to think I was giving in.

I needed him to think I trusted him so that he would trust me. I would have to play the role of a damsel and give him the ego boost he needed. That was something I could do. I had perfected playing the role expected of me over the years. It was the only way to avoid the migraines. I could do this. I just had to do it right.

I took a few sips, the cool water bringing me comfort that I would never admit. When I finished, the rogue seemed satisfied and began to add more wood to the fire. His gaze flicked towards me occasionally, as if checking to make sure I was still there. Where would I go? I had no idea where I was or how to get back.

"Where are we?" I asked after a few moments. "And don't say the Deadlands, because that's obvious."

"About ten miles away from The Union," he said without hesitation. "Halfway to Twain."

"Twain?" I asked as I closed the bottle.

"My city," he replied. "We will finish the journey in the morning. It's too dangerous to travel after dark, and carrying you slowed me down."

The tone of his voice made it feel like he was blaming me for the slow travel. If he hadn't had that stranger knock me out, he wouldn't have had to carry me. Looking around, I noticed that there were no other campfires or people close by. There had been others when he attacked. Yet, now we were alone. Had they been captured? If so, The Union would make them talk, and help would be on the way. I just needed to stay alive until they arrived.

"They will come for you," the rogue said, as if reading my mind. "But not tonight. By the time they find us, you'll be ready."

"Ready for what?" The words spilled out of my mouth before I could stop them. Grams had said something similar. Something about me remembering and needing my rest for what was to come. Yet, no one was saying what I needed to be ready for.

"We will get that off you tomorrow," he said, motioning to my communicator. Frustration boiled inside me as he ignored my question. I kept my face calm, though, playing my part. "The days after that will be rough, but you'll live."

"It's against the law to tamper with or remove a communicator!" I gasped, holding my wrist closer to my body protectively. There were a few laws that I feared. When I was younger, I had taken pleasure in finding ways around them. The migraines didn't come back then, back when I was free. But tampering with a communicator came with a death sentence.

"And why is that?" He raised an eyebrow at me as he sat back down across the fire.

I struggled to find an answer. It was well known that communicators could not be removed, and any attempt to do so was punishable by death. But why something so mundane, especially in The Edge, was so well protected, I had no idea. I wasn't about to admit that to him, though. Instead, I gripped my communicator tightly and shuffled further away from him.

"Tell me something," he continued. "Tell me a specific memory from before your sixteenth birthday."

"What?" This rogue liked to speak in riddles, and I was losing my patience with him. I already regretted not stabbing him when I had the chance. "My parents were killed by rogues when I was seven."

"How?"

"What do you mean, how?" I snapped. What did he care how my parents died? He was playing a game, and I already wanted out. I felt my mask begin to slip with frustration. "I wasn't standing there watching them butcher my parents."

"Surely your grandmother told you," he said smoothly. "Even if not the gory details, she had to have given some sort of explanation."

I tried to think back, to remember the day Grams had told me my parents were dead, but drew a blank. I knew it happened, but the memory of it didn't exist. "I was seven," I finally said. "All she told me was that they died in a rogue attack. That night, our house was burned to the ground. I lost them and everything else in one night because of people like you!"

"People like me?" he laughed. "I am roughly the same age as you, yet you blame me for their deaths."

"Your kind is responsible," I growled. "You are all the same, murderers who hate what we have and do everything you can to destroy it." So much for playing my part. My mask had completely disappeared as I glared at him.

"Then explain why, since the night your parents died, there hasn't been one rogue attack?" It felt like a challenge, and I refused to play. There hadn't been any attacks since that night. The Union soldiers had diminished their numbers and forced the few that remained to retreat into the Deadlands. "Explain why tonight, no one was killed, and not a single building was burned? Well, except for that hideous tent."

I had no way of knowing if he was telling the truth or not. I had heard the explosion when it shook the ceremony tent. People were screaming outside, and it sounded as if there was fighting. I found it hard to believe that no one was killed, but I had no evidence either way. The silence hung between us as we stared at each other across the fire.

"Tell me a memory before you got that thing put on?" he demanded. "Just one, and I will take you back right now."

My mind raced, trying to find a memory to give him. It didn't have to be much, just something. As I tried to think of one, I felt a headache begin to prickle at the back of my mind.

The longer I tried, the more intense it became. I didn't need to be helpless with blinding pain right now. It would make me more vulnerable than I already was.

"I can't!" I blurted out. "Even trying brings on these damn headaches."

"And why do you think that is?" His questions were going to drive me mad. Why did he care about such things anyway?

"The doctor said it was my mind's way of keeping me from remembering things that I couldn't handle," I said sternly.

"A Union doctor?"

"Of course! All doctors are Union doctors. What does that have to do with anything? As long as I don't do or say anything that tries to pull at those memories, I'm fine."

"And you see nothing wrong with the fact that you cannot even speak your mind without a splitting pain? Or that you supposedly saw a Union doctor when they only treat the inner rings? Someone could crawl to the door of the medical center with their legs cut off, begging for help, and would be turned away. But they made an exception to see you for headaches?"

I tried to remember seeing the doctor, but nothing came to mind. It was all blank. There was just something inside my mind, like reading a book, that told me I had. What he said made sense. Union doctors did not treat people on The Edge. That is what had caused the people to attack and attempt to raid the facility several times over the years. How would I have managed to get help for headaches?

I shook the thoughts out of my head before the headache could get worse. He was playing mind games, and I was done. I had answered his questions, and I was ready to get back to my life. Even if that meant marrying Ryan, it was better than being trapped out here with a rogue. There was no telling how much radiation I had been exposed to since I had been brought out into the Deadlands. People out here were driven mad by it.

That's why they were not permitted to join The Union. Maybe it would mean that I was no longer eligible to marry Ryan. Perhaps the exposure would force me to stay on The Edge. That thought made my heart begin jumping in my chest. Perhaps there was a benefit to this after all.

"Take me home."

"I can't do that," he smiled. "The beasts are hunting, and it's too dangerous to leave the light. Plus, you still haven't been able to tell me a memory."

I stood up, my frustration boiling over. The beasts that roamed the Deadlands were nothing but a bedtime story to scare children out of sneaking away from The Union. I looked up at the stars, remembering how they looked back home - a home, which, according to the rogue, was ten miles away.

"Thanks for the water," I smiled at him, a plan fully formulated in my mind, and the pain gone. I had a general idea of which way was home. It would have to be enough.

"But I really must get back. Grams worries that something terrible has happened when I'm late."

The rogue's face went white as the meaning behind my words hung in the air. I turned and took off in the direction of home, or the direction I thought home was. Looking back, I watched as he disappeared into the dark before he even got to his feet. I was grateful that I had elected to stay with the worn flats for the ball. Running in them proved easy as I made my way through the dark, not daring to look back to see if he was following me. If I kept up this pace, I could get back to The Union by dawn. Whatever fate awaited me there had to be better than out here.

The cool night air brushed over my face as I moved as swiftly as I could. I felt myself smile as I moved; the freedom I felt was almost intoxicating. However, as with all things in my life, the happy moments always come to an abrupt end. Something hard hit me in the chest, knocking me off my feet and the breath out of my lungs. I gasped for air as a heavyweight climbed on top of me, pinning me to the ground. The creature let out a growl that vibrated every bone in my body.

"Shit," I breathed as the creature's hot breath hit my face and its warm drool dripped onto my cheek. It was too dark for me to make out what it was, not that it would have helped me. Whatever it was, it was larger than me, and I had no way of fighting it off. Turning my face to the side, I closed my eyes and waited. I knew the creature wouldn't wait long to claim its meal. I could only hope that I died quickly so I wouldn't have to endure the agony of it eating me while I was alive.

The creature's weight suddenly disappeared from on top of me, and I heard it thump to the ground. I opened my eyes to see a dim light coming from a torch nearby. I rolled over to see the rogue with his arms around some sort of beast. I looked in the direction of home, something inside of me screaming to keep going. I looked back at the rogue, still fighting with the beast. The beast was stronger than him, taking bites at him with both of its mouths, which were full of sharp teeth. I think it used to be called a wolf, but the radiation had made them bigger, with two heads and their eyes sensitive to light.

Light! I grabbed the torch and hurried closer to where the rogue was now pinned to the ground. I shoved the torch close to one of the heads just as it snapped at the rogue's face. It immediately let out a howl and backed away. I continued thrusting the flame forward until it had gotten off the rogue and stood at a distance, growling at me. "Duo-wolf," the rogue said as he stood up and took the torch from my hand. "We should get back to the fire. Their pack is never far, and one torch is not enough to keep them all away.

I nodded, the pain in my head urging me to continue. However, I knew I could survive the migraine, but a pack of duo-wolves in the dark, I might as well kill myself now and get it over with."

The rogue took my hand and began to lead me back to the camp. The fire was still burning brightly as he led me close to it and helped me sit. I curled my knees to my chest, hiding my face from the light as my migraine ripped through my head.

"Drink," he said as he thrust a bottle towards me.

I shook my head no, fearing that I would throw up if I even tried. Besides, water wouldn't help.

"Drink," he said in a softer voice. "It will stop the pain."

I looked up at him, seeing the honesty in his face. I took the bottle and brought it to my lips. The fragrant smell reminded me of the flowers that had been at the ball, too beautiful to be real. I quickly chugged the water, not stopping for a breath until it was empty. When I finished, I tossed the bottle to the ground and returned to hiding my face. I didn't care if the water killed me. Either way, the pain would end. To my surprise, a few moments later, the pain was gone -

not even the normal pressure that lingered after the migraines remained. "What was that?" I asked, surprised.

"A tonic," the man answered. "It helps suppress the effects of a Silver Tongue for a short time. It's only temporary, but it will keep you from getting those headaches for a while."

I couldn't help but look at him like he was mad. I had no idea what insanity he was talking about with a Silver Tongue. But still, I was grateful for the relief. He tossed a bag beside me before standing up and turning his back to me. Inside it, I found a change of clothes. Looking down at my mother's dress, I could see that the once white fabric was covered in dirt. I tried to brush it off, but my hands only pressed the dirt deeper into the fabric. I needed to get out of it before it couldn't be saved.

Making sure that the rogue still had his back turned, I slipped out of my mother's dress and into the clothes he gave me. After carefully packing the dress back in the bag, I laced up the boots I found in there as well. Everything fit me surprisingly well, as if he had known my size and prepared the clothes. That was ridiculous, but still, I felt better and less exposed than I did in the dress.

"Thank you," I managed, causing him to turn back around. His expression was something I didn't recognize as he looked at me. He quickly made it disappear as he walked to the other side of the fire. "Do you have a name, or should I keep calling rogue?"

His lips twitched into a smile that sent shivers down my spine. "Calix," he said in a way that sounded dangerous. "Calix Harkin."

My blood ran cold. No one had seen the King of the Deadlands before, but everyone knew his name. His reputation was even worse than that of my intended husband. Not only was I with The Union's most wanted man, but also the one responsible for my parents' deaths. Looking at him, he was probably a child when they were killed, but he had to have taken his title over from his father. Just when I thought there was goodness in my kidnapper, I learned that he was the most vile man to ever exist.

He continued to smile as he pulled a bag under his head and lay down. I stared at him, words refusing to form as the realization that I was stuck in the middle of the Deadlands with a murderer. If I were going to survive, I would have to get as far away from him as possible. But for tonight, I was trapped. I couldn't fight off the beasts that lurked in the dark and needed the safety of the fire. I would have to wait until morning to escape, if he allowed me to live that long.

Chapter 8

I barely slept that night. I kept watching Calix, waiting for him to make a move to kill or perhaps rape me. But he remained still, sleeping as if this rough ground were the softest bed in the world. I never thought I would miss the prickly straw mattress, but that night I yearned for the small comfort it provided. Eventually, my body betrayed me, and exhaustion took over. When I woke, I was still clutching the bag containing my mother's dress, and Calix was gone.

Panic filled my head as my eyes darted around. Had he decided to leave me out here to die? If he were gone, I could start my journey back to The Union. All my plans of how to slip away wouldn't be needed. How disappointed he would be when he learned that I was stronger than he thought. He had left me to die, not knowing I would find my way back.

My hopes were dashed as I spotted him just a short distance away, watching as the sun rose over the hill. Beside me, I noticed a bottle of water, bread, and an envelope. My stomach growled, demanding the food first, which I gave it. He hadn't poisoned me yet, so I doubted he would now. Once I had eaten enough to silence my stomach, I picked up the envelope. Written in a neat handwriting that I knew too well was "The King". I traced my fingers over the curves of the letter, my heart aching for Grams at the sight of them.

I was so caught up in emotion, it took me a few minutes to wonder why, or even how, she had written to Calix. Another thing she hid from me all these years. Turning the envelope in my hands, I found that it was already cut open. I slid out the piece of paper folded inside, my heart pounding in my chest. Unfolding the paper, I saw a letter that I couldn't deny was written in Gram's handwriting. Carefully, I read the words, each proving that I didn't know her like I thought I did.

Calix,

I send this as both a formal request and an apology. For reasons that are too long to explain, I could not allow you to help Elizabeth escape until now. Trust me when I say that doing so would have cost her life. But now, we have a small window to not only finally free her from The Union but give her a chance to remember everything they took from her. At the ball tonight, her communicator will be deactivated as soon as she enters the ceremony tent. It has to go offline to be updated for her new ring of residence. That is the only opportunity we will have.

Despite your feelings towards me, I know that you will do the right thing. It is time for her to awaken and The Union to burn.

Gertrude

I kept re-reading the words as if they would change. Grams asked him to come for me, to take me away. She even told him how and when to do it. I thought back to what I heard her saying before I passed out. She said she was staying behind to protect those she could. She had gone through a lot of trouble and risked everything to get me out. She said there were things I didn't understand and told Calix it was time for me to awaken. None of it made sense, and my head was beginning to hurt. I ignored the pain as the thoughts continued to race through my mind. Regardless of everything, I knew that Grams only did what was best for me. If she thought that being out here and going to Twain was best, I would need to trust her.

I stood with resolve and determination, coursing through me as the pain continued to throb in my head. "Which way to Twain?" I yelled to Calix.

I watched as a smile spread across his face, and I felt a sudden flutter in my chest. Why did making him happy make me react like this? It wasn't him I trusted, but Grams. Still, I didn't know the way to Twain, and I needed him to show me the way. I smiled back as he began to close the gap between us. That's when it happened. The pain in my head intensified to a level it had never been before. I thought my head might explode. Grasping it, my eyes slammed shut, and I fell to the ground screaming in pain. My skin felt like it was on fire as the pain continued to intensify. It was as if my decision had signaled my brain to kill me.

"Liz?!"

Calix's voice sounded like it was coming from a distance, but I could still hear the worry in it. I tried to respond, but I was in too much pain to form words.

"Shit!" Calix yelled as I heard him fall to the ground beside me. "We should have had another day before the tonic wore off!"

Well, he was wrong. The pain continued to rip through me, causing my muscles to tighten and my entire body to hurt. I felt my body being lifted from the ground. I kept my eyes clamped shut, knowing the sunlight would be more than I could handle, and the pain was already threatening to kill me at any moment. I felt a coolness that surprised me. I buried my face closer to it, the cool mixing with the scent of fresh snow and a burning fire. The relief from the heat in my body helped to take a bit off the pain. I suddenly became aware that I had my face buried in Calix's chest, and he was running. I could hear his heart beating frantically in his chest. Whether from panic or running, I didn't know.

I should have felt shame and pulled away, but I remained as close as I could, desperate not to lose the comfort I was finding in his arms. He may have been evil, but in this moment, he was an angel. But then again, according to old scripture, so was Lucifer.

"Malic! Malic!" Calix's voice cried out with urgency and panic. The sound of it rang in my ears and caused the pain to intensify. I leaned in closer to him and tried to block out his screams.

"What the hell happened?" a voice that sounded almost out of breath asked with urgency. I recognized it from the ceremony tent. He had been the one to tell me to go to sleep, the one who held the case.

"The tonic wore off," Calix quickly explained. "The pain it's, it's killing her."

I felt my body returning to the ground and instantly clung tighter to Calix. Carefully, he peeled my arms from around his neck and held onto my hand. The coolness I felt while he was holding me remained as if it was radiating from his hand. The men's voices talked in hurried tones, but I was too exhausted from the pain to focus on them. I lay still, fearing that if I attempted to move, it would cause the pain to finally kill me.

While the prospect of dying had been my solution the day before, the thought of it now terrified me. I had too many questions that needed to be answered. I couldn't die with them all still hanging over me. I needed to live, but the reality of my situation seemed to be saying that wasn't an option.

"I have to have her permission!" someone shouted - a man whom I didn't recognize. His voice echoed in my head, causing even more pressure on my skull that felt as if it was already cracking.

"Get that fucking thing off her now!" Calix demanded.

I felt someone beside me, leaning close to my ear. "Elizabeth," he said softly. "I know you are in a great deal of pain, and I can help, but I have to remove your communicator. The removal may be painful, but afterward, your body will be able to heal, and you will never have these migraines again. However, I would never do such a thing without your consent."

I could feel the heat fighting to return to my skin, his offer flaring up my condition once more. It was a crime to remove it, but if he was right, not taking it off would kill me. I thought of Gram's, what she said in the tent, and her letter. She must have known that they would need to remove my communicator. I didn't understand how it was the source of my migraines, and I was too exhausted to try. For the first time, I was being given a choice. I could have them remove it and live, or keep it on and die. I chose to live. "Get it off," I said through clenched teeth.

The man wasted no time. I felt my wrist being held, the now scorching metal slowly being peeled off my skin. I let out a scream that echoed all around us and instinctively tried to pull my arm back.

"Hold her down!" the man yelled as he continued to pull on my communicator.

Suddenly, more pairs of hands than I could count appeared and held me firmly in place. I continued to fight against them as the pain ripped through my body. It felt as if my flesh was being torn away with my communicator. Despite the pain in my wrist, I could feel the pain in my head slowly begin to fade. The more of the communicator that lost contact with my skin, the less the pain lessened. The hands holding me remained firm, not allowing me to squirm or pull away.

"Fuck me," the man said as the pain became dull and my migraine became nothing more than pressure. "It's rotting her damn skin."

I was too exhausted to look at what was going on, but based on what they were saying, it didn't sound good. Rotting flesh was something that they weren't expecting. I felt a worry deep in my chest. If they had not expected it, perhaps it would mean I would die after all. I chose to live only to have that choice ripped away from me once more.

"She's strong," Calix said firmly. "She'll heal." The ground disappeared beneath me, and the familiar scent of snow and a campfire filled my nose. He held me close to his chest, careful not to touch my wrist that was rotting.

"With that kind of damage," a woman said with worry, "It will take everything she's got just to survive the detox. There's a good chance she won't remember..."

"We did this to save her!" Calix growled. "We will help her get well so she can make her own choices moving forward. We've set her free. We can't ask for more than that."

Everyone went silent, and the only thing I could hear was the sound of Calix's heart beating hard in his chest. It was a steady pace now, but each beat was strong. I focused on the rhythm of it, distracting myself from the fear that was growing inside me. After a few moments, I felt him start walking and could hear the footsteps of others behind us. I thought several times that I heard the sounds of people, maybe a market, but every time we drew closer, everything disappeared. The silence returned, and only the sounds of footsteps could be heard. It felt like the world was holding its breath while we walked by. I kept my face buried in Calix's chest with my eyes pinched shut. Part of me was too scared to even dare a glance at where we were, and the rest was too exhausted to try.

"Make sure everyone is on high alert," Calix commanded. "Close the gate. No one enters without my permission."

There was a murmur of voices and the sounds of footsteps walking away. We must have arrived in Twain. I wish I could have seen it, the rebel city that somehow survived the harshness of the Deadlands. Perhaps I would get the chance if I survived.

I felt Calix lower me onto a mattress. Not a straw mattress like I was used to, but one that was soft and formed to my body. I kept my eyes closed and remained still as I sank into a comfort that I had never experienced before. I hadn't moved, spoken, or opened my eyes since I permitted my communicator to be removed. Now, I hoped that Calix would believe I was unconscious. I needed space and quiet to recover and think through what had happened.

"I know you're awake," Calix said in his deep, commanding voice. "You have been the entire time."

I remained still, unable and unwilling to give up my ruse. I was caught, but I still had no desire to talk. Too much had happened. I just wanted to be left alone.

"The next week is going to be hell for you," he continued. "Like a drug addict going cold turkey. Ms. Timlin will come in and check on you throughout the day, bringing you food and water and changing the bandage on your wrist."

I felt my stomach knot. It sounded like he was speaking to me for the last time. I didn't know why that bothered me, but it did. He was the only person I knew here. Despite him being my Lucifer, I wanted to keep him close. I had lost enough and wasn't ready to be completely alone.

"You will stay in this room until Gertrude arrives," he continued. "Even after you are feeling better. After that, she will help you decide what you want to do next."

Grams was coming. Relief spread through my body. As soon as she arrived, everything would make sense. For now, I just needed to focus on getting better.

I listened as the sound of his boots thudded against the floor, and I heard the door close. Slowly, I opened my eyes, my vision blurry as I looked up at the metal ceiling. I tried to push myself up to sit, but the little food in my stomach threatened to come back up as the room spun around me. I collapsed back into the mattress, closing my eyes until the nausea passed.

"Stay still," a kind voice urged as a gentle hand pressed a damp cloth to my head. "It will be a while before you can sit up, let alone get out of bed."

I opened my eyes and looked at the woman who was leaning over me. She was older, probably mid-fifties, with silver hair tied back in a loose bun at the back of her neck. She wore a loose dress that hung over her large frame but looked to be well made. Of course, the granddaughter of a seamstress, I still noticed her clothing as I lay here an inch from death. As the image of her became clearer, I could see scars covering the skin on the right side of her body.

"It was a fire," she said gently as she dabbed something on my wrist. "Not everyone appreciates what a good healer can do."

I felt my cheeks go red with embarrassment. I hadn't meant to stare, but she had seen me do it. Turning my attention away from it, I lifted my arm so that I could see my wrist. I wanted to gag at the sight of the tainted skin, and the smell didn't help. My communicator was gone, but where it had been, the skin was blackened and looked as if it were rotting. The smell reminded me of when meat was left out in the sun for days. Desperate as we were for meat, no one would dare try to touch it. We would bury it under a mound of dirt to hide the smell while it decomposed and eventually disappeared.

That's what I was now. I piece of decomposing meat. They should have just buried me and allowed me to disappear. I wouldn't have blamed them. Yet, here I was with a strange woman trying to nurse me back to health. I had chosen to live. They were taking my choice seriously and trying to help me recover. How was that even possible? I didn't know. Rot couldn't be stopped once it set in. Regardless, Ms. Timlin applied an ointment to my disgusting flesh and carefully wrapped it. She had said she was a healer. Perhaps she knew something I didn't.

"Have you seen something like this before?" I asked, tearing my gaze away from my disgusting skin.

"No," she said, her honesty shocking me. I hadn't expected she had, but I thought she would at least pretend to make me feel more at ease. "But I am confident that it will heal up just fine. If it leaves a scar, I'll just buy you a pretty bracelet to cover it up."

I couldn't help the giggle that escaped me. I was in the Deadlands, my communicator was gone, and a strange woman was trying to heal my rotting flesh. Yet, the thought of her buying a bracelet to hide the scar was the ray of light I needed on an otherwise shitty few days. I could tell that I was going to get along with Ms. Timlin. She seemed like a kind, gentle person, but was also a straight shooter. She was kind yet honest. Honesty was something that was sorely lacking in my life right now. All the secrets that Grams kept felt like they were weighing down on me. But right now, hearing a kind woman talk about buying a nice bracelet to hide any scarring, I felt safe for the first time in days.

"What did Calix mean by the next week would be hell?"

Ms. Timlin finished wrapping my wrist and gave me a soft smile before sitting on the edge of the bed.

"Your communicator was injecting venom directly into your bloodstream. The venom was what was being used to control your mind and give you migraines when you did anything against The Union."

I remained silent as she explained. It sounded impossible, but the fact that the pain had disappeared and the skin on my wrist was now rotting, it was impossible to argue.

"Your body has learned that the venom is part of it," she continued. "Taking it away will cause you to go through withdrawal. With as high as your dose was, I guess that it will take a week for you to get it all out. You will feel sick, and the remaining traces of it will try to get you to put your communicator back on. You will be like a drug addict looking for their next score."

"Oh." The word sounded hollow, but I couldn't think of anything else to say. Whatever venom was, it was comparable to me being a drug addict and was used to control my mind.

"Don't worry," Ms. Timlin patted my hand as she stood up. "I promise not to let you have your communicator and not to hold against you any of the nasty things you may say while going through withdrawal."

Chapter 9

*M*ost of the next week went by in a haze of sleep and rants that made me feel like I was drunk. Ms. Timlin was kind and patient despite how ugly I was to her. Every few hours, she came to my room with food, water, and medicine. I threw things at her and cursed her for not bringing me my communicator. I heard myself demanding it. I felt that I needed it to be whole. But the whole time, part of me could hear how crazy I sounded.

Calix had said I had to go through detox from whatever the venom was. I had seen addicts in The Edge suffering without their drug of choice in the streets. It was never a pretty sight, but I never felt pity for them. They had made their choice, and now they had to suffer the consequences. Now, experiencing what I was, I couldn't help but change my stance slightly. Yes, most of the blame still lay with them, but part of it was with a government that pushed them to the breaking point, where they didn't have anything to live for. And now I knew how it felt trying to get clean, how your mind and body work against you to get back the very thing that was poisoning you. I hadn't chosen this, but I still understood their struggle a bit more.

After about a week, the shaking in my hands began to ease, and the constant sweating stopped. It felt like a fog was finally clearing from my mind, and I could breathe again. As I sat up in bed, I could feel the grime and dirt on my skin. A touch of my hair told me that it was a tangled mess and equally disgusting. I felt embarrassed as Ms. Timlin knocked and came in just as she had done all week. I was sure I smelled, and yet she showed no disgust as she looked at me.

"Good morning," she smiled as she walked in with a breakfast tray. "After yesterday, I thought maybe some bacon and eggs would be better than oatmeal. Easier to clean if you decide to fling it."

She never lost her smile as she walked over to the bed and set it down. My cheeks heated with embarrassment as I remembered throwing the bowl of oatmeal at her the day before. She hadn't been angry with me. She just gave me a gentle smile and cleaned up the mess. I had sat on the bed, hurling every curse word and insult I could think of at her. Still, she had returned a few hours later with a sandwich and a glass of water.

Her patience was unnatural, and I needed to find a way to set things right.

"Thank you," I said softly as I looked down at the breakfast. I knew that more than a simple 'thank you' was needed, but it was all I had, and it was a good start.

"Of course, my dear," she said as she took a step back. "To save myself some trouble today, I must ask if you will wash if I warm up the water, or should we just wait until tomorrow?"

"I can do it," I said as I took a bite of the eggs. "I've already given you so much trouble this week. Thank you for putting up with me. I'm not normally like that. It must have been..."

"Oh, thank the heavens," she said with a smile as she clapped her hands together. "Honestly, I was starting to wonder if it would take another week for that venom to clear out of your system. I've never seen someone given such a strong dose. I knew you were strong, though, and you would find your way back. I just wasn't ready to say I was wrong with my initial estimate."

I smiled politely, still embarrassed about my behavior over the past week. I took a bite of the eggs and realized how hungry I was. Despite her bringing me multiple meals every day, I rarely ate. It was like I thought if I starved myself, she would give in and give me my communicator back. Ms. Timlin was strong, though, and my crazed self never stood a chance.

As I ate, Ms. Timlin disappeared through a door on the opposite side of the room, and I could hear the sound of water running. She had ignored me, saying that I could draw my bath and was still taking care of me. I quickly ate my breakfast, my stomach angry with me for refusing so much food over the past week. Just as I ate the last bit of bacon, Ms. Timlin appeared, drying her hands on her apron.

"It's all ready," she smiled. "Just keep your wrist as dry as you can, and I'll return to change the bandage when you're done."

I looked down at the bandage around my wrist. This week had been so rough that I hadn't even looked at it again since that first day. When I looked back up, Ms. Timlin was gone. That woman could walk without making a sound. Carefully, I climbed out of the large bed, my bare feet unsteady on the wood floor. At some point, my clothes had been changed after I arrived. I was now in a long white nightdress that was desperately in need of washing or perhaps finding its way straight to the garbage. My opinion was that it needed to be put out of its misery.

I carefully walked crossed the room, taking it in for the first time. The large bed took up about half of the space. However, the space that remained was still larger than Gram's entire shack. On the other side was a wardrobe, a vanity with a mirror, a pair of chairs on either side of a small table, and a fireplace. While the furniture was lovely, I couldn't help but feel like it seemed empty. There were no decorations or personalization of any kind. Even as poor as people were in The Edge, they always found ways to decorate their homes in a way they felt made them warm and inviting. But this room felt almost cold and empty.

Stepping through the doorway, I found myself in a washroom. Back home, we had a bucket that we used to haul water and heat it over the fire. It was always a sponge bath, and then we used what was left to rinse out our hair. This room was more than just a bucket of warm water. A round, metal tub took up half the room. Water was filled three-quarters of the way up, and I could see the slight steam rising off it. I looked at the pipes and could see where a small flame was lit. If I had to guess, the water flowed in and was warmed in the pipes as it traveled to the tub. It was a brilliant setup and one that I would have to remember. Something like this could be life-changing for people back home.

I stripped the nightdress off and slowly lowered myself into the hot water. My muscles instantly relaxed the further I sank until I sat on the bottom. I closed my eyes and leaned back, deciding to enjoy the comfort of the bath before setting to scrubbing the filth off myself. Normally, heat bothered me, but not when it came to washing. I had tried cold baths once to avoid the anxiety that came from heat. But, after locking up my muscles several times from the cold water stabbing into my skin, my mind seemed to agree that an acceptance had to be made for bath water.

When the water began to cool, I decided it was time to wash. Carefully, I unwrapped the bandage around my wrist, hesitating before finally removing the final layer. I waited for the rotting smell to assault me and the sight of my blackened, rotting skin to overwhelm me. Instead, the skin was now a shade of light gray, the smell was gone, and it looked to be healing. Looking closer, I could see spots where my normal skin tone already appeared. Whatever Ms. Timlin had done, she was a miracle worker.

I used the soap on a small shelf to scrub the grime from my skin, carefully keeping my wrist as dry as possible. I could feel myself getting lighter as the dirt and grime washed away. It was like I was scrubbing off everything I had been through over the past week. Once I had scrubbed every inch of myself, I washed my tangled mess of hair. The soap was difficult to work through the mess and even more difficult to rinse. When I finished, I refused to look at the water. I climbed out, fearing that the dirt I would see would cause me to ask for another bath to keep washing. I felt lighter as I stepped back onto the floor, wrapping a towel around myself.

Back in my room, I found a fresh set of trousers and a blouse waiting for me on the bed. On the vanity, there was a brush that I couldn't help but look at like it was a murder weapon. I dried and dressed quickly before walking over and picking it up. My hair had been tangled before, but never this badly. As I tried to pull the brush through, I felt like I was trying to rip my hair from my scalp.

"This may help," Ms. Timlin's voice spoke behind me. I turned to see her holding a small glass bottle with a clear liquid in it.

"I think I should just shave it and start over," I said in frustration as I turned back to the mirror.

"Maybe," she nodded. "But could I at least try first?"

I turned and followed her over to the chairs. She sat in one, and I sat on the floor like a child. I remained still as she gently massaged the liquid into my hair and slowly began working the brush through. Whatever she was using turned the experience from torture to relaxation. I sat still as she took her time and worked the brush through all my hair.

"There," she said finally. "I think I managed to save it."

I smiled as she stood up and placed the brush back on the vanity. I reach up, feeling the soft texture of my hair once again.

"Now, in the chair."

I did as she said and stood up and took a seat. Ms. Timlin held out her hand, and I placed my wrist in it. After examining it for a moment, she pulled out an ointment from her apron and rubbed it on. I was surprised that it didn't hurt, even with as gentle as her touch was.

"Almost there," she said once she finished. "I think you may still deserve a pretty bracelet for making it through all this."

"Thanks," I laughed. "But I'm not big on jewelry, especially after this."

"I'll think of something then," she said as she finished wrapping it in a fresh bandage.

"Can you let Calix know I am feeling better?" I blurted out as she headed for the door. "So, maybe he could stop by and see me today."

I regretted the words as soon as I spoke them. I had no idea why I wanted him to know how I was doing or why I wanted to see him. Yes, he had saved me and brought me here to free me from the venom. But that didn't change who he was. It didn't matter how much kindness he showed me, he was still my personal Lucifer.

"I will let him know," Ms. Timlin nodded before she left.

The twinkle in her eye made me feel uneasy, but I managed to smile back. Once she was gone, I let out a sigh of frustration as I walked over to the window. I should have been asking about Grams. If there had been any news, or if she had arrived yet. Why had I asked about that murderous traitor of a king? Perhaps some of the toxin was still affecting me? That had to be it. Nothing to feel guilty over. It would surely take a few more days before I thought completely clear again. Until then, I just needed to rest and take my time.

I looked out my window, eager to distract myself from my thoughts. Below was a beautiful garden, something that I was sure most people would have marveled at. Not only because of its beauty, but also how well it was growing in such poor soil. My eyes traveled beyond it, beyond the tall fence that kept it contained, and to the city beyond. Even from a distance, I could hear the sounds of people laughing, children playing, and a city that was full of life. Not only was their life, but it sounded as if the people here were happy and thriving.

I stood there listening, only taking a break when Ms. Timlin brought me my lunch and supper. She never questioned why I was at the window, just seemed genuinely happy to see me out of bed. After dinner, she came back once more to change the blankets before wishing me goodnight. I returned to the window, listening as the city fell asleep.

Gone were the sounds of people and workers. Instead, the sounds of crickets and a cool breeze blowing filled the night air. All day, I had listened for sounds of violence, debauchery, or anything we had been warned the rebels did. I found none of it. This place was relaxed, and for the first time since my parents were killed, I felt at peace.

As I began to turn away from the window, my eyes swept over the garden. I would need to ask if I was allowed to visit it tomorrow. I had never seen this many living plants growing in one place before.

I almost didn't see him at first, walking through the dark. I leaned closer, watching as Calix made his way through the paths with flowers in his hand. I couldn't help but laugh that I was spying on the king going on a late-night rendezvous with some unknown woman. How scandalous. Maybe there was some debauchery here after all.

I watched with a grin until he reached a place where I could see four large stones sticking out of the ground. Carefully, he divided the flowers into two bundles and placed them on two of the stones. My smile disappeared as I realized he was not meeting a woman; he was paying respects. He stood there for a long time talking to the stones. He was too far away for me to hear what he was saying, but something in his expression showed the sorrow he was feeling. Part of me wanted to call out, to find a way to comfort him, but I remained silent. I was already intruding on a private moment, and the last thing he would want was me trying to comfort him.

I watched as he turned and walked away, back towards the house. As soon as he was close, he suddenly stopped. My heart thudded in my chest, and I gasped as he suddenly looked up at me. His piercing blue eyes cut through the dark as they reflected the full moon overhead. My heart froze as he looked at me, not in anger but with a softness that made my heart freeze in my chest.

I ducked away from the window like a scared child who had been caught trying to sneak out and ran to the bed. I dove onto the mattress and pulled the blankets over my head. I was grateful Ms. Timlin had changed them today. I didn't want to think about how filthy the old ones had been. I sat in the dark, hiding under the blankets, and tried to slow my breathing. Minutes seemed to stretch on forever as I waited for him to come to my door and yell at me for spying on him.

After I felt enough time had passed with no knock on the door, I slowly lowered the blankets. My eyes moved slowly around the room, half expecting him to be standing in the shadows. I had spied on him, so it would only make sense that he might take his revenge by doing the same to me. I breathed a sigh of relief

when I found the room empty and lay back on
the pillows.

I hadn't done anything wrong, not really.
Maybe I had spied on him a little, but he was
walking through the garden outside my room.
Really, could it be considered spying, seeing as he
walked into the only view of the outside I had? I
had been at that window all day observing. Other
than Ms. Timlin, I had been alone all week.
Maybe if he had come to check on me, I wouldn't
have needed to spy on him or listen to the sounds
of the city to feel connected to something other
than the furniture.

No, I didn't want him to check on me. I
was content to stay in this room until Grams
arrived. Well, except for asking if I could go to
the garden. Then maybe I could learn who he was
paying respect to. I snuggled into the pillow,
feeling content in my reasoning that it was his
fault that I was spying on him, just like it was his
fault that I was curious who was buried in the
garden. There were four stones, and I could only
assume that meant four graves. Was it possible
that there were four people that the great King of
the Deadlands cared enough about to mourn?

Chapter 10

A solid knock on the door caused me to look up from my work. The house was shut down for the night, and everyone had gone home- everyone except Ms. Tillman. I studied the door for a minute, considering telling her to go away, but I knew she wouldn't listen. She was one of the most stubborn yet patient people I had ever met.

"Come in," I said in a firm voice.

I set down my pen as Ms. Timlin opened the door and closed it behind her. While everyone else, except for my closest friends, always spoke to me with respect and a slight bit of fear, Ms. Timlin was not impressed nor intimidated by my title. She had been my mother's best friend and practically raised me after my parents were killed. It wasn't easy, but she had made the sacrifice without ever complaining. When I had insisted she move into the manor, I meant for it to be her home. But as soon as she learned that Elizabeth was being rescued, she demanded to be her nurse and caretaker. Honestly, there was no one I trusted more with the task. But I knew that this would give her reason to try and push me to do things I didn't want to do.

"The venom has worked its way out of her system," she said with a soft smile. "She wanted you to be informed so that you might visit her."

My stomach twisted into a knot. "Does she..." I couldn't bring myself to say the word.

"She remembers nothing still," Ms. Timlin continued. "Yet, it seems like she is still drawn to you without knowing why."

My heart thudded in my chest, and I hoped I was hiding how I felt. Ms. Timlin raised a knowing eyebrow at me, unfooled by my lack of reaction. Still, I kept my face as neutral as possible as I picked up my pen and went back to work. "It will pass."

I should have known better. Ms. Timlin was not going to let me out of this conversation that easily. I heard her feet stomp across the floor just before she ripped the pen from my hand. I looked up at her in disbelief as she put her hands on her hips. She was normally more subtle about her scolding, using her soft words to cut through you rather than physical acts. I had managed with three simple words to piss her off.

"Why not go to her?" She demanded. "I've watched you suffer these years, trying to find a way to bring her back. Now, she's right up those stairs and you sit her scribbling in a book!"

"I can't," I growled, my chair scraping against the floor as I stood up. "It's best if she never remembers. I have let her go, and now she will be free to live the life she chooses."

"How dare you!" I could see the flush of red spreading across her face like a tea kettle ready to blow. Nothing she could say would change my mind, but I braced myself for her anger. She had never struck me before, not even as a child. Not that a hit from her would truly hurt me. But still, it stirred a fear inside me that I didn't realize I had. "How would you feel if someone took it all away from you?! If you were alone in this world, not knowing where you come from or anything about who you are?!"

"Free," I replied firmly. "All that hurt and pain is gone! I would have asked Malic to take it away years ago if I thought there was a chance he would!"

We stood staring at each other, rage filling the space between us. I refused to be the first to break the silence, and she looked as if she was trying not to explode.

"Alone," she finally spoke. "They don't just take the bad when they change your mind. They take the good, the love. It leaves you alone in this shit storm without even knowing who you are. You aren't doing her a favor. You are leaving her alone to suffer."

I opened my mouth to retort, but she was already walking out of my office, slamming the door behind her. In truth, I had no idea what I was going to say. I thought it would be better for her to forget about our parents' murders, the fights, and the killing we survived. Every painful memory she had was tied to me in some way. If she didn't remember me, then she wouldn't remember the pain.

But what if Ms. Timlin was right? Was I leaving her alone to suffer without any of the good? Was I hurting her more by not trying to help her remember? I took a deep breath and ran my hand through my hair. Perhaps part of me did want her to suffer a little, just like I had over these past five years. It still felt like yesterday that I was standing in that cathedral, so long I swear I could see it rotting around me. The pain I felt when Gertrude came instead of her to tell me what happened. The emptiness in her eyes when I passed her on the street, and she didn't recognize me, was torture.

I had done that walk more times than I could count. It was a risk, being in the Union during the day, but I had hoped for years that one day she would look at me and see me again. For three years, I kept trying, and never once did she see me.

Suddenly, my office felt small and like the air was trying to suffocate me and suffocating. Grabbing the flowers out of a vase that one of the maids must have put in here, I walked out and into the back garden. It had been months since the last time I was out here, and part of me felt ashamed. I made my way through the bushes and flowers to the stones in the center.

Splitting the flowers in half, I placed them on the two center stones. I walked closer to the two on the right and knelt, closing my eyes before looking at the names. I ran my fingers over the engravings, seeing my parents' faces in my mind as I played here as a child. They had taken risks, too many in my opinion, to do what they believed was right. The last risk they took had put them in these graves. Even knowing that, I knew in my heart that given the chance, they would make the same choice.

That's what Elizabeth had done when she went to the medical center. We had talked about needing to get a communicator. Thomas had just mastered his ability enough to be able to manipulate the metal of which they were made. If we could get one and remove it without having to destroy it, we could use it to gain access to the Union's inner workings. Of course, Elizabeth had volunteered immediately. She was always so eager to take down the Union that she put herself in the most dangerous situation. It had been months since we had anyone try to leave the Union, and it was our best option.

Still, I refused. I could still remember our fight. In the end, she had said she wouldn't go. I should have known she was lying. She had that look in her eyes, she always had when she was about to do something she knew she wasn't supposed to do. She hadn't done it to hurt me or be selfish. She had done it for me, for the cause that our parents had died for.

I looked over at the other two graves where her parents rested. She was so close to them and didn't know. She deserved to know the truth about them, about what they fought and died for. It was a disgrace to their memory and everything they had done to allow her to believe they were killed by rogues, by my parents.

Perhaps Ms. Timlin was right. I was punishing her and making her feel alone out of spite. As I brushed the dirt from my pants while I stood, I suddenly became aware that someone was watching me. I made my way out of the garden the same as I had come in, careful not to look up at the window where I knew she was watching. As I neared the door, I couldn't resist anymore and looked up. It didn't matter how hard I tried to stay away from her, somehow, she would always end up finding me. I couldn't help but laugh as she scurried away from the window, embarrassed that I had seen her.

If she ever did get her memories back, I would never let her forget that for five years she was as timid as a mouse. The strong, confident, and rebellious woman I knew was still in there. I didn't know if she could ever get her memories back, but perhaps I could at least be the friend she needed. I could help remind her of her strength and help her regain part of who she was.

Chapter 11

"*N*o sleeping in today," Ms. Timlin's voice rang through the room.

I let out a groan as I opened my eyes to see that the sunlight was just starting to peek through the window. I had stayed up late, my mind refusing to give way to sleep, and instead kept assaulting me with thoughts about Calix. I had even considered trying to climb out the window to see whose graves he had visited the night before. In the end, I decided against it out of fear that I would break my neck.

"Fresh clothes are in the closet," Ms. Timlin continued as I stretched in an attempt to wake my muscles. "I suggest pants and a light shirt with a comfortable pair of boots."

Tossing back the blankets, I slid out of bed and onto the cool floor. I watched sleepily as Ms. Timlin set down my breakfast tray on the table and headed towards the door. While I did adore this kind woman who had done so much to help me since I arrived, her chipperness this morning had me wanting to punch her in the face.

"Maddison will be by to collect you in twenty minutes. She's not well known for her patience, so I suggest you not keep her waiting."

So many questions ran through my mind. Someone named Maddison was coming to get me. Calix had said I would stay in this room until Grams arrived. Was he sending someone to get me so he could punish me for watching him last night? This seemed a bit excessive for an accident.

"Who's Maddison?" I managed to ask.

My question hung in the air unanswered as Ms. Timlin shut the door behind her. I had been in this room for a week with no one but Ms. Timlin checking in. I couldn't help but feel concerned that I was suddenly being woken at dawn and told a stranger would be by to collect me. Whatever was going on, I wasn't going to face it in my pajamas.

I rushed to the closet and changed into the outfit Ms. Timlin suggested. I grabbed a piece of toast and the glass of juice off the breakfast tray as I made my way over to the vanity. Holding the toast between my teeth, I slid the brush through my hair. It was still smooth and untangled thanks to whatever Ms. Timlin had put on it the day before.

I ate as I rummaged through the vanity and found a hair tie in one of the drawers. Brushing my hair out of my face, I secured it with the tie. I had just finished my juice when there were three quick knocks on my door. I turned and watched as it opened, and a girl about my age with fiery red hair walked in.

"Maddison?" I asked as I set my glass down.

"Maddie," she corrected with a grin. "You look much better than you did when you arrived."

I recognized her voice immediately. She had been there when they removed my communicator. It felt like an eternity since the events of that day, despite it being just a week ago. Still, I felt comfort in knowing that she was in some way familiar, at least her voice was.

"I feel it," I smiled back. "Amazing what cleaning a bit of venom out of your system can do for a girl."

"Cal wants me to give you the grand tour," she nodded with a smile. "He thinks it will help you feel more comfortable to get to know and see the people here. That way, you don't feel so alone until Gertrude arrives."

So, this wasn't a punishment for last night. Calix was trying to make me feel more at home, more comfortable. I would have been happy just to have been allowed in the garden. But, instead, I was getting a full guided tour around the city. I tried to hide my excitement as I followed her out of the room.

I hadn't seen anything when I arrived, keeping my eyes shut and face buried in Calix's chest. I should have expected grandeur based on the room I was in, but it still took me by surprise. The walls were all wood, the slats nearly perfectly straight with no gaps in between, with a metal roof. And not the type of metal roofs I was used to. There were no signs of rust or holes that would require buckets under them when it rained. Everything was solid and very well maintained.

The hall was decorated with paintings and pictures. Photographs were something that we didn't have access to back home. Some painters would attempt to paint your portrait for a small fee, but it always ended up being more abstract than realistic. Small tables stood under the pictures with flowers or statues. Everything looked as if it were polished, or perhaps that dust was too afraid to tarnish its beauty. I turned as we walked, trying to take in everything.

I followed Maddie down the hall a short way to a staircase that led down into a large entryway. Everything was clean and elegant as people walked in and out carrying goods or in conversation. Maddison swiped a couple of apples from a basket as we walked by and led me out the door. I stopped, allowing my eyes a moment to adjust to the bright sunlight. Maddison waited patiently and tossed me an apple. I managed to catch it just before it hit me in the face.

"Not nearly as fancy as the capital," she said as she took a bite, "but it's home."

I stood holding my apple as I stared in awe at the city before us. The buildings were close together, each looking to be of solid construction with curtains fluttering in the windows and blooming flowers growing outside. The people who walked were all smiling, some waving and offering me a greeting as they passed by. I couldn't imagine what Maddison said was true. Nothing could be grander than this. It looked like a place where people not only survived but lived. Why had the Union told us that this place was nothing more than a wasteland filled with people who were driven mad by the radiation? By the looks of things, they were living better than people on The Edge.

"Come on," Maddie waved as she walked into the street, continuing to eat her apple.

I ran to catch up and followed her as she pointed at the buildings, telling me what goods or services were offered. I was surprised by the number of them that contained what we considered luxury items on The Edge. I glanced inside each as we walked by, marveling at the glass figures, racks of clothes, children's toys, and books.

Books were things I had only ever seen during my studies. They were much too expensive for anyone in The Edge to be able to afford. I stood at the door and watched for a moment as people browsed the shelves before leaving with their treasures.

"It's a library," Maddie explained. "Anyone is free to borrow as long as they return them. They also offer reading classes twice a week."

I couldn't find the words to express the wonder I felt. In the Union, knowledge was something you had to pay for, but here they were just giving it out. It felt surreal as I watched a small girl walk past me, clutching a small book to her chest. It didn't matter that she wasn't rich or from a wealthy family. Here, she was allowed to read and experience a world that only existed on pages.

"Cal has a small library back at the manor," she continued. "I can show you when we get back if you want."

I nodded as I turned and followed her deeper into the city. As we walked, I couldn't help but feel that some of the people looked familiar. I kept quiet, trying to place where or how I had seen them before. Maddie continued talking and pointing at the buildings, her words blurring into the city's noise as I struggled to absorb all the information.

"Why Twain?" I asked as we walked.

"The people who founded this place, Cal's great, great-grandfather, I think. He found an old, broken metal sign when he was gathering supplies and learning the land. It was broken in half, and the only word that remained was Twain. According to some books, this used to be a forest, the Mark Twain Forest. As the first was gone, he decided to keep the half of the name that remained, and Twain was born." She held out her hands and spun in a circle as she motioned to the city around her. "The sign hangs outside the gate, a tribute to the past."

I remembered from school days that there used to be an expansive forest in this area. They taught that the reason some of the land survived was because the center of the forest was so rich that even the radiation couldn't kill it. That's where they built the Union and claimed everything else was a wasteland. I was beginning to see the lies that were sprinkled with a bit of truth to make it more believable.

"What's this?" I asked her to stop at a shop we were walking by.

"Mirda's Trinkets," she smiled. "Mirda sells little figurines and such, sculpted from metal. Primarily, she helps take care of littles if their parents have to go outside the city."

I felt myself walk forward and into the small shop. I wanted to ask why anyone would ever want to leave this place, but something pulled me inside. There were shelves lined with little metal figurines, each uniquely beautiful. I gravitated towards one and picked it up in my hand. The metal felt cool in my hand, but there was something about it that felt familiar.

"First one's free," a kind voice said. I had been so absorbed in the figure; the voice caused me to jump with a start. I turned and saw a woman in her sixties sitting behind the counter on a stool. "The first one always seems to choose its person."

"It's beautiful," I said, looking back down at it. It was a simple scene, a small girl swinging on a tree swing, her hair flowing behind her as she glided up to the sky. Whoever had manipulated the metal in such a way was brilliant. The details of the tree and even the girl's face were amazing.

"How much is it?" I asked, my throat tightening as I realized I didn't have any money. I couldn't just take something so lovely without paying for it. "It's on me," she smiled. "Looks like you could use it."

"I can't..." I said, looking back at the figure.

I wasn't one to owe favors or money to anyone. It always caused problems when people had something they could hold over you. Looking at the woman, I didn't get the feeling that she was trying to show anything but kindness, but I still couldn't just take it.

"I've got it," Maddie said as she stepped closer to the woman and placed a few coins on the counter. "Lizzy here isn't one for taking things without giving."

The woman nodded and slid the coins into her apron pocket. I clutched the figure as I followed Maddie back out of the shop, feeling strangely protective of it.

"Thanks, Mads," I said once we were back outside. "I promise I'll pay you back."

I didn't know what had happened to the case that held the silver at the ceremony. But if Calix had it, the coins inside were mine. He could give me at least some of them to pay Maddie back and take care of myself. I looked up from the figure just in time to realize that Maddie had stopped and avoided colliding with me. Her face was one of shock as she stared at me. I felt uncomfortable under her gaze as I clutched the figurine in my hands.

"No worries," Maddie said with a shrug and a smile before turning and continuing like nothing happened. I shook off the tension I felt and followed behind her.

The rest of the day was spent without the tension of that moment. We stopped and had lunch at a small cafe. The owner was a robust man with a loud voice that made you smile when he spoke. He insisted he knew what I wanted and didn't allow me to order. I wasn't a picky eater, but it made me nervous not knowing what he was going to serve. The plate he set down in front of me was piled with steaming vegetables, rice, and chicken. My mouth watered at the sight of it. I should have been ashamed of eating it all in one sitting. That serving was more than Grams and I ate in a week. Still, the feeling of the warm food in my body brought me joy that overrode any embarrassment I had.

Everyone we met was warm and welcoming. I saw nothing of the savages we were warned about in the Union. These all just seemed like normal people, living their daily lives outside of the Union's rule. I made Maddie promise that we would visit the library as soon as we returned. I was eager to read every book, no matter the subject, and then move on to the next.

"I should get you back," Maddie said as the sun was setting. "Ms. Timlin will have my hide if you miss supper."

I nodded, still clutching my metal figurine. Today, I felt normal and free for the first time in years. I should have been afraid or trying to find a way out, but I couldn't think of a single reason to leave. Grams would be here any day, and I was determined to convince her to make Twain our new home. I had no desire to return to the Union, to a place that poisoned my mind and body.

"Thanks," I said softly. "For showing me around and being so nice to me."

"Just remember that when I need you to back me up with Cal one day," she smiled back.

I nodded, unsure what she expected me to do that would convince Calix to agree with her on anything. In our few interactions, he had beaten my groom to a bloody pulp, kidnapped me, saved me from a beast, and locked me in a room to detox from a venom. It wasn't like we were close or I had any sway over his decisions. He had only done those things because Grams asked him. Once Grams arrived, I felt confident that he would wash his hands of me and I would never see him again.

I followed Maddie through the streets, darkness settling in around us, and the manor finally came into view. She reached for the brass handle on the large wooden door just as a bright light broke through the dark. We both spun as the sounds of an explosion filled the air around us. In the distance, flames and smoke could be seen billowing into the sky. The streets that had been quiet were suddenly filled with people, all rushing towards the fire and shouting to each other.

"Get inside!" Maddie yelled as she ran past me. "Find Ms. Timlin and stay with her."

"I can help." My voice sounded stronger than I felt. I was tired of hiding or having to be rescued. If this was going to be my home, I wanted to help.

"Help by staying here!"

I watched as Maddie disappeared into the sea of people heading towards the fire. My grip tightened on the figurine as I looked at the closed door and then back at the fire. I couldn't just go inside and hide while a fire was burning in the city. It could easily spread, people could be killed, and I would have done nothing to stop it. Staying here wasn't helping; it was being a coward.

Setting the figurine down on the stoop, I ran to join the others. People crowded around me as I ran with them through the streets. I wasn't sure what I would do when I got to the fire, but I didn't care. An extra set of hands could only help the situation, not hurt it. I could help try to put it out, help move the injured away from danger, or just be there to help those who needed it. No matter what I did, I felt confident that it would be appreciated. Maddie was just being protective, she would understand why I had to help.

I was done being told what to do. It was time that I took control over my life and stopped letting people or headaches dictate who I was. I chose to live. The man who had removed my communicator had given me a choice, and I made it. It was time to step up and start living. Otherwise, I may have just told them to let me die that day. My life had meaning, it had to. Why else would the Union have poisoned my mind to keep me in line with their way of things? I was meant for more than being a wife who gave a husband the children he desired. I was meant for more than being just a scared girl hiding away while other people took care of things. I was Elizabeth Allard, and I was done trying to be what other people thought I should be.

Determination coursed through my veins as I followed the crowd closer to the fire. For the first time, I was doing what I wanted, and there was no pain trying to stop me. I didn't have to hold back. I didn't have to be scared. I could do what I thought was right without worrying about my decision trying to kill me from the inside. A smile spread across my face as I continued to run. This was exhilarating, dangerous, but exhilarating.

Chapter 12

$\mathcal{I}$ could feel the heat of the fire from a block away. People filled the streets, carrying buckets of water and dirt that they passed in a line to be thrown onto the flames. I considered joining them, helping to move the buckets, but pushed forward. A few looked at me in surprise as I ran past and into the chaos. In front of me was a two story building, part of it gone from the explosion, and the rest engulfed in flames. In the street, people were sitting, covered in soot and burns, but nothing that looked too serious. I stood in shock and watched as people threw dirt and water into the flames, trying to get the blaze under control.

The heat from the fire triggered my anxiety, and I began to second-guess my decision to come. Perhaps it would be better if I moved back and joined the bucket line further away from the flames. Just as I was about to turn and leave, movement caught my eye just inside the flames. A gasp escaped my lungs as I watched Calix step out of the building with a man. His skin was blackened and dirty, but he looked to be unharmed. I watched as he helped the man to where the injured were and carefully lowered him onto the ground.

"That's everyone," he said loudly as he looked back at the building. "Concentrate the efforts around it. There's no saving it, but we can keep it from spreading."

Shouts echoed throughout, and the people with the buckets began concentrating on any flames that tried to reach beyond the structure. I looked back at the fire, a sick feeling in the pit of my stomach. As much as I wanted to escape the heat of the flames, something wouldn't allow me to leave. My eyes began frantically searching the flames for something, anything. That's when I saw him. A young boy, no more than seven or eight, was in the second-story window. He was only visible for a moment before the flames pushed him deeper inside.

Swallowing my fears, I began to run towards Calix. My heart was hammering in my chest as I ran as fast as I could. Suddenly, a strong hand gripped my arm, pulling me to a sudden stop. The jar of being forced to stop caused a pain to radiate through my arm. I turned, ready to tell off whoever had stopped me.

My stomach twisted as I found myself staring at the man from the ceremony tent. He was no longer trying to play the part of a Capital errand boy and was dressed in nothing but a pair of pants. "What are you doing?" he growled as he began to pull me away from the fire.

"There's a boy inside," I cried, pulling against his grip. I was sick of these men thinking they could just force me to go where they pleased.   "Calix cleared the building," he replied, not even looking at the fire. "It was just the flames tricking your eyes."

I felt another flame spark, but this time inside me. I had been dismissed and pushed around my whole life. But this wasn't just something trivial like how to talk to someone or the proper way to fold a napkin. There was a boy inside that building who was going to die.

"Go back to the manor," the man said in a firm voice. "Go to your room and stay there until the king says you may leave."

His voice dropped to the same tone he used when he told me to sleep, and my body did as it was told against my will. I felt a tingling in my arm where his hand was still grasped. For a moment, I felt myself beginning to nod, and a desire to do as he said. The image of the boy flashed in my mind and immediately pushed thoughts of complying out. He wouldn't make me do as he wanted, not this time.

"No!" I yelled as I pulled back. As soon as I yelled, it felt like an energy burst out of me. The man was knocked to the ground, his grip on me broken. I swallowed the fear and confusion I felt as I turned back to the building. There was no more time to waste. I took off running, shouts ringing around me as I closed my eyes and jumped through the flames.

The flames licked at my skin as the unbearable heat threatened to suffocate me. Part of me wanted to run and escape the heat that now threatened to devour me at any moment. But I kept the image of the boy in the front of my mind as I forced myself to walk deeper inside. I covered my mouth with my arm as the smoke caused me to cough violently. Each cough grew more painful as I moved deeper inside.

The boy had been on the second story. The first thing I needed to do was find a way to reach him. I searched for a way up, feeling a wave of victory as I found the stairs. The railing was in flames, but at the top, I could see a small figure on the ground.

Slowly, I made my way up the stairs, feeling each step bend under my weight as the fire ate them away. When I reached the top, the boy was lying motionless on the ground. Burns covered his bare arms, and ash coated his tiny face. My hands shook as I reached down and touched his cheek. Relief washed over me as he stirred at my touch. He was alive. Now, I had to move quickly to get us both out of here. Carefully, I picked him up in my arms. He was a small thing and was light enough that I didn't struggle to hold him. I pressed his face into my shirt, hoping to filter out the smoke so he didn't breathe in any more.

Once he was safe in my arms, I began to make my way back down the fiery stairs. Every step I took felt like I was tempting fate. While the steps had held me on the way up, the fire had continued to burn them away, and I was now carrying the boy. I felt myself begin to celebrate as I grew closer to the bottom. I regretted it instantly as I stepped down and felt the board give way under my foot. My foot went through the board, causing me to fall forward. I tossed the boy with all my strength to try to clear him of the flames before I crashed against the stairs.

Pain radiated through my body as I hit and knocked the wind out of my lungs. It felt like something in my ankle snapped as it twisted in the hole it was now wedged in. Everything

<u>152</u>

around me went blurry as my head struck the stairs. I blinked rapidly, trying to regain my vision to ensure that the boy was alright. My situation didn't matter as long as he was ok.

As everything came back into focus, I could see him looking around in confusion at where he had landed. The landing from the fall must have pulled him back to consciousness.

"Hey!" I yelled before coughing so much that it brought tears to my eyes.

The boy looked at me wide-eyed, taking in the scene. He looked at me, lying on the stairs with my foot trapped in the broken board. Pushing himself up from the ground, he moved closer to me.

"Run!" I yelled at him, causing him to stop. "Get out!"

"What about you?" The concern in his voice weighed heavily on me. He covered his mouth as his lungs rejected the smoke and causing him to cough.

"I'll get my foot out and be right behind you." The lie tasted bitter on my tongue, but the boy seemed to believe me. He stared at me for a few more moments before a coughing fit racked him once again. Finally, he nodded and ran, disappearing out of the fiery building. I felt confident that he would make it out, but I wasn't so sure about myself.

Quickly, I turned my attention back to my trapped foot. The board had broken just enough for my foot to fit through. The wood had splintered downward, causing the wood to stab into my skin if I tried to pull it out. As the flames grew closer around me, panic took over my actions. I began to claw at the wooden step in an attempt to free myself. The splintered wood ripped at my skin, leaving my hands raw and covered in splinters.

Soon, the smoke that had filled my lungs caused me to cough uncontrollably. The coughing made it impossible for me to keep trying to free myself. I glanced around, searching for a miracle in the flames and smoke. Nothing but impending death was to be found. I tried one last time to pull my foot free with no success. As I lay on the stairs, I felt the last bit of energy I had left be suck out of my body.

I jumped as a pair of hands reached past me, pulling the remnants of the board apart in one swift motion. I looked back and locked eyes with Calix. His blue eyes seemed to shine in the fire-filled dining room. He said nothing as he pulled my leg free and helped me to my feet. As soon as I applied pressure, pain radiated through me. I let out a slight cry as I shifted my weight to my other foot.

Calix noticed and didn't hesitate before lifting me into his arms bridal style. I must have been in the heat of the fire too long, as his skin brought a cool comfort to my burning skin. I wanted to be defiant and tell him I would walk, but my body betrayed me. I leaned into his body as he held me close. He ran through the flames, seemingly unfazed as they lashed out at his skin. His grip on me tightened as he carried me out of the flaming doorway and back out into the night air.

The crowd let out a collective sigh of relief and applause as soon as we appeared. Calix said nothing as he carried me away from the burning building, his grip on me tightening even more. I expected him to take me over to where the other injured were gathered, but he walked through the crowd with me still in his arms. I realized that he was taking me back to the manor. My coughing lessened as the clean night air filled my lungs with each breath. After a few deep breaths, I felt strong enough to speak.

"I can walk," I insisted as I tried to climb out of his arms.

His grip on me remained firm as he held me against him. I struggled, but he was relentless. No matter how much I protested, he remained silent and refused to release me. His determined strides had us back to the manor in minutes. The door flung open as we approached, and I could see Ms. Timlin's worried expression as we entered. Calix walked through the door past her, making his way to the stairs.

"My figurine!" I yelled, pointing to where it still rested on the front stoop. Ms. Timlin looked and picked it up before closing the door. I felt comfort in knowing she had it as she followed us up the stairs. Calix kicked open my bedroom door, and I expected him to throw me on the bed with the anger I could feel radiating off of him. Instead, he set me down gently before stepping back and looking at me with concern.

I looked at him, confused, as Ms. Timlin rushed to my side, placing the figurine on the bedside table. As she set to work looking at my leg, I saw Calix eyeing the figure with an expression I could not place. Maybe it was my insistence on having it that piqued his interest.

"Just a bad sprain," Ms. Timlin sighed after a few moments. "I'll get a wrap, and she will be back up in no time."

I watched as she hurried out of the room, leaving me alone with Calix, who now had his icy gaze fixed back on me. He looked angry, and I could feel he was getting ready to tell me off. "What were you thinking?" he growled, clenching his fists by his sides. "You could have been killed."

"I had no choice," I retorted. "The boy was going to die."

"You should have told me!"

Anger caused my body to shake as I stared at him. Of course, he was blaming me for what happened. I had tried to tell him. That man had stopped me, and there was no more time to waste.

"I tried!" I yelled back. "But that man who made me sleep stopped me and tried to order me back to my room!"

Confusion flashed on his face, but he quickly composed himself. "If Malic had ordered you to your room, then you would have been in your damn room."

Well, at least now I have a name for the man. Malic was who Calix was yelling to when my communicator was killing me.

"I don't think so," I sneered. "I'm done being ordered around like some pet. I knocked him on his ass, and if anyone else tries, I'll do it to them too!"

We stared at each other, the tension hanging thick between us. Maddie burst into the room, causing us both to look at her. A wide smile was on her face as she stared back and forth between us. "Am I interrupting?" she asked with a sly grin.

"Perfect timing," I breathed. "Much longer with your king, and I'm afraid I would have killed him."

Maddie looked between us, not hiding the playfulness in her eyes. "All clear," she laughed as she walked further into the room.

I watched as three men followed her in. I recognized Malic, his gaze glued to the floor as he rubbed at his hand that had been grabbing my arm. The other two men felt familiar, but I didn't recognize them. One was tall with a smooth head where his hair should have been. His square shoulders and strong build made him look intimidating compared to the other. He was at least a head shorter with short hair shaved close to his head. His small frame matched the thin wire glasses that sat on his face. They all looked uncomfortable, but Maddie strode across the room unfazed.

"So," she said as she jumped onto the bed. "I heard you knocked Malic on his ass without lifting a finger."

Calix's eyes shot to Malic, who nodded. He was silent, but I could tell that Malic was just as confused as I was about what had happened. Calix looked back at me and seemed to be looking for something in my face. If he was looking for an explanation, I didn't have one. So much had happened, I hadn't had time to think about what had happened.

"It just happened," I breathed as Ms. Timlin rushed back into the room and wrapped my ankle. "I knew the boy needed help, and he tried to force me back to my room like a child. It just kind of exploded out of me."

I looked over at Malic, who was still rubbing his hand. Whatever that burst of energy was had hurt him. That had not been my intention. Regardless of how frustrated I was with him for ordering me around, he had helped to save me.

"I didn't mean to hurt you," I said softly. "I apologize."

"He'll survive," Maddie laughed. "It's not physical injury that makes him pout like a baby. It looks like you knocked the connection to his gift. I'm sure it's temporary, but he's still a little bit hurt."

My head was spinning once again. I hadn't hurt him, but knocked out his connection to his gift? What was she talking about? Everyone here was constantly speaking nonsense. Were they trying to drive me insane?

"Maddison," Calix said with an edge to his voice that seemed to be a warning. Whatever Maddie was talking about; he wanted her to stop. "Come on," Maddie said, rolling her eyes. "Surely she must be getting her memories back if she was able to do that."

"She couldn't do that before," Malic said, looking at Maddie sternly. "This is new. It doesn't mean anything."

"What are you all talking about?!' I yelled in frustration.

The smile on Maddie's face disappeared as she realized that I had no idea what was going on. I hadn't even had time to properly freak out about a strange energy bursting out of me before I was being hit with more things that didn't make sense. No one was explaining anything, and I was tired of them talking about me like I wasn't here.

"Not tonight," Ms. Timlin said firmly. "All of you out. She needs to rest."

None of them argued as they moved to do as she said. I watched as they all filed out of the room like children who had just been scolded. Calix was the last to leave, his gaze lingering on me. For a moment, I thought he would finally give me some sort of explanation for what happened.

"Tomorrow," he said as he walked out with Ms. Timlin and closed the door.

I wanted to get up and follow to demand answers, but the pain in my ankle warned me to stay where I was. Letting out a huff of frustration, I turned my gaze to the figurine on the bedside table. I still didn't understand why I felt so drawn to it. It was lovely, but I had never been one drawn to material things, especially those without a purpose. It was almost as if the little girl on the swing was trying to tell me something, as if I knew her somehow.

Chapter 13

The sun beat down, but I didn't notice as the cool breeze rushed past me. I gripped the ropes beside me tightly as I leaned back and pushed the swing upward. My small bare feet stretched out in front of me as I soared towards the sky. I was swinging high enough now. As I reached the top, I loosened my grip on the ropes and jumped.

The ground came rushing towards me as I landed, my feet sinking into the warm dirt. I looked back and smiled at the empty swing as it came down empty.

"Not fair! She only went farther because she weighs next to nothing!"

"A bet's a bet," I grinned back at Garrett as I walked towards him. Even as young as we were, his large build made him look almost as strong as a grown man.

"Fine," Garrett growled as he looked back towards the city. "But if I get caught..."

"If you get caught, you will take your licks and keep your mouth shut," Maddie said in a warning tone. "Or the whooping you receive from us will be far worse."

Garrett glared at her before turning and running off. I sat down next to Thomas as I giggled. Thomas wasn't one to get involved in our schemes, but he always enjoyed the outcomes when they were favorable. I looked over at the small piece of metal he held between his fingers, watching as the metal slowly turned and formed. The wrinkle on his nose held his glasses in place while he worked, showing that he was focused.

I continued to watch in silence as he morphed the metal into a small flower. "For you," he said as he handed it to me. "For your impressive victory." I took the flower, holding it carefully in my hand. The smooth edges and shimmer in the sunlight made it seem almost magical.

"The real victory will be if Garrett gets the sweets," I smiled back.

As if on cue, a roar of laughter grew closer.
I looked up to see Garrett and Cal running
towards us. Garrett's hands were filled with candy
and sweets. Cal had a sucker in his hand, teasing
Garrett about something as they ran towards us.

"Here," Garrett pouted as he tossed the
goods on the ground. "I almost died getting
those."

Everyone grabbed something from the pile
as Garrett and Cal joined us. I sat listening as
Garrett told his heroic tale of getting the candy.
When he finished, Cal filled in the missing pieces.
Garret had the candy in his hands when Ms.
Timlin walked in. She hadn't spotted him yet, and
he stood frozen, too scared to move and too
dumb to put it back. Cal had been on his way to
join us and saw what was happening. He ran in
and began asking Ms. Timlin every question he
could think of. It still took Garrett several
minutes to realize what Cal was doing and to run.

We all laughed, giving Garrett a fair amount
of trouble as we continued to eat the sweets.

"Did you make this?" I turned to see Cal
holding the flower that Thomas had given me.
"You're getting better."

"Not fast enough," Thomas sighed. "I tried to get another communicator off yesterday and was barely able to get the metal to respond."

Metal bending was not a common gift, and Thomas took his seriously. He wanted to be able to remove the communicators from those who escaped the Union and study them. Part of me was jealous that his gift was so useful. Mine did nothing but protect my mind. I glanced over at Maddie, who had her hand on Garrett's shoulder. Garrett could crush a boulder with his strength, but one touch from Maddie and he was butter. She had a way of calming people with her touch.

Malic sat a distance away from us, careful not to touch anyone. His gift was a bit more common but could be dangerous if used wrong. They called him a Silver Tongue. If he touched someone and told them to do something, they had no choice but to do it. He hadn't mastered control over it yet, mainly because he refused to practice, and feared what he could make someone due unintentionally.

Then there was Calix, my best friend since the moment I was born. His touch was as unique a gift as mine. Most parents don't have to worry about their child getting in a fight and giving the other person frostbite. They had forbidden him from going near me when we were little because of a single mistake he made that could have killed me. It was a good thing that gifts don't work on me, unless I choose to let them. They found him holding me because I looked like I was about to cry. My blanket was covered in frost, but I was perfectly safe.

The six of us had been inseparable from the time we could all walk. It was a well-known fact that if one of us were up to something, the others weren't far behind.

"Ms. Timlin told me that I needed to show more responsibility today," Calix sighed next to me, pulling me out of my thoughts. "Says a man should want to keep the girl he cares about safe and not lead her into danger."

"You led me into danger?" I laughed.

"No one believes that I only go along to help minimize the damage you do," he said, shaking his head.

"Well, you try," I teased, pushing his shoulder.

"She also said...." Calix's voice trailed off as he looked down at his hands. I could see the frost crystals on his skin, indicating that he was uncomfortable. "She said that here in a few years, we'll realize that we are more than just playmates or friends. That we're all meant for greater things."

"Normal parent stuff," I waved. "Nothing to worry about."

"She also said that I should want to keep you safe because one day you'll be my wife."

The candy in my mouth suddenly tasted sour. Wife? I was only twelve years old, and I had no intentions of being a wife any time soon, if ever. Calix was my best friend, not my boyfriend.

"Wife?" Garrett laughed. "The day Lizzy gets married is the day I agree to marry Maddie."

"You wish," Maddie said, rolling her eyes. We all laughed as Garrett pretended to be offended, holding his hand to his chest.

Chapter 14

The metal figure of a girl swinging met my eyes as soon as I opened them. The sight of it made my dream more real. I sat up in bed, trying to sort out my dream.

"What the hell?" I said to myself as I ran my hand through my hair. The hair on the back of my neck rose, and I realized that I wasn't alone. I turned and pulled the blankets close to my chest as I spotted Calix sitting in one of the chairs. "What are you doing, creeper?!"

"Creeper," he grinned casually. "Is that a step up or a step down from rogue?"

His air of arrogance had returned, and I wasn't in the mood for it. He watched me with an intense gaze that made me move against the headboard with the blanket still clutched in my hands. No matter who he thought he was, he didn't have the right to stare at me or make me feel like this. Grams had not asked him to make me uncomfortable. Yet, he still seemed to enjoy watching me squirm.

"Rogue creeper," I replied. "It's a step down, and you were already underground."

My words seemed to tickle him as he let out a soft laugh. This man was maddening. He looked pleased with my reaction as he leaned back in the chair and looked at his hands like he was bored.

"I'm here to keep Maddie from storming in and possibly killing you."

His tone was casual, as if he didn't just tell me that the woman I had spent the previous day with suddenly wanted me dead. My eyes looked at the door, a vision of the girl from my dream flashing in my mind. That girl had been friends with Maddie. I thought that Maddie and I were becoming friends. Whatever I had done, she now wanted me dead.

"Is this about yesterday?" I said, trying to hide the fear in my voice. "I didn't mean to do that to Malic. If that's what she's upset about, I will explain. Surely we can find a way to work this out that doesn't involve killing me."

"I know," Calix assured me. "It has nothing to do with that. She's not going to walk in here and stab you. She wouldn't even kill you on purpose."

"What are you talking about?!" I threw down the blanket in frustration and smacked the mattress. "I don't understand what the hell is going on!"

Calix stood from his chair and walked over to the bed. He was surprisingly calm, my outburst not appearing to rattle him at all. My body tensed as I felt the mattress dip as he sat down. Something about him being this close, looking at me like that, was stirring something inside me. Damn it! My Lucifer was making me question everything once again.

"I can't tell you everything," he finally said. "It's too dangerous."

That seemed to be a common theme with these people. Everything was too dangerous. I wasn't some child who needed them to protect me from every possible danger. They seemed to know more about me than I did. All of this talk about missing memories and gifts. They couldn't keep dodging my questions.

"At least tell me something," I sighed in frustration. "I feel like I'm going crazy!"

"I was hoping Gertrude would be here, but it appears she's been delayed," he said, looking at the door and back at me.

My stomach twisted. Grams was supposed to be here already. Something had gone wrong, and even he seemed concerned. I opened my mouth to speak, but saw Calix start to speak and stopped myself.

"You're a MUT."

I felt my mouth open in shock. I had no idea what a MUT was, but it felt like an insult. He said it like it was common knowledge. Like he expected me to know what he was talking about. My face must have shown that I was insulted, as his showed he instantly regretted his words.

"Let me explain," Calix continued, holding up his hands.

I wanted to tell him off, but I wanted to hear his explanation more. I kept my face stern and motioned for him to continue. He nodded and sat in silence for a moment. I didn't push, giving him a chance to get his thoughts straight. I

had a feeling that this was not going to be a
simple explanation.

I sat back and listened as Calix explained
that a MUT was a mutant with no physical
deformity, but instead a change in their DNA. It
was different from person to person. Some gifts
were common, and some were rare. He
continued, saying that the Union was aware of
these gifts, and those who weren't born into the
Capital or the first two rings were enslaved by the
governors. The governors forced the MUTs to
use their gifts to further their control and power.

With everything I had been through and
seen, I didn't doubt that he was being honest.
Grams had told me that some mutations were in
the blood. She hadn't told me that those
mutations held what Calix called gifts. Did this
mean that Grams was also a MUT like me?

"Silver Tongue," I said before I could stop
myself. He had said that the venom that
controlled my mind was from a Silver Tongue.
Was that a MUT?

"That is one type," Calix said, raising an
eyebrow. "There are a few of those that I know
of." He seemed impressed that I had made the
connection. "The Capital learned how to turn a

173

Silver Tongue's blood into a venom. Allowing them to control the person they infect without having to touch them. It only works as long as the venom is in the person's system."

"Malic is a Silver Tongue," I said slowly. "That's how he made me go to sleep at the ceremony tent."

Calix nodded. "He hates doing it, especially to you."

"He tried to use it again at the fire." It wasn't a question; it was the only thing that made sense. Whatever I had done had taken away his gift and kept it from working on me. For someone who hated using his gift on me, he seemed to do it a lot.

"But your gift fought back," Calix said. "Though we've never seen a gift work like that. All gifts require touch or venom."

I nodded in understanding. I had lived with the venom in my blood for years, and it explained why Malic kept grabbing hold of me before trying to tell me what to do. He needed to touch me for his gift to work. This knowledge only gave me the desire to let no one touch me.

"So, I'm a freak amongst freaks," I sighed, sinking into the bed. Calix remained silent, allowing me time to work through my thoughts.

"Why was I given the venom?" I finally asked. "Were they trying to control me?"

Calix shifted around uncomfortably because of my questions. Still, I needed to know.

"What is my gift?" I pushed. "What was it before they messed with my mind?"

He still wouldn't meet my gaze. I understood that he didn't want to push too much, try to force a memory, and turn my brain to mush. But this was important. Whatever it was, it was different than before. If I didn't understand what was happening, then I couldn't learn to control it. For all I knew, my gift could hurt someone if I wasn't careful.

"Your gift is unique," he said after a moment. "We've never seen anything like it, and neither has the Capital. Most people can't resist if a MUT gift is used on them. But you, at least before, could block it. You had to choose to allow a gift to affect you."

"So, I can shield myself?" I asked, feeling a little disappointed. Of all the MUT gifts I could imagine, mine seemed disappointing.

"Being able to block MUT abilities is unheard of," Calix insisted. "The Capital relies on their abilities and those indentured to them to keep their power. You posed a threat, not being one of them. They needed you under control to make sure that your gift was only used to benefit them.

It all suddenly made sense. The headaches occurred when I tried to disobey or go against the rules. It was the Silver Tongue's way of punishing me and making sure I stayed in line. They had found a way to control me and get me to serve them without question.

"That's not all the venom did," Calix continued. "They also altered your memories. Everything before your sixteenth birthday, you remember how they see fit. That's why you can't remember anything specific. It's like your mind is reading from a script that they wrote."

"What?" I felt like I was learning too much information at once, but I still needed more. "What did they change? What don't I remember?"

"That's what I can't tell you," Calix said with a hint of remorse in his voice. "Your mind may not be able to handle it if we try to force your memories back to the surface.   At best, it could drive you mad."

"At worst, it could kill me."

He didn't have to answer. I was just talking out loud, not asking. I understood. Maddie wanted me to remember, and was even trying to give me clues to remember last night. But if Calix let her, it could kill me. I suddenly remembered my dream. Or was it a memory? I looked over at the figurine on my bedside table, almost able to feel the breeze on my skin as I swung up.

"Thomas made this," I said, not taking my eyes off it. "It was from the day Garrett and I had a competition to see who could jump the farthest. The loser had to go and sneak candy from the manor. He lost and almost got caught, but you distracted Ms. Timlin so he could escape."

The silence was deafening when I finished. Slowly, I turned and could see the surprise on his face. My eyes glanced at his hands, and I could see the ice crystals forming on his skin. I remembered how cool he had felt when he carried me. Had he been doing that on purpose because he knew it would comfort me?

"I saw it in my dream," I said softly. "The six of us all by the swing, eating candy and laughing about Ms. Timlin saying one day I would be your wife."

"What else?" Calix said, his voice sounding forced, almost hopeful.

"That's all," I shrugged. "I thought I made it up because of this." I motioned at the figurine and then looked back at him. "But I didn't, did I?"

"No," he said, shaking his head. "Perhaps your mind is giving you back memories as things naturally pull them to the surface."

"So, I just have to walk around and wait for something else to trigger a memory?"

It sounded ridiculous even saying it. I had remembered that day on my own. My mind was ready. But I could tell by the look on his face that he still wasn't going to do anything to help me remember. I needed Grams.

"What about Grams?" I asked. "She said she had a blood mutation. Is she a MUT?"

"She is," Calix nodded. "But please don't ask what her gift is. That is something she will need to tell you for herself."

Of course it was. Grams seemed to be the only one who could answer my questions, and she wasn't here. He had said she was delayed. Had he heard from her?

"When will she be here?" I asked. "Are you going to get her?"

"Gertrude will make her way here as soon as it is safe."

"But the beasts, the duo-wolves?" Panic filled me as I thought of Grams alone in the wasteland, trying to fight off the beasts.

"Trust me, Gertrude can handle herself. I pity the beasts that get in her way."

He laughed as he spoke, but it didn't do anything to calm my nerves. Grams wasn't a fighter. Her hands shook when she sewed, and I wasn't sure she would have the strength to make the journey to Twain on her own. Why he was so confident, amused even, I didn't understand. Still, I didn't have the strength left in me to argue or question him more. Everything I had learned already felt like too much. My brain was tired.

I wanted to know, to learn everything, but I was starting to see why it couldn't be rushed. If learning just the little bit I did today was this exhausting, I couldn't imagine handling all the truth at once. Calix was right. I needed to give it time and let it come to me as it saw fit. I wouldn't tell him that. He didn't need any bigger a head than he already had; his crown wouldn't fit.

I giggled at the thought of him sitting on a thrown and wearing a crown. I knew that the title was just symbolic, a way of saying the people of Twain followed him. But still, the thought gave me a sense of joy that I so desperately needed.

"Care to share what's so funny?" Calix asked with a raised eyebrow.

"No," I grinned back. "I think I'll keep it to myself."

"Right." The way he looked at me caused heat to flush in my cheeks. "Ms. Timlin says you need one more day in bed to heal that ankle," he said, standing up. "After that, I think it's time you started doing more than sitting in this room and shopping with Maddie."

"You're the one who kept me on a leash," I pointed out. "I would rather be out doing stuff, but you're the king and you make the rules."

"That I do," he laughed. "And it's probably going to come back to bite me in the ass, but I have the perfect task for you."

I leaned forward, excited to hear what he was thinking. Instead, he shook his head as he smiled and walked towards the door.

"Be ready at dawn," he said, turning back to me. "And make sure you get your rest. I heard Garrett still wants revenge for all the times you bested him. It doesn't matter if you don't remember; he will take joy in any victory he can get."

"Who said he'll win?" I smiled.

"That's my girl."

Calix's face went pale as the words slipped out of his mouth. He quickly walked out, and the door shut a little too hard behind him. The smile was gone from my face, and I stared at the door in shock. His words echoed in my head. Everything he had just told me, all the shocking things I had just learned, and it was his parting words that left me stunned.

"That's my girl." The words repeated over and over in my mind. I hadn't met him until he took me from the ceremony tent, but he was already calling me his. No, we had known each other before; that was obvious. He knew about my abilities, and there was a reason Grams had asked him not only to come for me but to help me. He also knew Grams. The way he and Maddie had spoken about her was like they knew her better than I did.

Maybe I was reading too much into it. It could just be something people out here say among friends. But that didn't explain his reaction after he said it. He had practically sprinted out of the room and was probably miles away by now. It did, however, explain why he tried to keep his distance and why he was so protective.

Nestling back against the pillows, I shook the thoughts out of my mind. It was nothing. Maybe we were friends before, but I felt confident that's all it was. He was just comfortable around me, like Maddie. No need to worry myself about possible romance when I had much bigger issues to deal with. Garrett was expecting to win tomorrow. Win what? I had no idea. But I felt determined to make sure he didn't. I couldn't remember our past rivalry, other than the swing, but I knew I didn't like to lose. Poor Garrett. He had no idea that the girl with no memory was still going to beat him.

Chapter 15

"*A*gain," Garrett said with a commanding tone as he spun a knife in his hand. The frustration in his voice made me grin. I spun my knife and prepared to go once again.

As it turned out, Calix's idea of the "perfect task" was combat training from dawn to dusk. Garrett had arrived at my door that morning, a little too eager to start. We had started with knives, since it was the only weapon I had. It felt like a good decision to learn how to use it. Part of me was still struggling with the idea that there was a large part of my life that I had been forced to forget. But as soon as we started sparring, my body proved that Calix was telling the truth.

It was as if my muscles remembered what my mind couldn't. I wielded the knife like it was part of me, dodging Garrett's attacks with ease. We had been sparring for hours, and he had yet to best me even once. Maddie and Thomas sat on the edge of the training area. Thomas, with a look of worry that seemed to be permanent, and Maddie, yelling teases at Garrett each time I bested him.

"Really," I said, adjusting the knife in my hand. "I may not remember, but I get the feeling that you've never beaten me."

Garrett's face reddened as Maddie laughed. Dropping his blade to the ground, he charged. It felt like jumping out of the way of a raging animal, but I managed to get out of the way just in time. I landed in the dirt with a huff as he stopped where I stood.

"You may best me with a blade," he sneered. "But I will always be stronger.

"Always?!" I yelled back as he turned his back on me. "I doubt that!"

Something felt familiar about this. He and I mouthing each other. I felt sure that to a stranger, it looked like we hated each other. But it felt like we were pushing, even encouraging each other to be better.

Garrett turned and reached out a hand to help me up. I took it cautiously and felt it as soon as his skin touched mine. The same strange tingling feeling I felt when Malic had tried to use his gift on me. I still didn't know what his gift was for certain, but I had a feeling it had something to do with strength. I smiled as the feeling built in my skin as I got up to my feet.

"Do you know how to fly?" Garrett grinned as he held onto my forearm.

"Do you?" I asked playfully. Garrett's face fell just as the energy burst out of me. He flew several feet back and landed with a thud in the dirt.   "Oh shit!" Maddie yelled as she jumped up and ran over with Thomas right behind her.

"Not fair," Garret groaned from the ground. "I forgot you could do that."

I walked over, leaning down with a slight smile on my face. "Do you say that every time I win?" Garrett let out a laugh as I offered him my hand and helped him back up. "You learned to control it!" Maddie clapped excitedly.

"Not really," I admitted. "It's more like a reflex when I sense someone is going to use their gift on me. But at least I know when it's going to happen now."

"A useful reflex," Thomas added. "One that could save your life."

For a moment, the worry on his face lessened. I smiled at him as I nodded in agreement. I was happy to see him more relaxed, even if it was short-lived. Thomas seemed to be the natural worrier of the group. Even knowing that, he seemed more worried about the explosion that had happened. I had tried to ask him about it several times, but he always changed the subject.

"I remember you thinking you weren't learning fast enough when you were making me flowers out of metal," I smiled, placing my hand on his arm. "And now you can remove the communicators. You saved me."

"And almost got you killed."

Thomas was suddenly back to being sullen as he backed away. So that was it, somehow, he thought he had put me in danger. But I still didn't understand. He hadn't done anything but remove the thing that poison from my wrist.

"How?" I blurted out as I pulled him back. "How did you do that?"

Thomas looked surprised at my reaction, but did not try to pull away. He glanced at the others, who nodded at him. Whatever it was, they agreed it was safe to tell me.

"Your communicator," he said, turning back to me. "We hadn't removed one that updated before. I was studying it, trying to hack into the system to get more information on the Capital's plans."

"That's a good thing," I said, confused. "The more we know, the better."

"Except, they had planned for it," he continued. "Or at least put in a safeguard in case they lost you."

"What do you mean?" I felt sick but stood steady as I waited for Thomas to answer.

"I had just transferred all the data and encryptions," he continued. "The screen lit up, and I thought you were receiving a notification. The damn thing had been leaking venom since the moment I got it off you. I wanted to destroy it, destroy the venom, so we didn't run a risk of you coming into contact with it again. But I knew that I had to see what the notification was. When I looked, it said one and then...."

"The explosion," I said, letting go of him. "The communicator exploded, that's what caused the fire."

"The fire you ran into to save someone I put in danger," Thomas continued. "All because I wanted to try to get all the information I could. I should have destroyed the damn thing right away!"

Thomas blamed himself, and I felt myself wanting to take the blame from him. It was my communicator after all. But the truth was, it wasn't either of our faults. He was doing what he could to help, what he thought was right. I had worn the damn thing here, bringing a bomb into their city. But the true blame lay with The Capital and the governors. They had set all this in motion, not us.

"Did you learn anything from the data?" I asked, causing him to look at me in surprise.

"There's still a lot to go through..."

"Keep looking," I said firmly. "You did the right thing. No one died that night, Thomas, and if they hadn't, it wouldn't be your fault. Don't let fear stop you from moving forward. If we can get any information from that damn thing that will save even one life, this was all worth it."

Everyone was staring at me in disbelief. I didn't fully understand why I felt so strongly about this. But that's all it was, a feeling. The only memory I had was of all of us as children. We had been here, Twain, not the Union. With the venom out of my system, I was free to speak what I thought and felt without worry of pain. Still, my determination and words surprised even me.

"Liz?" Maddie asked carefully, as if she was afraid to push.

"You all used to call me Liz, didn't you?" I smiled. "I don't remember anyone calling me that before, but I like it. Maybe one day I will, but until then, I want you to keep doing it."

"Good enough for me," Garrett laughed. "Now, who wants to get something to eat? I'm feeling a little weak after all this training."

"You'll be lucky if you can open the door to the kitchen," Maddie laughed. "That energy blast knocks out your gift, remember? It took Malic a full day to get his back."

"Fuck!" Garrett yelled, realizing she was telling the truth.

I couldn't help but laugh as Garrett attempted to storm back towards the manor. Something about the way he walked even seemed weaker. I had been right, his gift was strength, and I had made him as weak as a kitten. The irony of it all was not lost on me. I laughed with the others as we watched him storm away.

"Speaking of Malic," I said once Garret was gone and we had settled down. "I haven't seen him since that night."

"He's hiding from you," Thomas replied. "He knows that you got a memory back, and he's ashamed that he used his gift on you. I may be the worrier, but Malic is the master of sulking."

I looked at Maddie as she nodded. Malic had nothing to be ashamed of. If he hadn't made me sleep, I would have never left. And the night of the fire, he was trying to protect me. I had no ill feelings towards him. Still, I remembered his face as a young boy, sitting away from all of us because he feared his gift. I couldn't let him hide away again.

"Where is he?" I asked. I watched as they exchanged worried glances. "You can either tell me or I will find him myself."

"The dungeon," Maddie said quickly. "It's where..."

Thomas held up his hand to make her stop talking. Frustration boiled inside me, knowing that it was another thing I couldn't remember. Without asking where the dungeon was, I turned and made my way back to the manor. As I walked inside, it felt like my feet knew exactly where to go. I walked across the entryway and to the far wall.

Turning towards the staircase, I pressed on a wooden panel that gave way and opened to reveal a staircase. As I looked at the stairs, I felt something stir in the back of my mind.

"Why do we need a dungeon?" I asked, following the others down the stone stairs. "We don't take prisoners."

"It's for us," Calix called back. "No one comes down here, so we can use it. We can hide down here, and no one will know where to look."

I breathed in the damp air as the memory faded. That was two things now that had come back. Maybe walking around and waiting for them to come up naturally wasn't such a bad idea.

Carefully, I stepped onto the stone steps and closed the panel behind me. Looking down, I could see a dim light in the darkness below. As I made my way down the stairs, the only sound I heard was water dripping somewhere in the distance. When I reached the bottom, I smiled as I looked around the room. Hints of its original purpose could still be seen in the metal shackles bolted to the walls and the iron cells with their doors hung open. But it was all covered in a fresh purpose. Childhood drawings, stuffed animals, blankets, pillows, and makeshift bookshelves filled with items consumed the space. It felt like I was coming home after being gone too long.

I could see Malic sitting in one of the cells towards the back at a small table. He remained focused on what he was doing, and I felt confident that he didn't know I was here. Slowly, I made my way through the main entry and down to the cells. Each cell was filled with things and made to look more like bedrooms than cells. I looked in each one as I went, guessing from what was inside whose space it was. Stopping at one, I felt stumped as to who it could belong to. I looked around at the belongings for a moment and spotted it. A small metal flower was sitting in a cup near a stack of pillows that looked like it had been used as a bed. This was mine.

The small space was filled with books and treasures that I must have collected over my childhood. I started to take a step inside, but stopped myself. Forcing my memories was dangerous, to say the least. As much as I wanted to look through it all, it wasn't safe. Besides, I had come down here with another purpose. Turning away, my attention returned to Malic. His cell was only a few feet away. Inside, I could now see that he was writing in a journal. His pen was tearing across the pages, each movement threatening to slice through.

"You're abusing that paper," I said.

Malic jumped, dropping his pen to the floor as he turned towards me. His eyes were full of fear and panic. I could tell that he hadn't expected to see me here. He had chosen his hiding place carefully to avoid me, and now here I was. He looked around as if searching for a way to flee, but I stood blocking the only door.

"You're avoiding me," I continued. "Even hiding from me in our sanctuary."

"How?" His face filled with the realization that the others must have told me.

"They told me you were in the dungeon," I answered. "But I remembered the way on my own."

"You shouldn't be here," he said, picking up his pen and going back to what he was writing. "You need to leave. It's dangerous for you here.

I couldn't tell if he was worried about me trying to force a memory or that he would use his gift on me. Either way, I didn't move. I watched as he continued to write, glancing at me out of the corner of his eye.

"Thank you," I said, stepping further into the cell.

Malic looked at me, confused as if I had lost my mind. Well, what little bit of it I still had. I considered letting him remain that way, confused, but decided he had been through enough. I would take pity on him, this time.

"Thank you for saving me that night," I continued. "If you hadn't, I would have refused to leave and died."

"You wouldn't have died," Malic said, shaking his head. "Even if you hadn't left, you would have discovered the truth and fought your way out on your own. I never should have messed with your mind like that. I did exactly what they did."

"No," I said firmly as I walked closer. Malic pulled back, causing me to stop. He wanted to keep some distance, and I didn't want to push him too hard. "I would have died. When I realized who I was marrying, I planned to kill myself in that tent once the contract was signed."

"You what?" Malic asked in disbelief. My plan that night did not match up with who I was before. I could see on his face that he didn't understand.

"The only thing that I had left to care about was Grams," I continued. "Once I was married, I would never see her again. I could make sure she had the silver she needed to be comfortable. But once that was done, I had nothing else to live for except a vile husband who hurt me every chance he had. You saved me, Malic."

"You're telling the truth?" he said after a moment. "You planned to kill yourself?"

"Yes," I nodded. "They thought they were in control, but all they did was take away any reason I had to live. I still don't remember life before, but here, with all of you, I finally feel like I'm alive. And you gave that to me, Malic. I know you hate your gift because too many use it for bad things. But you, you have a good heart. You used something that most people see as terrible for something good. You saved me even though I didn't deserve saving."

Malic stood from his chair and pulled me into a hug. I wrapped my arms around his solid frame, feeling a warmth and safety I had rarely known.

"I never want to hurt you," He said as he held me. "But if you ever say you're not worth saving again, I will kick your ass."

"You can try," I said as I pulled back to look at him with a playful grin. "And if you try, I'll knock you on your ass."

Malic let out a deep laugh that made my heart happy. I could see the wall around him crumbling down and the tension disappearing from his body. I didn't need my memories to know that he was a good man. He had taken a big risk standing in that tent and being there for me.

If anyone had looked at him, he would have been caught in an instant.

Turning, we walked out of the dungeon together, neither one of us in need of its sanctuary anymore. I made a mental note to return later and look through the things in my cell, but now was not the time. Being here, with people who were my friends, made me feel alive again. I couldn't remember anything but that day at the swing, but it was enough for now. Everything with them felt natural and real. I knew I wanted to protect them just as they wanted to protect me. I could talk to them without worrying about what I said or them thinking I was crazy.

Well, with all of them except for Calix. For some reason, I was drawn to him the most, yet I couldn't bring myself to confront him. It was as if there was something I felt I needed to apologize and beg forgiveness for, but I had no idea what it was. Not to mention the backwardness of his calling me "his girl". I had decided to pretend it never happened. But he had gone with a different approach. He stopped in on the training sometimes, watching from a distance and leaving without saying a word.

The men here seemed to wield avoidance as the ultimate coping mechanism. I would have to talk to Maddie about it. Maybe she knew

something to get them to stop, though I doubted
it. Still, I wouldn't give up. Each day here brought
me closer to being myself, and it was them who
made it possible. I would drag each one of them
out of the dungeon if I had to.

Chapter 16

$\mathcal{T}$he next week went by in a blur of training and laughs. Everyone joined Garrett and me at the training grounds each morning - everyone except Calix. Each day, someone would try to use their gift on me, and I would use my ability to block it. The more I practiced, the more control I gained over it. I could now use it without being in danger myself. I could feel when one of the others was summoning their gift and pushing out the energy, effectively knocking them away from whoever they were going to attack and blocking their gift.

I was no longer just a shield who could protect myself. I could now protect others as well. I could still remember feeling disappointment in my gift, but that was gone. The others still applauded me each time, saying that I was the first to be able to project my gift in such a way. I still didn't know how it happened, but I knew how to channel it.

"There has to be more to it," Thomas said as Maddie helped him back to his feet.

He had been the volunteer for today. Only one person volunteered each day. That way, only one had to go without their gift at a time. I had been surprised when Thomas volunteered. He didn't seem the type to willingly go into a fight. Yet, with his gift, his skills were amazing. He was able to quickly bend any type of metal with just a touch. My blade had been twisted and bent more times than I could count as we sparred. Each time I thrust it, he bent the blade away from his body and back at mine. It was fascinating to witness.

"Not kick-ass enough for you?" Maddie teased back.

Thomas wrinkled his nose at her, but I could tell his mind was deep in thought. My gift had changed since they last saw me. According to them, I had always been able to block other MUT's gifts from affecting me, but the energy push and taking of gifts were new. Thomas couldn't help but wonder if there was more I could do or if others could use their gifts in ways they were unaware of. We had been trying to explore his theories, but so far, nothing had worked.

"Do you feel any different afterward?" Thomas asked.

"A little," I admitted. "It's as if my body is still buzzing from it."

Thomas's face lit up, and he held up a knife. "Concentrate on this," he said, holding it away from himself. "Try to push it away like you do with us."

I looked at the knife and him, confused. I couldn't manipulate metal like him. We had already tried to test that, and all I got was a cut for my trouble. Still, I decided to try despite my doubts. I concentrated on the knife, willing it to move. My skin felt like electricity was surging through it. I let out a gasp as the knife flew out of Thomas's hand and landed in the dirt several feet behind him.

"Yes!" Thomas clapped while everyone else stared in disbelief. "You're not blocking our gifts, you're absorbing them."

I looked at the others, who seemed just as confused as I was. "I what?" Thomas let out a sigh of frustration as he ran his hand through his hair.

"She was able to affect the metal of the knife because she just absorbed my ability," he explained. "I would be willing to wager that if she were to absorb any of yours, she would be able to access some of your gifts too."

"Let's find out," Maddie said, stepping forward.

Of course, Maddie was willing to volunteer. Nothing seemed to scare her. I took a step back, suddenly feeling out of place. This gift was dangerous, even more dangerous than Malic's. If Thomas was right, I could steal others' gifts and use them as I wanted. We all already knew the dangers that came from the wrong people controlling gifts. The fact that I could gain and control them all was terrifying. This also made me a bigger target for the Union if they found out. They wouldn't need an army of MUTS to do their bidding. Just me absorbing the gifts and using them. I didn't like it and I didn't want it.

"No," I said, shaking my head. "I don't want to. It's not right."

I hadn't seen Maddie use her gift, but I had a feeling it affected people's emotions. I could still see the way she had calmed Garrett in my dream. I had no idea how to control what she did, and I didn't want that kind of power over people. I didn't want the gift I had, let alone hers.

I was already desperate for Thomas's gift to return to him, and then I would never absorb another again.

A strong hand gripped my shoulder. I looked back to see Malic standing behind me with a knowing look on his face. I knew he could recognize the fear in my eyes. Out of everyone, he knew what it was like to have a gift that felt more like a curse.

"Fearing our gifts make them dangerous," he said smoothly. "I feared mine for years, but someone told me that I needed to embrace it so I could control it and use it for the right reasons."

The way he raised his eyebrow told me that I must have been the one to say those words, though I didn't remember. "Like saving a friend who has been brainwashed?" I asked with a slight smile.

"Exactly," he nodded. "Now, let me help you master this so you can save someone in the future." Malic walked over and stood next to Maddie. I watched as he put his hand on her shoulder, and I felt the familiar tingle in my skin telling me he was accessing his gift. I concentrated on him, allowing that energy to flood to the surface. I felt the surge through me, but Malic remained standing.

"I can't," I said, letting out a heavy breath.

"You did," Malic grinned. "I can't feel my gift."

"I didn't," I insisted. "You didn't get pushed away or knocked down." It seemed obvious, but Malic continued to grin. "Would you stop smiling like that? It didn't work!"

"Make me."

I glared at Malic, wanting to smack the smile off his face. It was hard enough to fail at something I could do just moments ago, but to have him mock me made it worse. I thought I was gaining control, but I was wrong. Maybe what had happened with the knife was just a fluke. Right now, I just want that stupid smile off his face.

"Stop smiling!" I yelled.

Malic's smile suddenly disappeared from his face, but I could still see the joy in his eyes. Had I made him stop? Is this what it was like to be a

Silver Tongue? I couldn't believe it and just stared at him.

"But you didn't get..." I stuttered.

"Because you didn't want to push me away or knock me down," Malic said calmly. "You only wanted to take my ability, so that's all you did.

Now, if you could please permit me to smile again, I would greatly appreciate it."

"Of shit, of course," I stuttered. "Malic, smile whenever you want."

A smile immediately spread across his face, reaching up to his eyes. "Now, try the knife again." I looked back at where the knife lay on the ground. I focused as intently as I could, but it remained still.

"One at a time," Thomas said, picking up the knife and causing the blade to bend slightly. "As soon as you took Malic's gift, I felt mine return."

So, there were limits on what I could do. It made me feel a bit more comfortable knowing that I could only absorb one gift at a time. This new gift was still dangerous, but limits would help keep it in check.

"But I can't give it back," I said, turning back to Malic.

"Fine with me," he grinned. "I could use a night off."

A wicked thought ran through my mind. I realized I could ask them all the questions about my past, things they refused to tell me, and they would have no choice but to answer me. It would allow me to get the information I wanted and return Malic's gift to him. If it wasn't for the fact that I knew it was wrong and that it could kill me, I would have started asking immediately. Instead, I bit my tongue so hard that the taste of copper filled my mouth.

"There has to be a way I can give it back," I insisted. "I don't just want to wait for it to wear off. Especially since I don't have to touch people for it to work. It's too much."

"I'm impressed." Calix's voice drew everyone's attention. "I expected you to start forcing them to tell you things you know they're not allowed to. Instead, you are eager to find a way to give it back."

"It crossed my mind," I admitted. "But I decided against it. I don't want to force anyone to say something they don't want to. It's just...wrong."

Calix let out a light laugh and looked at Malic. "I think I will take over your training for the day," he said, turning back towards me. "Less temptation to ask forbidden questions if it's just one person you have to interrogate."

An unease washed over me as the others began to take their leave. I had not been alone with Calix since that morning in my room, and even that had been awkward.

"Follow me," he said, motioning towards the manor.

"Wait," I insisted as I turned back to Malic.

My eyes remained locked on him, and I could feel the tingle in my skin. I willed for it to go back to him, to leave me immediately. I felt the rush of energy leave me, and my limbs felt heavy. Malic flexed his fingers and was grinning at me.

"Can't have you take a night off," I said with heavy breaths.

"You returned it?" Maddie asked, looking between us. "She returned it?"

"I told you she was strong," Calix grinned. "With just a week of using you all as training dummies, she has mastered skills we didn't even know were possible."

Calix took my arm and began to lead me away from the others. I walked with him in silence, still exhausted from returning Malic's gift. I would need to practice more so that it wouldn't exhaust me each time. I may not like my gift, but Malic was right. It was more dangerous to fear it and not learn how to control it.

Calix led me around the house and to the garden. Even with my freedom, I still had not found the time to visit. With training all day and spending time with the others, I was too exhausted by the time I was alone. I realized that he was leading me to the stones I had seen him place flowers on when I had detoxed from the venom. I had wanted to see who was buried here in an attempt to understand him a bit more. Now, he was leading me to what felt like a great secret.

As we stood in front of the stone, he brushed the dirt away from each of them slowly. The first two I didn't recognize, but they had been the ones he was talking to that night. I felt safe in assuming that they were his parents. I watched as he cleaned the others, my heart rising into my throat. This wasn't possible. The Union had cremated them, and their ashes were scattered with the others who fell in the attack.

"No," I mumbled, shaking my head. That was my mind still reading from the script. I glanced between the stones, noticing that the dates on all of them matched. They had all been killed on the same day, and then brought her to be buried. I forced myself to ignore the script trying to play in my mind, and focused on the stones.

"My parents," I said, stepping forward. Carefully, I traced over my parents' names that were carved into the two stones to the left.

"And mine," Calix nodded to the other two.

"Why are they here?" I asked with more accusation in my voice than I intended. "I was told that they were cremated. Their ashes were spread with others who were killed that night. What really happened?"

"I brought them here." The coldness in his voice sent shivers down my spine. "I brought them back one at a time and laid them to rest. This was their home, after all. They deserved to at least be put to rest in a place where they felt loved."

While I couldn't remember, I knew that I had been in Twain as a child. Logic told me that my parents must have been here as well. However, hearing Calix say that this was their home still felt surreal. I looked back at the stones, the familiar sting of tears burning my eyes that I blinked away. Tears wouldn't bring them back or change anything. He was just as young as I was when they died. Yet, he had managed to bring their bodies back here one at a time. I could understand his parents, but he had also taken care of mine.

"Thank you," I heard myself say. "I don't know if I thanked you before, but thank you for bringing them here."

I wanted to ask him how they died, but knew better. He was already breaking the rules by showing me their graves. It didn't trigger a memory, but I felt certain that the truth of their deaths would. That moment was important; it changed everything in my life. If remembering anything before my mind was ready was going to break me, that would be it.

"And, I'm sorry," I said softly.

"For what?" Calix spoke, turning to look at me.

"I don't know," I admitted. "I just have this feeling that I owe you an apology. That I should be begging for your forgiveness."

"You don't owe me anything," he said firmly as he placed his hands on my arms and stared into my eyes. "And you don't beg anyone for anything. Understand?"

I nodded in agreement even though I didn't. Calix relaxed and turned back to the stones. I had decided to pretend that what he said before running out of my room had never happened. But the way he looked at me built me up and stirred something inside me that I didn't understand, and it was more than I could take. I had to know.

"Calix, I..."

The sound of bells cut through the air, echoing around us. My words were cut off by a feeling of dread. I didn't know what the bells meant, but it couldn't be good.

"The gate," Calix said before running back through the garden.

I ran after him, my feet thudding against the ground as I struggled to keep up. People filled the streets but moved aside as Calix ran towards them. I could feel the tension in the air and see the fear on everyone's faces. When we reached the gate, it was shut. In my time here, I had never seen the gates shut.

I followed Calix as he ran up a set of stairs to the top of the wall. I was breathing so hard my chest burned by the time we reached the top of the wall. The others were already there, their faces pale when they looked at us. I was right, something was wrong. I could already tell that they were ready to get me as far away from here as possible. They wanted to protect me, but I was done being protected.

"Elizabeth," Maddie said, stepping forward. "Maybe you should go back down and..."

I pushed my way past her and looked down. Nothing could have prepared me for what I saw. Below us was a floating disk. I recognized it from the depot back in the Union. The wealthiest families used them for deliveries so they wouldn't have to travel to our part of the city. This one was large, and it looked like there was a person on it. No, not just a person, it was Grams. I barely recognized her. Her clothes were torn and dirty, and dried blood clung to her skin and matted her hair. Around her ankles were large silver cuffs that held her on the disk.

"Grams!" I yelled.

I watched her frail body stir, and her tired eyes looked up at me. Calix was right; she was delayed. They had been torturing her while I was here. She had done everything for me, and I had left her to be hurt by them.

"We have to help her." I looked back at the others, trying to contain the panic I felt raging inside me. Why did I even have to say it? I didn't understand. They all knew her, and yet they hadn't done anything to help her.

"We can't," Calix said, stepping forward. "She yelled for the gates to close when she approached. It's a trap."

"I don't care." I looked down at Grams and felt my heart shatter in my chest. She was the only family I had left, and I had to save her. I didn't care if it was a trap; there had to be a way.

"Lizzy," Garret said, stepping forward, but I pushed him away. I didn't need comfort right now. I needed them to do something to save her.

"Elizabeth," Grams's voice called out. I looked back and fell to my knees. I couldn't hold back the tears that streamed down my face. "Elizabeth, don't you dare try to come out here."

"Grams!" I yelled back through sobs. "We can save you!"

"You saved me years ago," Grams replied as she forced a weak smile on her face. "You saved so many people the day you were born. You gave us the courage to fight back."

What was she talking about? She had to be delirious from whatever they had done to her.

"I don't understand," I sobbed.

"You will," she said. "Just trust that those you need to finish this arc with you. My part in this is done, and I am honored to have been able to help."

"Grams!" The disk below her began to glow, and even from a distance, I could feel the heat. "Please," I begged. "Please don't!"

"I love you, little one," Grams said as she closed her eyes.

"Grams!" The scream burst out of me just as the disk erupted in flames. I would have fallen off the gate if a set of strong arms hadn't wrapped around me and pulled me back. My body shook as the realization of what just happened washed over me. I fought against whoever was holding me and looked back down. The flames engulfed the disk, the heat burning my skin. My head felt light, and everything around me became a blur. I could hear distant voices, but they were too muffled for me to understand. This couldn't be real. It was a nightmare, and I needed to wake up. I closed my eyes, willing myself to wake. Grams couldn't be gone; she just couldn't.

Chapter 17

"*You* didn't have to come," I said, looking back at Calix as we walked through the dark streets. He had been complaining since we left Gram's house an hour ago about the horrible smell of the city. "Our parents said we would be back in the morning."

"And I was supposed to trust that you would visit Gertrude and keep yourself out of trouble?"

I let out a giggle as we continued to walk. He was right, of course. I had planned to sneak off and cause a bit of mischief while our parents were having their meeting. But, of course, he had to tag along and keep me in line.

"How about a race?" I said, eager to do something fun. Calix was always so serious when he thought he was protecting me. Just because he was a year older and his father was king was making him into a sour old man at the age of eight. Without me, he would have grey hair and be talking about back when he was young.

"I don't know," Calix said, looking around. "We aren't supposed to draw attention to ourselves."

"Ready, set, GO!"

"Hey!" I heard Calix yell behind me, but I was already running. There were only a few blocks left until we reached my parents' city house. I knew it was safe enough, especially since it had been dark for hours. Everyone was either sleeping or doing things they didn't want to be seen doing. No one would notice us, and Calix needed to relax.

Cold water splashed on my leg as my foot landed in a puddle. Mother would scold me for ruining my good shoes, but Father would help me out of trouble. I glanced back over my shoulder to see that Calix was catching up, though it was hard to see him through the smoke that was now filling the street. Panic rushed through me as the smell of the fire assaulted my nose and the smoke stung my eyes. Something was wrong. I pushed my legs harder, rounding the final corner.

The blaze caused me to stop mid-stride. Calix crashed into me, nearly knocking us to the ground. I stared at the flames and the men standing around them. In front of me, my parents' house was ablaze. Tears stung in my eyes as I pushed myself up and started to run to the fire. Calix wrapped an arm around my waist and pulled me back behind a building.

"Why aren't they trying to put it out?" I gasped as I tried to push my way past him.

Calix looked back at the fire and then at me as he held me against the wall.

"Our parents!" I gasped. "We have to help them!"

"Their gone," Calix said, holding me in place. "If we go out there, we will die too."

I could feel the warm tears running down my face. Calix looked out once more, and I was able to look. The men were mostly dressed as soldiers. All were standing and watching the flames. I fought against Calix, but he held me in place. I couldn't understand how he was being so calm about this. Our parents were in that building, and he was acting like it didn't matter.

219

"You all have your assignments." I looked and saw a man wearing a finely tailored black suit with silver hair. The look on his face showed no emotion as he brushed a piece of soot from his sleeve like it was nothing more than a fly. "Set the fires and kill any who try to escape."

The soldiers let out a grunt of understanding and began to move through the empty streets. Within minutes, fires began to light throughout The Edge, with the screams of those trapped by the flames cutting through the night. As the screams continued, the silence coming from the house in front of us was deafening. All I could hear was the crackling of the wood as the fire consumed it.

"We have to go," Calix said as he gripped my arm and pulled me away. I tugged away from his grasp and ran towards my parents' house. The man with silver hair still stood, watching the flames. He looked down on me as I ran up, searching the flames for any sign of my parents. I barely noticed him as I looked for a way to get inside, a way to save them.

"Well, now," the man said with a sick grin. "This is unexpected."

"My mom," I cried. "Where's my mom?"

"Mom?" The man looked back at the fire and then at me. "Well, she sure did a good job of hiding you, now didn't she? You look just like her when she was young."

Calix appeared beside me and pulled me back as the man reached for me. "Sorry, sir," Calix said smoothly. "I must be taking her back to her grandmothers. She snuck out, and her grandmother is worried sick."

"Gertrude, I presume."

The way the man said Grams's name sent a shiver down my spine. Something inside me was screaming for me to run. How did he know I looked like my mom when she was a child? There were no pictures of her, and she had told me she had no family other than the one she made. Calix tightened his grip on me as he nodded. I glanced at the fire once again and then back at the man.

"That won't be necessary," the man sneered. "I will see that this young one is taken care of." "No offense, sir, but we must be going." I allowed Calix to pull me away as realization washed over me. The man knew my parents, and he had killed them. The heat of the flames stung my skin as the man's steps closed the distance between us. He grabbed my arm and tried to pull me back. I struggled against him as Calix pulled my other arm.

"Can't you see you're hurting her?" the man sneered at Calix. I felt confused. As they each pulled on my arms, it felt like there was more to what the man was saying.   "Her arm, it's BROKEN."

As he said the word, I felt the tingle in my skin. I knew it all too well. He was trying to use his gift on me. I allowed it to wash over me and glared back at him. Whoever he was, his gift was to inflict pain. I stared at his face, memorizing every detail. It wouldn't be tonight, but he would pay for what he did. I could see that he was taken aback by my lack of reaction. I seized the opportunity and yanked my arm free. Together, Calix and I turned, running as fast as we could. It didn't take us long to reach Gram's house. She was waiting for us outside and pulled us both into her arms.

"He knew you were her grandmother," Calix told her through heavy breaths. "The man setting the fires. He tried to take her."

Grams looked at him with wide eyes and took both of our hands. She led us through the streets and to the secret entrance that led out of the city. I stood with Calix as she pulled the lever, opening the small door and leading us outside. Grams said nothing as she led us through the wastelands with a torch. Her eyes darted around like she was prepared to fight off any creatures who dared try to attack us. I thought I heard a few growls in the dark, but as soon as Grams looked in the direction they came from, everything went silent.

When we arrived back in Twain, she took us both upstairs and laid us down in my parents' bed. Her face was tight with worry as she tucked us in and told us to try and rest. Rest was not an option. Our parents had been murdered, and the man responsible for it wanted me. I didn't know who he was, but I knew I wanted to kill him.

"He's a MUT," I said as she walked towards the door. Grams stopped and turned towards me with a knowing look on her face. "He tried to break my arm, but I blocked it."

"Good girl," Grams smiled softly.

"When I'm bigger," I continued. "I will kill him. I'll start by breaking his arm and finish by setting his home on fire with him inside."

Gram's face went sullen. I could tell she wanted to tell me not to say such things. It wasn't normal for a seven-year-old to be planning how to torture and kill someone. However, most seven-year-olds didn't have their parents murdered. Instead of scolding me, she simply nodded. I watched as she closed the door, leaving us alone in the dark.

"I'll help," Calix said beside me.

Chapter 18

*M*emories are tricky things. Sometimes, people take them for granted, not realizing how important each one is. For me, the memory of my parents' death was the key to all others. As I opened my eyes, feeling Calix's cool skin against mine, I remembered everything. It felt like I had been sleepwalking these past five years, and now I was suddenly aware of everything.

"I will kill him," I snarled.

Calix pulled back, searching my face. "I will start by breaking his arm and then finish with him chained in place as I set his home on fire, while those he cares about are forced to watch."

"I'll help."

I fell back against his chest, my tears forming ice where they trailed down his skin. He pulled me close, holding onto me as if I might slip away again. I wanted to get up, to get planning, but I remained still. I owed him an apology, and in no way deserved his forgiveness. How could I deserve forgiveness after I lied to him and left him alone at the cathedral the night we were to be married? I had hurt him in the worst way for nothing. Yes, I had gotten my communicator, but in doing so, I had allowed myself to be brainwashed by the same man who killed our parents.

"Who are we killing?" Garrett asked.

Calix loosened his grip and helped me to my feet. I looked at the others, memories of our childhood together racing through my mind. I trusted each of them in ways I couldn't describe. I had left them all, without warning or explanation. Yet, they had all come for me and still stood with me despite it. My tears stopped, and I would not allow them to return. I had spent enough time crying; it was time to take action.

"The governors," Calix replied. "Just as we always planned.

"But my grandfather," I spoke up. "He is the one who has to suffer."

Now, Calix looked confused. Grams had always refused to tell us who the silver haired man was and why he tried to take me. The most we learned was that he was one of the governors. We had decided that they were all evil and therefore all deserved to die. I was changing things. Now, I was the one who knew something that none of them did.

I looked back down at the fire, my heart aching in my chest. Grams was gone, and there was nothing I could do about it. When the flames went out, I would lay her to rest in the garden with my parents. I asked the guards to inform us when the fire was out and motioned the others to follow me. It felt surreal to be myself once again. When my mind was twisted, I felt meek and scared all the time. Now, I felt like I had grown two feet and could stand face to face with anyone and feel no fear.

The others followed me back to the manor and into Calix's office. Once we were all inside, Thomas closed the door behind him, and they all looked at me. I owed them all an explanation. Yet, standing here with all of them, the words felt heavy. I took a deep breath and looked at each of them.

"First, I'm sorry about what I did," I started. "I should have told you all what I was doing. I didn't because I knew you would try to stop me. We needed that communicator if we were ever going to have a chance at getting into the Capital."

None of them spoke, so I continued before I lost my determination. "When I got there, everything seemed to be going according to plan. They put me through an examination and a blood test. But when the results came back, that's where things went bad."

"They discovered you were a MUT," Thomas spoke, and I nodded.

"I thought they would tell me I was normal, give me my communicator, and remind me of my choices for marriage. I couldn't have been more wrong."

They all listened intently as I spoke, detailing that day at the medical facility. I could still see the shock on the physician's face when the computer screen showed my results. I knew something was wrong when he rushed out of the room. My first instinct was to flee. Something was off, and I needed to get out. But he had locked the metal door and sealed me inside. I tried everything I could to get out, banging my fists on the metal until they bled. I was trapped and had no choice but to sit and wait.

When he returned, the silver-haired man was with him. He had looked at me just like he did that night. I felt more like a prize than an actual person. There was no compassion in his eyes, just victory.

The man's name was Samuel Abbott. He was one of the governors, the only one without an heir to his position. I was forced to listen to him explain that he was my grandfather. My mother had been raised in the capital, and a marriage had been arranged for her at great expense to him. She had never shown signs of her gift, but he assumed she was hiding it to try to get out of the marriage. But her test results came back that she was normal. Not a MUT, not a mutant, just normal. Normals were unheard of. He had thought it a disgrace, given his and his wife's gifts. She would be impossible to wed and cost him his legacy. He would rather choose a new successor than live with the shame that his bloodline had failed. The governing families had always had the strongest abilities. That's what allowed them to gain and remain in control.

He banished my mother that day to The Edge and never looked back. Over the years, he had heard whispers of rebels sneaking in and out of the city, but had no idea how. Every attempt they made to catch them failed. He had come to The Edge to investigate himself when he saw her again. She was walking with my father through the streets, happy and carefree. He had not expected her to find happiness, not when he was robbed of his own. He immediately tried to access the communicator of the man she was with. But the system didn't work. The communicator had been tampered with, only allowing messages to be received. He checked my mother's and found the same thing. Their tracking was disabled.

He watched them for days, trying to figure out what was going on. A man was arrested during an attempt to raid the medical facility, forcing him back to the Capital. He had tortured the man for days for information about the rebels. However, he learned that he was hurting the wrong person. The man had a child who was sick, so Samuel had her brought to the capital and made the man watch as he tortured her. The man broke down and begged Samuel to stop, and offered to tell him everything.

It was then that he learned that she had wanted to escape him and was one of the leaders of the rebels who threatened the Union. Her gift was to affect frequencies around her. She had manipulated the computer to show the result so she would be banished. After he learned the truth, he tried to get her to come home, marry, and produce him an heir. My mother had spat in his face and cursed him while clinging to my father. He decided in that moment that he had been too kind before in just banishing her to The Edge. It wasn't enough that she was dead to him; she needed to be erased. My parents had withstood hours of torture, not giving up any information on Twain or the rebels' plans.

In the end, Samuel decided it was a waste of time to keep trying. He ordered the house to be burned with them inside, along with anyone they had ever been seen interacting with. He was sure that they were the source of the rebels' information. He would kill them, stop the leak, and return to his life. It wasn't until that night that he learned I existed. He couldn't find me again after that night, until I walked in to be tested.

I had tried to fight, to escape, but soldiers came in and held me down. As soon as the communicator touched my skin, I could feel the venom burning. I blocked it at first, but it was too strong. I couldn't fight it forever, but I kept trying. I thought if I could just stop the effects long enough, I could get it off and escape.

It was then that Grams arrived, calling Samuel by name. The two of them fought, most of which I couldn't understand, as I was forced to keep focused on blocking the effects of the venom. Eventually, Samuel stepped away and allowed Grams to come closer. I begged her for help, but she hushed me while stroking my hair. She told me it was too late to get out of this. I needed to give in and allow the venom to alter my mind. I tried to argue, but I was growing too weak. She leaned down and whispered that it was just five years. In five years, I would be free. Until then, she would keep me safe.

I asked her to go to the cathedral to tell Calix and the others what happened. She agreed and promised to do so as soon as she got me home. I hated myself in that moment. I was losing everything because I thought I was smarter than a system. Samuel had laid a trap and waited patiently for me to walk into it. After that, I couldn't fight the venom anymore. I felt it take over and lived the next five years oblivious to what had happened.

"She told you to give up?" Maddie said in disbelief as I finished. "Gertrude always told us never to accept defeat. There was always a way to win; we just had to fight harder for it."

"She made a deal," Calix answered. "Gertrude knew that if she could buy time, we would find a way to get her out. But if Samuel took her that day, Elizabeth would have been lost to us."

"But why make us wait until her damn ceremony to get her out?" Garrett said in frustration. "Thomas could have removed her communicator years ago."

"The update." I nodded at Thomas. "My communicator didn't have access to the Capital information until it was updated at the ceremony."

"She knew that the sacrifice needed to be worth it," Malic agreed. "Please tell me you were able to get the information we needed off the thing."

"It's a lot to go through, but I'm working on it," Thomas answered. "I feel confident that I will be able to rig up some of the old communicators to grant us access to the inner rings."

"I still don't understand something," Garrett said. "Why would Samuel make a deal with Gertrude to wait five years. He had Liz. What did he gain by waiting?"

Grams told very few people about her gift. It was terrifying, to say the least, and probably would have gotten her killed if too many people knew.

"He had to make the deal if he wanted me alive," I explained. "Haven't you ever wondered how she was able to travel at night and never get attacked. Even the beasts knew that she could end them in a second. Grams could stop hearts. I can guarantee you that she told Samuel that if he did not give her the five years, she would stop mine."

"Fuck," Garrett breathed. "I knew she was terrifying, but I never thought..."

A knock on the door brought the conversation to a halt. I knew what it was about before Calix even opened it. I listened as a guard talked to him in a hushed tone. Calix nodded and closed the door, turning back to us.

"The flames have stopped," he said in a ragged voice. "We should lay Gertrude to rest before we do anything else."

Everyone nodded in agreement and headed for the door. I followed close behind, stopping only when Calix gripped my arm. I looked up into his light blue eyes, confused. Whatever he wanted to talk about could wait until Grams was laid to rest. I knew we had some things that needed to be discussed, but this wasn't the time.

"You should wait here," he said firmly. "We will come get you once she is..." His sentence trailed off, as if he was afraid finishing it would somehow break me. I tried to pull my arm free, but his grip remained firm. "You shouldn't see her like that."

"I can handle it," I said. "It's not the first time."

"It would be the first time you've seen it."

My heart ached at his words. I remember him not being in the bed the next morning after our parents were killed. I had searched for him but learned he had left to go to the Union. I didn't see him until that night. I spotted him digging the graves out of my bedroom window with our parents' bodies under a cloth behind him. I had tried to rush out to help, but Grams stopped me.

I had tried to fight her, but ended up locked in my room. I watched from my bedroom window as Calix, just eight years old, dug all four graves and laid them to rest. When he finished, he came up to my room, his eyes swollen from tears and his hands bleeding with blisters and splinters. I had taken care of him and cleaned his hands as best I could. He shouldn't have had to go through that alone. My parents were down there too. I should have helped. But the only thing I was allowed to do was take care of him after he handled the hard part.

"I'm not a little girl anymore," I said, yanking against his grip.

I was so busy struggling against his grasp that I hadn't noticed he was slowly turning. For a moment, I thought I had won when my arm pulled free. I stumbled backwards and nearly fell to the ground. When I looked back at Calix, the door was slamming shut, and I heard the lock click into place. Running over to the door, I twisted the handle and pulled with all my strength.

"Damn you!" I yelled as I beat my fists against the door. "Calix! Let me out!"

"She stays in there until I come to get her," Calix said to someone. "Understood?"

I heard someone grunt that they did. I continued to beat against the door, the curses and swear words flowing really at whoever was on the other side. Despite the rage and pain I felt, I didn't cry. Crying and mourning were pointless and a waste of energy. Control and focus were the only things I needed. Grams and my parents were gone. No amount of time, tears, or reflection was going to change that. All I could do now was kill the man who took them from me before he took anyone else I cared about.   Calix couldn't keep me from getting my revenge, no matter how many doors he locked.

Chapter 19

$\mathcal{T}$he dull ache in my hands was the only comfort I had as I sat on the small couch. I had continued to pound on the door long after Calix had left. It felt like hours had passed since Calix locked me in. I had tried everything I could think of to get out, but he had sealed it well. He even froze the door leading to the garden shut. I rubbed my hands, red and sore from pounding on the door. The lock clicking echoed around me just before the door opened.

"She's taken care of," Calix said in a soft tone. "You're free to visit her when you're ready."

"You had no right!" I shot up off the couch and pounded my hurt fist against his chest. "You had no right to lock me in here, to deny me seeing what he did."

Calix remained silent, letting my fists pound against him without flinching. My hands hurt with a fresh rush of pain with every strike I landed. Realizing that what I was doing was having no effect, I stepped back. My chest fell and rose quickly with each heavy breath I took. I stared at him for a moment, my anger trying to take full control. I could take his ability. Freeze him like a statue right here; force him to feel like I had - trapped in this room. Helpless and unable to move because someone else said so.

The thought sent a shiver of fear up my spine. Using gifts for personal vengeance was something Samuel did, not me. My skin buzzed, begging for me to cross that line. Before it could, I pushed past him and stormed up the stairs to my room. Opening my door, I looked around and, for the first time, realized why it felt so empty. Everything I had here before had been taken away. Probably in an attempt to keep my memories from being triggered before I was ready. A lot of good that did. Seeing Grams set on fire had brought them all back in an instant.

"I want my stuff back!" I yelled over my shoulder before slamming the door behind me.

I glanced around the room, regretting my decision not to go outside. The air was stuffy and hot, just as it had been in the office. Marching over to the window, I threw it open and leaned out into the cool night breeze. I closed my eyes and breathed deeply, hoping that it would help calm the rage inside me. After a few moments, I opened my eyes and looked out over the garden. I tried to avoid it, but my gaze eventually landed on the graves. A fifth stone had been added. I stared at it, replaying the moments in my head when fire took those I loved.

Everything I did, I did to avenge them. That's the way it had been since I was a child, all I knew. But downstairs, I had almost allowed myself to be just like the man I hated. I almost used my gift to punish someone innocent. Yes, Calix had no right to stop me from seeing Grams and laying her to rest myself, but that was not a crime that deserved having his ability stolen and used against him. I needed to get my head straight and refocus on the task.

A light knock on my door pulled my attention back inside. I turned just as Ms. Timlin opened the door and walked in. I could tell by the look on her face that she was here to talk, and there was a good chance I wasn't going to like what she said. I turned and leaned against the windowsill, keeping the cool air on my back. "So," she said, walking closer. "You remember."

"I do," I nodded.

Ms. Timlin had a way about her that demanded respect. She had been one of my mother's best friends and was more like family to me. The silence was heavy as she walked over to a chair and took a seat. A glance at the chair beside her told me she wanted me to sit. Part of me wanted to protest and remain where I was, but I didn't dare. Pushing away from the cool comfort of the window, I walked over and joined her.

Silently, she held out her hand to me. My fingers recoiled, desperate to avoid her touch. Her gift was unique and scared me more than any other. She could sense someone's pain, physical or emotional, and help ease it. The tonics that had been used on me since my arrival were made by her. Each contained her blood and helped speed up the healing process considerably. It was a blessing that the Union didn't know about her. They would have her making them practically invincible.

But now, she wasn't here to cure me of poison or help with a broken ankle; she wanted to see my emotional pain. I had avoided letting her see that side of me for years. I could block it if I wanted, but now she was asking me to let her see. I looked at her face and saw nothing but patience and compassion. Slowly, I lifted my hand that felt heavy as a brick and set it in hers. I felt the tingle in my skin, the warning that a gift was being used on me. I remained still and allowed her in.

As her hand wrapped around mine, she closed her eyes. I watched for several minutes as tears slowly fell down her face. I couldn't know what she was seeing, what was causing her to cry like this. I sat frozen, silence my only companion as she looked into my pain. When she opened her eyes, she gripped my hand tightly as she wiped her tears with the other.

"I can handle it," I said. "It keeps me going."

Shaking her head, she let go of my hand. I pulled it back into my lap, turning my attention back to the window. I wanted nothing more than to run to it and jump down to the garden below. It wouldn't be the first time I used it to escape something. I knew how to land and avoid getting hurt. But running from Ms. Timlin was something my conscience would not let me do. Instead, I remained in my chair, staring out into the night.

"You've never let yourself mourn," Ms. Timlin finally spoke. "You've never allowed any of yourself to heal."

I didn't look at her. Mourning was a sign of weakness. I didn't need my face covered in tears and snot. What good would that do? Vengeance, that's what I needed. When I got my vengeance on the man who took everything from me, then I would heal, not before. Until then, I needed the hate, anger, and everything else to keep me going. How could she not see that?

"It's not weakness," she spoke as if she could hear my thoughts. "It will make you stronger in the end."

"I don't have time for that," I growled. I was done with the conversation. The only reason I hadn't told her to leave was out of respect, but I was beginning to reach my limit. My fists clutched at my shirt as I continued to stare out the window. I needed this, all of it, and I wasn't going to let her or anyone else tell me to let it go.

"I'm glad that you and Calix did not take your vows."

I whipped my head around and stared at her in disbelief and anger. I didn't have many regrets in this world, but not being able to take my vows that night was one. I was supposed to meet him that night, the night I got my communicator. He was waiting for me at the cathedral with our friends, ready to bind ourselves together forever. Now, the woman who had seen our love before we even knew what love was glad that I wasn't able to make it.

"How dare you?!" The words came out as a growl through my locked teeth. I may respect her, but she was pushing me too far. I stood up out of the chair so fast that it fell to the ground. Ms. Timlin didn't react as she kept her eyes on me. I wanted to tell her to get out, to leave me the fuck alone. Instead, I glared at her, my chest rising and falling with angry breaths.

"You misunderstand," she said softly. "When taking vows, you are offering yourself, your entire self, to the other person. You can't do that."

"Why not?" I yelled. "Why am I destined not to have anyone I love?"

"How can you offer yourself to him when you are consumed by another?"

My hands balled into fists at my side. Calix had been the only man I had ever loved. Now, here sat the woman who practically raised him, accusing me of cheating. "Samuel consumes you," she continued. "Every thought, every driving factor, everything you do is for Samuel."

I stared at her in shock. She wasn't saying that I loved someone else. She was saying that my hatred for the man who killed my family and trapped my mind for five years was my obsession. Of course, he was. I wanted to watch him die slowly, screaming for mercy, as the world he loved so much burned around him. But that didn't lessen my feelings towards Calilx, not in the slightest.

"Calix is willing and able to give himself completely to you. But you cannot do the same."

"I can!" I shot back. How dare she tell me how I felt and what I was capable of?

"Really?" she asked as she raised her eyebrow. "When you got your memories back, what was the first thing you did?"

I knew what I did. I had told the others what I learned about Samuel and made sure they were still with me in destroying him. What else was I supposed to do? It was our mission to destroy him and everyone like him.

"Did you run to Calix?" Ms. Timlin asked. "Did you apologize for leaving him alone, for the pain he endured when he lost you?"

It felt like a vice was being squeezed around my heart. Honestly, Calix hadn't been my first thought when everything came rushing back. But he understood. He knew why I had to kill him, and he had always stood by my side.

"When you vow yourself to another, they are your priority. They come before everyone else in this world. Calix isn't that for you, not yet."

I felt dizzy as my hands relaxed and the realization of her words came crashing down. For five years, I was oblivious to everything I had done, the pain I caused. I knew she was right. Despite my love for him, it would have been wrong for me to take vows. He wasn't my priority; vengeance was. It had been since I was seven, and even now, that hadn't changed.

In the time I had been back, really been back, all I had thought about was Samuel and my revenge. I hadn't even spoken with Calix in that way. He had shown his affection in the way he held me, laying Grams to rest and trying to protect me. I, on the other hand, had done nothing except try to make plans of attack and yell at him. Shame filled me as I watched Ms. Timlin stand, smoothing her dress as she did.

"When you can do that," she said softly, looking at me with knowing in her eyes.

She didn't need to finish. I watched her as she made her way out of the room, closing the door behind her. As soon as she was gone, it felt like the walls were closing in around me. I needed out now.

Running to the window, I lifted myself onto the ledge and looked at the ground below. I was on the second story, not a small drop. I had mastered it years ago, but it had been five years since the last time I attempted it. Would my muscles remember what I needed to do, or would I snap a bone when I landed? I sat there, debating what to do for several minutes.

A knock on the door made me jump. I looked back at it. My fingers gripped the edge of the window frame as the strong knock sounded once more. My heart hammered in my chest as I looked back at the ground. I wasn't up for any more conversations, not right now. As the door handle began to turn, I pushed myself off the ledge.

The ground came at me fast, faster than I thought it would. My muscles instantly remembered what they needed to do. I rolled as I hit the ground, a stinging pain from the sudden stop on my skin, but nothing else. I glanced back up at the window above. I could still hear the faint sounds of someone knocking. Pushing myself up from the ground, I ran into the garden.

My feet carried me on their own, and I had no idea where I was going; not until I found myself standing in front of five stones. I knew what they were now. My eyes stung as I read the names that were engraved. First Calix's parents, then my own, and finally, Grams. The dirt in front of Gram's marker was recently disturbed, showing that she had just been laid to rest. I fell to my knees, my hands landing on the loose soil.

"I'm sorry, Grams." My voice was barely above a whisper, but I could hear the tremble in it as I spoke. "I will make him pay for what he did. I swear it."

The words tasted like ash in my mouth. For the first time, my vow for revenge felt hollow. Ms. Timlin's words still swam through my head. I thought about Grams and the five years we had together, when I couldn't remember my promise for revenge. We had grown closer than we had been before. Our time, conversation, and love for each other weren't clouded by the need for revenge. While those years had cost me more than I could bear to think, they had also given me more than I thought I could ever have.

"What do I do?" I wasn't sure if I was asking the dead or myself. I lay down on the dirt, curling myself into a ball as I hugged my knees. Getting my memories back had felt easy, like I could pick up where I left off. Now, with what Timlin had said, nothing seemed easy anymore. I felt the sting of tears and didn't fight it. I let them flow freely down my face and wet the soil. I knew it wouldn't help, not in the grand scheme of things. But right now, my heart needed to let go of some of the hurt and sorrow that consumed me. I had cried when I couldn't remember, despite trying not to, but it wasn't the same. I couldn't release any of the pain that was cut so deeply into my soul that it had begun to fester like an infection.

The sounds of the city went silent as I lay there. Even after my tears had run out and my body felt void of everything, I remained. A new thought entered my head, a dangerous thought. Perhaps I wasn't meant for this world. Perhaps I was capable of nothing but death and pain, whether I inflicted it or people suffered it for caring about me. Perhaps my place was here. In the soil beside those I lost, just another stone with a name that would be forgotten over time.

My eyes grew heavy with exhaustion, and I let my heavy lids close. The cool soil beneath me was slowly trying to lull me into a sleep and away from my dangerous thoughts. I could lie here, join the dead, and no one would even notice. The only change would be that they would no longer have to shoulder the burden of my need for revenge. They would mourn, perhaps some tears would be shed, but in the end, their lives would be better for it.

As I accepted my thoughts, I felt myself being lifted from the ground. The coolness the soil had provided still touched my skin, but now flesh and muscle were supporting me. I knew it was Calix who had found me, but I was too tired to open my eyes or say a word. My head fell against his chest as he adjusted me in his grip. It would be hardest for him to let me go, but it was for the best.

I remained still, partially in a state of sleep, as he carried me through the garden. I heard the sound of the door opening and closing as he carried me inside and up to my room. The soft mattress sank beneath my body as he lay me down and pulled a sheet over my cold skin. While I was exhausted, I felt a new sense of resolve and determination. Tonight, I would rest and allow the weight of my decisions to press down on me a bit more. I deserved the suffering of it for more than one day. Tomorrow, when I was alone, I would set them all free. I would make it quick, using the knife I had planned to use to kill myself the night of the ceremony. By tomorrow evening, I would be in the dirt beside Grams. Just another stone that would soon be forgotten.

Chapter 20

I felt lighter as I woke the next morning. The resolve had settled deep in my chest that this would be the last time I woke. After today, everyone would be free of the cancer I had become. Pushing off the sheet, I sat up and rubbed the sleep from my swollen eyes. - the only reminder that I had cried so much the night before. My plan was already running through my head. I would go through my morning as normally as possible. Then, when everyone was busy with their day, I would go back to the garden and put an end to myself there. It was simple and would provide the least amount of fuss.

"Only the dead sleep in the garden."

My head turned quickly towards the voice. I knew who it was before I saw him. Calix sat in a chair, watching me from across the room. He was still dressed in the clothes he had been wearing the day before. Dirt and sweat stains could be seen even from a distance. His eyes were cold, full of anger, as his hands gripped the chair arms. I could see the ice forming under his hands and a few spots where the brittle wood had given way to the cold. There was no way he could know what my plan was. But after tonight, he would be free of me. He could live his life, find someone to give him what he deserved, and be free.

"Dead inside," I quipped as I stood up and placed my feet on the cool wood floor. I didn't remember taking my boots off, in fact, I was positive I hadn't. Calix must have removed them once I was asleep. That was him, taking care of me despite me being the source of his suffering. He reminded me of the poor souls you heard about trying to take care of a wild beast, not knowing that one day the beast would kill them.

As I glanced over at him, I could see that my words had only caused him to tense more. The wood under his hands cracked and splintered as he froze it and crunched it under his grasp. I pretended not to notice as I made my way to the wardrobe. Quickly, I grabbed a fresh set of clothes. I could feel his gaze locked on me as I moved. I made my way to the bathroom, thankful to be free of his eyes.

I slipped out of my clothes from the day before, kicking them into a pile. It wasn't until I dressed in the fresh shirt and pants that I realized something was missing. I rushed to where my dirty clothes lay on the floor, searching through them. I rushed back out into the bedroom and continued searching. Calix watched me as I made my way through the room, never moving from his chair. My hands were shaking as I realized that my knife was nowhere to be found. Maybe I had dropped it in the garden?

Yes, it had to be there. I moved for the door and reached for the handle.

"It's not out there." Calix's voice made me freeze. I turned and looked at him slowly. "Your knife," he continued.

"You took my knife?" I growled at him as I stormed closer.

He nodded, flexing his fingers around the arm of the chair. This was impossible. He had no way of knowing what I was going to do. Yet, he had sat here and watched me all night and taken away my tool to end my life. Just like when he had not allowed me to lay Grams to rest, he had taken something from me once again that wasn't his to take.

"Give it back," I ordered as I held out my hand.

Calix looked at my hand for a moment and then shook his head. I growled in frustration as I ran my hands through my tangled hair. This man was doing everything he could to try to keep the person who led to his death and suffering close. I had already failed him by loving him, and now I couldn't even leave him to find the happiness he deserved.

"You have no right!" I yelled. "It's mine!"

"And what will you do with it?" he asked. His voice remained steady and calm despite the tension I could see in his body. I could have lied to him; told him I just like having it to protect myself. But he would see through it if I tried. He could always tell when I was lying. Instead, I folded my arms over my chest and stared back at him.

"That's none of your business."

He stood up so fast that I hadn't noticed him moving until the chair hit the ground. I didn't flinch away and remained still as he leaned down close to my face. I could see the air with each breath he took, his control over his gift slipping away. The tingle on my skin showed that his gift was working overtime. I blocked it and kept my gaze locked on him. Anyone else would have probably gotten frostbite from the drop in temperature, but I could take it. He couldn't hurt me. I was the one who caused the pain. I hurt him more times than I could count, but all of that would be over today.

"None of my business?!" he snarled as he grabbed my arms.

"It's not," I insisted as I tried to pull out of his grasp. His hands only gripped me tighter, holding me in place. I could have fought him off, but I held my hand. I had already caused him enough pain. I wouldn't make this harder than it needed to be. Even if he knew what I was planning, I would let him have this. Perhaps it would help him heal when I was gone, being able to say he tried everything he could to stop me.

I let out a gasp as Calix lifted me from the ground and threw me over his shoulder. He didn't say a word as I thrashed around. He carried me through the house, everyone staring at us as we went. As if I weren't going through enough, now I had to suffer through this humiliation on my final day. Perhaps I deserved it, but that didn't mean I had to like it. My fists pounded against his back as he carried me down the stairs. He stopped only for a moment while the sound of a familiar door opening rang out. I continued to squirm as he carried me down the stone steps into the dungeon.

"Are you kidding me?!" I yelled as he dropped me onto the floor. Calix said nothing as he walked over to where the old metal shackles hung on the wall. I watched as he adjusted them, checking to make sure they were secure, before turning back to me. I pushed myself backwards on my hands as he reached down and pulled me up. I continued to try to pull away as he dragged me over to the shackles.

"Calix!" I yelled just as the first one closed around my wrist. The sound seemed to echo in my ears. It was more than just being trapped. The sound signaled that I wouldn't escape; my plan had been stopped. Calix didn't respond as he grabbed my other wrist, lifted it above my head, and snapped the second shackle closed.

He stepped back and began pacing back and forth. Each breath he took was heavy and fast. He looked wild and uncontrolled. I pulled at the chains that now held my arms above my head. He had adjusted them just enough that my feet were able to comfortably touch the ground. My wrists began to grow raw and sore from tugging on the chains that showed no signs of giving.

"What's your plan then?" I asked in frustration. "Just keep me chained up down here forever?" Calix kept pacing, but only a glance showed that he heard me. "What I do is my choice," I continued. "You have no right..."

"I have every right!" he snapped as he stormed back towards me. "How dare you say I don't?!"

His words stung with so much pain and anger that I pressed myself against the wall in an attempt to avoid them. I turned my face away and closed my eyes, desperate to escape the situation anyway I could. I heard his breaths begin to even out slowly, and I turned back to face him. The anger was still radiating off him in waves, but he seemed calmer in a way. - maybe I could make him see. Not that killing myself was the best option, he would never agree to that, but that I wasn't good for him and he was in no way bound to protect me. If I could get my freedom back, I could do what needed to be done.

"We're not vowed," I said softly. His eyes flashed with another wave of anger, but he remained still, his breathing almost regular. "I can never be vowed," I continued. "I can't be the person you need, the person you deserve."

"You are," he said firmly.

I shook my head in disagreement. "I'm not. I'm broken, Calix, too broken. You deserve better. Someone who can give you their whole self freely. I can't do that."

He eyed me carefully, as if trying to find more information. "Tell me you don't love me." His words caught me off guard. This had nothing to do with love. Of course, I loved him. I loved him before I knew what love was. I loved him even when I couldn't remember he existed. That hadn't changed. But love wasn't enough, it was never enough. I wasn't able to give him what he deserved, and he needed to be free to find someone who would.

"This isn't about that," I sighed. "I will always love you, Cal. But..."

"No," he interrupted. "You don't get to tell me what I do and do not deserve."

I stared at him, trying to hide the emotions that were swirling through me. "I see your broken bits and love each sharp piece. I will let them shred me for all of eternity if it means I get to be close to you."

My words caught in my throat as his hand brushed my cheek. My skin burned where he touched, begging for more.

"If someone else keeps you from giving yourself to me, I will see them destroyed," he continued. "I have always been yours and always will be. I won't let you leave unless you tell me you don't love me. I will keep you chained here as long as it takes to make you see what I do."

A tear fell down my cheek, which he gently wiped away. My resolve was fading despite everything. I could feel my walls crumbling with his words, his touch reaching parts of me that no one else could get close to.

"Vows are just words. You and I are connected in ways beyond that. In ways that other people dream of finding. I have never let that go, and I never will. If you die, I will join you."

"Cal, you can't..."

"Dying is easy," he interrupted. "You've never been one to choose the easy way."

I let out a light laugh despite myself. He was right, of course. I had a knack for choosing the hard path and relishing in its challenges.

"Living, that's hard enough. Living with me, that could be the hardest thing of all. So what will it be? Easy or hard?"

His face was so close to mine that I could feel his breath on my skin. Every part of me was burning, trying to reach out for his touch. I gripped the chains above me in my hands, trying to steady myself as my mind spun.

"What will it be, love?"

I couldn't resist, not anymore. I leaned my face forward and crushed my mouth against his. He met my enthusiasm as he pulled me closer. Opening my mouth slightly, I felt him eagerly begin to explore mine. I felt him grip my hair as he angled my head back and deepened our kiss. I heard myself let out a slight moan that caused a growl to rumble through his chest. He suddenly pulled back, breaking our contact and causing me to pout. I pulled against the chains, eager to touch him once more.

A mischievous smile spread across his face as he stepped back and pulled his shirt over his head. My eyes wandered over his bare chest, taking in every detail and muscle that sculpted his perfect body. His smile grew as my eyes locked on the bulge that was visible through his pants. I forced my gaze back up to his eyes, feeling my cheeks flush with embarrassment.

I watched as he pulled my knife from his pocket and stood back towards me. I eyed the blade as he held it closer to me.

"Tell me you're mine," he demanded. "Tell me that you want me."

I swallowed hard, my body heating up at his words. Something deep inside my core ignited at what he was saying, and I felt a dampness between my thighs.

"I'm yours," I said, looking deep into his eyes. "I want you, Calix, I need you."

In one swift motion, he slid through my shirt. I heard the knife fall the floor as he carefully pushed open the ruined fabric, exposing my bare chest to him. I went still as his hand gently touched my bare flesh, causing everywhere he touched to instantly ignite. My eyes closed as I lost myself in his touch.

"Absolutely, perfect." I opened my eyes to see that his gaze was locked on my hard nipples. I let out a gasp as he pulled one into his mouth, swirling his tongue and sucking on the sensitive bud. The wetness grew between my thighs as he released it and moved to the next one. My thoughts and body were fully consumed by him and his touch.

His hands traveled down my body, his fingers teasing at the waistband of my pants. I felt my hips thrust towards him, begging for more. Releasing my nipple, he knelt in front of me and carefully pulled my pants off. I watched as he tossed them away and gently rubbed his hands up my thighs. I felt a twinge of embarrassment as he reached the dampness that was now covering my upper thighs. He didn't seem to notice as he ran his tongue over my skin, tasting my arousal. Gently, he pushed my legs apart, exposing my wet center to him.

I gripped the chains tightly as he lifted my legs and rested them on his shoulders. I could feel his breath against my center as his hands continued to rub my thighs.

"You may be broken," he said in a deep breath. "But I will see to it that everyone kneels before my queen."

Before I could respond, he began running his tongue against my folds. My hands gripped the chain tightly as he gently eased his tongue inside and began running it over my clit. The nerves let out a spark with each touch, causing my entire body to shudder. My thighs squeezed around his head, but that only seemed to make him more hungry. His tongue worked mercilessly, pushing me closer and closer to an edge that I hadn't known existed.

Just as I thought I was about to go over it, Calix stopped and eased me back to my feet. My body shook with anticipation as he stood and removed his pants. I felt myself lick my lips as they fell to the ground, and he stood ready. His gaze washed over me, and then at the chains holding me in place.

"Should I let you down?" he asked, stepping closer.

I help my grip the chains tightly in my hand. Something about being restrained like this was turning me on. I always needed to feel in control, like I had all the power. But like this, fully at his mercy, I felt free for the first time. There were no thoughts of revenge or the battles outside. I was able to finally give all of myself to him. I shook my head and slowly lifted my leg, running my foot up the side of his bare leg.

"You give yourself to no one but me," he said, gripping my thigh and pulling me close.

"I'm yours," I said, struggling to find the breath to form the words.

Calix's lips crashed against mine in the next moment, taking away the last bit of breath I had left. His hands gripped my backside as he lifted my feet off the ground. I wrapped my legs around his waist as he positioned myself at my entrance. He broke the kiss and stared deeply into my eyes. No words were needed; I knew what he was asking. I nodded at him as I tightened my legs around him.

Slowly, Calix lowered me down onto his hard length. I felt myself stretching around him as he continued to move deeper inside me. Once he was fully in, he remained still a moment. The stretching hurt, but the pleasure of him inside me was greater. Carefully, I began to rock myself back and forth. He gripped my hips and joined in my rhythmic movement. The pain faded with each thrust until I felt nothing but ecstasy.

I could feel my orgasm building inside me, pushing closer and closer to the ledge as Calix increased the spread of his movements. Moans and gasps escape me unchecked, echoing around us. The only other sound other than our heavy breathing was the chains clanging against the stone wall.

Calix moved his hand from my hip and began rubbing my clit with his thumb. It was more than I could take. My orgasm exploded, shoving me over the edge and into a bliss I didn't know existed. Calix moved at a steady pace, working me through each blissful moment. As I neared the end, I felt him shudder as he found his release deep inside me.

We stood still for several moments, my back against the stone wall and his head against my shoulder. Once our heart rates began to slow, Calix held me carefully as he undid the cuffs on my wrists. I held onto his neck as soon as I was free, and he lowered us both to the floor as he pulled out of me. I suddenly felt empty without him inside, but still at peace somehow.

As we sat on the cold stone floor, Calix's hand gently rubbing my back as I leaned against his chest, I realized I was wrong. I couldn't leave him, not now, not ever. Maybe Ms. Timlin was right. I couldn't give myself completely to him now because of the vengeance that burned inside me. But, until I took care of that need, I could give him this. I could give myself to him completely in these moments. Calix knew who I was, how broken and torn up I was inside. He still wanted, no, needed me despite it. She may not have seen how we belonged together, but that didn't matter. Calix and I were all that mattered. And right now, in the dungeon, naked on the floor, we had taken a vow with no words or grand ceremony. I was his and he was mine. And by whatever God still existed, I pitied whoever tried to tear us apart ever again.

Chapter 21

The thing about peace when you are at war is that it never lasts long. I wish Calix and I could have stayed in the dungeon longer, forever even. As we climbed the stone steps back upstairs, I fought the urge to pull him back down. As we reached the door, he looked back and kissed me on the forehead. He had given me his shirt to wear, as mine was destroyed. Once we were dressed, he had taken great care returning my knife to where it belonged on my thigh. Some people would have called him crazy, giving a girl who was determined to kill herself back her weapon, but he did it as a sign of trust. He believed it when I told him I loved him and that I was his. He trusted me to make the hard choice and live this life with him.

When the door opened, I felt a flush rush to my cheeks. There stood our friends, all clapping with giant smiles plastered on their faces. Calix pulled me closer to him as he rolled his eyes and shut the door. They continued as we walked past them and into the office. Calix flipped them off just before slamming the door shut.

"Maybe I should have tried to be a little quieter," I said as he turned back towards me. "Never," he smiled. "It is my goal to see how many moans and screams I get you to make. Let them hear you at the Capitol."

"Calix!" I teased as I hit his shoulder, and my cheeks flushed.

He caught my wrist and pulled me closer. I felt the warmth begin to pool in my core once again. "Later," he grinned as he let me go and stepped around me. "We have to get some form of work done today."

I followed him over to the desk and sat down on it as he sat in the chair. I watched as he looked through stacks of papers, making notes and sighs as he went.

"I could help," I said finally.

He looked up at me and gave me a soft smile. "This is all the data Thomas was able to get off your communicator. But, even with all this, I can't see a way that we go in and make it out alive."

I picked up the papers one at a time and began to look through them. The communicator held more information than I realized. There were maps of the Union, even the Capital. I looked closer at the lines, noticing some light markings that seemed to connect the rings.

"What's this?" I asked, pointing it out to Calix.

He took it and shrugged as he handed it back. "It's nothing, probably just guidelines or something."

I looked back at the paper and studied the lines. "I don't think so," I firmly said. "See here, this one starts where the medical center is and goes into Ring Four."

Calix set down the papers he was reading and took a closer look at where I pointed. "How did I miss that?"

"Everyone knows that I'm the smart one," I teased.

Calix ignored it as he rummaged through some more papers and pulled out another map. This one had locations marked. I watched as he slid it under the paper I had, and we both looked closer. Each faint line started and ended at a medical center, connecting The Edge to the Capital.

"It makes sense," he sighed.

"Ok, now I'm missing something."

"The day of the ball," he explained. "We thought it was strange they had you evaluated at the depot, but we just thought they wanted to keep you separate from the other brides. But we were there all day and never saw the other brides arrive. They all just walked out of the medical center when it was time, but we never saw them go in."

"It's the same with the staff," I pointed out. "They are never seen coming or going, but all the doctors are from the inner rings."

Calix pulled me into his lap and kissed me hard. I smiled as his lips pressed against mine, his hands firmly on my hips.

"You did it," he breathed when he pulled away. "You found the weakness we have been searching for. This tunnel system is how we will get into the Capital. They won't even know we are there until it's too late."

He was so excited that I decided not to point out that there would still be obstacles. The tunnels would surely have some sort of security that we would have to deal with, but we were closer than we had ever been before. It was always too much of a risk to try to take things head-on. Even with the communicator allowing us access to open the gates, each of the inner rings would be prepared for us before we arrived.

Now, we had an alternate route that would provide us some cover and hopefully allow us to reach the Capital with minimal resistance. There was still a lot of work to do, but we were making progress.

"We will be ready to move in the next couple of days," Calix grinned. "Soon, this will all be over."

"Slow down," I insisted. "Rushing is the wrong move. We need to make sure we are fully prepared."

Calix raised an eyebrow, surprised by my saying to slow down. Honestly, I was surprised to hear myself say it. For years, I had been the one insisting we rush in. However, the last time I rushed in unprepared, it cost me five years of my life. I was not eager to repeat that mistake. The Capital had broken my mind so deeply that I had considered suicide twice in the past few weeks and also gotten both Grams and my parents killed. I wanted revenge more than anyone else, but if we didn't do it right, it would cost us even more.

"We need to figure out how I project my gift," I explained. "And see if anyone else can do the same. It would give us the upper hand, and the Capital wouldn't be ready for it."

"You're serious?" Calix asked skeptically.

"Deadly," I nodded. "They've taken so much and nearly cost me everything. If we are going to do this, then let's hit them with everything we've got."

Calix's grip on my hips tightened as he pulled me close. Leaning my forehead against his, I closed my eyes. The need for revenge still ran deep in me, but I finally understood that it wasn't enough; that revenge couldn't be the only reason I had for being here. It was the people I cared about who made it worth living. I loved them all more for their willingness to stand beside me in this fight. I owed it to them to do everything I could to make sure we made it out alive.

I couldn't be the only one who was able to project my gift. We had all just accepted that only touch or contact with our blood was the only way to use it. But I had felt it during my training. I could feel it as soon as people were accessing their gift, long before they even reached for their target. If they were accessing it without touch, perhaps they could wield it without it as well.

A soft knock came at the door, and I tried to stand up. Calix gripped me firmly and pulled me back down on his lap. "Come in," he called out. I watched as Thomas slowly pushed the door open and stepped inside.

"I have forty communicators that I can reprogram with the information to give us access to the Capital," he said slowly. "But it will take a few weeks to have them all ready."

"Perfect," I grinned. "That will give us time to train all of you."

"Train?" Thomas asked, confused.

I remained in Calix's lap as I explained how anyone who was going into the Union would need to report for training starting tomorrow. He listened as I told him my theory about others being able to project their gifts; we just needed to learn how to do it. Calix remained silent as I spoke, his hand stroking gently on my arm. I could feel goosebumps forming everywhere he touched. He was trying to distract me, and it was almost working. By the time I finished, my thoughts were proving impossible to hold together.

"You're an ass!" I slapped him as soon as Thomas was gone. "I was trying to focus."

"I know," Calix grinned. "And I was focused on you."

This man was impossible. When I couldn't remember anything, he seemed dark and mysterious. But now, his playful side was back, and he only wanted to play one game. Gone was the focus on the papers or anything else. I had found something, and he was eager to get back to something more enjoyable.

Unfortunately for him, it wasn't going to happen. Despite having enjoyed our time in the dungeon, I was quite sore. Probably because it was my first time. I felt my heart sink at the thought. It was my first time, but it didn't seem like it was his; the way his tongue had expertly worked on my clit. I wouldn't have even thought that was something people did, or that I would enjoy it.

"What's wrong?" Calix asked as I pushed myself out of his lap.

His eyes watched me intently as I passed back and forth. I had left, forgotten him, and now I was jealous if he found comfort in others when he knew there was a chance, I was lost to him forever. I knew it didn't make sense, but it didn't stop the jealousy that was swelling inside me. I may not have remembered him, but my heart never forgot. I never had any desire to be with anyone. That was a part of the reason I had opted for an arranged marriage. But he... he had been able to move on.

"Liz?" Calix's voice was thick with concern as he stood and grabbed my arms. I stopped pacing but still refused to look at him. "You better not be thinking about leaving me again."

That's what he thought this was about? Did he think I was considering killing myself again? I had already decided to do that twice. Each time, I was stopped before I could even begin to act upon it. No, I was done with that. I was going to live and be a pain in his ass until the day I died old and grouchy.

"How many?" Taking a step back and crossing my arms over my chest, I glared at him. I could tell me the expression on his face that he had no idea what I was talking about. "How many women?"

"Are you serious?" he laughed in surprise. "That's what you're upset about?"

"I'll go first," I spat. "Zero before today. Your turn."

With a heavy breath, he ran his hand through his hair and closed his eyes. "I don't know," he finally said. "It's all a blur."

A blur? Is that what I was to him? Just another blur for him to add to the list of women he couldn't remember. I took a step back as he reached for me. I couldn't stand the idea of him touching me right now.

"You are really going to hold it over my head, what I did?" He sounded upset, but I wouldn't give him the satisfaction of a reaction as I continued to glare at him. "You were gone for five fucking years! Do you have any idea what that did to me? I fought for three, threatening war with Gertrude if she didn't let me save you! When she told me to leave and never return, or she would stop people's hearts that I did have left, it nearly killed me!"

I could hear the raw emotion in his voice. He was telling the truth, and I felt my hardened stance relax slightly.

"After that, I just wanted to feel something," he continued. "Anything, with anyone. So, yes, I slept with women. I can't even remember their faces. Every time, the only face I saw was yours. Only to have my heart ripped out when it was over, and I saw a stranger in my bed. Even today, I was afraid you would disappear and it would be another stranger."

He was right. I had put him through hell and left him alone. It wasn't fair to judge him for what he had done. I had planned to kill myself, and he hadn't judged. He had protected me from myself and reminded me of all the reasons I had to live. He was there for me when I was at my lowest. But when he was, I was nowhere to be found.

Surprise washed over me as Calix dropped to his knees, tears glistening in his eyes.

"I can never undo what I did," he said softly. "But, if you let me, I will spend the rest of my life trying. I will never look at another woman. I will never let anyone keep me from you again. I will worship you from this moment until my last, my queen."

My chest swelled with his words. Dropping down to my knees in front of him, I cupped his face in my hands. His eyes were full of a mixture of hope and fear.

"I'm yours," I spoke softly. "And you are mine, my king."

Relief filled his chiseled features as I pulled him closer. His lips pressed softly into mine as his hands held my body firmly. The things we had done in the past five years didn't matter. Through it all, we had found our way back to each other, and we always would. Grams had told me stories when I was younger, stories about true love and soul mates. Her stories always reminded me of my parents, how they came from different worlds but were meant for each other.

As a little girl, I had always dreamed about finding someone like that. Someone who was my other half, who was on this earth for me. I wish I could go back and tell that little girl that we found him. He was our best friend from the moment we were born. Things would pull us apart, but somehow, we would always find our way back to each other.

I would tell her about this moment. The moment when the entire world melted away and we kneeled before each other. This was more than a fairy tale; this was our life. It was far from perfect, but I would treasure every moment of it going forward.

Chapter 22

"*D*am it, Cal!" Garrett hissed. "No touching. Are you trying to give me frostbite?"

I sat on the sidelines watching as the others tried to project their abilities. Over the past few weeks, no one had been successful. Frustrations were growing more with each passing day. The soft grumbles were growing more loud that it wasn't possible, and wanting to move ahead with our plan.

Calix felt the pressure more than me but still insisted we keep trying. The communicators still weren't ready, so it wasn't like we were wasting time. Still, it was hard to keep failing every day.

"Sorry," Calix breathed. "Instinct."

"And why are we trying to go against that?" Maddie asked her with her hands on her hips. "We all can use our gifts just fine in a fight. Our instincts know what to do. Why do we keep pushing for more?"

I could see Calix glancing in my direction before explaining to the others what the benefits would be once again. His words didn't register as my gaze drifted over to the tower. Maddie was right. I hadn't been trying to project my gift. It had just happened when my instincts told me it needed to be done. That's what we were doing wrong. They were able to project because they didn't have a real reason to push themselves to.

As they all continued to argue, I made my way over to the tower. It was used to train guards for wall duty. Aiming at a target below you was different than even ground. No one noticed as I began to climb the wooden stairs. My lungs were burning by the time I reached the top, the others' voices barely registering as a mumble. From up here, I could see the entire city. It was truly remarkable what the people here had managed to build.

"Liz!" Maddie's voice rang out. "What the fuck are you doing up there?"

Ignoring her, I tore my gaze away from the city and walked closer to the edge. They needed something to force them to project their gifts. This was a stupid plan, but it had to work.

"Elizabeth!" Garrett yelled up. "This isn't funny. Get your ass down!"

I smiled as I looked at all of them. "You assholes better not let me die!" I yelled down.

They all moved like they were going to run to the tower, but it was too late. I stepped off, my body plummeting to the ground below. I closed my eyes as the air rushed around me, trusting that this plan would work. If it didn't, well, they wouldn't be able to yell at me.

I opened my eyes as I felt something solid appear under me, and I began to slow down. I looked down to see a piece of flat metal under my body. I continued to slow, and the metal tilted to slide me off. The cold of an ice slide sent shivers up my spine. I felt like a child as I giggled my way to the bottom.

I was still laughing when I stopped, slowly looking up at all the angry faces that were staring down at me. "It worked," I laughed. "I knew you guys could do it."

"You could have killed yourself!" Maddie yelled. "What is it with you and trying to kill yourself every time we turn around?"

"I wasn't trying to kill myself," I laughed as I stood up. "I knew you guys would save me."

"And what if we didn't?" Calix's voice was low and dangerous. "There was no way of knowing that we could get it to work, especially under conditions like that."

I glanced at Malic and Thomas, both of whom were quiet. I could tell by their expressions that they were starting to understand my reasoning.

"I couldn't project before," I began. "Not until the night of the fire. When Malic tried to stop me, I knew that boy would die if he succeeded. My gift reacted to the desperation I felt. It took a life-or death situation for me to do it at first. I'm sorry if I scared you, but you all needed the push."

"That was more than a push." Calilx's face did not relax as he stared at me. "That was reckless and..."

"Me," I finished for him. "That was me doing what I had to. I would do anything for you guys to be stronger. Anything to give you all the best chance of surviving what we are about to do. That fear you all felt when I was falling, I face that every time we talk about attacking the Union. So, if you want to be pissed at me for pushing too hard, fine. At least you'll be alive to glare at me."

"She's right." Malic's voice interrupted the thick silence that filled the air after my words. "It was risky, but she got each of us to project our gifts."

Calix took a step closer to me and gripped my chin in his hand. "Never again," he growled.

"No promises," I replied. "I'll do what I have to if it means you all survive. Tell me you would do it differently?"

He shook his head with a light smile. I was right, he would have jumped off a mountain if it meant keeping us all safe. He knew he wouldn't win this argument. It was better to save his strength for one that he had a chance at.

"So, I know about the metal and the ice slide," I said as I pulled away and looked at the others. "But you said all of you were able to project."

They all looked at each other for a moment, and I waited for them to explain.

"We all freaked out a little," Maddie admitted.

"A little?" Malic asked with a raised eyebrow.

"Okay, a lot," Maddie continued. "Malic yelled at me to calm everyone down. I felt like I had no choice, damn Silver Tongue. At first, I was confused because he was nowhere near me. Still, I concentrated, and everyone's heartbeats slowed just enough that they were able to think straight."

"The plan was going great," Garret said. "Until the damn ice slide started to fall when you were on it. I don't know how, but I wanted it to stay up. I couldn't reach it, and yet I could feel the weight of it. I kept it up until you were safe."

They all had worked together and kept me from becoming a mush pile on the ground. Now, they would just need to practice without someone's life being on the line.

"How much longer do we have until the communicators are ready?" Calix asked, looking at Thomas.

I watched as Thomas shifted uncomfortably on his feet. His eyes remained fixed on the ground, but his silence was speaking volumes.

"Last week," he finally spoke. "I had them all ready last week, as well as the part to hack others once we're in."

"What?!" Garrett boomed. "You've been ready and didn't tell us?!"

"Liz was right," Thomas said defensively. "We needed to learn to project before we attempted to go in. It put the odds of winning more in our favor and..."

Garrett's fists were clenched at his sides. He had always been hot-headed. We used to joke that all of his strength left no room for patience.

"Enough," Calix said firmly. "Thomas, you should have told us, but you did what you did with all of us in mind. It was a gamble that paid off, and we all owe you our thanks."

Garrett's jaw clenched so tight I thought he was going to shatter his teeth. His glaring gaze shifted between Calix and Thomas, and I felt that familiar tingle in my skin.

"Garrett," I said cautiously. "Don't..."

No sooner than the word left my mouth, I felt it. His gift was projected directly at Thomas. I absorbed it just before it collided with Thomas. Garrett's rage-filled eyes locked on me in an instant. He knew what I did as soon as he lost access to his gift.

"I'll give it back when you can behave," I said, like I was talking to a child. "We are supposed to be fighting the Union, not each other."

"Keep it," Garrett growled. "It will be mine again soon enough."

I felt Calix tighten his arm around my waist and pull me closer to him. Garrett was one of our best friends, but Calix wouldn't hesitate to stop him if he tried to hurt me.

"Not until you cool off," Calix said firmly. "If that takes days, then she will take it from you every day."

"You can't be serious!" Garrett roared. "After everything, you are going to let her..."

Calix stepped forward, tucking me protectively behind him in the blink of an eye. I could see the ice crystals forming on his skin as he stood nose to nose with Garrett.

"Watch yourself," Calix warned.

"You are seriously going to choose her over me?" Garrett snarled. "After everything."

"Yes." Calix didn't hesitate even for a moment. "I will always choose her."

Maddie took a few cautious steps towards Garrett and placed her hand on his arm. I watched as he tensed at her touch but didn't pull away. The tension was thick for several moments. Maddie whispered something to Garrett that I couldn't hear. He glared at me one last time before turning and walking away with her.

As soon as they were gone, Calix pulled me back to his side. I hated to see him and Garrett fight. They were best friends, well, we all were. If we didn't pull it together and stop this madness, the capital would win before we even left Twain.

"She'll get him to calm down," Malic said with a light smile. "Even without her gift."

I nodded slowly as I continued to stare in the direction where Maddie and Garrett had disappeared. Malic was probably right. Still, something about this just didn't sit well with me.

"Why don't you relax?" Calix asked. "We still have some time left. The three of us can keep practicing."

I nodded and walked back to the edge of the training area, taking a seat on the dirt. I watched as Calix, Malic, and Thomas each took turns projecting their gifts. As the sun started to set, they all had mastered it in unimaginable ways.

Maddie and Garrett returned just as we were about to head back to the manor for dinner. Garrett looked calmer and exhausted. Calix stood beside me, my hand in his, as they approached.

"I'm sorry," Garrett said as soon as they were close. "I lost it for a moment there. If you hadn't stopped me..."

"That's what friends are for," I smiled at him. "To tell each other when we are being a pain in the ass."

I could feel Garrett's gift still rippling through my skin. With a deep breath, I released it and felt it disappear. Garrett immediately perked up and looked at me, surprised.

"I trust you." I let go of Calix's hand and stepped closer to him. "Even if you are a big meathead sometimes."

"I may be a meathead, but at least I have the brains not to step off the tower."

We both let out a light laugh. Things were back to how they were supposed to be, and everything felt right again. Calix took my hand again as we all walked back to the manor. Inside, Ms. Timlin had dinner ready for us when we arrived. We all gathered around the table. The air was filled with light conversation as each of them talked about what it felt like to project.

I sat in silence, listening and enjoying the sight. We had all lost everything. Our families were gone, and all we had left was each other. But somehow, that was all we needed. We were our own family. Sure, we had our issues and could be dysfunctional as hell at times. In reality, though, what family doesn't have those issues?

"One more day," Calix said, causing the chatter to disappear. "We will meet in the morning and practice projecting until noon. After that, we all need to prepare to move out. We will meet at the gate at six. That will give us just enough time to make it to The Edge before dark."

His words sat heavily on my shoulders. After all the years of preparation, all the setbacks and losses, it was finally time. We were making our move on the Union. No matter the outcome, this would be the end of our battle, one way or another.

Silence hung in the air, and only the sound of forks scraping against plates cut through it. Everyone was probably feeling the same as I did and trying to wrap their minds around what we were about to do. We all knew the plan, but it somehow felt different now that it was time.

The six of us would make our way to The Edge, staying out of sight. Our allies inside would get their communicators altered by Thomas's program, and any bombs that may be in them disarmed. After that, we would take the medical center and gain access to the tunnels. Once it was secured, the army from Twain would join us. We would repeat this process all the way to the Capital. Our number of allies in each ring would decrease as we went. Ring two, and the Capital would provide us with no friends.

We finished the dinner in silence, each of us walking away to deal with our thoughts. My feet felt heavy as I slowly climbed the stairs and walked to my room. As I closed the door behind me, I felt the weight of what we were about to do come crushing down. I leaned against the door, my heart hammering in my chest. I thought I was going to collapse under the weight of it all until a sharp knock pulled me out of my thoughts.

Straightening myself, I slowly opened the door. Calix was standing on the other side with his hands in his pockets. I could see that it was weighing on him just as much as it was on me. I opened the door wider and motioned for him to come him, closing the door behind him once he was inside.

"Did I make the right choice?" He asked, not looking at me.

"I don't know," I admitted. "We've talked about it for so long. But now that we are about to do it, it feels different."

He nodded as he walked over to the bed and sat down, dropping his head into his hands. The downfall of being in charge was that everything landed on him to decide. It didn't matter if it was tomorrow or years in the future;

this fight was going to happen. The Union would never stop exploiting MUTs for power. Twain was full of people who had barely managed to escape. The Union wasn't going to let this place stand forever. There was too much power, and the Union had to control it.

I walked over to him and forced his face up to look at me. As his arms fell to his sides, I climbed into his lap, my knees on either side of him.

"We have to do this," I said softly. "This is about more than revenge. We have to do it to protect everyone here. To save everyone who they still have trapped."

Calix wrapped his arms around me and nodded softly.

"After this, we won't have to fight anymore," I continued. "We will finally be free. We will get to live our lives without the constant worry of them trying to rip us apart."

I felt his skin grow cold as his muscles tensed. Even the mention of me being taken away again put him on edge. I leaned forward against him, allowing him to hold me tighter.

"They have taken so much from us. Don't let them take tonight, too."

Calix lifted his face, and his lips found mine. My body pressed closer to him, begging for his touch. I felt the edge of my shirt begin to lift, and I raised my arms. Calix pulled it off in one swift motion before dropping it to the floor. Grabbing the edge of his shirt, I pulled it off just the same and dropped it.

Calix pulled me back to him as he lifted me and turned, laying me down gently on the bed. His tongue explored my mouth as he tasted every part of me, eager for more. I could feel his length pressing against my thigh through his pants. My breathing became heavy as the moisture in my core grew, eager for more.

A soft whimper escaped me as he pulled back and stood up. He smiled at me knowingly as he undid his pants and let them fall to the floor. Holding my breath, I watched as he leaned forward and undid mine. Slowly, he pulled them off until he was kneeling beside the bed. After throwing my pants aside, his hands slid up my thighs until they reached where my arousal was pooling.

"So eager for me, my Queen," he smiled as he pulled back his hand and slid his finger into his mouth. He let out a low growl as he tasted my arousal on his skin. I felt my core tighten at the sight, my body screaming for contact. "Tell me what you want." His voice was causing me to quiver. He knew what I wanted and was toying with me.

"You," I breathed. "I need you."

That was enough. The bed dipped under his weight as he climbed on top of me, positioning his length at my entrance. "As you wish, my queen."

My eyes rolled back in my head as he pushed deep inside me with a single thrust. I felt myself stretch around him, filling an emptiness I hadn't realized I had. There was no pain this time, just pleasure. Calix moved slowly, each long movement causing my body to beg for more. I bucked my hips, trying to increase the pace.

"Patience," Calix smiled as he held my hips in place. "I'll give my queen what she needs."

With that, he thrust into me hard and fast. White flashes appeared in my vision as I let out a gasp. Calix began moving at a relentless pace as he thrust inside me. I clung onto his shoulders, my nails digging into his skin as incoherent words came out of my mouth. I felt myself moving closer and closer.

"Calix!" I cried as my orgasm reached its peak.

My legs were shaking around him as Calix slowed his pace slightly. Through the haze of my euphoria, I could see the smile that played on his lips as he worked me through every second of my orgasm. As I felt the rush of it end, I expected Calix to find his own release. However, his pace only increased. My body trembled, my strength gone from the pleasure I just experienced.

"One more time," Calix grinned. "I want to feel you come one more time for me."

My body responded immediately. I could feel myself tightening around his length as he worked every nerve ending inside me. I couldn't form words as I felt my body reach its peak once more and come crashing down.

"That's my good girl," Calix grinned as he closed his eyes.

The second orgasm was just as powerful as the first. It ripped through my body, giving me a pleasure that was beyond words. As it neared its end, Calix let out a low growl, and I felt him find his release.

We were both breathing heavily as he collapsed on the bed beside me. Our bodies were both covered in a slick sweat. I could feel his release beginning to run down my thigh, but I didn't have the strength to move. Calix pulled me closer so my head was resting on his chest. We both seemed unbothered by our current state. The need to be close overrode any shame we should have felt. This is how we belonged. Together, they worried about nothing but making sure the other was as close as possible.

Chapter 23

$\mathcal{T}$he next morning came too quickly. I let out a groan as Calix kissed my head and woke me. The night before had been one of the happiest of my life. We had lain in bed, not speaking for a long time, before Calix drew us a bath. We sat in the water, carefully washing each other until the water went cold. I was not ready for him to untangle his limbs from mine as he drew back the blankets and crawled out.

"I need to meet the others." His voice showed that he hated the idea of having to get up as much as me. "Maddie and Garrett need to practice before we head out."

"You talk like I'm not going with you." I stretched and let out a yawn before forcing myself to sit up.

"I need you to go meet with Thomas," he said, looking back at me as he tied his boot. "You need to get your communicator and convince him that he hasn't made any mistakes. You know how he is."

"Communicator?"

My stomach twisted, and I drew my legs up to my chest. I knew that we were all going to have to wear one; it was the only way we could move through the districts without triggering alarms. Even still, I could see Samuel's face as a communicator was forced onto my arm, the rotting flesh and pain when Thomas had taken it off, and the sinking feeling of being forced to forget who I was again.

"Hey," Calix said, taking my hands. "Everything will be fine. You're old one was destroyed. This one is safe."

"You don't know that." I hated the tremor of fear in my voice, but I was safe with Calix. I didn't have to hide my fear in front of him.

"I do," he said softly. "And so do you. Thomas programmed all of them himself. He would never do anything to put any of us in danger, especially you."

I leaned against his cool chest and let his words wash over me. He was right, the communicators would be safe. I had to get it together. Thomas would be second guessing everything right now. If he saw that I had any doubts or fears, he would scrap them all and start over. Thomas was good at what he did. He was probably more skilled with electronics than anyone in the Capital. I couldn't let my irrational fears push him into self-doubt.

"Better?" Calix leaned back and looked down at my face, tucking a strand of loose hair behind my ear.

"Better," I nodded. "I will make sure Thomas is good and gather our supplies. I'll meet you at the gate."

After kissing me on the head, Calix left the room. I forced myself up and quickly put on my clothes before heading out. Word of what we were planning had spread overnight. The manor was full of people rushing to get things ready and making sure that Twain was prepared in case something went wrong.

Weaving my way through the people, I managed to reach the front doors and step out into the morning sun. Outside, everyone was just as busy as they rushed through the streets. I walked slowly, taking my time as I made my way to Thomas's workshop. The building was only partially finished, the structure rising out of the ashes where it had burned.

Standing outside was a boy I recognized. His face was no longer covered in soot, and his green eyes were full of life.

"Ms. Elizabeth!" he yelled as he ran forward and wrapped me in a hug. I hugged him back with a light laugh. I hadn't seen him since the night of the fire, and I was glad to see that he had made a full recovery.

"Is Thomas inside?" I asked once he broke our embrace.

"Yes, ma'am," he nodded. "But it's best not to go in. He's a bit cranky today." "I think I can handle him," I smiled.

With a tussle of his hair, I headed for the door and stepped inside. Thomas was rushing between tables, looking at devices, screens, and scattered papers. I watched as he continued rushing around and muttering to himself. Calix was right; he was trying to find a flaw in what he had done. Even as I watched, I could tell that he wasn't having any luck.

"Your first victim has arrived," I announced. Thomas froze and slowly turned to face me. "Here to get my communicator before I start gathering our supplies."

"No." Thomas backed away like I was going to attack him. "I've made a mistake. They're not ready."

"They look ready to me," I shrugged as I picked one up. "What's wrong with them?"

Thomas's eyes darted around, never meeting mine. "I'm not sure."

"You mean you haven't been able to find anything wrong then?" I set down the communicator and walked closer to where he stood. This time, he didn't back away. "I'm sure you've gone over them multiple times since last night," I continued. "And haven't found a single thing wrong with your work."

Thomas finally looked at me, the worry and exhaustion showing on his face. I held out my arm, giving him my wrist. I had to look closely to see the slight scar that remained. Thomas let out a shaky breath and picked up a communicator from the bench. I watched with fascination as he compelled the metal to stretch and slid it over my hand. Once it was in place, the metal shrank back down until it sat firmly on the skin.

"Much better than last time," I said as I rubbed the cool metal. "If you weren't one of us, you would have a heck of a career in the Capital."

Thomas let out a sigh of relief and turned back to the computer. I watched over his shoulder as his fingers flew across the keys. "It's stable," he said after a moment. "I was worried that when it made contact, the program would corrupt. But, the only way to test it was to..."

His voice trailed off. "Glad to be the test subject," I teased. "I had no doubts it would work, of course. So, there wasn't a risk for me."

I watched as Thomas's shoulders relaxed and he let out a deep breath. He picked up another communicator from the table and put it on himself. After checking the computer once again, he turned back to me.

"It's programmed with all the information about the Capital," he explained. "It will allow you to open the gates between the rings and see all emergency broadcasts they send out. It will also allow us to communicate with each other. You will have full access to their systems, but they won't be able to access these." He held up his wrist with a smile. "The level of encryption I have on these would take their top hacker years to break. They won't be able to track us or withdraw our access."

"You're a genius," I smiled at him.

"Once we get inside," he picked up a small device from beside the computer," I can use this to reprogram other communicators. They will be able to see them go offline, but hopefully, they won't pay too much attention. It should look like a system glitch. I doubt they will be in a hurry to address it until it gets closer to the Capital."

"And by then it will be too late," I nodded.

"I'm next," Malic's voice rang out. "Seeing as she seems fine, I guess there's no point in stalling."

I stepped aside and watched as Thomas slid Malic's communicator on. Malic looked uncomfortable once the device was secured. He had been born in Twain and never worn one before. I looked down at my own, surprised at how comfortable I felt with it on.

"How's the training going?" I asked when

Thomas turned his attention back to the computer. "They're done," Malic nodded. "The Siren and Wrecking Ball are ready to go."

"Siren and Wrecking Ball?" I laughed.

"We gained access to the Capital's records a few years ago," Thomas said, still typing. "That's what they call MUTs with those abilities. I'm a bender." "What about me and Cal?" I asked. "I want a nickname, too."

Thomas stopped typing and looked at Malic.

"You don't have one," Malic said slowly. "There was no record of any MUTs with abilities matching yours."

While it was true I had never met anyone with abilities matching ours, I had just figured that the Capital had them locked away. Learning that we were the only ones was something I never expected.

"Then they won't know how to fight us." I hoped that my smile was enough to hide how much this realization shook me. "I still have some things to do. I'll meet you guys at the gate."

I hurried out of the building before either of them could speak. If our abilities were really that unique, it explained why Samuel was so eager to have me. My blood tests must have given them some kind of indication that my gift had not been seen before.

As for Calix, they would have no idea what he was capable of. That would go, however, the first time he used his gift. They would fight harder to add us both to their collection.

I walked through Twain in a haze. I gathered the supplies we needed and took them all to the gate, where they were loaded into backpacks. When I finished, I noticed that the weapons had already been gathered. I grabbed my knife, securing it to my thigh like a safety blanket. I wasn't going to win this war with a small blade, but it still made me feel stronger having it close. I looked down at the other weapons but decided to wait for the others before arming up.

I still had time before the others would be here. Standing there seemed to make the minutes drag by even more slowly. I felt like I was going to explode out of my skin if I didn't do something. Turning away from the gate, I headed back into town. I didn't think about where I was walking until I found myself standing at the door to the dungeon. Pressing the panel, I slipped inside and down the stairs. I let out a sigh of relief when I saw the cells were empty. Rushing down the aisle, I went into mine. Determination filled me as I rummaged through the shelves and blankets, looking.

"Gotcha," I said in victory as I pulled out a small wooden box.

I opened the lid and looked down at the two treasures inside. Two silver rings, each perfectly round with a smooth polish that made them shine even in the dim light.

I had been carrying them with me five years ago when everything went to shit. Of course, Grams would have found them and put them somewhere safe. This was the only place that she could have hidden them, where I would not have accidentally stumbled across them. I hadn't even thought about them until I found myself standing at the door down here.

We were going to be using the Cathedral as our base when we arrived - the same place that Calix and I had planned to say our vows. Most people avoided it, except for the odd couple that wanted to have a traditional ceremony. Over the years, a random priest would make it his mission to bring religion to The Edge. He would rebuild sections of the church and try to get people to attend services. After a few months, they would always give up and leave.

We were about to head into something big, and there was no guarantee we were going to make it out. I had lost the opportunity once to marry Calix. I wouldn't make that mistake again. If he would have me, my Lucifer and I would be husband and wife tonight.

I shut the lid and tucked the box into my pocket just as my communicator chimed. I looked down at the screen and could see a message from Thomas that read "Fifteen Minutes".

I rushed out of the cells and back upstairs. I ran through the streets and was breathing hard by the time I reached the others. All of them were rubbing at their communicators, still not used to the foreign metal they were now shackled by.

Maddie walked up to me and secured a belt around my waist before placing a pistol in the holder. "You ready for this?" she asked with a slight smile.

"Yeah," I nodded with a glance at Calix. "I'm ready."

Chapter 24

The journey to the Union had been tense. None of us spoke as we made our way through the Wastelands. I was sure everyone was wrestling with their thoughts. Mine were consumed by the weight of the ring box in my pocket. Maybe I shouldn't have brought them. There was enough going on without my springing a surprise wedding on everyone. How did I know if Calix was even still interested in taking vows?

We had sealed our relationship in ways that a simple ceremony could never match. Yet, the need to see this all the way through burned deep inside me. If he wasn't ready, I could find a way to be okay with that. But if I didn't at least try, I would never forgive myself.

The streets were silent as we crept through the dark towards the cathedral. The last of the sun's light had just disappeared as we made our way through the hidden doorway. Normally, people would still be working or rushing around to take care of things they hadn't had time for during the day. The silence was unnatural. Everyone seemed to notice, but no one dared to talk. It was as if speaking would cause the world to shatter around us.

We all paused in the shadow of an abandoned shack and looked at the cathedral. It had probably been lovely once. The rumor was that it stood before the Great War. It had taken a beating and still survived. The large stones that made it up showed their age and the scars of what it had been through. The roof had collapsed in several spots, though the stone had quickly been taken away for other uses. The large windows that once housed beautiful stained glass now sat empty. The dark emptiness of the large structure behind them gave them a feeling of dread. But, despite all of that, I still found it beautiful.

I followed the others as we made our way across the street and up the crumbling stone steps. The large wooden door let out a moan as we pushed it open just enough to slip inside. The darkness consumed my sight, and I had to wait for my eyes to adjust. The others were already moving, draping large black cloths over the windows and covering any holes that may allow people to see inside.

As soon as they were finished, we all gathered on the pulpit and lit a few small candles. My gaze traveled up to the high ceilings, now covered with a makeshift straw roof by the last priest. Despite the roof looking out of place, the pillars were magnificent. Each one was carved to the top. Most of the statues were damaged or broken over time. Yet, it was still a marvel to look at.

Everyone went tense and reached for a weapon as the door let out a moan. I let out a breath and relaxed as Joe came into view. Not only had he been kind to me when my memories were gone, but he was also one of our closest allies in The Edge. His position at the depot gave us access to information and a way to transmit messages to allies further in.

Joe came closer and pulled me into a hug. "I'm so sorry," he said after a moment. "I tried to get her to run, but she wouldn't go."

He had promised me to look after Grams, and now he was carrying the blame for what happened to her. I pulled back and looked him in the eyes.

"Grams knew what she was doing," I said. "No one will taint her memory by blaming themselves or thinking they could have made her do something different."

"You sound just like her," Joe laughed lightly as he wiped a tear from his eye.

Joe and I sat down and joined the others. After they all had said their greetings, Calix's face turned serious.

"What's going on?"

The question had been on everyone's mind. Something had felt off since we arrived.

"Curfew," Joe sighed. "Everyone is required to be indoors before dark. Any caught are killed on the spot.

I looked at Calix in shock, but his face remained free of emotion. He was still looking at Joe, as if waiting for more.

"Those who follow the curfew aren't safe," he continued. "They have been removing people from their homes, questioning them, and if they don't believe what they hear, they kill them on the spot. Everyone has also been required to report for follow-up genetic testing. They claim there was a system update that makes it more accurate, but everyone who goes comes out with a new communicator."

"Have you been yet?" I asked nervously.

"No," he said, shaking his head. "I've been able to keep my family in the clear for now. But we can't hold back much longer."

"You won't have to," I said, placing my hand on his arm.

Thomas moved forward and attached the small device he had shown me earlier to Joe's communicator. The screen lit up and flashed several messages so fast I couldn't see what they were.

"You're free," Thomas said as he disconnected the device and sat back down. "You are disconnected from them and connected to our network."

"What about my wife? My son?" The fear and panic on Joe's face broke my heart. I wanted to take it all away from him.

"Bring them here," Calix answered. "As soon as you are able, along with all our allies. Make sure to bring them in small groups to avoid getting caught. Thomas can free them all."

Joe nodded and hurried out of the cathedral. A few minutes later, he reappeared with his wife, Harmony, and their small boy, Alic. I watched as Thomas reprogrammed each of the communicators, freeing them from the Union.

"I will work through the night," Joe said once his family was safe. "But that means I can't protect them."

"They can stay with us," I blurted out.

Everyone looked at Calix as an amused smile played on his lips. "The queen has spoken."

"Speaking of," I said, reaching into my pocket. "The last time I was about to do something reckless, I decided to do it before meeting you here." The box felt like it weighed a ton in my hand as I held it out. "What do you say we make my title official?"

A grin spread over Calix's face as I opened the box and revealed the rings. Grabbing my wrist, he pulled me close to him and kissed me softly.

"Only you would want to get married before we start a war," he smiled.

"They started the war," I replied. "I'm just not letting it stop me from living my life anymore. That is, if you still want to..."

"I would marry you as hell itself rose if I had to," Calix interrupted as he reached down and pulled my knife off my thigh.

Everyone moved off the pulpit and gathered around the base of the stairs. I knew they were watching, but my gaze was fixed on Calix. I held out my left hand, which he took and softly kissed.

"I am yours."

With that, he took the tip of my blade and carefully cut into my ring finger. I didn't flinch as the blood ran down my hand. When he finished, he rinsed the cut with a bit of water and then held a cloth to the fresh cuts. Once the bleeding stopped, he kissed my hand once more and slid on my ring. I didn't have to see the cuts to know what they were. It was his initials, CH. Rings were nice, but easily lost. More often than not, they were sold to make sure a family didn't

starve. The cuts, those were forever. He had just
bound himself to me.

After cleaning the blade, Calix handed the
knife to me and held out his left hand. Carefully, I
repeated the process of carving my initials into
his ring finger and then placing his ring.

"And I'm yours," I smiled when I was
finished.

Just when I thought I was going to get my
happy ending, reality snuck up on me. I forgot
that happy endings only exist because the story
stops. If everyone knew the real outcome, they
wouldn't believe in such foolish things.

Calix wrapped his arms around me just as
the slow clapping echoed throughout the
cathedral. I turned to see everyone frozen in fear
as a man walked slowly towards us, his clapping
still echoing. His expensive suit looked out of
place with his long silver hair. I narrowed my eyes
in hatred as Samuel grinned back at me.

"So, touching," he bellowed as he stopped.
"My invitation must have gotten lost."

That bastard was acting like this was a
game. He had killed my parents and Grams, and

now he was ruining my vows. My skin began to tingle as I felt everyone access their gifts. They were all ready to attack him here. But this was too easy. While he was an evil man, he wasn't dumb. He wouldn't have just walked in here unprepared.

I focused harder on the gifts I felt and cursed under my breath. His MUT soldiers were right outside, ready to take us down at a moment's notice. Even with the ability for everyone to project their gifts, we would not win.

Garrett was the first to act. I felt his gift rise to the surface and push out towards Samuel. I reached out, absorbing it and snatching it away. Garrett spun to look at me as I returned his gift to him. He looked confused, but thankfully, Samuel seemed unaware of what had happened.

"What do you want?"

I stepped away from Calix and down the stairs. Samuel seemed pleased with my courage, though that was something I planned to make him regret.

"To take you home," he said with false sincerity. "We are family after all."

"You'll let them go?" I asked, not looking at the others. I could feel the cold radiating off Calix. He needed to get in control before I had to take his gift, too.

"Of course," Samuel nodded. "They will all need to go to the medical center for new communicators as theirs appear to be malfunctioning. But after that, they will be free to return to their lives."

"Their lives are in Twain," I said firmly. "You will let them return, unharmed."

Amuel looked at me for a moment, but I stood firm. I knew I couldn't trust him, but I could still see Alic out of the corner of my eye. His face was white with fear as he tried to hide behind his mother's dress. The others could fight for themselves, but I had to try to get him out.

Samuel snapped his fingers, and the soldiers from outside came filing in behind him. Everyone's stance tightened as the soldiers piled in, filling the cathedral, and more could be seen just outside.

"Everyone can leave except for him."

My heart sank as Samuel's bony finger pointed behind me. I didn't have to turn to know he was pointing at Calix.

"I can't let the King leave without a proper discussion."

"You can't..."

"Deal."

I spun around and looked at Calix. His face was hard as he stared at Samuel. I wanted to punch him and call him an idiot, but there was no time.

"Garrett, get the others out of here," Calix ordered.

Garrett looked between us before walking with the others to the far side of the cathedral. The only exit was now blocked by soldiers, but that wouldn't stop him. I watched as he punched into the stone several times, opening up enough of a hole for them all to crawl out.

Samuel stayed true to his word, not moving or ordering his soldiers to stop them. Several minutes passed before Calix's and my communicators dinged. I glanced down at the screen and felt relieved, "Clear." Now, I just had to find a way to get my idiot husband out of here alive. It would have been simple for me to escape. Absorbing gifts and fleeing until I was free. Now, it was complicated.

"My dear." I looked back to see Samuel holding out his hand to me. "It's time to keep up your end."

I glanced back at Calix, his jaw tight as I took Samuel's hand. Samuel pulled me close, leading me back out of the cathedral. Panic filled me as the soldiers moved in closer.

"I thought you wanted to talk to him." I struggled against Samuel's grip as he continued to pull me on.

"I did," Samuel said as we neared the door. "But the second you vowed yourself to him, you left me no choice. Your union with Ryan cannot be done as long as you are vowed. Even if it is to that worthless boy they call king. Traditions and so forth. Your first husband must be dead for you to take on another."

My heart froze in my chest as I fought to turn back and look at Calix. His hands were up in surrender as the soldiers surrounded him. He must have seen the panic, the terror, on my face.

He gave me a half-smile and winked before the soldiers blocked him from my view. I could hear the sounds of fists and feet striking flesh.

Samuel held me still, seeming to take joy in watching my pain as his men killed Calix in front of me.

"It's done," a deep voice rang out.

I watched as the soldiers moved away, revealing Calix's broken body. His shirt was torn, and blood covered his skin and hair. I watched, pleading for the slightest movement to tell me there was still life in him. Nothing came.

I felt numb as I allowed Samuel to drag me outside. I didn't even try to get away as he shoved me forward. I felt myself hit someone and looked up into a set of cold eyes.

"There you are," Ryan sneered at me. "I assume you're no longer pure. That's fine with me.

I prefer my women to be a bit more experienced."

"Fuck you!" I spat in his face and tried to pull away.

The slap came hard and fast, knocking me to my knees with its force. Running my tongue along my lip, the taste of iron assaulted my taste buds.   "I will beat that defiance out of you," Ryan said as he bent down closer to my face. "You will bend to do me."

Calix's words echoed in my mind. I bowed to no one. Calix may be gone, but I was still here. I would keep fighting for him. I hardened my face and matched Ryan's eyes.

"You hit like a bitch."

Chapter 25

 ighting flashed across the sky, followed by a rumble of thunder that shook me to my core. I kept my stern gaze locked on Ryan as I rose from my knees, the sting on my cheek empowering me. Ryan's face showed a look of murder as we stood glaring at each other. The sky lit up again as rain began to fall around us. It was as if the weather was mirroring the anger and pain I felt.

I stood steady and braced myself as Ryan raised his hand to strike me once more. He appeared to think he would be able to smack me into submission. Little did he know that each hit only gave me the strength to continue fighting.

"Enough!" Ryan's hand stopped inches from my face at the sound of Samuel's voice. "Lillian will punish us both if we deliver her all banged up."

Ryan's hand remained ready to strike as he glared at Samuel. "This bitch needs to learn her place. I am her-"

"She isn't yours yet," Samuel interrupted. "Once the contract is done, you can deal with her as your wife as you see fit. Until then, we both still answer to Lilian."

Ryan let out a frustrated grumble as he lowered his hand and took a step back. I finally looked away from him and glanced at Samuel. He was still maintaining his arrogant composure as the rain covered his suite. The lighting flashed again, and I spotted something unexpected in his eyes - fear. Whoever Lillian was, she was powerful enough to command respect and fear from Samuel. I wasn't sure if I should respect or fear her, but I already knew I would hate her.

"We need to get moving." Two of the soldiers grabbed my arms as soon as Samuel spoke. I tried to pull out of their grasp as they began to draw me to move.

"Tell Lillian I regret not being able to make it," I said between clenched teeth as I continued to struggle. The soldier's grip only tightened as they continued to pull me along. Everyone remained silent as I was led through the rain, which was now falling in sheets around us. I knew I wouldn't be able to overpower them and escape, but I refused to give up. I continued to fight against them as they pulled me through the muddy streets and to the medical center.

A wave of cold blasted my wet skin as they pulled me inside. The sound of wet steps on the shiny white floors echoed around us as they led me through the building.

When we reached a dead end, Samuel stepped forward and opened a hidden keypad. I tried to watch as he quickly entered a code and closed the cover. As soon as he finished, two doors slid open, revealing an elevator. The soldiers pulled me inside after Samuel entered. I felt claustrophobic as everyone squeezed in before the doors closed, and the elevator began to descend.

After a few minutes, the doors opened once again, and everyone spilled out. Everyone moved quickly as they walked across the small terminal and to a train. I didn't struggle as my eyes tried to take in everything. White tiles covered every surface, and rows of black metal benches filled the area between the elevator and the train. The train was black and shiny, looking futuristic compared to the buildings just above it.

I was led away from where the soldiers were boarding and to a separate car. Samuel entered a code on the door before stepping inside. The soldiers shoved me in behind him just before the door slid shut.

"Sit," Samuel instructed as he walked over to a small bar and poured himself a drink into a thick, clear glass.

I felt disgust as I looked around the lush car. Fancy chairs and tables with heavy cloth and plush cushions. The people of The Edge are struggling to survive, and the amount of resources used for a fancy train car was disgusting. Samuel looked back at me, glancing at my clenched fist before walking over to a high-back chair and sitting.

"Feel free to stand," he said as he crossed his legs and lifted his drink to his lips. "It will take a little over an hour to reach The Capital."

My eyes remained locked on him as I moved to the simplest-looking chair and sat. I didn't want to waste my energy standing. I had a fight ahead of me, and I needed all my strength. Samuel smiled slightly before taking another drink.

"Who's Lillian?" My voice was void of emotion as I spoke. In truth, I preferred the awkward silence, but I needed to try to learn more about this new enemy.

"My wife," Samuel replied smoothly.

I couldn't help the laugh that escaped me. It was hard to imagine Samuel being ordered around or fearing a woman, even his wife.

"Laugh if you wish," Samuel replied as he took another drink. "Soon you'll learn why no one goes against her."

"My mother did." Samuel's hand froze as he was lifting his drink once more. His gaze locked on me for a moment before he lowered the glass.

"And you know how it ended for her." I couldn't believe it, but it sounded like there was a hint of sorrow in his voice. "A bit of advice: do as she says. It will save everyone a world of pain." "I'm not one for being told what to do," I replied with a smirk. "But, you know, since you poisoned me with venom to make sure I complied."

"It was a mercy," Samuel said, leaning forward. "I was trying to spare you the pain of her methods."

"Mercy?" I snorted. "Taking my memories and giving me a mind-splitting pain when I did anything you dreamed of as misbehaving was mercy?"

"Yes." The look on Samuel's face gave me pause. I knew the man was evil, but something in his expression made me feel a twinge of fear. "It is a mercy you will not be granted a second time. "Samuel leaned back and closed his eyes. I could tell he was done with the conversation. The rest of the train ride, the only sound was the whirl of the train as it traveled.

Trapped inside, I allowed my mind to wander. As I closed my eyes, the image of Calix's body on the floor, lifeless and unmoving. I felt a pain in my heart. It was a pain I knew I would feel for the rest of my life. I hated that I had to leave him there and hoped the others would find him. He deserved to be taken back to Twain and laid to rest. It should have been me doing it, and I would regret not being able to forever.

I refused to cry; there would be time to mourn him later. For now, I needed to focus on finishing what we started together. I would avenge our parents' deaths, his death, and free the people of the Union. I couldn't help but feel that would be the easy part. It would be life after the war that would be hard. Part of me wanted to join him in death, but I knew that wasn't an option. I had to continue living and seeing our vision for the people through. When I joined him, I wanted him to be proud of me.

The thoughts of Calix were pushed out of the front of my mind as I felt the train slow to a stop. I opened my eyes just in time to see Samuel stand and return his now empty glass to the cart. I was still sitting as he turned towards me, straightening his wetsuit jacket.

"Will you walk willingly, or do I need to have them drag you again?"

I considered his question for a moment before rising to my feet. In no way did I want to appear as being complaint, but at this point, I knew I had no choice but to go meet with Lillian. My body was already exhausted and could not afford to waste any more strength.

"Lead the way," I replied firmly.

Samuel nodded and walked over to the train door and opened it. Outside, I found myself in a terminal that looked exactly like the one in The Edge. Unlike The Edge, however, people were filling the benches. They all remained still as their gaze followed me and Samuel as we made our way across the space and into the elevator. As the doors closed, the people moved from their seats and began filing into the train cars.

"If you're planning to run once we get above ground, don't," Samuel said as the elevator began to rise. "The soldiers will be waiting for us, and I do not want to have to answer for any more bruises you would receive."

Of course, we wouldn't be making the journey to Lillian alone. I nodded to show I understood as I continued to stare at the doors. Just as Samuel said, as soon as the doors opened, there was a scene of soldiers waiting for us. Their faces were unfamiliar, and they were not the same ones that had been in The Edge.

I followed Samuel out of the elevator into a grand building full of people who were bustling around. I expected to be in another medical building, but it didn't look to be the case.

"Where are we?" My voice came out barely above a whisper, and I wasn't sure if Samuel heard me.

"The Hub," Samuel replied as he walked towards a set of large glass doors. "The stations are only concealed in The Rings. Here, we don't have to worry about people trying to rebel and raid against us."

Stepping outside, I had to hold up my hand to block the sun from my eyes. It was very early in the morning, but the night had ended while we traveled underground. I felt a soldier nudge my shoulder, urging me to move forward. I looked and saw that Samuel was already climbing into a round, black vehicle that was hovering above the ground. I slowly moved forward and climbed inside, and sat down on the soft leather seats. As soon as I was seated, the door shut, and the pod began moving forward with a slight whine of what I assumed was an engine.

Samuel appeared bored as he leaned back against the seat and closed his eyes once again. I moved closer to the window and tried to take in the world that was moving by outside. The shiny buildings looked as if they were reaching for the clouds. Through the windows, I could see people in fine, fancy clothes moving through their everyday lives. The furniture inside that I could see reminded me of the furniture that had been at the ball. The shops we passed were full of objects that I was unfamiliar with, and many of which I didn't know their purpose. There were flashing signs showing more products, and people who looked out of place compared to what I was used to.

What amazed me the most was what I didn't see. There weren't any homes that looked to be still standing against all logic. There weren't any starving or sick people begging for help. There weren't any children looking beyond their years from long days of hard work. Everyone looked to be comfortable, happy, and oblivious to the struggles of the people outside The Capital.

The people and buildings disappeared as the pod moved through a large set of gates. I continued to watch as we moved around a circular drive where three large mansions stood. The pod slowed and stopped in front of the one in the center. Samuel opened his eyes and climbed out with a word. I followed him out and up a walk with vibrant flowers lining the sides.

"She's waiting for you inside," Samuel said as he opened the large wooden door.

I walked past him and felt a shudder run down my spine as the door closed behind me with a thud. I glanced back to discover that he had not followed. I turned my attention back to the shadow filled room in front of me. The large windows on either side of the door were covered with heavy curtains that were drawn shut. The only sources of light were dim lights on the walls.

The floor was made up of dark tile with stark white in between. There were tables against the wall with vases of fresh flowers on top. The walls had several paintings of people I assumed were related to me, but I had no desire to look closer at them. There were dark wooden doors that were closed on either side of the room. At the far end, there was a grand staircase. As my eyes traveled up the stairs, I spotted a figure walking down. I straightened my stance as the figure reached the floor and took a few steps closer.

Lillian had an air around her that commanded attention and respect. Her dirty blonde hair, which mirrored my own, had a few grey streaks and was pulled back into a sleek bun. With her hair pulled back, her smooth, stern face was unobstructed as her brown eyes appeared to be evaluating me with her lips pressed into a thin line. She was dressed in a dark blue gown with beading that lined the bodice, which flowed onto the floor around her.

"You're late," she said with a hint of annoyance in her voice that caused my blood to boil and my fists to clench.

Chapter 26

"*You're* late." The words echoed in my mind as I struggled to keep my composure. As much as I hated Samuel, I knew that I was going to hate Lillian more. She was either oblivious or simply did not care about the anger I was sure was evident on my face. She glided across the floor, her heels clicking in an even rhythm, as she made her way towards me.

"For heaven's sake," Lillian sneered with a wrinkled nose, "You smell like one of them."

"If you mean I smell like someone who has known a hard day's work, I'll take it as a compliment." Anger and annoyance flashed in her eyes as she looked over me once more. I waited for her next insult, but it didn't come. Instead, she motioned with her hand for me to follow and took a few steps towards the staircase. A heavy sigh filled the silence when she turned back and saw I had not moved.

"I'm sure Samuel told you that it is not wise to defy me," she said firmly as she turned back towards me.

I remained planted where I stood, staring at her. I wasn't going to be intimidated by a sixty year-old woman who had no power over me. My goal had been to reach The Capital. There was no need to go any further.

"Just like your mother," Lillian said, shaking her head. "Have you ever wondered why she remained compliant as long as she did? Why didn't she fight against me while she was here?"

I still refused to move or speak. My mind was now racing with questions. My mother had fought against The Capital once she escaped, but not before that I knew of. She had been here, in this manor, with access to these vile people while they slept. Why hadn't she ended this a long time ago?

"I feel safe in assuming you have her same weakness?" Lillian looked almost bored as she smoothed the front of her dress. I could feel what she was doing. She was summoning her gift. A slight smile played on my lips as I blocked it and prepared to absorb whatever it was. However, as soon as it washed over my shield, I felt my stomach turn. I didn't know what her gift was, but it felt as evil as her. I kept my shield firmly in place, refusing to absorb it. I wanted to win; to show her she wasn't in control, but not at the risk of having her vile gift inside me.

"Don't worry, child," Lillian said with a smile. "I just wanted to see if Samuel was right or if it was up. Impressive, I must say."

I didn't relax, keeping my shield firmly in place, but her gift was no longer focused on me. Before I could react, screams began echoing around the house. Panic rose in my chest as my eyes darted around in the direction of the screams.

"Like I said," Lillian spoke casually. "Just like your mother. Caring for the pain of those beneath us."

"Stop," I yelled, stepping forward. "Whatever you're doing, stop."

The screams disappeared in an instant, and only a few muffled sobs could be heard. Lillian motioned for me to follow her once again before turning and heading up the stairs. I felt defeated as I followed her. Once we reached the top, she turned left and led me down a dark hallway. I was beginning to think she was allergic to light, as all the curtains were pulled shut and only dim bulbs cast a creepy light across the dark walls and wooden floor.

I followed Lillian as she walked into a room with a set of open double doors. I barely managed to stifle a gasp at the sight of the maids who were waiting inside. I could tell they had tried to clean themselves up, but the blood stains were still visible running down from their eyes and ears. I glanced at Lillian, but she didn't seem to notice or care.

The room was large with a four-post bed in the center and more pillows than a person would ever need. Every bit of cloth in the room was dark purple. This didn't feel like a spare room. It felt like it had belonged to someone.

"They will get you cleaned up and into proper clothing," Lillian said as she turned back to me. "Once they are done, they will lead you to the dining room. I expect it will be lunch hour by then."

I stared at her in disbelief as she glided out of the room. The maids moved forward and shut the doors before they reached for me in an attempt to remove my clothes. I pulled away and watched as they stared at each other with fear.

After a moment, the younger of the two stepped forward. She was slightly younger than I, with heavy blonde curls that were pulled back.

"Please," she said in a low pleading tone. "She will punish us if we don't."

"The blood," I said, motioning towards her face. "She did that?" The girl nodded but remained still, waiting for my permission. I glanced at the other maid, a woman in her late thirties with hair that was already turning silver. "I'm here to stop her," I whispered.

I expected to see hope or relief on their faces, but they looked even more terrified. It was as if their eyes were pleading with me not to. I didn't try to push further. Instead, I began to remove my clothes, piling them on the floor. Both women's eyes remained fixed on the floor until I finished. Then, they led me into a room where a bath was already waiting for me.

I settled into the water and reached for the soap. The older maid picked it up in the blink of an eye. I looked to see them both holding scrub brushes, a look of embarrassment and pleading on their faces. I nodded in understanding and positioned myself in the center of the tub. The woman scrubbed for what felt like hours. I kept waiting for the water to turn red with blood as I was positive, they were removing layers of skin. By the time they finished, my skin was raw and the water had gone cold.

Back in the bedroom, they moved quickly, drying my skin, trimming my nails, and styling my hair. I felt like a doll that was being dressed up. Once they were finished, they helped me into a cream-colored gown that looked ridiculous for every day. I stood still as they expertly applied makeup to my face and made sure every detail was perfect.

When they were satisfied, I braved a look at myself in a tall mirror. I felt like I was looking at a stranger. The only part of myself that I recognized was my eyes. Their deep brown color still shone with the defiance that burned under the layers of fluff and frill.

"You're ring," the older woman said, holding out her hand. I clenched my hand, shielding my wedding ring from her. They could take everything, dress me up however Lillian wanted, but they couldn't take that.

"I have an idea," the younger woman said as she rushed over to the dresser and opened what looked like a jewelry box. She rummaged around inside for a moment and then returned with a silver chain. "We can put it on here, and you wear it around your neck. She won't be able to see it, and then you can have both of them with you."

"Both of them?" My voice squeaked out.

"This is the heir's room," the girl answered. "This chain belonged to - "

"My mother," I finished as I slowly slid off the ring. As I handed it to her and watched her put it on the chain, I told myself it was temporary. Once this fight was over, it would return to my finger and stay there. Until then, I still had Calix's initials cut into my skin. The girl stepped forward and helped me secure the necklace and tucked it within the bodice of the dress.

The man walked back to the door and pulled it open. I stood, looking around the room that I now knew once belonged to my mother. If I had to guess, I would say that nothing in here had been touched since she was banished. Perhaps this was my chance to get to know her a little better. She may have left secrets behind, secrets that I could find. If she had, it might have finally told me why she waited so long to stand up to her parents and why she didn't do it until she was free of them. "Ma'am," the young maid said. "Lunch will be served soon, and if you're late, she won't be happy."

"Is she ever happy?" I asked with a raised eyebrow as I looked back at her. "Seems to me like that stick is permanently shoved up her ass."

The maids looked at each other, their eyes seeming to have a secret conversation.

"Only once that we know of, ma'am," the oldest spoke.

"What, when she discovered that she could use people like her personal puppets?" I laughed.

Both maids remained serious as they stared at me.

"No, ma'am," the youngest spoke. "It was the day of the ball. The day she was supposed to get her heir back."

Of course, Lillian had only shown happiness when it benefited her. She probably had my life mapped out the moment Samuel told her I existed. She had lost control of my mother, but now she had me. All she cared about was ensuring that her family's legacy, her legacy, lived on the way she wanted it to. That black hearted woman cared nothing about me.

I could feel the cool metal of the ring on my skin as I took a deep breath. Lillian didn't know love and never would. She probably saw it as a weakness or, at least, some kind of defect. She would never know that what I shared with Calix is what would give me the strength to bring her legacy, entire world, crashing down.

Chapter 27

The manor was as silent as a morgue as the maids led me downstairs. We passed several more maids as we walked, all of whom quickly turned to avoid meeting my gaze. They seemed just as fearful as the two who had helped me get dressed. If I were being honest, I didn't blame them. Lillian had a presence and commanded respect. Those who didn't comply paid a severe price, as well as everyone else in the manor.

Downstairs, I followed the maids into a large room. The heavy curtains were cracked in here, allowing lines of sunlight to cast across a long wooden table that stretched the length of the room. The table was filled with steaming food and fresh vegetables. There was enough food and chairs for a small army to gather. My eyes swept over the feast and stopped when I reached the only person seated at the table. Lillian was sitting up straight in a highbacked wooden chair.

<u>344</u>

I straightened myself as I took a few more steps into the room. Lillian locked her eyes on me as I moved towards the table. The maids followed close behind, seeming to guide me to a seat closer to Lillian. I stopped a few chairs away from her, refusing to get any closer. The younger maid pulled out the chair, and I sat, never taking my eyes off Lillian as I did so.

"Much better," Lillian nodded in approval as the maids began to move and fill our plates with food. "Once we get your behavior correct, you will be an acceptable heir."

My blood boiled as I watched her take a small bite of salad. "I don't want to be your heir," I said flatly.

"You have no choice," she replied before taking another bite and dabbing her mouth with a napkin. "It is your purpose, and I will not allow you to bring more shame to our family. Your mother was useless, but at least she had the common sense to provide me with you."

"My mother wasn't useless!" Lillian appeared unfazed by my outburst as she took another bite. I forced myself to take several deep breaths to calm down. Losing my temper wasn't going to help me. It would only cloud my mind and push me to make mistakes.

"My daughter threw away her future," Lillian said, setting down her fork. "And nearly destroyed everything our family built. I should have known her test results were altered. But in truth, I didn't think her either smart or powerful enough to accomplish such a thing."

I continued to take deep breaths as I stared at Lillian. My memories of my mother were limited. Lillian saying such things about the wonderful person I remembered was threatening to push me over the edge.

"My mother had a strength and grace that you will never know," I said through gritted teeth. Lillian let out a light chuckle as she adjusted in her chair.

"Dear child, you are naiver than I thought. Perhaps this is a good place for us to start. It is time you learned the truth about your heritage and your place in continuing our legacy."

Squeezing my thighs with my hands, I managed to keep my mouth shut. Lillian took this as permission to continue her lesson. She took a small sip of water from her clear glass. After placing the glass back on the table, she made herself comfortable in her chair.

"The history you know of The Union leaves out some important information," she began. "The Union was founded after the Great War, but not by the three governors everyone believes. It was founded by my grandmother, Edith Marnell. She was the first to release her gift and the power it gave her over the remaining people. She was a smart woman and knew that no one would accept a woman as ruler. So, she devised the three governors as the face of power. Her husband and his two best friends filled the roles. She ensured that they were all talented with their gifts, though none of them compared to her own."

"So, she had no spine," I sneered. "She hid and destroyed lives while the men she chose took the blame."

"She was a brilliant woman," Lillian answered. "She protected herself from anyone who chose to target those in charge. She designed the communicators we wear today, though they have been updated over the years."

<u>347</u>

Instinctively, my eyes went to her wrist, and for the first time, I noticed she wasn't wearing one.

"That's right," Lillian smiled. "I have a false one that I wear for public appearances, but other than that, the Empress has never worn one."

Things were starting to make more sense. The windows being closed throughout the house were to ensure that no one saw her bare wrist. I couldn't help but feel there were more secrets that she was concealing. I didn't have to wonder for long as Lillian took another sip of water and continued.

"Women in our family have always had a unique, powerful gift," she continued. "It has always had something to do with frequencies. Your mothers affected technology, which is what allowed her to change her test results."

"And yours?" I asked before I could stop myself.

Lillian let out a light laugh. "Mine affects the frequencies of the human body. If I choose, I can force a frequency into a person that sends their nervous system into shock. It can cause death if I choose."

I felt my stomach drop. No wonder everyone in the manor was afraid of her. She could kill them all in a matter of moments if she chose, and they knew it. Lillian and her relatives had figured out how to project their gifts, an ability they thought was unique to their family.

"I am sure that your gift will not disappoint," Lillian smiled. "With a bit of training, you will be able to project and rule."

"I have no desire to rule," I replied. "I want to set the people free from your tyranny. I won't let you do to anyone else what you did to my mother, Grams, or Ca-" I couldn't say his name as sobs threatened to rack my body. I looked away from Lillian and back down at the plate in front of me. It was still filled with food that I had no desire to eat. I closed my eyes, trying to hold back the tears that threatened to spill. "I won't let you hurt any more innocent people."

"Innocent?" Lillian laughed loudly. "Gertrude was anything but innocent. Stopping hearts is not something most people would consider innocent."

"She couldn't help her gift. She used it in the best way she could."

"Did she?" Lillian continued to laugh. "That woman used her gift to her advantage. She was determined not to marry and continue her bloodline like the law required. At her ball, anyone who danced with her nearly died as she stopped their hearts. No man was brave enough to bid on her and take her as a wife. They all feared she would kill them in the ceremony tent."

"But she did marry," I shot back. "And she had my father."

"Did she tell you she got married?" Lillian continued to laugh.

I thought back to Grams and all the times I asked about her husband. The truth was, Grams had never said anything about him other than that my grandfather was dead. I had always assumed it was too painful for her to talk about, but looking back on it, she seemed angrier than upset. She never called him her husband or by his name, just my grandfather.

"When it became clear that her ability and bloodline would die out instead of grow and evolve to better The Union, my mother decided to take matters into her own hands. She sent a Silver Tongue to befriend her and then make her compliant as the situation was corrected. It only had to be done once as she fell pregnant immediately. Once

Gertrude learned what had happened, she was furious. She used her gift to kill both the Silver Tongue and the father of her unborn child."

"She was raped," I gasped. "And you try to portray her as evil for killing her rapist and his accomplice."

"She killed two people who were following orders," Lillian said flatly. "In truth, my mother was impressed. She invited Gertrude to the Capital and to become one of the governor's wives. It was an opportunity to rule and help our cause."

"She refused," I smiled. "She told you all to fuck off, and if you came near her or her child again, she would kill you."

"But fate has a funny way of setting things back on course," Lillian continued. "When I learned of your mother's deception, I couldn't help but feel joy when I learned who she had married."

"Then why kill them?" I demanded. "You had everything you wanted, but needed a child to continue your bloodline. Samuel didn't know I existed until after they were dead!"

"Your mother made a rash decision," Lillian said, shaking her head. "Your parents had been together for years and, as far as we knew, never had a child. They were given a choice: burn alive or return to The Capital and have a child. Your parents chose to die and abandon you."

Her words felt like a knife to my heart. She saw it as a choice, but I could see the truth. My parents had died, but they did not abandon me; they protected me. They knew that they would have to reveal my existence, and Lillian would have turned me into her puppet. Lillian had still learned that I existed, but hadn't been able to sink her claws into me.

"Now, we have a lot of work to do to make you into the woman you should have been." Lillian scraped her chair across the floor as she stood. "Tomorrow, we will begin. By the end of the week, you will be ready."

"Ready for what?" I asked, seething with anger.

"For the marriage ceremony and to take your place by my side," Lillian said matter-of-factly.

"Never," I sneered.

"We will see," Lillian said flatly as she strode out of the room.

I shoved myself back from the table and stomped out of the room. I could hear the rushed footsteps of the maids rushing to keep up with me. I stormed through the manor and back up to my mother's room. As soon as I was inside the doors, I slammed them shut and locked the maids outside. I needed to be alone.

Lillian thought she had everything figured out. Little did she know she had provided me with the perfect opportunity to do what needed to be done. Over the next week, I would play her game and slowly convince her that she was winning. Then, at the ceremony, I would strike. I felt positive that she would make it a grand event, ensuring that all the governors and their families would be present. Having all of them together would give me the opportunity I needed to kill them all.

Chapter 28

Exhausted from the day before's events, I passed out in my dress. My dreams were haunting, not allowing me a restful sleep. I saw Calix's face as we took our vows, and then his lifeless body lying on the floor of the cathedral. I woke up, sweat beading on my face, and my now messy hair clinging to it.

"Breakfast, ma'am."

I looked to see the younger maid entering the room with a silver tray. I hadn't eaten the day before, and my stomach growled at the sight. Still, I didn't want to appear too eager to accept it. I watched as the young maid set the tray down on the table and turned to leave.

"Wait," I blurted out. The young maid stopped and turned back towards me with her head bowed. "What's your name?"

"My name is of no consequence." It sounded like a line she had been forced to say. Of course, her name was important. She was a person after all.

"It is to me," I said firmly. "I refuse to eat or do anything else until you tell me your name and how you ended up serving Lillian."

Panic shot across the young maid's face. She stared at me for several moments before her shoulders slumped in defeat.

"I'm Mara," she said in a weak voice. "My family lives in Ring 4. I was brought here to serve the heiress when she arrived. My deformity cannot be seen, so my appearance does not offend the Empress."

While she answered my questions, she did so by giving as few details as possible. Still, I knew the conditions in Ring 4 weren't much better than those of The Edge.

"You came to work here to help provide for your family?" The question hung in the air for a moment before she slowly nodded. This poor young woman was as much a prisoner here as I was. I climbed out of bed and walked over to where the tray of food waited on the table. Mara watched as I picked up a piece of bacon and took a bite. Relief washed over her face that I was keeping my word. "It won't be like this forever, Mara. I promise."

Mara said nothing as her eyes moved back to the floor, and she left the room once again. Alone, I quickly ate the food that she had brought, silencing the pain that was forming in my stomach. I looked around the room, the walls and dark curtains feeling as if they were closing in on me. I stomped over to the window, grabbed the thick curtains in my hands, and flung them open. Sunlight burst into the room instantly. Pressing my hand against the cool glass, I looked out onto Governor's Hill.

The grounds were covered in thick green grass that looked just as soft as the bed I had just slept in. Lush beds of bushes and flowers were everywhere, along with stone fountains with flowing, clear water. A tall stone wall surrounded the grounds, keeping Lillian and the governors separated from the citizens. I quickly moved to the other side of the bed and flung open those curtains. Lillian may be able to hold me prisoner, but I refused to feel like I was locked inside a dark box. It was a small act of rebellion in the grand scheme of things, but I would take what I could get.

I heard the doors open, followed by a low gasp. I turned to see Mara, and the older maid had returned. Their eyes were locked on the curtains that were now open, allowing the sun to filter in. "They stay open," I said firmly as I walked towards them. "Is that understood?"

They both turned their faces back to natural expressions and agreed. Mara made her way to the closest and pulled out another dress. As they walked closer to me, I took a step back and looked at the older maid.

"I have no name," she said. Mara must have told her about my threat when she left the room. "Or if I did, I've long since forgotten it. My mother worked in the manor, so I was raised here. She has long since passed, and I began working as soon as I could walk."

My heart hurt for this poor woman. She had nothing to hold on to for hope because all she had ever known was Lillian's cruelty. Still, I could tell she had a strength and wisdom about her. I studied her for a moment, taking her in.

"You look like a Mildred," I finally said. "Perhaps that should be your name."

The woman looked shocked for a moment before she schooled her expression. She muttered a "As you wish" before stepping forward once again. This time, I did not move away. I stood still and allowed them to do their jobs of dressing me like a doll. The two of them worked quickly as they fixed my hair, applied makeup, and helped me step into a fresh dress. Yet again, I felt ridiculous under the layers of material. I had seen fine garments such as these when I worked with Grams. I always thought that the people of the Capital attended a lot of balls. I never imagined this was how some people dressed every day.

"The Empress has been pulled away for urgent business with the Governors," Mildred said once they were finished. "She regrets that she will be unable to see you today to begin your training. However, she has asked that we inform you to work on your ability today. Every woman in your family has been able to project their gifts, and that is where their real power comes from. We are to remain for you to practice on."

"No need," I said as I turned back towards the window.

"Ma'am," Mara spoke up in a small voice. "There will be punishment if we don't."

I let out a heavy sigh and turned back towards them. I could tell them the truth, that I knew how to use my gift, but I had a suspicion that Lillian's grip on them was so strong that they wouldn't hesitate to tell her.

"I'm a shield," I said flatly. "I guess family tradition ends with me. Please inform Lillian that I am a disappointment and will not be continuing her legacy."

Mara and Mildred looked at each other before lowering their heads and leaving. Once the door closed, I allowed myself to relax. Lillian would be furious with me, but that was part of the plan. She would be suspicious if I gave in and did what she said right away. Besides, I needed time to myself to search this room. I had been too exhausted to search the night before, and Lillian's urgent business gave me the opportunity. I refused to believe that my mother had been complacent with what was being done.

In all the memories I had of my mother, she always had a journal. She wrote everything down. I could still remember her telling me that sometimes it was safer to put her thoughts, feelings, and memories in writing. Then no one could try to convince her that it wasn't real. Being in the manor, I had a feeling that was something she learned as a child. I searched through the drawers and the closet, but came up with nothing.

"Damnit!" I slammed the doors to the wardrobe closed as I came up emptyhanded again. The sound of something hitting the floor drew my gaze down. The piece of wood that lined the base of the wardrobe had fallen off. Getting down on my knees, I looked into the small space underneath, and there they were. Stacks of old journals were hidden and covered with a layer of dust. I reached in and pulled out the first one.

Wiping the dust off the cover, I revealed a neat script on the cover. "Lillia, Age 15". This had to be my mother's last journal before she escaped this place. I replaced the fallen piece of wood and scurried over to the bed. It felt like an invasion of my mother's privacy as I opened the cover and began reading over the words. Each page proved that I had been correct; my mother hated Lillian. She spoke of how she tortured the servants for fun and used her gift to ensure her position and power. My mother spoke often of her plans to change things once she was in control.

About halfway through, my mother stopped talking about what she would do as Empress and instead spoke of her escape plan. Something had happened that she no longer wanted to wait to be in control; she wanted to help the people take it back immediately. I flipped through the pages quickly, feeling as if I were sitting beside my mother as a young girl, pouring out her thoughts on paper. It wasn't until the last page that I slowed, reading the words carefully.

Tomorrow is the day. I have hidden my gift for all these years, and it is about to pay off. I will finally be free and help free the others that she rules over with her tyranny. She will think she broke me when she banishes me for being normal. She won't learn until it's too late that she set me upon a path that would lead to her destruction. She will think I will have nothing in The Edge and expect me to wither and die, removing the black stain from our family's legacy. She will try to have another child, a thought that both terrifies and makes me laugh. She has been drinking the tea for months now. I can only imagine her rage when she learns that she can't. She will suffer in agony, losing everything she holds dear and watching our legacy disappear each day that she gets closer to death. Not knowing that I will not only survive but thrive. Philip will be waiting for me when I reach The Edge. We will be able to begin our life together and destroy Lillians. While there are some things I know I can't predict, there is one thing I know for certain. If Philip and I have a child, I will ensure that they do not know the darkness I was raised in. They will know what it feels like to be loved and appreciated from the moment they come into this world. I will die if it means protecting them from Lillian and her darkness.

My fingers traced over the words as tears fell down my face. My mother knew my father before her testing and had planned everything that had happened that day. She had sworn to protect me before I even existed and kept her vow. She had died to protect me. My heart swelled as the tears continued to fall. Closing the journal, I hugged it tight to my chest. My mother may not have been able to finish what she started, but I could. I wouldn't let her death be in vain. The last thing Lillian would know before I saw the light leave her eyes was that I am my parents' daughter. She can't break me or make me be who she wants. I will smile as she takes her last breath, knowing that I was the one who ended our family's legacy bathed in the blood of those they sought to control.

Chapter 29

"*S*it."

Lillian's voice was commanding as she pointed to a metal chair in the center of the room. I had not seen her at all the day before. Mara and Mildred had brought me my meals, saying each time that Lillian was still busy handling urgent business. It wasn't until they delivered my supper that I managed to get Mara to tell me what was going on. The Capital had lost all communication with Rings Five and Four. Word was spreading through The Union that a rebellion had started, and the King was fighting his way to The Capital.

I understood the truth of what was happening. The others were continuing the plan, but Calix was not with them. He was dead, and my grandparents knew it. However, that didn't stop the others from continuing the fight and, knowing them, trying to find a way to rescue me.

My communicator had been silent since that night. I had thought about sending them a message and letting them know I was safe. But in the darkness of my room, it seemed too risky. I couldn't be sure if Lillian had a way of intercepting or seeing the message. Perhaps my friends feared the same thing, and that is why they hadn't reached out. In the end, I decided that it wasn't worth the risk.

This morning, as soon as I was dressed, Lillian came to collect me. She was in a foul mood from the moment she walked through the bedroom doors. She had snapped at me to follow her and led me down to what I thought was a basement. This large space appeared to have been converted into some type of secret headquarters. Large screens lined the walls with images and text filling them. No one looked up from their stations as I walked over to the chair Lillian had pointed to and took a seat.

Lillian stood in front of me with her arms crossed over her chest as she motioned for a man to walk closer. The man looked exhausted as his eyes drooped. He lifted my wrist and began to look over my communicator. Sitting still, I allowed him to work while I stared at Lillian. The man plugged a wire into the port that I had seen Thomas use for reprogramming. He looked over a screen as his fingers worked quickly on a keyboard.

"This is quite impressive," the man said to himself. "It has been recoded to block our system from accessing any functions."

"I don't need your praises for the rebels," Lillian snarled. "I need you to do as you're told!"

The man began typing faster, pausing a few times as he read lines of code that I couldn't understand. "This should..." Before he could finish, the screen of my communicator lit up. I looked down at the screen, and a smile spread across my face as I read the words that were now displayed.

"Long Live The Queen."

Lillian's eyes glanced down, and I could see her anger grow as she read the words. Instantly, the man's eyes and ears began to bleed, the red blood running down his face as he let out a scream. I resisted the urge to reach out with my gift and stop the man's suffering. After a few moments, his face relaxed, and the blood flow stopped.

"Empress," he began with a shaky voice, "I'm afraid that I cannot do as you ask. This coding is beyond anything we have encountered."

"Then we will remove the damn thing, and you can continue working until you figure it out!" Lillian yelled.

"I'm afraid we can't." The man's voice shook with fear as he looked at the floor. "According to what I see here, that would be devastating for our system. Now that I've connected it, if we remove it from her, there is a worm that will shut down everything."

I let out a light laugh. Thomas was a genius. He had prepared for the worst-case scenario. Lillian couldn't take away my communicator without losing the control she had over the remaining Rings.

"Get out of my sight," Lillian growled. The man didn't hesitate before running out of the room. I watched as Lillian paced for a few moments, taking several deep breaths. When she finally managed to calm herself, she stopped in front of me. "We will just have to move faster than expected." Something in her eyes told me that she had a plan. I heard the door open behind me and watched as a group of children was led into the room. They all stood in a line in front of me, their tear-stained faces and threadbare clothes telling me they weren't from The Capital.

"All women in our bloodline can project their gift," Lillian said. "You just need the proper motivation to learn how. Once you master it, we will be able to see the real power you possess."

I did my best not to react as Lillian grinned and turned to the children. In an instant, all the children were screaming, blood running down their faces. I tried to stand up and force Lillian to stop. A strong set of hands pushed me back down into the chair. Whipping around, I saw Samuel standing behind me, his voice void of emotion. My eyes went back to the children, most of whom were now on the ground. I couldn't let these innocent souls suffer a moment longer. I reached out my shield and wrapped it around them.

The sound of sobs filled the air, but the screams and blood came to a halt. I could feel Lillian trying to break through, but I kept my shield firmly in place. I pushed her gift away, not allowing myself to absorb it but keeping the children safe from further harm. "Excellent," Lillian sneered. "Now your ability will grow."

"You evil bitch!" I shot back. "Their kids!"

"Their nothing." The way Lillian said it so dismissively made my blood boil. "Just rats from The Edge."

"I'm from The Edge," I responded.

"And if it wasn't for you having my blood, you would be just as disposable as they are."

That's how she saw the people that she ruled over: disposable. There was nothing good in this woman. I found it hard to believe that I was related to her. She believed that because our family gift was the first to evolve that it made her better than everyone else. She was partially right; our family gift had evolved and grown strong. She just didn't see that it was all leading to her and her legacy's destruction.

"I'm sure by now you've heard the whispers," Lillian continued. "Rings 3, 4, and 5 have gone dark. They are building an army of misfits with the traitors from Twain. Another attempt at taking over when none of them are fit to rule. Though the message on your communicator confirms my suspicions, and that my plan will succeed."

My stomach twisted in a sick knot. Whatever her plan was, I couldn't let it succeed.

"The wedding ceremony will take place tomorrow. All of this nonsense will stop once they see that their "Queen" is one of us. Those from The Rings will return to their jobs, and those from Twain will have no choice but to flee. Not that they will have anything to flee to."

"What do you mean?" I asked. The fear and apprehension in my voice showed.

"We knew as soon as you and that King left Twain," Lillian smiled. "We've sent a couple of our own to live among them right after you turned sixteen. Tonight, the Sparks will burn Twain to the ground."

"You can't do that!" I blurted out.

"Really?" Lillian grinned as she leaned closer. "How about a deal then, granddaughter?"

I knew that any deal with this woman would be the same as signing my soul over to the Devil. My mind instantly went to Calix, my handsome Lucifer. I had lost my soul the day he died. I had nothing left to lose.

"Do your part," Lillian offered. "Stop fighting and plotting against me. Give yourself willingly at the ceremony and produce an heir. You get a comfortable life, and the people of Twain can continue to live."

I nodded my head in agreement. Lillian needed to feel like she was in control, and I could play the part of a broken, submissive woman for a day. Once at the ceremony, I would kill her and all the others. I just needed to make her believe me to keep the people of Twain safe until them.

"Good girl," Lillian smiled. "But if I get even the smallest feeling that you're lying and I will burn it all to ash. Understood?"

I lowered my gaze to the floor and nodded again. I felt Samuel grip my arm as he pulled me up from the chair. I walked like I had lost the will to fight as Samuel led me out of the room and back to my room. Shoving me inside, he slammed the doors shut, and I heard the lock click into place. The room felt smaller as I stood there. The air was heavy with what was to come, and the curtains were shut once again. I stormed across the floor and flung them open once again.

I let out a heavy breath as I turned back around. The sunlight shone on something I had not seen when I first entered. I walked over to the wardrobe where a glittery white dress now hung. I walked closer and gripped the silky fabric in my hands. Lillian had planned this the entire time. She had every detail figured out, down to my wedding dress.

I wicked grin spread across my face as I released the fabric and smoothed out the wrinkles. It was a beautiful dress and perfect for the ceremony. Though I always thought I looked better in red. I felt confident that by the time the ceremony concluded, it would be dripping in the perfect shade of red. I hadn't managed to be able to secure a weapon since I arrived, and my thigh knife had been left in the cathedral. But I felt confident that I could find something at the ceremony. I would use the damn pen if I needed to.

I could already picture myself plunging it into Ryan's neck, the start to the river of blood I planned to spill. I would leave Lillian and Samuel for last. Their deaths had to be slow, and I would ensure they felt the pain of all those they killed. I would take pleasure in beating them until they pleaded for death. Then I would tie them up in the manor and set it aflame. I could practically feel the soft grass under me as I would sit on their lawn and listen to their screams as the flames erased any trace of their existence.

Chapter 30

$\mathcal{M}$ara and Mildred burst into my room just before dawn to begin getting me ready. Before I even managed to climb out of bed, Lillian strolled in with a swarm of maids I didn't recognize behind her.

"This will take hours," Lillian said as she looked me up and down with disgust. "We may have washed the filth off her, but she still looks like one of them."

My fists balled at my sides as I bit my tongue to keep from speaking. Fighting with Lillian wasn't going to help my plan for today. If anything, it would make it harder. Lillian snapped her fingers in the air, and the maids instantly began moving. As soon as the chaos started, Miria reached around my neck and pulled off the chain with my wedding ring. She gave me a small nod as she tucked it into her apron. Despite her

fear of Lillian, she was helping me to keep the
one thing I had left of my husband.

Only Mildred and Mira followed me in as I
took off my nightgown and climbed into a bath.

The water was too hot, but the burning on my
skin was just what I needed. Mildred reached in
to wet a sponge and pulled her hand back. Her
face was covered in shock and worry. Yet, she
remained silent. I continued to let my skin boil in
silence as the water slowly cooled. I nodded to
them both once it had reached a decent
temperature, and they immediately set to
scrubbing. By the time they finished, my skin was
a bright shade of pink from a combination of the
heat and cleaning.

Once out of the water, a smooth white robe
was dropped around me, and I was led back into
the bedroom. Everyone was busy working, and I
was led to a chair by the vanity. I sat still as the
maids worked to comb and dry my hair, showing
no emotion as they pulled out the knots. When
they had finally finished, layers of makeup were
applied to my skin. In the mirror, I could see
Lillian behind me, watching the process with cold
eyes.

I couldn't help but think of Gram's. The care and love she had shown me in preparation for the ball were something I appreciated even more now. I wouldn't find the same comfort or love with Lillian. To her, I wasn't a granddaughter. I was simply a body she needed to ensure that her family line lived on. By the time the maids were done, hours had passed, and it was already early afternoon.

"Get her into the dress," Lillian ordered.

My stomach growled, and I turned to face her without standing. "Perhaps I should have something to eat before putting it on. I would hate to..."

"Eat?" Lillian laughed. "Your next meal will be with your husband after he claims you. Hopefully, before long, you will be eating for two."

This woman had no decency whatsoever. I turned back to the mirror and forced myself to take several deep breaths. It was almost time; it would be over soon.

"Speaking of," Lillian said as she produced a small glass bottle and stepped forward. I watched as she unlocked the top and held it out to me. "Drink."

"What is it?" I asked as I took the bottle.

"Insurance," Lillian said in a flat tone. "It will ensure that you are ready for Ryan's seed."

I tilted the bottle back and allowed the liquid to pour down my throat. No harm in something that would help fertility. Besides, Ryan would be dead in just a few short hours.

"We can't have that rogue king's bastard being born."

The bottle slipped from my hand and shattered on the floor as the realization of what I had drunk struck me. It wasn't something to help me get pregnant; it was to ensure that I wasn't pregnant.

"Stupid girl!" Lillian yelled as she took a step back and snapped her fingers. A maid rushed forward and quickly cleaned up the shattered glass. As I looked down at the tiny pieces, I could feel that my heart had been shattered even more. I had no way of knowing if I was pregnant. It wasn't like Calix and I had done anything to prevent it. But now, any chance I had of having something left of him was gone. I felt tears stinging in my eyes as I glared up at Lillian.

"No sense in getting all emotional," Lillian rolled her eyes. "You will have a baby soon enough, and it will be of proper breeding."

Proper breading was all she cared about. I couldn't wait. It would be harder to get them all, but Lillian did not deserve to see another moment of life. I pushed out of the chair and took a step forward. Shock covered Lillian's face for a moment, and she took a step backwards.

Suddenly, I felt a gift being used in the room. It brushed against my skin, almost as if asking for permission instead of trying to force itself. Something about it felt familiar. I didn't block it, and instantly, I felt my heart rate lower, and my anger disappeared. Looking at Lillian, I still hated her, but my need to kill her that moment was gone.

I turned and strode over to where the wedding dress was hanging. The maids rushed over and began helping me into it. There were so many layers that it felt like I was being strapped into a suit of armor. I didn't care, though, and allowed the maids to dress me like a doll. I could still feel the gift working on me, keeping my emotions under control. I scanned each face as the maids came close. I only knew one person who could control emotions like that. While yes, it was known that there were other Sirens, Maddie was the only one who would know about my shield and ask permission to use her gift on me.

The dress was finally secured in place. Lillian was bored with the activity, her eyes wandering around the room. Mira quickly slipped the chain and the ring around my neck, and I tucked it out of sight. I felt a maid kneel beside me and lift the edge of my dress. I assumed that she was helping me with the shoes. I felt the shoes and slid my feet into them without much thought. But then, I felt something wrap around my thigh, and the maid tied it firmly in place. My eyes shot down to the maid just as she lowered the dress and looked up at me.

Maddie was here. I don't know, she managed to sneak in, but she was here. I wanted to wrap my arms around her and let out all the emotions I had been holding in. Somehow, I managed to keep myself in check and remain still. Maddie stood from the floor and gave me a wink before she joined the other maids near the door.

Lillian paced around me several times, inspecting their work. "Acceptable," she finally said. "You will wait here and not mess a thing up. Philip will be here in the next few hours to collect you and escort you to the ceremony."

I nodded to show I understood, trying not to look at Maddie directly. I was afraid that she would disappear at any moment, and I desperately needed her right now. Lillian snapped her fingers, and the maids quickly began to file out. I opened my mouth, trying to think of something to say that would allow Maddie to stay. Another wave of calm washed over me, and my mouth snapped shut. Maddie tapped her thigh before following the other maids out of the room.

Lillian followed them and closed the doors. I heard the lock click into place, signaling that I was trapped and alone. Immediately, my hands flew to my skirts and lifted them until my fingers felt the familiar cool steel handle of my knife. I pulled it out of its hiding spot and allowed my skirts to fall back to the ground. Around the blade, a piece of paper was secured with a piece of twine. Pulling the paper free, I unfolded it with shaky hands. My heart caught in my throat as I read over the words.

My Queen,

I am sure by now you already have a plan to end the
rebellion on your own. Patenice was never what you were
known for, but I need you to try.

Things are bigger than we thought and require more
than your anger to win. Go to the ceremony. I will come
for you, just like I did last time.

Valix

The paper crumpled in my hands as I held it to my chest. I didn't know how, but Calix was alive. I let out a light laugh as I pulled the paper back and looked over the words once more. He was coming for me and would break up another attempt at a marriage between Ryan and me. I tucked the knife back into its hiding place and the note into the strap. As I smoothed my dress, I could hear footsteps approaching. I kept a neutral look on my face as I stood still and waited.

Chapter 31

*I*t had been days since I last saw Liz.

Having her stolen away like that right after we said our vows was unbearable. Yet, part of me found a slight humor in the timing of it all. Liz hadn't wanted to wait, afraid that something would tear us apart again. I hadn't shared that fear, but knew that I wanted no one but her. The look on her face as they dragged her away was seared into my mind. Liz wasn't one to get scared, but in that moment, I could see the terror she felt. I tried to tell her, give her a sign that everything would be fine. Yet, I had no way of knowing if she understood it with the chaos that was going around us.

"She should have been back by now."

I looked up a Garrett and could see the frustration and worry on his face. Maddie had left us the night before to slip into the manor and deliver a message to Liz. She wasn't late, but was cutting it close.

"She's fine," I assured him. "Maddie knows how to take care of herself."

Garett let out a huff as he stormed away and took a seat where the others were huddled around a small fire. I let out a deep breath of my own as I walked over to join them. Around us, people were busy setting up tents, checking supplies, and doing other things to make our makeshift camp sustainable. This hadn't been part of the original plan, hiding in an underground cavern waiting for the right moment to strike. But things had changed once we reached The Capital.

Our plan of striking fast and hard fell apart when we learned the truth of what was going on. There were research centers and prisons, scattered throughout, that most citizens were unaware of. They were all full of MUTs that the governors deemed necessary but dangerous. The MUTs were being tortured to do the governor's work and experimented on to find new ways to harness their gifts. Attacking the Capital like we had originally planned would only lead to all of them being killed.

It was Maddie who pointed out that Liz would never agree to letting them all die if there was a chance to save them. So, we moved to the tunnels and came up with a new plan. We would make our first strike today. Two groups would be moving on the prisons to free as many MUTs as they could, while another group and I would go to the manors. The chaos of being hit on multiple fronts should give us enough time to do what needs to be done and slip back into the tunnels.

"Did you miss me?" Maddie's teasing voice instantly perked up everyone as we turned to look at her. Without hesitation, Garrett jumped up and pulled her into a hug. Maddie closed her eyes as she leaned into his chest and they embraced. I couldn't help but feel a twinge of jealousy as I watched. I needed Liz back now.

"Were you able to get in?" I asked, causing them to break apart.

"I was," Maddie nodded as she walked closer and sat down. "I paid a maid off to loan me her uniform and slipped into her room to help her get ready for the ceremony. I had to use my gift to stop her from killing the old bag right there, though."

"Old bag?" I asked.

"Lillian," Maddie answered. "Her grandmother. That is one evil bitch. The maid warned me not to make her angry or her gift would cause everyone in the house to bleed, except for Liz, of course."

I clenched my teeth as Maddie began to talk about Lillian's gift to make people bleed from their eyes and ears. Not just one person, but the entire house at once if she wanted. I knew this information was important, but right now I just wanted to know about Liz.

"She knew I was there," Maddie said, drawing my attention. "I was able to slip her the knife and the note. She looks fine, dressed up like a princess, which I can tell she hates, but fine."

My shoulders relaxed slightly, knowing that Liz was unharmed.

"The ceremony is scheduled to start in an hour," Maddie continued. "None of the staff are MUTs as far as I could tell. I don't think their loyal, just afraid to fight back."

"As long as they don't try to stop what we are there to do, we won't force them to make a choice."

"There is something else," Maddie said softly. "There is a group of kids, all under 10, that are being held as collateral. If Liz goes back on her word to marry Ryan, Lillian will kill them."

Of course, that's the only way Liz would have been able to control her temper for this long. We had to get those kids out at the same time.

"If they're being used as leverage," Thomas spoke, "Then it stands to reason they will be at the ceremony. Lillian will want a constant reminder to Liz of what will happen if she doesn't follow through."

"Then we get them all at once," I said, standing up. "Tell everyone it's time."

The others stood and nodded before disappearing into the tunnels. I turned and walked towards the exit that came up just outside the Governor's wall. The others, along with a group of fighters from Twain and The Edge, would join me shortly. I looked down at the ring on my finger and closed my eyes.

"I'm coming," I whispered.

Chapter 32

$\mathcal{S}$amuel opened the doors and gave me a fake smile. I remained still, the knife strapped to my thigh anchoring me to remain calm. When Samuel held out his arm, I took it without glancing at him. He walked me downstairs and into a grand ballroom. The dark wooden floor gleamed with a fresh polish as the chandeliers overhead cast down bright light. The large windows remained covered in heavy curtains that were pinched shut. In the center of the room, a podium stood where Ryan and a governor were waiting.

My eyes continued to scan the room until I saw the group of children huddled to the side. Their tear-stained faces were covered in fear as they cowered and held each other. I stopped and felt Samuel tug on my arm.

"She'll kill them," he whispered. "Just keep going."

I forced my feet to continue to move, my eyes sweeping over the group of maids that stood near the children. Fear crept over me as I realized Maddie was not with them. I would need her help to get the children out; there was no way I was leaving them behind. When I looked back, I realized that we had reached the podium. Ryan's smug expression loomed over me as Samuel left me and went to stand beside Lilian.

"We are all gathered here today to witness the union of Elizabeth Allard and Ryan..."

"Harkin," I interrupted. I could hear Ryan grinding his teeth in frustration beside me. "Elizabeth Harkin."

The governor looked past me, confused. I knew he was looking at Lillian for some kind of guidance on how to proceed. After a moment, he returned his attention to me and regained his composure.

"We are all gathered here today to witness the union of Elizabeth and Ryan. The terms of the contract have been negotiated and agreed upon by the intended families."

The speech was a lot shorter this time than last. There was no asking if I agreed or even saying what the terms were. I watched as Ryan picked up the pen and signed his name. As soon as he finished, he thrust the pen at me with a sickening grin. Taking the pen in my hand, I glanced back at the doors, half expecting Calix to walk in as he did before.

The sounds of the children screaming turned my attention back to the ceremony. I could see the blood running down their small faces. I couldn't stall any longer. I touched the pen to the paper and quickly signed before pushing the contract back towards the officiant. He picked it up and quickly rolled it and tucked it into his robes. "I now pronounce you man and..."

BOOM!

The entire manor shook around us as what sounded like an explosion echoed around us. Another loud sound followed, and I looked towards the far wall. Even from a distance, I could see the cracks forming in the otherwise perfect structure. Ryan grabbed my arms and pulled me close to his body.

"You're mine!" he growled.

Another blow struck the wall, causing debris and dust to fill the room. Ryan's grip on me tightened to pull me closer. From a distance, it would have looked like he was protecting me. The truth was, he was claiming me, determined to keep me to himself for his sick pleasures. The warmth of the sudden burst of sunlight disappeared as frost spread across the floor. The dust was beginning to settle, and I could see a figure walking closer. My heart skipped a beat as I fought my eyes to see his face through the thick air.

"Get your fucking hands off my wife!" Calix, he was here.

"Sorry," I said to Ryan with a smile. He looked down at me with a look of fear and confusion. "My husband's here."

Before Ryan could react, I lifted my knee and hit him between the legs. His grip on me disappeared as he fell to the ground, moaning in pain. Seizing the opportunity, I ran to where Calix was waiting. Others filtered around him, weapons drawn and gifts ready. As I ran, I stretched out my shield and protected the children and as many of the fighters as I could. When I reached Calix, I didn't stop. I ran and jumped into his arms. His cool skin instantly soothed my nerves, and I felt a sense of relief I didn't know was possible.

"Enough!" Lillian's voice rang out.

Calix's grip on me loosened as he placed me back on the ground and pulled me to his side. I could see the frustration and anger on Lillian's face. I could feel her gift reaching out, but I had managed to shield everyone I could see. Maddie rushed past me with the children, ushering them to safety.

"This is a civilized union!" Lillian continued. "She signed. You have no claim to her anymore!"

"Did I?" I asked with a grin.

Calix's grip on me tightened as Lillian stormed over to the officiant and pulled the contract from his robes. I watched as she looked at it and then at me. The realization of what I had done caused all the color to drain from her face. Continuing to smile, I swiftly held up my middle finger to signal what I had written on the contract.

In a fit of rage, Lillian tore off the contract and threw it to the ground.

"It doesn't matter!" she screamed. "She is my blood and will do as I say!"

Calix loosened his grip on me and stepped forward protectively. "Your command is that she is to marry that piece of shit?!" he called out as he pointed to where Ryan had finally managed to stand.

"Ryan understands the ways of our society," Lillian said firmly. "He is from good breeding and will help to ensure..."

My focus moved to Calix's hand as the air temperature around him dropped drastically. I watched as an icicle formed in his grip with a sharp point. Before anyone could react, he lifted his arm and thrust the icicle towards Ryan. I watched as it sailed across the room and plunged into Ryan's chest. Everyone stood silent as soon as it struck its mark. Ryan looked down at the icicle for a moment before a coughing fit brought blood to his lips. In the next moment, his lifeless body hit the floor.

"No one touches my wife and gets to live," Calix growled, breaking the silence.

I stepped up next to him, ready to kill them all with Calix by my side. Surprise took me when Calix grabbed my hand and pulled me to run in the opposite direction.

"No!" I yelled, pulling against him. "We can end this!"

"Not today," Calix said as he began to run faster. "You have to trust me."

I looked back at the manor over my shoulder, regret already washing over me at the fact that Lillian and Samuel were still alive. However, I knew that Calix would have a good reason for letting them live. They would get what they deserved. I just had to trust him. I looked back and quit fighting against him. I ran, matching his pace as we made our way to a hole that had been punched into the stone wall.

Calix's pace slowed as he climbed through the opening and reached through to help me. Once on the other side, I had a full view of the chaos that was happening in The Capital. Gifts were being used everywhere around us, and my skin felt like it was humming as I felt them all.

"Well, if it isn't the blushing bride?" His voice was hoarse, but I turned around and found Garret a few feet away, leaning against the wall. His hands were clenched at his side, and I could see the red liquid slipping between his fingers. Calix and I rushed and knelt beside him. "It's just a scratch," he insisted.

Calix forced him to lift his hand, and it became apparent that it was far more. Garrett pulled his hand back down in an attempt to stop the rush of blood that came out of the wound. I plunged my knife into the skirt of my dress and cut away the fabric. "Sit him up," I instructed. Calix pulled Garrett into an upright position as I wrapped the fabric around him.

"Liz, I think your husband is the one who's supposed to get you out of your dress," Garrett teased. "Not that I'm complaining."

I pulled the knot slightly tighter, causing him to wince. Only Garrett could be bleeding out and trying to make inappropriate jokes at the same time. Once the makeshift bandage was in place, Calix and I pulled him to his feet. Garrett was quite a bit taller than I, so I wasn't much help in keeping him up. Calix dropped Garrett's arm over his shoulders and began walking into the chaos of the city.

"Where are we going?" I asked as we grew closer to the fighting.

"A few blocks up," Calix replied. "We have an exit to a safe place, but we have to get there before it closes."

I opened my mouth to ask what he meant just as a guard rushed towards us, his gun at the ready. Nearby, I could feel Thomas's gift and spotted him a short distance away. He nodded at me, and I chose to take that as permission. I absorbed his gift just as the guard pulled the trigger. I had used Thomas's gift before, but never like this. I focused everything I had on the bullet, feeling it continue to push against my will as it began to slow. I pushed with everything I had, and in an instant, it flew back and struck the guard in the chest. As soon as his body hit the ground, I released Thomas's gift back to him.

"Nice work," Garrett said after releasing a deep breath. "Don't think I could take getting shot again."

"Move!" Calix ordered as he pulled Garrett further into the fighting.

More soldiers and guards attacked us as we went. Calix froze some or flung ice that cut into their flesh. Others I managed to take down with my blade. What remained of my wedding dress was covered in splashes of blood that only grew the further we went.

"It's there," Calix said, motioning towards what looked like a tunnel popping out of the ground. "We just need..."

An explosion nearby cut off his words as we all fell to the ground. My ears were still ringing as I looked around, everything blurring together for a moment. When my vision finally cleared, I spotted Malic a short distance away, surrounded. His hands were held up in surrender. I could feel that his gift was weak, almost as if he had depleted its energy.

"Liz!" Calix's voice called my attention back to him. "I have to get you both to the tunnel!"

"Go," I said, looking back at Malic. "I'll be right behind you."

Before he could protest, I pushed myself up and ran towards Malic. His eyes filled with surprise as I pushed my way through the soldiers and stood beside him.

"You want him," I sneered. "You'll have to kill me."

One soldier raised his weapon before another pushed it down. I hadn't been sure if they would know who I was, but relief washed over me. My mind was racing, trying to come up with a plan for how to get both Malic and me to the tunnel, when a beeping sound began emanating from Malic's communicator.

"It's too late," he whispered. "The tunnels are closed."

"Shit," I muttered. "We need to run."

"Don't move," Malic said as he pulled me closer to him. "And remember to roll when you land." "Roll?"

As soon as I spoke the word, the ground beneath us shook and opened up. Everything disappeared as we fell into the earth. I glanced up as we fell, seeing the whole city above us as we moved. Glancing back down, I could see solid ground quickly approaching. Remembering Malic's advice, I did my best to roll as we hit. Still, I landed hard and felt the air rush out of my lungs. I lay still for several moments, gasping to refill the air in my lungs. Malic appeared above me and offered me his hand. I took it and allowed him to help me to my feet.

"Where are we?" I asked, looking around at the dark tunnel.

"Basecamp," Malic answered as he struck a match. "Think of it as an underground Twain."

Chapter 33

$\mathcal{M}$alic lit a torch he plucked from the wall and led me down the dark tunnel. The further we walked; I began to hear the sound of voices in the distance. At first, it was all just a muffled sound, but then I heard him.

"Where is she?" Calix was yelling. I could hear the panic thick in his voice, though he was trying to disguise it with anger.

"Calix!" I called out. Out of the corner of my eye, I could see a slight smile spread across Malic's face. Before I had time to say anything about it, the tunnel filled with light, and Calix came running into view. He sprinted towards me and pulled me into his arms. I could feel the tension leaving his body as he held me.

"What happened to no exceptions?" Malic teased.

"We all knew I wouldn't leave anyone behind," Calix replied as he released me. "You, maybe, but not her."

Malic let out a light laugh as he shook his head and walked in the direction that Calix had come from. I noticed for the first time that Maddie and Thomas had both come with Calix.

"Nice job on the worm," I smiled at Thomas while motioning to my communicator. "They had no one who could override what you did."

"And it's not even my best work," Thomas said with a grin.

Maddie didn't say anything as she closed the distance and pulled me into a hug. "You have to stop getting yourself kidnapped," she said as she held me tight.

"I swear, this time it wasn't on purpose," I laughed. "And, I got to keep my mind."

Maddie laughed as she let go of me and took a step back. Calix immediately took my hand. It felt both possessive and protective, as if he were afraid, I would disappear at any moment.

"How's Garrett?" I asked.

"They were patching him up," Maddie said as she looked back the way she had come. "I should probably head back and check on him."

Holding Calix's hand, we followed Maddie back up the tunnel. The sight when we reached the end was breathtaking. A large, open cavern the size of a city appeared before us. Around the open space, tents and small fires were set up. Malic hadn't been joking when he said it was an underground Twain.

"Twain!" I suddenly gasped. "Calix, we have to get there now! Lillian said she had people there who would burn it to the ground if-"

"It's been taken care of," Calix said softly. "The sparks have been killed, and most of the people have moved to an underground camp similar to this one."

Questions swirled through my mind, but I couldn't hold on to one long enough to ask it out loud. What were Sparks? How did he know about Lillian's plan? How had that tunnel opened under our feet? But, most importantly, why did we let Lillian and the others live?

Calix gently pulled me forward deeper into the camp, and I forced myself to keep my questions to myself. There would be plenty of time to get answers. We walked through the rows of tents, the people all bowing their heads at us as we walked by. I felt like royalty, even though my title was nothing. I wasn't a queen, just an orphan girl whose parents were killed by the government. A government that now needed me to marry and give them a grandchild to carry on their family destiny. If anything, these people should be demanding that I be thrown out.

Calix seemed not to notice as we worked our way deeper into the cavern. "Garrett!" Maddie yelled as she took off running. My eyes followed her as she ran to a small fire where Garrett was sitting on a stone. His torso was wrapped in thick white bandages, but he was at least strong enough to sit up on his own. Maddie flung herself into his arms. Garrett winced in pain but pulled her tightly against him. I glanced up a Calix, who was grinning.

"Started right after you were taken," Calix explained. "Looks like Garrett was waiting for us to go first. Be warned, new love can be sickening at times."

I playfully slapped him across the chest as we walked closer and sat down. Calix immediately pulled me against his body, not willing to be parted from me for even a moment.

"They didn't hit anything vital," Garrett explained as Maddie settled in next to him. "It will just take a few days to heal."

Everyone nodded, and I couldn't help the relief I felt. Garrett could be an ass, but he was like a brother to me. I had felt my world start to shatter when we found him bleeding out. I couldn't handle watching another person I love die.

"How are you alive?" I blurted out as I turned to look at Calix.

Garrett let out a hearty laugh that caused me to turn back to him. "If you think it's weird, imagine how we felt when we were about to put him in the ground and his eyes sprang open."

I turned back to Calix, who was smiling and shaking his head. He looked down and lightly brushed the tips of his fingers across my jaw. "You figured out how we all could project our gifts," he said softly. "I decided to see if there was a way for me to absorb mine, like you do with others' gifts. It's painful as hell, but it turns out I can freeze my own heart."

"You froze your - " I couldn't finish. I thought back to the wink Calix had given me just before the soldiers surrounded him. He had a plan, but no idea if it would work. The cocky bastard had risked everything and nearly been buried.

Calix pulled me close and gently kissed the top of my head. I breathed deeply, his scent invading my nostrils and bringing me comfort.

"All the tunnels are closed off." I looked up to see a woman about our age standing there in dirt-stained closed. She was so covered in dirt that I almost didn't notice the trickle of blood coming from her nose. I watched as she quickly wiped it away on the back of her hand.

"Did you get hurt in an explosion?" I asked, leaning forward.

"An explosion?" the woman laughed.

"There were no explosions," Calix explained. "Meri and her brother Phelip are Moles; they can control the earth. They opened the tunnels we use to get in and out of the cavern, which they also made."

"Then, how were you injured?" I asked, turning back to Meri. "Do you need a healer?"

"Just a little over exhausted," Meri smiled. "Wasn't planning on having to open an emergency tunnel and stretched myself a bit too far. Nothing a good night's rest won't   fix."

It suddenly made sense. The tunnel that had opened under Malic and me, Meri had created and sealed behind us. She had pushed her gift to its limit and still kept going to get us here.

"Thank you," I said meekly.

Meri held up her hand to stop me from talking. "No thanks needed, my queen. If you don't mind, I would like to borrow Thomas for a moment. We are having some issues with some of our equipment, and though he may be able to help us out."

"Of course," Thomas said as he jumped up eagerly.

"Love is in the air," Garrett teased loudly as Thomas walked away with Meri.

We all let out a laugh while Thomas shot us a dirty look over his shoulder. Everything went silent between us, the sounds of the camp echoing around the cavern. I wanted to be content, enjoy this moment, and stop trying to understand everything. Some of my questions had already been answered, but there was still one that was burning away at me.

"Why didn't we kill them?" I asked, breaking the silence. Everyone looked at each other, but no one spoke. "I trusted you, but I need to know why."

"It started with Meri and her brother, Phelip," Calix spoke. "We were working our way here and took shelter in what we thought was an old warehouse."

He took a deep breath, and I waited for him to continue. Calix took his time as he explained that the warehouse was a holding facility for MUTS, ones that were deemed necessary but untrustworthy. He and the others managed to take out the few soldiers that were present and set them free. Most chose to take their freedom and run, not wanting to spend another second in the Union. But some, like Meri and Phelip, joined our fight. They wanted to take down The Capital and free other MUTS who were being held hostage. Calix continued to explain that there were other facilities spread throughout The Capital. Some were holding facilities, and others were research labs. While Calix had been rescuing me, other groups moved to free people in some of the facilities they had been able to locate.

"The research facilities are the worst," Maddie added. "They are trying to find ways to extract a MUTS gift and give it to another. The torture they put those people through is sick."

"But that doesn't explain why Lillian and the others couldn't die." Everyone looked at me with a look of pity that I hated. I had been gone for only days, but was already behind. So much had happened that they were going to have to help me catch up. At least this time, I wasn't so stupid as not to remember anything.

"The facilities are all linked to a heartbeat," Calix said in a gruff voice. "If that person's heart stops beating, the facilities will all self-destruct, killing those inside."

"Who's?" I asked even though I felt as if I already knew the answer.

"The matriarch," Garret said with disgust. "She's the bitch that's really in charge and running the show. We figure it has to be one of the governor's wives, but we have no idea which one."

"Lillian," I said through gritted teeth. "She's the tne pulling the strings on everything."

"Are you sure?" Calix asked, a hint of doubt in his voice.

It was time for me to fill them in on what I had learned. I told them about Lillian, the founding of The Union, and everything else I had learned while I was being prepped to be a birthing vessel to carry on their sick legacy. By the time I finished, Calix was squeezing his fists so tight that his knuckles were white.

"We will kill them," he said firmly. "Once the facilities are all cleared out, I will listen to her screams as fire consumes her."

Chapter 34

$\mathcal{T}$hings around the fire grew tense after that conversation. As time crawled by, the others began to fade away to their tents until only Calix and I remained. He sat silent, his strong, cool arms holding me against him. I felt safe, but I could feel the tension radiating from him. He had me back, but now his mind was focused on vengeance. I knew from experience how dangerous that could be. I needed him to focus on something else, to feel something else.

"So, do we have a tent or do we just sleep here by the fire?" Calix looked down at me with a hint of surprise. "I just found out my husband froze his own heart on our wedding day and came back from the dead," I explained. "I think you owe me a proper wedding night."

Instantly, heat and desire filled his eyes. His arms grew warm around me, and I knew I had sparked something. I stood up, my destroyed wedding dress now covered in dirt and blood.

Calix remained where he was, eyeing me like a predator. The look in his eyes reminded me of our time in the dungeon. Only this time, I had the feeling he would not be so gentle.

A shiver ran down my spine as I stood up slowly, his eyes never leaving mine as he moved. I felt a current course through my skin as he ran his fingers down my arms. I felt him take my hand in his and allowed him to pull me away. He took large strides, causing me to have to jog slightly to keep up. On the opposite side of the cavern, there was a smaller indent dug out in the wall. Calix stepped into it, revealing a smaller cavern. In the center, a large tent was set up. It was large enough for our entire group to share, though I hoped they were all somewhere else tonight.

Calix pushed open the tent flap and pulled me inside. I couldn't help the giggle that escaped me as the anticipation built. As soon as I was inside, Calix pressed against me. His strong lips found mine and began kissing me as if he were a starving man who had finally found food. I returned his passion, pulling myself even closer so that our bodies felt as if they were trying to become one.

I felt Calix's hands run across my back until his fingers found the zipper on the dress. In one swift motion, he pulled it down, his hands now exploring my exposed skin. Breaking our kiss, I took a step back. Anger flashed in his eyes until I reached up for the straps on my shoulders. Teasingly slow, I pulled them down, allowing the dress to fall into a crumpled mess on the ground.

I knew my skin was filthy with dirt and blood, but Calix didn't seem to notice. He looked at me like I was the most beautiful woman he had ever seen. In one smooth motion, he pulled his shirt over his head and closed the distance between us. His mouth found mine once again, and he continued to devour me. I felt his strong hands on my hips and jumped slightly to allow him to lift me from the ground. Wrapping my legs around him, I gave him full control over me. He moved his mouth to my neck, kissing and nipping in all the right spots that were causing the moisture in my core to build.

I let out a gasp as Calix released me and dropped me down onto a bed. It wasn't as nice as the one we shared in Twain, but that didn't matter right now. I watched as Calix walked over to where a small trunk sat and opened it. After just a few moments of digging around, he found what he wanted and allowed the lid to slam shut. My breath caught in my throat as he turned, and I saw the rope in his hands.

"I guess the only way to keep my queen from getting taken is to keep her tied up," he said with an evil smirk. "Put your hands together."

I immediately did as he asked. Calix knelt on the bed beside me, carefully tying the rope around my wrists and the other end to one of the tent poles above the bed. When he finished, he stood up and looked down at me.

"Too tight?" he asked.

I shook my head no. Calix immediately moved to the foot of the bed and kneeled. Before I had time to register what was happening, I felt him run his fingers up my slit.

"So wet for me," he growled, slipping one of his fingers into his mouth and sucking it clean. He then moved closer, and I could feel his hot breath on my wet folds. I squirmed against the rope, desperate to feel him. "So eager," Calix laughed before plunging his tongue into my center. I gripped the rope above my head as my entire body tensed. His tongue instantly found my nerve bundle and began swirling around it in a way that shot electricity through me. I could feel myself building, moving closer to the edge where my orgasm waited. This madman knew how to push me into pure ecstasy in a way that shouldn't exist.

As my body continued to tense, I felt Calix thrust two fingers deep inside me. White spots filled my vision as he began to work his fingers on my spot. I felt a warm gush on my thighs just as my orgasm reached its peak. Calix didn't slow down, his tongue and fingers still working expertly to help me get every second of ecstasy I could. As my body began to relax, his fingers slowly disappeared, and I felt him look up at me. I looked down, my breathing heavy, and saw the evil smile spread across his face. His lips were wet with my excitement, and I felt my core clench at the sight. My perfect Lucifer.

"Such a good girl," he grinned as he crawled up closer to me. I gripped the rope tightly as he kissed me deeply. I could taste my arousal on his tongue, and it made me want him even more. "I think it's time for my good girl to return the favor," he sneered as he undid the ropes around my wrist. I watched as he stood and undid the button of his pants, and they fell to the ground. I could see that his length was ready for me, but I was unsure of what he wanted. "Come here."

I obeyed as I crawled across the bed and sat on the edge. Calix took a step closer and wove his fingers into my hair. With his other hand, he gently placed his thumb on my lower lip and opened my mouth. I suddenly understood what he meant. He gently eased my head down towards his length and slowly slid it into my mouth. Closing my lips around him, I pulled him deep but had to stop when I felt myself begin to gag. Slowly, I began pulling him in and out of my mouth, my tongue swirling around his length as I did so. Calix let out a low growl, his grip tightening on my hair. I took this as a sign that he was enjoying himself and began to move faster.

"Stop," Calix commanded as he pulled back on my hair and pulled his length from my mouth. I could feel the spit running down my chin as I looked up at him with needy eyes. Calix pushed down against the bed and spread my legs. I was breathing hard as he positioned himself at my entrance and thrust deep inside me. I gripped the blankets tightly as Calix continued thrusting into me faster and faster. He reached down, and his thumb began working on my nerve bundle once more. I couldn't hold back. I felt myself fall over the edge once more into an orgasm that shook my entire body. Calix joined me a few moments later, thrusting deep one last time as he found his release.

I lay still as he slowly pulled out of me and then collapsed beside me on the bed, his arm dropping over my stomach. We lay in silence for several minutes. Once our breathing returned to normal, I felt a sense of content wash over me.

"So," I asked, causing him to open his eyes and look at me. "Is tying me up going to be our thing?"

Calix let out a light chuckle. "I didn't hear you complaining."

"And you never will. But there may be a day I want to tie you up instead," I teased.

Calix moved fast, and soon he was on top of me. His chest pressed to mine, and his nose inches from my own. "Just say when, my queen."

Chapter 35

I slept well for the first time since I was captured. Calix held me close, his breath against the back of my neck a consistent reminder that he was alive and with me. Even after I woke, I lay still, not ready to leave the comfort of his embrace. The sounds of the camp waking up began echoing around the cavern.

"Good morning," Calix said in a raspy voice as he began to stir.

"How can we be sure it's morning?" I teased.

Calix let out a laugh before kissing my hair and letting me go. I turned and watched as he threw back the blanket and climbed out of the bed. I couldn't help but admire him as he stretched, his clothes still on the floor beside my ruined dress. Calix turned to see me watching him, and an evil smile spread across his face. He walked over to a trunk and quickly changed into a fresh set of clothes.

"Yours are in there as well," he said, pulling down his shirt.

"Maybe I don't want to get dressed."

His eyes flashed dark as he looked down at me. "As much as I would love that, we have work to do. I don't want to have to kill everyone for seeing what is mine."

I felt a heat spread through my face as he spoke. Tossing back the blanket, I took my time standing up and going over to the trunk. I could feel the tension radiating off of him as I bent over and slowly looked through the trunk. My clothes were easy enough to find, but I loved teasing him. After a few moments, Calix let out a sigh, and I heard him leave the tent. I would pay for that tonight, and I looked forward to it.

I quickly put on the clothes and tied my hair back out of my face. I found Calix outside the tent with Malic and Thomas. Their conversation stopped as I approached. "What's going on?" I asked as I joined them.

"We have a new location," Calix answered. "We had planned to wait a few days before we attacked, but it seems that Lillian is sticking back at losing you."

"What do you mean?"

"She's destroying anything she thinks can be used against her," Malic answered. "Two holding facilities were wiped out last night on her orders. If we don't move on the remaining one, she will kill them."

"What are we waiting for?" I asked as I took a step forward.

Calix grabbed my arm and pulled me closer to him. "Every time I let you join us, you get taken."

I could hear the fear in his voice. He was right. I was their target. Lillian would stop at nothing to get me back. I knew going back above ground would be a risk, but I couldn't stay here. This was my fight, and I refused to hide.

"And you always get me back," I replied.

Calix's face showed that he knew I wouldn't stay. He hated it, and I was sure he would rather take me back in the tent and tie me up. That would have to be saved for after we returned. For now, we had work to do.

I walked with them and joined the others around the fire we had sat at the night before. Garrett was loudly voicing his feelings about having to stay behind due to his injury. The way his eyes kept darting towards Maddie told me that he was worried about her going without him. I felt Maddie activate her gift and watched as Garrett relaxed slightly. They were perfect for each other.

Malic led the meeting as we were joined by several people I didn't recognize. He explained that the building was a testing facility that was disguised as a specialized medical building for the terminally ill. In truth, they were testing gene extraction on people and transferring the abilities to infants. They planned that they would raise the infants to be loyal to The Union. They were trying to build an army of MUTS that would never question their authority because they knew nothing else. They had yet to be successful; all the infants had died during the transmission process. However, they were set to do a new trial in the next day or two that they believed had a chance of success. That was the reason that the facility had been spared, but we needed to move fast.

"We need to save as many as possible," Calix said, looking around. "The infants, especially since they have no way of defending themselves."

"They will kill the kids as soon as they realize we're attacking," Maddie pointed out. "We can't do this like we have before. We need to get someone inside to protect them before the rest of us make our move."

"I'll go," I volunteered. Calix gave me a look that I feared would freeze my heart with how cold it was. "I can use my shield to keep them safe until you all get inside and help me get them out. No one else can keep them as safe as I can."

"And if they recognize you?" Calix said in a stern voice.

"I'll go with her," Malic volunteered. "I can make sure they don't."

Everyone was silent for several breaths until Calix nodded in agreement. I listened quietly as he talked the others through their part in the plan. Once everyone understood, they left to gather their weapons, agreeing to meet in ten minutes.

"You can take your knife," Maddie said, walking towards me. "Most people don't realize you have it unless they make you use it. Any other weapons would raise too many questions."

"I agree," I nodded. "Good thing I'm good with a blade."

I turned to walk towards the meeting spot when Maddie grabbed my arm and pulled me back to face her. "Don't get taken again," she said with concern. "He can't take it, none of us can."

"No plans for it," I assured her.

Maddie nodded in understanding and released me. I walked to the meeting spot and found Malic waiting for me. He was dressed in simple black clothes. They were loose-fitting, and I had a feeling that he was hiding weapons in the loose fabric.

"When this is all over, I think we need to find you a nice girl to settle down with," I said, desperate to fill the silence.

Malic let out a hearty laugh, wiping a tear from his eye. "I'm not opposed to settling down, my queen," he said, shaking his head. "But my tastes run different than most."

419

"Well, tell me what you're looking for," I said, crossing my arms.

"Well, to start with, not a girl," Malic answered.

"Ok, woman," I nodded.

"No," Malic said, raising an eyebrow.

"Oh," I said, surprised. "Alright, a nice man." Malic looked embarrassed, as if he was waiting for me to judge or scold him. "You haven't told anyone, have you?" I asked.

Malic shook his head and looked down at his feet. "My ability was too much already. I didn't think anyone would accept me if they knew."

"They will or they can feel the queen's wrath," I smiled. "As soon as this is over, we will find you your fella."

Malic let out a laugh as he relaxed his shoulders. It looked as if a giant weight had been lifted from it. I had no idea how long he had been carrying that secret, but it was over. He was an amazing man and deserved all the happiness this fucked up world had to offer.

"Ready?" Calix asked as he and the others joined us.

"As ready as we can be," Malic answered.

Meri and a man whom I assumed was Phelip stepped forward. I watched in awe as they held up their hands and concentrated on the wall of dirt and rock in front of us. The dirt slowly began to slide away, taking the rocks with it. In just a few moments, a smooth tunnel opened in front of us.

"You will come out a block away from the facility," Meri explained. "Send a ping through the communicators when you are in position. It will take the cavalry two minutes to reach you after you send the signal."

"Simple enough," I smiled, hoping that I was hiding the nerves that were beginning to swell inside me.

Calix stepped in front of me and pulled me close to him. I leaned into him, taking in every bit of him I could. "I'll be right behind you," he said before kissing me deeply. "See you soon," I smiled back as he let me go.

Together, Malic and I made our way down the tunnel. The ground slowly slanted up, and as we neared the end, the ground cleared away and revealed the sunlight outside. Malic climbed out first, making sure that we had not been discovered. I waited patiently until he signaled for me to follow.

Outside, it was obvious how much had changed from the day before. The streets had few people in them; despite the bustle I had seen the day I had arrived. There was still debris throughout the streets from the battle.

"Stay close," Malic instructed as he led us out into the open. It felt as if our footsteps echoed around us as we walked. We both kept our heads down as we hurried across the block to the facility. As far as I could tell, we managed to keep from drawing any attention to ourselves. Malic opened the glass door and ushered me inside. The smell of sanitation filled my nostrils as soon as we entered. Malic followed behind me, the door softly closing behind us.

"No visitors," a stern voice said as a guard stepped into view. "You need to leave."

Chapter 36

$\mathcal{E}$very muscle in my body tensed as the guard stared at me with cold, dead eyes. I felt Malic step closer, causing the guard to shift his gaze.

"We are not visitors," Malic spoke smoothly. "The doctor here was requested to look over the subjects before testing begins."

The guard glanced back at me and then back at Malic. "No one informed me," he said flatly.

"I wasn't aware that the Matriarch was required to report to you," Malic said, his voice thick with sarcasm. "We will inform her thusly that the exams were not completed because of you. May I have your name?"

Panic flashed across the guard's face. He shifted for a moment on his feet before letting out a grunt. My muscles relaxed as he stepped aside and motioned for us to continue. I walked as confidently as I could, pretending that I not only belonged but knew where I was going. I had a feeling that asking for directions would just cause more suspicion.

Malic followed close behind as we made our way down the empty, sterile-looking halls. I was about to stop and ask him which way he thought we should go when I heard it, the cries of a baby. We turned down the hall and followed the cries. At the end of a long hall, there was a set of doors, locked with what appeared to be a key card. I looked back at Malic, but he gave no signs that he knew how to get in. Perhaps this is why the guard at the front was so easily swayed. He knew we couldn't get into the room unless we had a key. I wouldn't be surprised if he appeared in the next few minutes, ready to prove that we were lying.

"Couldn't your mother disrupt electric frequencies?" Malic asked in a whisper.

"Yeah," I nodded. "But she's not here."

"But maybe someone else in here can too," Malic continued. "If they can, you could borrow their gift long enough to get us in."

I closed my eyes and reached out, looking for the gift we needed. The number of gifts in this building was overwhelming. Every infant beyond the door already had a gift; Lillian just wanted them to have more. I could feel beads of sweat forming on my brow as I continued to reach, invading others as I felt out their gift.

"I can't," I breathed after a few minutes.

"Doctor!" A chipper voice called out behind us, causing us to both turn. A young man was running towards us in a white doctor's coat. "I'm sorry I wasn't there to greet you at the door. The guard informed me of your arrival. I do apologize. I wasn't expecting you until this afternoon."

"With everything going on, things have been accelerated," I replied.

"Of course," he nodded. "Everything is ready."

Malic and I watched as he pulled out a card and tapped it against the sensor. I heard the lock click and the door swung open.

"We have twelve infants, all just under six weeks, who have signs of the gene. Each has been paired with a donor, and the injections are ready to be administered once you clear them."

I followed the doctor as he led us into a small room with twelve small plastic cribs, each barely big enough to hold the infants that lay inside. Looking around, these children were not treated like anything but lab rats. There was nothing in the room that one would expect to find in a nursery.

"Their files?" I asked, looking back at the doctor.

"Of course," he said as he rushed towards a table and fetched a stack of folders. "Each one contains the medical history we were able to obtain from the parents. All of them were conceived and delivered on the farm, so we were able to ensure the best breeding conditions."

My stomach turned as he spoke. The parents of these children did not bring them into this world willingly. They were paired up and forced to conceive to have their child ripped away once they were born.

"Are the parents available for the exam?" I asked, pretending to glance at the files.

"No," the doctor said with a hint of confusion. "They were disposed of to ensure that the children would not have any attachments should the procedure turn out to be a success."

I nodded, trying to hide the rage that I was feeling inside. Setting the files down, I walked closer to the first small crib. Inside, dressed in a stark white onesie, was a little girl. Her dark hair and light blue eyes instantly caused my heart to warm and melt at the same time. Reaching towards her, I looked her over, pretending to do an exam. I could feel the doctor's eyes on me as I worked. I moved slowly, counting in my head the seconds. After a minute, I carefully reached out my shield to protect each of the little ones.

The cribs were on wheels, so I carefully pushed them closer together. My shield wouldn't protect them from physical threats, so having them in a small group would help Malic and me keep them safe. The doctor watched me, glancing at Malic, probably looking for an explanation. Time was nearly up when I finished and turned back to the doctor.

"I regret to inform you that none of these children will be able to be part of your experiment," I said flatly.

"That's not possible!" the doctor growled. "They have all been examined several times since their births, and each is perfectly healthy!"

"You misunderstand," I said calmly. "They are all healthy but will not be able to participate."

The doctor looked at Malic as if I had gone insane. Malic remained still, his eyes locked forward, as if he didn't notice the doctor looking towards him for help.

"I disagree," the doctor said after a moment. "Lillian herself approved them all. You were requested as nothing more than a formality."

Just then, the building shook around us. Placing my hands on the crib to keep the babies steady, I continued to stare at the doctor. Malic made his move just then. It was so fast, I don't think the poor doctor even saw it coming. As the echoes of screams and fighting filled the halls, the doctor's neck audibly snapped before his body hit the ground.

Malic moved closer and helped me to keep the babies in place and shield them from any threat that may appear. As the doors burst open, we both tensed, ready to fight. Maddie swept into the room, stopping when she saw us. We both relaxed, and she stepped closer.

"We can't exactly walk them out the front door," she said, looking at the infants.

I watched as she pressed on her communicator and then took a few steps back. The ground began to shake beneath us, and a tunnel opened. We moved quickly, rolling the cribs into the tunnel where they were taken back to our camp.

"Calix wants you to go with them," Maddie said as the last crib went into the tunnel. "I told him you wouldn't, but that I would deliver the message."

I looked back down at the tunnel where Phellip stood waiting. "Seal it up," I instructed before turning and heading for the doors. "We have more work to do." I pushed the door open with Maddie and Malic right behind me. Out in the halls, fighting was everywhere. We made our way through, helping our allies as we walked.

"Calix is on the second floor," Maddie said as she shot a guard in the chest who was rushing us. "He went to download information from the mainframe."

"I don't remember that being part of the plan," Malic grunted as he slammed another guard's head into the wall with a sickening thud.

I could feel my heart beating, pumping blood through my veins as I continued to fight. Of course, most of the guards were MUTS, each of them depending on their abilities to save them. Each one died swiftly as they realized that their abilities would not work on us.

A few hallways over, we found Thomas helping a group of people into a tunnel. "Where's Cal?" I ran over to him. I had expected Thomas to be with Cal if it was something technical he was after.

"We got the download," Thomas said, not meeting my eyes. "And this is the last of the people. We should get back."

"Where's Calix?" I repeated more firmly. "Go!" Calix's voice boomed.

I looked up to see him running at us at full speed down the hall. My heart swelled for a moment before I felt it. I couldn't see her, but I could feel Lillian's gift. Calix grabbed my hand and pulled me down into the tunnel just as she rounded the corner. The murderous look in her eyes shot shivers down my spine. A moment later, I was surrounded by dirt, and the tunnel entrance was sealed.

Chapter 37

"We need to move," Calix said firmly as he pulled me deeper into the tunnel. "Make sure this is sealed."

As we walked, the tunnel began to turn into solid earth behind us. Calix was covered in cuts, but none of them seemed life-threatening. None of us spoke as we made our way back to base camp.

"See what you can get off that drive," Calix ordered Thomas as soon as we returned.

Thomas looked a bit taken aback by the sharpness of Calix's tone, but nodded before taking off. The others seemed to want to get away from him and his foul mood as well, and they quickly muttered things they had to check on before heading off themselves.

"We should get you cleaned up," I said softly, watching Calix's chest rise and fall hard.

He didn't seem to hear as he continued to stand, his grip on my hand so tight it was starting to hurt. "Calix, what happened? What is the download about?"

Calix looked at me for the first time since we had returned, his shoulders relaxing slightly and his grip on my hand loosening. "It could be nothing," he finally sighed. "But when the MUTS started talking about it, I knew I had to get it just to be safe. I didn't expect that bitch to be there."

I didn't speak as he took several deep breaths. I waited patiently for him to continue.

"One of the MUTS claimed he wasn't from the Union," he explained. "He said he arrived here just a few years ago as part of a trade."

"Trade?" I said before I could stop myself.

"He claimed there are other cities, each one different and spaced far enough apart that people don't realize," Calix continued. "Thomasa and I went to download the files from the main server to see if it was true. We had barely finished when she walked in, killing the man. Thomas and I barely made it out. She was weak, like she had used most of her energy already."

My head felt like it was spinning. I knew the Union had lied about many things, but this seemed like too much, even for them. This was supposed to be the only land that survived the Great War. How could there be other cities that we know nothing about?

"We should go check on Thomas," I said flatly. "See what you guys downloaded."

Calix shook his head. "It will take him days to work through the encryption on those files," he explained. "He was geeking out over how sophisticated it was when he downloaded it."

So, we wouldn't know what, if anything, they had managed to find out any time soon. Thomas would break the encryption, of that I felt certain, but I wasn't sure any of us were ready to know if the man they had met was telling the truth. If there were other cities, other people, were they used like slaves as we were? Their governments couldn't be any better than ours if they were trading MUTS. Even if we won our own freedom, would our fight truly be over? No, it wouldn't. We couldn't leave others to suffer as we had. It didn't matter if we knew them; no one deserved to be traded and used like pawns in a sick person's game. For now, though, we needed to focus on our fight before starting a new one. If there were other cities, we couldn't do anything to help them until Lillian and the others were destroyed.

Calix softly kissed the back of my hand, pulling me out of my thoughts. His eyes showed that he had calmed down, the adrenaline finding its way out of his body. "We should go and make sure everyone is getting settled."

I nodded in agreement and followed him deeper into base camp. A few people were injured, but nothing too concerning. Our plan had worked in catching The Union off guard. In total, we had managed to save fifty-four people, including the infants. Of those, nine were willing and able to join in our fight. Calix quickly set to making arrangements for the others to be moved to the underground Twain. The twins were exhausted from the tunnels they had done for our attack, and the transport would have to wait until the next day. For now, we have plenty of room and supplies to keep everyone comfortable.

I had just finished setting up a tent for an older woman when I felt someone tug on my shirt. I looked down to see a little girl who was no more than eight years old. Her big brown eyes looked up at me with an innocence I had nearly forgotten could exist in this world.

"Excuse me," she said softly. "I'm not sure where I'm supposed to go."

My heart broke as I knelt. I opened my mouth to ask her if her parents were in the facility before shutting it again. The words of the doctor rang through my mind. They killed the parents to keep the children from having an attachment outside of The Union. I looked around, watching as the broken people we had saved settled into their temporary housing. I looked back at the little girl and gave her a sweet smile.

"I'm Liz," I said softly. "What's your name?"

"I don't have one, ma'am," the little girl said. "Names aren't needed for someone like me. I'm MUT 22876."

I felt my rage rise inside me, but managed to keep my face cheerful and calm.

"Well, I say that everyone deserves a name. Maybe you could pick your own?"

The girl looked surprised, and her eyes grew wide. She shook her head gently as she looked down at the ground.

"That's alright," I assured her. "You don't have to choose one today. A name is important. You should take your time and pick the perfect one."

She looked up at me slowly but did not speak. I thought about taking her back to Calix's tent to stay that night with us. I heard shuffled footsteps behind me and realized that the old woman I had set the tent up for was walking closer. I turned my head and met her eyes.

"She can stay with me," the old woman said softly. "It would be good for an old woman like me to have someone to take care of."

I looked back at the little girl, and she nodded in agreement. I stood and watched as the girl walked over and took the woman's hand.

"I don't have a name either," the woman said with a soft smile. "Maybe you could help me come up with one."

The little girl smiled as she walked into the tent with the old woman. My heart swelled with the sweetness of the moment. Watching them together reminded me of Grams. She had always been so kind and patient with me, making sure I felt important even when no one else did. The girl would be safe, of that I had no doubt.

Walking through base camp, I found that everyone was settled, and some were already fast asleep. I wandered around, checking on those I saw until I eventually found my way to our group's fire. Everyone else had already arrived and was sitting around with half-eaten plates of food. Maddie leaned back against Garret, his eyes partially closed, with his arms wrapped around her. Thomas was sitting beside Merri, his eyes locked on a screen as his fingers flew across the keyboard. Meri sat quietly beside him, watching as he worked. Malic was settled by himself, watching the small flames of the fire dance.

As soon as I walked up, Calix extended his arms and pulled me into his lap. I settled in as he wrapped his strong arms around me. I leaned against his chest and watched the flames and listened to Thomas's fingers click across the keys. Now and then, he made a grunt, showing he was frustrated, but the clacking never stopped. "We should call it a night," Malic said. "I think we could all use some rest after today."

The sound of the keys stopped as Thomas finally looked up from his screen. The look on his face showed that he was just noticing we were all there for the first time.

"Anything I should know about tomorrow?" I asked, leaning forward and stretching.

"I want you and Maddie to lead the group to Twain," Calix said behind me. "Most of them are terrified, and I think a gentle hand will be best."

I looked at Maddie and nodded in agreement.

"You boys better not go starting any trouble while we're gone," Maddie said as she stood up. "We could use a day with no action."

"No promises," Garrett smiled at her, earning him a playful slap to the chest.

Chapter 38

$\mathcal{E}$xhaustion weighed heavily on me as I walked into our tent, Calix right behind me. I looked over at the bed, still a mess from the night before. Kicking off my boots, I had every intention of collapsing into it and sleeping for the next few days. Calix's arms wrapped around me before I made it even close.

"You weren't planning on going to sleep, were you?" he breathed into my ear.

I felt my body respond immediately, but I tried my best to hide it.

"I was," I admitted. "Were you planning on stopping me?"

Pulling my hair back away from my neck, Calix began to lightly kiss my skin. I resisted the urge to melt against him and give in to our desires. Instead, I pulled away and felt joy at the shocked look on his face.

"Just because we're married, you expect to get what you want every night?" I teased as I backed away from him. "You think you don't even have to work for it?"

Calix's eyes darkened with both desire and intrigue. He took a step closer, and I took two more back. He raised an eyebrow at me, and I couldn't help but smile.

"I think you need to earn it," I teased.

"What did you have in mind?" His voice was deep and dripping with desire. I nearly gave in right there, but managed to hold on to what little strength I had left.

"Catch me," I answered. "If you can catch me before I make it to the bed, you get what you want. If I make it to the bed, I get what I want."

"What do you want?" he asked, tensing all the muscles in his body.

"Afraid you're going to lose?" I teased. There was no need for him to know that I now wanted the same thing as him. That would take the fun out of our little game.

"Never," Calix growled.

<u>**441**</u>

With that, Calix lunged at me. I barely managed to scramble out of the way and avoid his grasp. He was now blocking me from the bed. He smiled like a predator who had cornered his prey.

"You'll have to do better than that," I grinned as I rushed behind a table and put it between us.

Calix grinned again and stepped closer to the table, knocking it over. Letting out a squeal, I ran through the tent, trying to hide behind some furniture and knocking other pieces down in an attempt to slow him down. We were making quite a mess, and part of me was surprised that no one came to see if we were being attacked. Calix continued to chase me, nearly catching me several times. Finally, I found an opening and sprinted towards the bed. I could hear him behind me as I jumped and landed on the soft mattress.

"Well done," Calix said as he stepped closer. "Now, what is your prize?"

I moved to the edge of the bed on my knees and pressed my body against his. Grabbing a fistful of his shirt, I pulled him down on the bed and climbed on top of him.

"I'm in control tonight," I said with a grin.

I could feel his length under me and knew that he approved. Slowly, I pulled my shirt over my head and tossed it behind me. Calix reached up, and I slapped his hands away.

"Did I say you could touch?" I scolded.

He put his hands back down and balled up the blankets in his fists. I scooted back so that I was sitting on his legs.

"Sit up," I instructed, and he immediately did as he was told. I couldn't help the joy I felt of having him under my control as I pulled off his shirt and tossed it. With one hand, I pushed him back down on the mattress. His eyes never left mine, but his fists were clenched so tightly that his knuckles were white. After undoing his pants, I climbed off the bed and pulled them off. Instantly, I could see I was right; he was turned on by me taking control. Undoing my pants, I slowly pulled them down, carefully stepping out of them one leg at a time before crawling back on the bed.

Once I was back on top of him, I positioned myself so that he could feel the heat and moisture of my core, but didn't allow him access. Instead, I slowly ran my nails across his bare chest, accidentally grinding myself against him. I could tell he was nearing his breaking point each time I moved. Yet, he kept his hands down as I had told him. Perhaps it was time for a reward.

I lifted myself and positioned him at my entrance, slowly sliding him into me. I watched as his eyes rolled back and he let out a groan.

"Fuck," he breathed once he was completely inside me.

Slowly, I began to rock back and forth. Each movement pushed me closer to the release I so desperately wanted. This position was perfect as I was able to angle myself in such a way that my clit brushed just right with each thrust.

"My queen," Calix groaned, gripping the blankets tighter.

That was enough; I was torturing myself now. "Touch me," I breathed.

There was no hesitation as Calix's hands shot up off the bed and grabbed my waist. His hands slid up my body until they reached my breasts. He began squeezing and pinching in just

the right ways. I could feel the edge of my orgasm
getting close and knew that I would fall over it at
any moment. Calix must have felt it too, as his
hands returned to my waist and he helped me
keep our rhythm as he thrust under me. That was
it. I fell over the edge as my orgasm ripped
through my body. I couldn't hold back the moan
that burst out of me as I threw my head back.

Just as I reached the end and began to
come back down, Calix found his release. He
thrust deep inside me, holding my hips firm as he
filled me. When his grip relaxed, I collapsed onto
his chest, his length still inside me. We were both
breathing hard, but the moment was perfect.
Once our breathing returned to normal, I
carefully slid off of him, and we both cleaned up.

Once we were back in bed, we instantly
tangled ourselves into each other, my head lying
on his chest.

"You are perfect," Calix breathed as he held
me close.

I knew I was far from perfect, but I didn't
want to argue right now. Perhaps I was perfect
for him, and that was enough. Instead, I kissed
his chest and snuggled closer.

"I love you," I said as my eyes grew heavy.

"I love you more," Calix replied, kissing my hair."

Lying on his chest, I could feel that there was something more that he wanted to say. Slowly, I traced small patterns on his skin, waiting for him to speak.

"There's one thing I don't understand from your time at the manor," Calix finally spoke after a heavy breath. "You said that Lillian's gift repulsed you and you refused to absorb it."

"That's right. It felt like it was so evil that just absorbing it would somehow make me evil," I explained.

"But, if you did take it, it would save so many from her wraith," Calix continued.

My muscles tensed at the words. Of course, he was right, but the thought of feeling her gift inside me made me shudder.

"It wouldn't change you," Calix continued, sensing my tension. "You're nothing like her."

"I would be if I used her gift," I sighed. "Even if I didn't intend to use it as she does. I would end up being exactly who she wants me to be."

Calix's hand rubbed up and down my arm, his cooling touch helping to relax me.

"I just want you to know, if you ever had to do it, I know you're strong enough to handle it," Calix said softly.

Words refused to come out of my mouth, so I nodded against his chest. I was desperate for this conversation to end. I had already decided that I would never absorb her gift. It was too much of a risk, and I would defeat her without becoming her.

Chapter 39

I woke early the next morning; my body and limbs tangled with Calix's. He was already awake, gently stroking his fingers over my messy hair. "Good morning," I said in a sleepy voice.

"Good morning," he replied before kissing the top of my head.

I let out a groan as Calix untangled himself from me and climbed out of bed. I knew we had work to do, but I still wished we could stay here forever. Throwing back the blankets, I followed his lead and quickly got dressed. Just as I finished, a voice sounded outside our tent.

"Are you decent?!" Garrett called out.

Calix looked over at me before responding. "Unfortunately!"

Garrett through back the tent flap and walked inside. I could tell instantly that he was feeling better as he had returned to his normal stride. He looked around the tent at the mess Calix and I had made the night before. Half the furniture was still knocked over, and our clothes from the day before were flung in random places. I felt my cheeks grow hot as Garrett looked at me with a wicked smile.

"Jealous?" Calix asked, making Garrett turn to him.

"A little," Garrett nodded. "I need this war to be over so I can make an honest woman out of Maddie and make our own fun."

I let out a laugh as I finished lacing up my boots and stood up. "Not sure if you can handle that," I teased. "I get the feeling she's a wild one."

"I'm counting on it," Garret said with a wink.

"Enough," Calix said, shaking his head. "I'm sure you didn't come here to talk about our or your potential sex life."

Garrett's face went stern as he nodded in agreement. I admired how fast he could make the switch from playful to professional.

449

"Everyone is ready," he stated. Meri says the journey will take about two hours

each way. She is going to be doing this one alone. Phelip will be staying behind in case we have an emergency."

"What type of emergency?" I asked, walking closer.

"We don't expect anything," Calix assured me. "But it's better to be safe just in case."

I nodded and followed them out of the tent. Being underground was still an adjustment. I still couldn't tell if it was day or night. I missed the feeling of the sun and breeze. I kept telling myself that this was temporary, but it felt too much like being trapped in a cage for my comfort. As we made our way back to the center of the cavern, I saw that the others were already waiting for us.

"Everyone is gathered and waiting," Maddie said as soon as she saw us. "You boys going to be alright while the ladies are away?"

"We'll be better once you're back," Calix replied, pulling me close. "I hate being away from you."

"I hate it too," I smiled at him. "I'll make it up to you tonight."

An evil grin spread across Calix's face, and I could feel his excitement as he pressed up against me. My mind turned to mush, and I instantly wanted to take him back to our tent.

"Gross," Maddie said loudly as she grabbed my arm and pulled me back. "People are watching."

Calix never took his eyes off me as Maddie led me to where the group was waiting. As soon as we were at the front of the group, Meri started her part. It was fascinating to watch as the earth and rocks shifted, forming a tunnel. Meri walked in, continuing the process as we went. She was focused and dared not interrupt her while she worked. For all I knew, it could cause the entire tunnel to collapse around us. Looking back over my shoulder, I made sure that everyone was keeping up.

I spotted the little girl from the night before running up to me. I slowed down slightly and waited for her.

"You're the queen?!" she asked excitedly.

"That's the rumor," I laughed. "But you can just call me Liz."

She nodded happily as she skipped along beside me. "And you can call me Abigail," she chirped. "And the woman who's taking care of me is Grace."

"Lovely names," I smiled. "Did you come up with them?"

"I named Grace, and she named me. Families are supposed to pick your name, and we are each other's family now."

Tears welled up in my eyes, and I quickly wiped them away. In less than a day, this small child had gone from being nothing to being part of a family. In the grand scheme of things, it probably seemed like nothing. However, it was little things like this that proved we were doing the right thing. I looked back and could see Grace a few steps behind us, a smile on her face. When this was over, I would make sure that they were both well taken care of. They were part of my family now.

Abigail chatted a bit longer before returning to Grace. Time went faster than expected, and soon Meri had opened the tunnel into the underground Twain. I saw familiar faces as we made our way through the tents. I watched as the citizens accepted those whom we had brought and began getting them settled in.

"Nice ring," Ms. Timlin said as she appeared beside me.

I turned and pulled her into a hug. She hugged me back with a warmth that only a mother figure could possess. When she released me, I could see the tears glistening in her eyes.

"Took you two long enough," she smiled.

I let out a laugh. Of course, she wasn't surprised. She had been telling Calix since we were kids that I was going to his wife. At the time, it seemed ridiculous, but now I knew it was just meant to be.

"Merri just needs an hour to recharge, and we can go back," Maddie said as she joined us. "I could use something to eat."

"Follow me," Ms. Timlin smiled. She led us through the camp and into her tent. It felt like home as we sat around her makeshift table, eating and drinking. The conversation flowed freely as

453

we informed her of everything that had happened.

"I met Lillian once," Ms. Timlin admitted as our conversation slowed down. "She had demanded that I heal her."

"From what?" I asked, confused.

"After they exiled your mother, Lillian was determined to have another child. However, she had become infertile," Ms. Timlin explained. "No one could explain it, as she was still young enough and in good enough health. She had demanded that I cure her of whatever it was."

"But you couldn't," I said lightly.

"No," Ms. Timlin confirmed. "She was furious. She was the one who..." I looked at her as she motioned to her face. She had told me that she had received it from someone who could not appreciate her ability. I hadn't realized it had been my grandmother whom she had angered. "After that, I fled The Union and haven't been back since."

"I'm sorry," I said softly. "My mother..."

"I know," Ms. Timlin interrupted. "When she learned what happened to me, she told me about the root. Quite clever, I must admit. It aged Lillian beyond her years and took away her ability to have more children. As strong as my abilities are, I can't reverse the ageing process."

"Wait," Maddie spoke up. "What's rot root?"

"It's an herb," Ms. Timlin explained. "It was said to grow on the oldest of graves. It was used as a form of punishment and population control. However, after Lillian was poisoned with it, she ordered it all destroyed, and people were no longer allowed to be buried."

"Damn," Maddie sighed. "Bitch went nuclear."

"More than you know," Ms. Timlin nodded. "It will do everyone good to have her wickedness scrubbed from this earth."

I sat silent, listening to the two of them talk for several minutes. Ms. Tilmin was a source of information, but none of us had ever asked her the difficult questions before. I thought about the man Calix and Thomas had met, claiming he was traded from another city.

"Did you ever hear any talk of other cities?" I asked.

Ms. Timlin and Maddie both went silent and looked at me. I felt like I had grown a second head with the way they were both staring at me. I sat straight, ready for her to say she didn't. I wasn't crazy, but until Thomas got into those files, I had to try to find out what I could.

"Just stories," Ms. Timlin said after a moment. "Mostly fairy tales of other places to help children have hope that there were better places out there. Why do you ask?" "There was a man that Calix and Thomas met," I explained. "He claimed he was from a different city and was traded to The Union a few years ago."

"Really?" Ms. Timlin gasped. "What else did he say?"

"Nothing," I admitted. "He helped them download some files that Thomas is trying to get into, but was killed."

"Is that what he's been working on?" Maddie asked. "I tried to ask him what he was working on, but he was in total tech mode."

I nodded. "I get the feeling our fight may not end when we free The Union," I admitted. "If these other cities do exist and are trading MUTS with The Union, they are probably just as corrupt."

Ms. Timlin nodded and thought in silence for a few minutes. "First, you must get your own house in order," she finally said. "Then, if there are other cities, you can do what you can to help them. But don't get consumed by war and forget to live your own life."

Ms. Timlin had a way of knowing just what I needed to hear. I was afraid that I would never find my happiness and enjoy my life with Calix. If there were others, I would do what I could to help them, but I needed to remember myself as well. We talked for a bit longer before Meri appeared. She said she was ready for the return trip. Maddie and I each hugged Ms. Timlin and promised to check in again soon before following Meri back into the tunnel.

"So," I said to Maddie as we walked. "Garrett is talking about making an honest woman out of you."

Her cheeks instantly flushed as a smile spread across her face.

"I told him I wouldn't take vows until after the war," she admitted. "I would appreciate it if we could speed things up and get this over with already."

"I'll do what I can," I laughed.

Meri walked behind us, closing the tunnel as we went.

"Thomas tends to focus on things too much," I said to her. "But I can tell he cares about you."

She smiled and looked away for a second. "I care about him, too," she finally said.

"Just don't break his heart," Maddie warned. "He's like a nerdy little brother to all of us."

"I won't" Merri laughed.

Chapter 40

"*F*inally!" Thomas yelled out.

I rushed over to him and looked down at the screen.

"You opened the files?" I asked.

"Just one," he explained as his eyes hurried over the screen.

I watched over his shoulder as he scanned the screen, his face giving nothing away as he read.

"But it's a good one," he finally said. "I know how to stop Lillian from blowing up half The Union if we kill her."

"I'd say that's a good thing," Garret spoke up as he leaned forward.

Thomas nodded as he looked back at the screen and began typing.

"It's quite a primitive system," Thomas explained. "Looks like it's been in place since The Union was founded. Each matriarch is implanted with a chip, which is why they don't have to wear communicators. The chip is removed from the current matriarch and implanted in the new one, one year after she is wed and takes her place."

"How does this help us?" I said in frustration. "Liz isn't going to marry some ass hat for a year and wait for Lillian to pass the torch."

"She won't have to," Thomas continued as his fingers flew across the keys. "The chip isn't hard to remove. We just need someone to get close enough to her to cut it out of her wrist."

"Easier said than done," Garrett sighed. "Liz won't even be able to get close to her."

"Once the chip is out," Thomas continued, ignoring Garrett, "It has to be implanted in the new matriarch within ten minutes. If it's not, it will trigger a catastrophic event."

"How catastrophic?" I asked, my stomach twisting in a knot.

"The Union will be no more," Thomas said softly. "A blast like this would even take out Twain."

I let out a sigh and began pacing back and forth. We knew how the fail-safe worked, but now we needed a way to use this information.

"What if one of us just went in, cut off the physio's hand, and put the chip in ourselves?" Garrett offered.

"Won't work," Thomas said, shaking his hand. "The chip looks for a DNA match. If you're not related to the matriarch, it will detonate."

Perfect! It may be an outdated system, but it was still pretty damn effective. I continued to pace until an idea came to mind. It was a horrible idea, and Liz would never agree to it, but Liz wasn't here. Perhaps it was time for me to be the reckless one.

"I know how to get the chip," I said flatly, causing them both to look at me. "Liz is going to be pissed, but it's the only way."

461

I began to explain my plan to them, each step causing their eyes to grow wider.

"She won't let you," Garrett said when I finished. "She'll break your damn legs to stop you."

"They won't be back for a few hours," I explained. "I will be gone by then. I need you two to push her. Tell her the story and make sure she doesn't fall. She can do this; she just needs a little push."

"A little push?!" Thomas gasped. "This is jumping off a cliff and hoping that there's water at the bottom. It's suicide!"

"Liz has been pretty damn clear that she won't absorb Lillian's gift," Garrett added. "If she doesn't, she will be spent before either of you can get close enough to get the chip."

"It's the only way," I insisted. "I need you both to be on board with this, or I'm doomed before it starts."

They looked at each other and then back at me.

"I'll get Philip," Garrett said, standing up.

"You'd better hurry."

I looked at Thomas, who nodded in agreement. Rushing back to my tent, I found a piece of paper and wrote as fast as I could. When I finished, I set the note on her pillow and looked around. She would be a wreck when she came back and discovered I was gone. My heart ached to think of the pain that she would go through, but I knew it was necessary. I was never meant to be a leader; she was. Her pain and compassion always made her more skilled at it than I could ever be. I just needed her to remember that. She could fight for others, especially if she cared for them. But I knew she would burn everything down to get me.

Swallowing hard, I headed out of the tent. I looked back once more, remembering the night before. The next time I saw her, it would be at the final battle. The memory of that night would have to be enough to carry me through. I pushed back the flap and headed outside. It was time for me to become the one who was captured.

Chapter 41

$\mathcal{W}$alking back into base camp, I could feel something was off. No one would look at me and seemed to scurry away as we approached. I looked over at Maddie and Meri, who both shrugged, signaling they were just as confused as I was. The further we walked, the hairs on my arms began to rise. Something was wrong.

"Garrett!" I yelled out as we approached the fire pit that was our designated gathering spot. "What's going on?" Garrett's eyes darted to Maddie and then back at me. I looked at everyone who was gathered and noticed that the one face I needed to see was missing. "Where's Calix?"

Maddie made her way over to Garrett, who whispered something I couldn't hear. My heart felt like it was hammering in my chest. When Maddie looked back at me, her eyes were filled with worry. I felt an anger brewing inside me that I couldn't control. They were hiding something from me, again, and I couldn't take it.

"Where the fuck is Calix?!" I yelled. The
entire cavern fell silent, and I could feel everyone
staring at me. My eyes remained fixed on my
friends as my chest fell up and down with heavy
breaths. Thomas set down his device as he and
Malic joined the others.

"Gone," Garrett finally spoke. I could hear
the fear and hesitation in his voice. I waited for
him to say more, but he remained silent. I was
tired of this game. My face remained stern as I
took several powerful steps towards him.

"It's not his fault!" Thomas blurted out,
causing me to stop and turn my attention to him.
"Calix made a choice and left us to tell you about
it."

"What choice?" I sneered.

Thomas rushed to pick up the device from
the ground and cautiously approached me. I
looked where he pointed to the screen as he
began to explain the file he had unlocked. At first,
it made no sense why Calix was gone because of
this.

"There's more," Thomas spoke as if sensing
my confusion.

I watched as he clicked another file and began speaking again. "You're DNA is the key, but without Lillian thinking she has a power play, we will never get close enough to use it," Thomas explained.

"So," I said slowly, "Calix left and allowed himself to be captured by that evil bitch so she could use him against me? And what if she decides just to kill him on sight and hope that I'm broken enough to come crawling back to her?"

Everyone remained silent as the weight of my words hung in the air.

"We don't think she will," Malic said, breaking the silence. "She had you when you thought he was dead before, and you still fought her. She's not stupid. She knows that she needs him to get you to cooperate. Plus, if you, too, had a child, it would be the most powerful MUT The Union has ever seen. It would give her exactly what she wants."

"An heir she can raise and brainwash," I said, the words dripping with venom.

"For the record," Maddie said, crossing her arms, "this is the stupidest plan I've ever heard."

"Stupid or not," Garrett shrugged. "It's what Calix has done, and there is no going back now. Thomas saw the notification an hour ago that Calix has been captured and delivered to Lillian."

Grabbing my forehead, I let out a growl of frustration. After everything, all the times he begged me to be more careful and not sacrifice myself, he had done just that. I would find him and get him back, and then I would kill him myself.

"So," I said once I steadied myself. "What's the next move?"

Awkward silence hung in the air again as the guys all looked at each other and then down at the floor.

"There's no plan?" Maddie gasped.

"Calix left orders that Liz is in charge," Garrett finally spoke. "He said that only she could figure out a way to get him back with her knowledge of Lillian and the manor."

"Of course he did," I said, throwing my hands up.

Thomas opened his mouth to speak, but I was done listening and talking. Turning, I stormed off in the direction of our tent. Throwing back the flap, I stomped inside, praying that none of them would follow me. Immediately, my anger was replaced with a flood of emotions as I looked around. The tent was still a disaster from our game the night before, and his scent immediately filled my nose.

Hot tears began streaming down my face, and it felt like a hole had been punched in my chest. How could he do this? I wasn't a leader. All I was capable of being was an evil dictator like Lillian. My feet ran to the bed. Collapsing on the mattress, I buried my face into Calix's pillow and let the sobs shake me to my core. As they began to slow, I tightened my grip on the pillow and felt a piece of paper. Grabbing it firmly, I pulled it out and wiped the tears away from my face to see it.

lizabeth,

I am sure by now you have both cursed and mourned
e and scared the others. Please know that I took my lead
om you. If you had discovered that the secret to taking
wn The Union was for one of us to sacrifice ourselves,
u would have done it without hesitation. But this time, it's
y turn.

Lillian underestimates you; they all do. I know how
rong and capable you are. It's part of the reason I know
at our rebellion will succeed. You aren't like Lillian or any
the others before her. You have a heart and soul that
ake you capable of anything. I know you will come for me.
hen we meet again, we will finish what they started all
ose years ago.
on't let your fear or anger consume you, my love. It is
me to use that brilliant brain of yours. I will be waiting
r you.
ith all my love,
alix

I read over the words several more times, feeling my heart slow and emotions go dormant once again to be replaced by determination. He was still an idiot, and he would still pay for making a stupid decision without talking to me. However, there was no time for fits or rage. I needed to be focused and finish this fight.

Folding the paper, I tucked it into my pocket and cleaned up my face. Once I was presentable, I opened the flap to the tent and saw everyone standing there with a look of concern.

"I need everyone here immediately," I said firmly. "Garrett, I need your help in setting up the furniture. Thomas, bring all the files and maps you have on The Union. Malic, get everyone who helped Calix with planning and attacks. Meri, fetch your brother as we will need him too. Maddie..."

My voice trailed off as I struggled to find the words. Maddie nodded and walked over beside me. "I'll stay with you," she said with a soft smile as she squeezed my arm.

I nodded, and the others immediately set off on their tasks. Maddie and I followed Garrett inside and helped set up the furniture and arrange a war room. Just as we finished, the others returned, and the tent began to fill. Everyone settled around the table, looking to me for instructions.

"Let's get started," I said, placing my hands flat on the table.

Chapter 42

$\mathcal{T}$he conversation became heated once again as Garrett made the same suggestion for probably the hundredth time. At this point, I had no idea how long we had been here. Had it been hours or days? My head was throbbing with a headache, and we were no closer to having a plan than we were when we started. If I were supposed to be the leader, I was already doing a shitty job.

"Enough," I said with a sigh. "We've gone over this from every angle. Just walking up to the front door isn't an option."

"But what if we-" Garrett began.

I shot him a look that immediately made him close his mouth.

"We will never be able to sneak an entire army or even a group in and get close enough to

Lillian to chop off her hand," I said, rubbing my temples. "The only option is that I go in alone."

"That's not an option either," Malic spoke up. "Then she will have both of you, and the fight will be over."

"My shield should be strong enough..." I began, but the looks on their faces told me to stop. As soon as I was seen in the manor, the assault would begin. I knew I was strong, but that would be a lot. By the time I got close to Lillian, there would be no chance of my being able to shield both myself and Calix. She would immediately turn her gift on him and kill him without hesitation.

"I have to take her gift," I said flatly.

Everyone fell silent and looked at me in surprise. "Once I have her gift, the soldiers will stand down, and Calix will be able to get that chip."

"I thought you said..." Garett began and then trailed off.

"I know what I said," I replied. "But there is no other choice. Just promise me if I go bat shit crazy like her, you'll end me."

I watched as everyone looked at each other.

"We need a moment," Maddie said firmly.

Without hesitation, the twins stood up and left along with several others that I couldn't remember their names. There was too much buzzing in my mind to even try. "What do you mean, end you?" Malic said once the five of us were alone.

"If her gift drives me mad or you see that I'm becoming like Lillian, you end my life," I clarified. "Calix won't be able to do it, so I need you all to promise me that you will."

The last of the calm immediately evaporated from the tent as they all erupted with their arguments. The main theme seemed to be that my fear would never happen. I sat patiently and let them all say their peace, shouting over each other. After several minutes, they ran out of breath, and the tent fell silent. Rubbing my temples, I took a deep breath.

"If it won't happen, then there's nothing to worry about," I said firmly. "Just consider it insurance to put my mind at ease and give me the courage to go through with this."

"Fine," Thomas finally spoke. "If you go crazy, I will put you out of your misery."

"Thomas!" Everyone else yelled in unison, but it was too late; the promise was made. I nodded and returned my attention to the maps on the table. Everyone except Maddie stormed out of the tent. I knew they were angry, but I was alright with that.

"Calix will kill him," Maddie said. "If Thomas even tries to keep his promise."

"I'll leave a note," I said as I marked the location of where one of our attack tunnels would be. "Just like he did before leaving me."

"This is different," Maddie insisted. "He didn't plan on dying, you do."

"I don't plan it," I clarified. "I just need insurance in case things go wrong."

"It still feels like you're playing with fire," Maddie said, looking down at the map.

A small laugh escaped me at her choice of words. It was fire that started this entire thing, so it seemed fitting that I had to play with it to end it. Maddie and I worked in silence as we marked the tunnel locations on the map. The twins were probably already working on them, but it helped me to see it laid out.

By the time the others returned, I felt exhausted. I sat in a chair, rubbing my eyes, trying to will them to stay open.

"Are we on target?" I asked as soon as everyone sat down.

"The first set of tunnels is complete, and everyone has been informed of their assignments," Malic said, sitting down beside me. "The twins were able to build a tunnel to the safe room under the manor. They stopped a few feet short to keep from being detected, and we have some people working on a way to blast through."

"Perfect," I nodded with a yawn.

"There's one more thing," Thomas said, stepping forward and handing me a device. "This has been broadcasting everywhere for a few hours."

I looked at the screen and my eyes shot open, exhaustion no longer pulling them closed.

"It's her offer," I said as I handed the device back to Thomas. "She's saying that if I return, I can keep Calix."

"I agree," Thomas nodded.

"We should respond in some way," Malic said. "We need her to think you accept and buy ourselves a bit more time."

I nodded in agreement. "Can you hack the broadcast channel?" I asked Thomas. A grin spread over his face as he nodded. A few minutes later, he handed the device to me, a blinking cursor showing that it was ready for my message. I quickly typed it in and handed the device back to Thomas. He looked it over and let out a slight laugh.

"We will meet again in the morning," I told the others, the exhaustion returning like a wave crashing over me. They all gave me a hug or a reassuring shoulder squeeze before leaving. I made my way back to the bed and collapsed onto Calix's pillow once again. This time, it wasn't to cry or to feel sorry for myself. I breathed in scent and let out a light laugh as my eyes slid shut. The message I had typed was showing vibrantly on the inside of my eyelids.

Chapter 43

The next two days were full of activity, but I didn't mind. It kept my mind busy, so I didn't focus on what torture Calix was having to endure at Lillian's hands. Everything seemed to be according to plan, and I could only hope that our luck continued.

As I walked through base camp, I realized for the first time that it felt more like a military camp. All people who were not part of the fight were moved to the underground Twain. Most of the tents were cleared away, and the faces I gazed upon were ready for battle. Today was going to be rough, to say the least. I knew that not everyone was going to make it to see the freedom we were fighting for. It was a bit unsettling to know that they were following my plan, my orders, and it may lead them to death. I swallowed down the nerves and held my head high as I walked through them to where my friends, my family, waited for me.

As I walked, people bowed and muttered "My Queen" as I passed. I accepted the title as I took my place at the front of the crowd with my family on either side. This would be the last time we would be together until the fight was over.

Looking out over the people, I realized I needed to say something to encourage them and prepare them for what was to come.

"Today is the day we have been waiting for," I yelled, my voice reverberating over the walls. "I can't promise you we will win, that after today, MUTs and Mutants will both be free, but I can't. What I can promise you is that they will remember us. I can promise that I will fight to end the tyranny they have used to control us until my last breath!"

Roars began echoing through the crowd. I could feel the energy radiating from them and filling me. I stood straighter and took a step forward.

"Today we fight so tomorrow we can live!"

The crowd immediately erupted in cheers and battle cries. Looking back at the others, the looks of pride on their faces cemented my resolve.

"To your assignments!" Garrett yelled.

Immediately, the crowd began to disperse, each heading to their assigned tunnel. Malic stepped forward first and pulled me into a tight hug.

"I'll see after we win," he whispered to me.

"We still have to find you that fella," I teased as I hugged him back.

Malic let out a laugh as he squeezed me tighter and then released me before walking off.

Garrett was a man of few words as he gave me a nod and walked off as well. Maddie was an emotional mess as she jumped and wrapped her arms around me. I could feel the tears rolling down her chest as she held me tight. When she released me, her face was wet with tears that she quickly wiped away. She quickly walked away. I thought she was afraid that saying anything would cause her to begin crying once again. I respected that and didn't push.

"And then there were two," Thomas said, stepping forward. "Merri is waiting for us at the tunnel to the manor."

I nodded as I turned and led us towards our tunnel. I knew the plan, but still kept running it through my mind as we walked. Thomas had worked with a few others and made a device that was capable of melting through the walls of the safe room at the manor. He, Merri, and I would reach the wall and plant the device. Then we would wait for the others to make their moves. Our army was being divided between twelve main attack points. All of them with the same goal of converging on the manor. The plan was that this would push Lillian and her people into the safe room.

Merri was waiting for us and gave a nod as we approached. None of us said a word as she turned and led us down the tunnel. The trip took longer than I would have liked, but I needed to remember that patience was key to this working. When we reached the end, Merri made quick work of the remaining dirt and stone, revealing the metal wall. Thomas stepped forward and removed the device from his bag. It only took him a few minutes to secure it before he instructed us to step back. Now, there was nothing to do but wait.

Thomas had a device that allowed us to track the movements of our troops. I held my breath as the time counted down and the little dots burst out of their hiding spots. I knew I should have been watching their movements to make sure everyone was going where they were assigned. My attention became fixated on the dots that disappeared. It was just a dot on a screen, but I knew what it represented: one of our people had lost their life.

"Their nearly in position," Thomas said, pulling me out of my thoughts. "I just want to say, so we're clear, if you need, you are free to take my gift."

"Same," Merri added without hesitation.

"Thank you," I nodded. "But there is only one gift I will take today."

We watched together as the dots moved over the line we had designated as our mark. Thomas slid the device back into his bag and concentrated on the device.

"It's going to get hot," he warned before flicking his hand.

A silver piece of metal flew upwards and hit the ground. Instantly, the device began to glow, and the metal followed suit. Thomas was right, the heat felt instant as the beads of sweat formed on my face. Part of me wanted to back away, but

I forced myself to stand still. It was the head of the fire that killed my parents that sparked this rebellion for me and the others. I would use this heat to fuel that fire inside me.

In moments, the entire thing was glowing bright red, and I could see it slowly melting away.

"What the fuck is going on?!" Lillian's voice rang out through the thin metal. "You told me that this place was impenetrable."

"It is," a man with a shaky voice said. "This isn't possible."

A sharp sound that I recognized as a slap was the only thing that followed. Immediately after, I could feel Lillian's gift reaching out for us. It wouldn't take her long to realize I was here as I shielded us. I considered absorbing it now, but forced myself to wait. Moving too soon would allow her too much time to flee or take lives in other ways. I needed to look her in the eyes when I stole the very thing that made her powerful.

"I think you misunderstand what impenetrable," Calix's voice floated in the air with a hint of laughter. "Not your fault. I have yet to see anything that can stop my wife."

"Elizabeth?" Lillian breathed as the last of the wall melted away.

"Hello, Grandmother," I said with venom as I took a step forward.

Chapter 44

Lillian's face was a mixture of surprise and fear. I couldn't help but be surprised to see the fear in her eyes. I thought she feared nothing, but I had just been proven wrong. There was something she feared, and it appeared to be me.

"I thought you accepted my terms?" Lillian snarled, regaining her composure. "I'll let you keep your pet, and you take your place."

"Pet!?" Calix exclaimed.

My gaze shifted to where he stood shackled to a wall. Metal shackles, he was choosing to remain restrained. I knew he could freeze those shackles enough to make them shatter. He was waiting for the right time. I flicked my gaze back to Lillian and could feel the hatred now radiating off her.

"That's the difference between us," I said as I stepped into the room with Thomas and Merri right behind me. "He isn't an object, he's my husband. People aren't servants, their assets."

"Just like your idiot mother!" Lillian yelled. "No matter. With you here, I can take what I need to make the next heiress."

Her gift was still pushing against my shield, and I felt a surge of more come down on it. I stretched it to protect Calix, but could feel myself growing weaker. I glanced at Calix and could see the frost building on his restraints. Though I wasn't moving, my muscles began to shake from overexertion as I continued to hold off the attacks.

Finally, I heard the metal shatter and the shards fall to the ground. Lillian didn't have time to react before I pushed out my energy and knocked everyone in the room to the floor. In my weakened state, most only went down to a knee, but it was all I needed. I seized the moment of confusion and allowed Lillian's gift to sink under my skin.

It felt like it was burning in my veins as it filled me, and it took everything I had not to vomit and push it back out.

"Well, someone was hiding a few tricks," Lillian sneered as she stood up. "Grab her!"

Two of the soldiers moved forward, and I focused on them. They froze as blood started to leak from their eyes, nose, and ears. They looked towards Lillian, panicked as she stared at them with her mouth open.

"How?" Lillian stuttered as she looked back at me.

"A real queen doesn't use her gift to force others to bend to her will," I said, stepping forward. "She uses it to protect."

Calix had moved behind her, and I could see the blade in his hand.

"You wanted me to take my place, and I am here to do just that," I continued. "But first, you have something I need."

With that, Calix grabbed her arm and, in one swift motion, severed her hand from her arm. He tossed the bloody hand to Thomas, who immediately set to removing the chip. Lillian's screams filled the air as she fell to the ground, the blood pooling quickly around her. I stepped over her as Calix reached down and froze her nub.

"Why?" Lillian sneered at me.

"You don't get to die here," I explained as I put my foot down on her chest. "You will feel the pain of all those you killed before your light is finally extinguished." The elevator suddenly opened, causing us all to look at it and prepare for a fight. "Did it work?" Garrett asked as soon as the doors opened.

I let out a laugh as I looked back down at Lillian. I tried to remember the woman I had met when I first arrived at the manor. Her pride and demanding presence were all but gone. Now, she was nothing but a broken shell of that woman.

"It's ready," Thomas said as he appeared beside me. "Remember, this isn't forever. I just need more time to deactivate the protocol."

I nodded and held out my wrist to him. I felt the pinch as he shot the chip into my body. I held my breath as we all remained still as the ten-minute timer ran out. I let out a heavy breath as we all remained. It was done, I had the chip, and Lillian was defeated. I looked around the room and eyed each of the governors and their families.

"Where's Samuel?" I asked, realizing that he was missing from the lineup.

"He disappeared right after I arrived," Calix answered. "I heard Lillian screaming about him fleeing and how she would see him pay for deserting her."

"Filthy coward," Lillian snarled. "He thinks he will be safe, but I already sent word for him to suffer."

"Sent word?" I asked, kneeling. "To whom?"

Lillian let out a twisted laugh as she lay on the floor. "You expect to get all the secrets just because you took a little chip?" she laughed. "I look forward to watching you lose everything you think you've won."

Something twisted inside me, and I needed her to shut up. I balled my fist and hit her hard in the face. Her laughter stopped as her face fell to the side and her eyes closed.

"Didn't see that coming," Garrett laughed behind me.

"I'm not surprised," Calix said, and I looked at him. His face was bloody and bruised, and I considered punching him as well.

"Really?" I said as I stood. "So, you wouldn't be surprised if you got one as well?"

Calix stood and held up his hands in surrender, and slowly stepped towards me. "It was the only way," he explained. "And it worked."

I stared at him for a moment, thinking of all the "punishments" he had given me for making reckless decisions like he had. A smile spread across my face, and I took a step back.

"Kneel," I ordered.

Calix immediately grinned and kneeled in front of me. "As you wish, my queen."

Chapter 45

Lillian's gift felt like it was burning under my skin, begging to be used. My nails raked at my skin as I tried to resist the urge to use it. I wanted to send it out, but I had to hold it a bit longer. Lillian would face her punishment soon, and it would disappear with her.

The Capital streets were packed with people standing shoulder to shoulder. I looked out over them as I sat on a large wooden platform that had been built in front of the gates to the governor's manor. It had only been a day since the battle, but the feeling in the air had already begun to change. As I looked out, I could see mutants and MUTS, standing together as equals. They were all gathered here today to witness the end of the old regime and welcome in a new way of life.

In front of the platform, the governors and their families all stood chained, each looking dirty and defeated as their eyes stared down at the ground. In the center, on a smaller platform, was Lillian. Her clothes were little more than rags, and her once neat hair was now ratted on top of her head. She looked to have aged ten years overnight as she stood with her arms chained behind her to a wooden pole. Kindling was stacked around her feet, and a torch waited nearby. Despite her position, she stood with her head held high, glaring at the citizens. Even though her death was only minutes away, she still stood like she was in control.

The crowd fell silent as Calix stood from his seat beside me. He stood silent for a moment, looking out at everyone before holding out a hand. I took it and slowly rose. My body felt weak from containing Lillian's gift, but I refused to show it.

"Citizens of The Union!" Calix called out. "This day signifies both a beginning and an end. The end of brutality and the beginning of peace."

The crowd erupted in applause. I noticed that the mutants seemed more excited than the MUTS, but that was to be expected. The MUTS that were allowed the privilege of living in luxury were losing their prized positions. Not that all MUTS shared that opinion. Those who had been used as slaves and tortured cheered proudly alongside the mutants.

"Today, you have all accepted my wife, Elizabeth Harkin, as your new leader. A position earned not by her bloodline or gift. Instead, she earned it through the blood she spilled, sacrifices she made, and strength she showed in defending all the people equally."

The cheering grew louder as Calix kissed my hand and I took a step forward. Today I was a Queen, but I still felt like an insignificant girl from The Edge. I waited for the crowd to quiet down before speaking.

"We have all lost so much; some of us gave it willingly, and others had it taken from them." A grumble spread through the crowd, some of the people shouting curses and hate at Lillian and the others. "Our lives were merely pawns in a game we weren't aware we were a part of," I continued. "But today, we rise victorious over those who dared to think of us as weak and disposable."

The crowd erupted again as I walked down from the platform with Calix, our friends following close behind. I walked around and stood in front of Lillian. Her eyes showed nothing but cold hatred as she glared at me.

"While all those here today are guilty in some way, they were also pawns. All controlled by an expert in manipulation and torture." Lillian straightened her stance as if my description of her gave her a sense of pride. "Her fate is set as she will feel the pain of all of those she tortured in her life," I continued, shifting my gaze to the others. "The others will be given a choice."

The people immediately stopped cheering as sounds of rage and confusion filled the air. I held up my hand, and they all fell silent once more.

"For things to change, we must do things differently," I said. "And that starts today. They will be given a choice and decide their fate. They can either join Lillian and share in her end or." The silence hung heavy in the air, and I waited until I swore I could hear that everyone was collectively holding their breath. "Or they can feel the weight of those they stepped on for so long. They will be stripped of all titles and wealth, sentenced to live out their lives in a cell, and work hard labor in exchange for meals. Every year, our council will meet and vote on whether they have paid their debt and if they can be allowed to join our society."

The crowd remained silent as they waited. Each of the governors and their families knelt on the hard ground and bowed their heads in surrender. I nodded as Calix motioned for several soldiers to step forward. We waited as the people were pulled into a line away from Lillian, their shackles remaining in place.

"Do I get the same choice?" Lillian sneered as she looked down at me.

"No," I said firmly. "You will get to feel the pain of all those who died because of you."

Lillian let out a laugh that shook me to my core. Something about it rattled my very soul. Calix stepped forward and placed a firm hand on my shoulder, helping me to steady.

"It's time," he said softly enough that only I could hear him. I nodded in agreement and stepped forward, and took the torch.

"For those you burned," I said as I tossed the torch onto the kindling. It took flame immediately. Lillian remained still, showing no signs of pain as the flames began licking at her skin. "And for those you cursed."

Focusing on Lillian, I allowed her gift to flow out of me. Through the flames, I could see the blood running down her face. I continued to let the gift flow out of me, attacking its former master. Lillian held out a few moments longer, but soon her screams filled the air. As the last of her gifts left me, I collapsed to the ground. My eyes remained locked on Lillian, trying to find the strength to take her gift once again if she were able to use it. If she did feel it return, she was too far gone to use it. The smell of burnt flesh and hair filled my nose, and her cries finally stopped.

I felt the tears well up in my eyes as Calix helped me to my feet, and I faced the crowd once more. "Let us let the wind carry away the ash and build something new, something better!"

Everyone applauded, and I felt my friends move in closer around me. It was finally over. We had our revenge. We were finally free. Now, we had a lot of work to do. We may have won the war, but

now we have to work to keep what we fought for.

Chapter 46

"The people are adjusting better than we expected," Malic said as he walked into my office.

Calix and I had taken up residence in Lillian's manor. It wasn't an easy decision, but eventually I agreed. We tore down the stone wall and the other manors. One of the first things I did was remove all the curtains, letting the light into the manor. It felt as if the rays cut through all the negativity that Lilian had left behind and breathed new life into the house.

We took out the portraits and everything belonging to Lillian and her family. There was talk of building a museum containing the artifacts to teach future generations about what we had overcome and keep them from repeating the same mistakes. The manor was too big for just Calix and me, so I insisted that the others join us. Now, the council resides with us in harmony in a building once designed to showcase separation and fear.

The manor wasn't the only thing that had changed. The walls between the rings were destroyed, and people now moved freely among each other. It was hard at first, redistributing the wealth and resources, but things seemed to get easier with time. It was still surreal to walk the streets and see the people together as one instead of separated by walls because of things they had no control over.

The people of Twain moved into the city, taking up lives and helping show those of The Union the proper way of things. Their presence seemed to help the others adjust to the new way of things.

"I knew they would," I said, setting down my pen and rubbing my eyes. "Now, about finding you a fella?"

Malic let out a laugh and shook his head. "The search may be over."

"What?" I gasped, shooting up from the chair. "Who? When?"

"Let me keep him to myself just a bit longer," Malic grinned. "When I'm ready, you'll be the first to meet him."

"I better," I insisted.

A knock on the door drew our attention.

"Are we interrupting?" Thomas grinned as he walked in, followed by Calix, Maddie, and Garrett.

"Not at all," I said, welcoming them in and sitting back down. "Have you had any luck with the files?"

Thomas set down his tablet in front of me on the desk and began tapping on the screen. The images changed so fast, I gave up trying to look at them and waited for him to finish.

"It was a lot of work, and most of it we had already figured out," Thomas said. "But there is one file that I think you need to see."

My eyes watched as Thomas clicked once more, and what appeared to be a map showed on the screen. I leaned closer and felt my heart freeze in my chest. On the map, there was a symbol towards the center, and I could see that it was marked "United Union". My eyes began darting around the map at the three other dots that were marked.

"Are these?" My voice trailed off as my fingers touched the screen.

"Other cities," Thomas finished. "It appears that each one has its setup, running things differently. However, they all appear to be connected in one way."

"What's that?" I asked, looking up at him.

"They all have treaties with each other for peace and trading," Thomas continued. "And an agreement to tell their citizens that they are the last civilization left."

"Just like The Union," I said, shaking my head.

"But they all appear to answer to one person or government," Thomas said as he adjusted his glasses. "I believe there may be a fifth city, but there is no information on it that I can find. In the files, Lillian simply refers to whoever she reported to as American Lord."

My mind was racing with all the new information. The MUT Calix and Thomas had met were telling the truth; there were other cities. Not only were there others, but they all reported to someone else. Someone who saw how Lillian ruled over the Union and approved. Whoever this Lord was, he was a greater threat than Lillian.

"That's not all," Thomas continued. "Lillian notes that she reported to the American Lord regularly, though not how she did it. Whoever it is, they will know she is no longer in control when she doesn't report in."

That's why Lillian had laughed as she was killed. The chip wasn't the only thing she was supposed to pass on to the next heiress. She knew that I wouldn't know how to report in and the repercussions of failing to do so. She knew we were doomed to fail and took joy in it.

"No sense in worrying about it if you ask me," Garrett said casually. "All we can do is prepare and keep doing what we're doing."

"You're right," I laughed. "No sense in worrying about it. Let's just continue to focus on the work that needs to be done."

Every left but Calix, whose eyes were fixed on me. As soon as they were gone, I allowed the smile I was forcing to fall and looked back down at the map.

"This is bad," I said without looking up.

"It could be," Calix admitted, stepping closer.

"These other cities, they probably need help, but what good does it do to free them if this American Lord is going to come slaughter us all anyway?"

Calix leaned forward and looked down at the map. He studied closely and then leaned up with a look of confusion. "Where does it say those other cities need or even want help? Or that this American Lord will slaughter us?"

I looked at him with frustration. Of course, it didn't say that, but I thought it was evident from the tone of things. Calix took my hand and pulled me close to him, ignoring the glare I was casting at him.

"If these other cities send out a call for aid, we will go," Calix continued. "And if this Lord thinks he is just going to steal in here and murder our Queen, I will take great personal pleasure in watching the light slowly leave his eyes." Calix placed a finger under my chin and tilted my face up so I was looking at him. "But today, your people need your full attention."

"And what about my king?" I asked, playfully biting my lip.

"Oh," he grinned, "Your king requires a special kind of attention. After all, we do have this manor to fill."

A gasp escaped me just as his mouth crashed into my mine. I could taste the hunger and desire on his lips as he tilted my head back and deepened the kiss. We had fought hard to get here and lost so much. He was right, we needed to focus on our victory and stop looking for another battle. If we had to fight again, we would. For now, I just wanted my husband and nothing else.

Epilogue

" Sir, perhaps we should turn back."

I let out a heavy sigh as I stopped and turned back to the soldier. His constant insistence on returning had been grating on my last nerve for the past two weeks. "It's over!" I yelled at him. "Lillian and the others are dead!"

The soldier shifted on his feet and looked uncomfortable.

"If I hear any more talk of returning, I will break your legs and let the creatures feast on you!"

They all nodded in understanding as I turned and began walking east once more. I should have planned my escape better, but I had been rushed when she captured that King. She saw it as a victory and refused to listen. I knew it was a trap, and she walked right into it. Elizabeth wanted us both dead, and I knew it wouldn't be quick. We killed her family and tried to kill her husband. There was nothing that would stop her from getting to Calix.

I had rushed, gathering the few soldiers I could to make the journey. I had agreed to be Lillian's husband, but not because I had any feelings for her. I wanted to be in control, and I seized the opportunity for power. I wasn't going to die and lose everything just because Lillian thought she was invincible. She could burn alone, but I would live on. The bitch had all the best soldiers assigned to protect her, leaving me with slim pickings. Still, they were adequate to keep the duowolves and other beasts away.

Once we arrived, I would offer them in exchange for residency. This pathetic city was always in need, insisting on living in the past instead of embracing new ways. Where we used technology to keep our people in line, they rejected it in every way they could. Living underground despite their lands recovering from the fallout. Some say it is because their lands received the least of the attacks and were healthier before everything. Still, living in mining tunnels and only sending up a few citizens to gather resources on the surface, all using primitive ways, made no sense - even the citizens of The Edge had more technology than these savages.

Still, Blaylin was a close ally of mine. We formed a friendship of sorts over the mutual hatred of my wife, of all things. The other rulers would have turned me away out of fear of what the American Lord would do for taking me in. Baylin, however, lived by a different set of rules. A laugh escaped me as I thought about what his reaction would be when I told him that a King and Queen now ruled the Union. He surely wouldn't take it well. He didn't take well to such titles.

That was the way of it. Each of the cities was ruled differently, like a giant experiment set up after the Great War. Blaylin's city was set up to run as what was formally known as a democracy, of sorts. It was similar to the Union, with all the elections rigged, of course, but they didn't hide who was in charge, and it was always a man. Something I was always a bit envious of.

I was breathing hard as we crested the top of a mountain and looked down into the valley. This area was once covered with thick trees and wildlife. Now, the trees were sparser, and grass grew in random patches. Still, compared to everywhere else, it was a lush paradise. Of course, things were even better the closer you got to the tunnels, where people worked and tended the land. Our destination lay up the next mountainside. It was easy to overlook if you didn't know it was there. A small mine entrance from before the Great War led into the underground mine city.

I was breathing hard as we finally reached the entrance. I could see the soldiers eyeing it like I had gone mad. Its crude construction did not indicate what it led to.

"Lights!" I ordered once we were in the entrance.

This was part of how the city remained hidden. While lights ran the walls of the city, in the entrance, travelers were greeted by a heavy darkness that made it impossible to see anything. I waited impatiently as the soldiers fumbled to retrieve their flashlights. Once their bright beams cut through the dark, we continued. It was nearly a mile to the main entrance, but it seemed longer in the quite dark.

I breathed a sigh of relief when the large metal door blocking the tunnel came into view. Outside of it stood two guards. Their clothes were covered in coal dust, and they wore mining helmets that flicked on as we approached. I watched as their grips tightened on their pickaxes, primitive but effective.

"Governor Samuel to see President Blayin," I announced.

One of the men moved to a small box on the wall and began speaking into it, never taking his eyes off me. His voice was too low for me to hear, but I wasn't worried. After a few moments, he nodded to the other. They stepped to the side just as the large, metal door slowly groaned open. I walked inside, not sparing them another glance. As expected, another coal-covered soldier waited for me on the other side.

"Follow me," he said in a deep voice.

I followed him through the dimly lit tunnels. I had to be careful not to trip over the old track that ran through it. The soldier led us through so many turns I knew I wouldn't be able to find my way out alone; perhaps that was by design. Anyone who managed to get in would get lost, while the citizens could navigate these tunnels with the lights off. Strategically, it was a sound system.

"If you have come for what you gifted me," Blaylin bellowed as we entered a large chamber. Blaylin sat on top of a stage, looking like an old fashioned judge; all that was missing was the powdered wig. "I'm afraid you will be disappointed."

I glanced to his right, where a large man stood. My head tilted up as I took in his large form. He stood over six feet tall with arms as big around as my torso. Judging by his coal-stained, hardened skin, probably from long days in the mines. He held a pickaxe nearly as large as some of my soldiers. I had nearly forgotten about him, my bastard. Lillian had been furious when she learned that I had been satisfying myself with the maid. She hadn't learned about it until the child was born, and the maid came seeking help to raise it. Damn fool, she thought, telling Lillian would get her some kind of sympathy. All she got was a slow death when Lillian bled her out. After that, we had sold the child to Blaylin in exchange for a couple of MUTS.

"Of course not," I said, shaking my head. "He is yours to do with as you wish. Though it does appear that our agreement was quite beneficial to you."

"It has," Blaylin laughed. "Egon is our finest warrior."

"Glad to hear it," I nodded, already bored of hearing about my bastard's accomplishments. "I come to ask a favor, my friend. I find myself needing to relocate and would like to take up residence among your people. I am sure that I would make a great asset as your advisor."

Advisor was a lower station than I would have liked, but one that I could live with. Blaylin looked at me, and I saw something flash in his eyes that made my blood run cold.

"And what could you advise me on?" Blaylin said in a deep voice as he sat forward. "Could you help me be tricked by my daughter, allow her to start a rebellion, kill her, and then watch everything I built be torn down by my granddaughter?"

Shit. I knew word would spread among the rulers once Lillian failed to report in. I had hoped that I would be able to make it here before that had happened, but I didn't. I straightened myself and tried to hide the nerves that were fluttering inside me.

"As you know, I did not rule over The Union," I said in a level voice. "Lillian controlled things as per the arrangement. She refused to listen to my warnings and advice, which eventually led to our downfall. I come here to offer the same advice to you, my friend."

Blaylin looked at me with hard eyes as he shook his head. "You have no advice that I could trust, friend." The last word came out as an insult, but I remained standing tall.

"Blaylin," I said, taking a step closer. I stopped as Egon moved for the first time and tightening his grip on his pickaxe.

"The order came in this morning," Blaylin said grimly. "You are to die for failing to protect your city."

The calm mask I was wearing began to slip away. I hadn't failed at anything. They put Lillian in charge, her bloodline, and always women. Now I was being blamed for that failure? No, I wouldn't let this stand.

"Surely there is something we can do," I offered. "An arrangement, perhaps? I have brought soldiers to join your ranks, a gift."

A flurry of arrows whizzed around me as I ducked to the ground. Seconds later, my soldiers all lay dead around me. I stood up slowly, looking at Blaylin. With a curt nod, two of his soldiers stepped up and forced me to my knees. I fought against them, but I was too exhausted from the journey. I tried to break their arms, but my gift refused to surface. I should have rested before coming in here.

Loud steps echoed around me, and I looked up to see Egon standing in front of me, his pickaxe looking even more deadly up close.

"Son," I said in a shaky voice. Drastic times called for desperate measures. "I'm sorry about your mother and sending you away. I had no choice. If I hadn't, Lillian would have killed you."

Egon said nothing as he looked down at me. I could feel myself shaking as fear took over my body. This wasn't how it was supposed to go. I was a governor, the second most powerful person in The Union. Reduced now to a sniveling shell of a man begging for mercy from his bastard son.

"Father," Egon's voice pulled me out of my thoughts as I looked up at him. "I forgive you."

I let out a sigh of relief and tried to stand, only to have the soldiers push me back down. I looked back at Egon just in time to see his pickaxe raise and come down at me.

Author's Note

Thank you for joining the rebellion. I hope you enjoyed this story as much as I did. If you could please review it, it would be greatly appreciated.

Are you looking for more? Please check out my other books.

Scan the QR code below for links to my social media, mailing list, and other books.

J.D. Crist

www.ingramcontent.com/pod-product-compliance
Lightning Source LLC
Chambersburg PA
CBHW011921300726
48970CB00008B/2533